ACTS OF FAITH

By Erich Segal

Novels

LOVE STORY

OLIVER'S STORY

MAN, WOMAN, AND CHILD

THE CLASS

DOCTORS

ACTS OF FAITH

For Children

FAIRY TALE

Academic Books

ROMAN LAUGHTER:
THE COMEDY OF PLAUTUS

EURIPIDES:
A COLLECTION OF CRITICAL ESSAYS (ED.)

PLAUTUS:
THREE COMEDIES (ED. AND TRANS.)

THE OXFORD READINGS IN GREEK TRAGEDY (ED.)

CAESAR AUGUSTUS:
SEVEN ASPECTS (CO-ED.)

PLATO'S DIALOGUES (ED.)

PLAUTUS:
FOUR COMEDIES (ED. WITH CRITICAL NOTES)

Erich Segal

ACTS OF

FAITH

BANTAM BOOKS

New York · Toronto · London · Sydney · Auckland

A Bantam Large Print Edition

ACTS OF FAITH

A Bantam Book

Publishing History
Bantam hardcover edition published April 1992
Bantam large print edition / May 1992

ISBN 0-385-42343-8

Published simultaneously in the United States and Canada

Bantam Books are published by Bantam Books, a division of Bantam
Doubleday Dell Publishing Group, Inc. Its trademark, consisting of
the words "Bantam Books" and the portrayal of a rooster, is Regis-
tered in U.S. Patent and Trademark Office and in other countries.
Marca Registrada. Bantam Books, 666 Fifth Avenue, New York, New
York 10103.

PRINTED IN THE UNITED STATES OF AMERICA

RRH   0 9 8 7 6 5 4 3 2 1

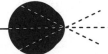

**This Large Print Book carries the
Seal of Approval of N.A.V.H.**

To Karen, Francesca, and Miranda
. . . who sustain my faith

*Sero te amavi, pulchritudo tam antiqua et tam
nova, sero te amavi! Et ecce intus eras.* . . .

St. Augustine, Confessions X.27

*Too late came I to love you, O Beauty both so
ancient and so new! too late came I to love you—
and behold you were within me all the time.* . . .

PROLOGUE

1
Daniel

I was baptized in blood. My own blood. This is
not a Jewish custom. It is merely a fact of history.

The covenant my people made with God requires
that we affirm our allegiance to Him twice each day.
And lest any of us forget we are unique, God created
gentiles everywhere who constantly remind us.

In my case, the Father of the Universe placed an
Irish Catholic neighborhood midway between my
school and home. Thus at regular intervals, as I was
walking to or from my yeshiva, the Christian Soldiers from St. Gregory's would catch sight of me
and hurl verbal abuse in my direction.

"Kike!"

"Sheenie!"

"Christ-killer!"

I could have run when they were still several

dozen yards away. But then I'd have to drop my books—my prayer book, my sacred Bible. And that would have been a desecration.

So I would stand there, book-laden and afraid to move as they swaggered up to me, pointed at my skullcap, and continued their ritual.

"Look at this guy—how come he's wearin' a hat and it ain't even winter?"

"He's a Hebe. They need their hats to hide their horns!"

I just stood there, helpless, as they encircled me and started shoving.

Then came the punches, raining from all sides, hammering my nose and lips, reverberating in my skull. After all these years, I can still feel the pounding and taste the blood.

With time I learned a few defensive tactics. For example, it is better if the victim in a brawl does not fall down (lean against a wall, if possible). For if you are prostrate, your attacker can employ his feet as well.

Furthermore, big books can serve as shields. Not only does the Talmud hold the most important comments on religious matters—it is large enough to fend off any kick aimed at the groin.

Sometimes I think my mother lived her life waiting behind the front door, for no matter how quietly I stole into the house after one of those encounters, she would be there waiting.

"Danny, my little boy—what's happened?"

"It's nothing, Mama. I just fell."

"And you expect me to believe that? It's that bunch of Irish cossacks from the church again, huh? Do you know the names of those hooligans?"

"No."

I lied, of course. I could remember every pimple on the sneering face of Ed McGee, whose father ran the local tavern. I had heard that he was training for the Golden Gloves or something. Maybe he was only using me for practice.

"Tomorrow I'm going to have a talk with their superior mother or whatever she's called."

"C'mon, Ma, what can you possibly say?"

"I'll ask her how they would have treated Christ himself. She could remind those boys that Jesus was a rabbi."

All right, Mama, I thought to myself, have it your way. They'll just come at me with baseball bats next time.

———

I was born a prince—the only son of Rav Moses Luria, monarch in our special kingdom of believers. My family had come to America from Silcz, a small town in Carpathia, which at different times had been a part of Hungary, then Austria, then Czechoslovakia. External rulers changed, yet one thing remained unaltered: Silcz was the home of the *B'nai Simcha*—"Sons of Joy"—and every generation saw a Luria honored by the title, Silczer Rebbe.

Several months before the Nazis would have annihilated his own community, my father led his flock to yet another Promised Land—America. Here they recreated Silcz in a tiny corner of Brooklyn.

The members of his congregation had no problems dealing with the customs of this new land. They simply ignored them and continued to live as they had for centuries. The frontiers of their world did not extend beyond an easy Sabbath walking distance from the pulpit of their spiritual leader.

They dressed as always in lengthy coats of solemn black, with beaver hats during the week and round *shtreimels* trimmed with fur on festive days. We boys wore black fedoras on the Sabbath, grew sideburns down in ringlets, and looked forward to the day when we could also grow a beard.

Some of our clean-shaven and assimilated coreligionists felt embarrassed to have us in their midst: we looked so odd—so conspicuously Jewish. You'd hear them mutter, *"Frummers,"* under their breaths. And while the word simply means Orthodox, their tone betrayed their scorn.

My mother, Rachel, was my father's second wife. Chava, his first, had borne him only daughters—two of them, Malka and Rena. Then she died in childbirth, and the little boy she had been carrying survived her by a mere four days.

Toward the end of the prescribed eleven months of mourning, a few of Father's closest friends discreetly started to suggest he seek another wife. Not only for dynastic reasons, but because the Lord decrees in Genesis that "it is not good that the man should be alone."

Thus it was that Rabbi Moses Luria wed my mother, Rachel, who was twenty years his junior, and the daughter of a learned Vilna scholar who was deeply honored by Rav Luria's choice.

Within twelve months a child was born to them. Yet another *daughter*—Deborah, my older sister. But to my father's great joy I was conceived in the following year. My first cry of life was regarded as a direct response to a pious man's most fervent prayers.

The next generation was assured that the golden chain would not be broken. There would be another Silczer Rebbe. To lead, to teach, to comfort. And, most important, to be an intermediary between his followers and God.

It's bad enough to be an only son—to see your sisters treated almost as invisible because they aren't brothers. Yet, the hardest part for me was knowing how much and how long I had been prayed for. From the beginning, I could sense the burden of my father's expectations.

I recall my very first day of kindergarten. I was the only child whose *father* took him. And when he kissed me at the schoolroom door, I could feel tears upon his cheeks as well.

I was too young to realize that this was an omen.

How could I have known that I would someday cause him to shed far more bitter tears?

2
Timothy

Tim Hogan was born angry.

And with good reason. He was an orphan with two living parents.

His father, Eamonn, a merchant seaman, had returned from a long voyage to discover his wife pregnant. Yet Margaret Hogan swore by all the saints that no mortal man had touched her.

She began to hallucinate, babbling to the world that she had been blessed by a visit from a holy spirit. Her outraged husband simply sailed away. Rumor had it that he found another "wife" in Rio de Janeiro, by whom he had five "mortal" children.

As Margaret's condition worsened, the pastor at St. Gregory's arranged for her to be given shelter in a sanitarium run by the Sisters of the Resurrection in upper New York State.

At first, it seemed that Timothy, flaxen-haired and

cherubic with his mother's porcelain blue eyes, was also destined for an institution. His aunt, Cassie Delaney, already burdened with three daughters, did not think it possible to feed another mouth on what a New York cop brought home each week.

Besides, Tim had arrived just after she and Tuck had decided, despite the dictates of their religion, to have no more children. She was already exhausted from years of sleepless nights in the penitentiary of diaper changing.

Tuck overruled her.

"Margaret's your own flesh and blood. We can't just leave the lad with no one."

From the moment he entered their lives, Tim's three sisters did not disguise their hostility. He reciprocated fiercely. As soon as he could lift an object, he would try to strike them with it. His trio of antagonists never exhausted their plans for persecution.

On one occasion, Aunt Cassie walked in just in time to stop them from pushing three-year-old Tim out the bedroom window.

After this hairsbreadth rescue, it was Timothy she slapped for provoking her daughters.

"Nice boys never hit girls," she chided, a lesson Tim might have better assimilated had he not on several Saturday evenings overheard his uncle roughing up his aunt.

Tim was as anxious to leave the house as they

were to be rid of him. By the time he was eight, Cassie had given him a key threaded on a braid of yarn. Worn around his neck, this talisman gave him the freedom to roam abroad and vent his innate aggression in appropriately masculine activities like stickball and street-fighting.

He was not faint of heart. In fact, he was the only boy who dared to challenge muscular Ed McGee, the undisputed leader of the grade-school pack.

In the course of their brief but explosive battle in the playground, Tim caused extensive damage to Ed's eye and lip, although McGee had managed to unleash a mighty left, which nearly broke Tim's jaw before the Sisters pulled the pugilists apart. The nuns' intervention, of course, made them fast friends thereafter.

Though an officer of the law, his uncle nonetheless took pride in Tim's fighting spirit. But Aunt Cassie was livid. She not only lost four days' work in Macy's lingerie department, but had to make endless ice packs for her nephew's jaw.

———

In the Delaney family album, Tim had seen his mother, Margaret, and could discern a pale reflection of her in Aunt Cassie's face.

"Why can't I go and visit her?" he pleaded. "I mean, just say hello or something?"

"She wouldn't even recognize you," Tuck asserted. "She's living in another world."

"But *I'm* not sick—I'd know *her.*"

"Please, Tim," his uncle insisted. "We're doing you a kindness."

Inevitably the day came when Tim learned what everyone else in his world had been whispering for years.

During one of their Saturday night bouts, he heard his aunt shouting at her husband, "I've had just about all I can take of the little bastard!"

"Cassie, watch your language," Tuck upbraided her. "One of the girls might hear."

"So what? It's true, isn't it? He's my slut of a sister's goddamn bastard and some day I'm going to tell him myself."

Tim was devastated. In one blow he had lost a father and acquired a stigma. Trying to control his rage and fear, he confronted Tuck the next day and demanded to know who his real father was.

"Your Mom was very strange about it, lad." Tuck's face had turned crimson and he refused to meet Tim's eye. "She never mentioned anyone— except this holy angel business," he said. "I'm really sorry."

After that, Cassie continued to find fault with whatever Tim said or did and Tuck simply avoided him whenever possible. Tim began to feel as if he were being chastised for his mother's sins. How else could he describe his life with the Delaneys, except as perpetual punishment.

He would try to come home as late as possible.

Yet when darkness fell, his friends would all disperse for dinner and he was left with no one to talk to.

The playground was dimly illuminated by a soft kaleidoscopic haze from the stained-glass windows of the church. Careful to avoid detection by the likes of Ed McGee, he would go inside. At first it was merely to warm himself. Gradually he found himself drawn to the statue of the Virgin and, feeling abandoned and lonely, he would kneel in prayer, as he had been taught.

"*Ave Maria, gratia plena*—Hail Mary, full of grace, the Lord is with thee, blessed art thou among women . . . Holy Mary, Mother of God, pray for us sinners, now . . ."

But even Tim himself could not fully understand what he was seeking. He was not old enough to comprehend that having been born in a web of questions, he was asking the Virgin Mother to deliver him from ignorance.

Why was I born? Who are my parents? Why doesn't anybody love me?

Late one evening, as he wearily looked up, he thought—for a single fleeting instant—that he saw the statue smile as if it were saying, "One thing must be clear in this confused life of yours. *I* love you."

When he went home, Cassie slapped him hard for being late for supper.

3

Deborah

Deborah's earliest memory of Danny was the glint of the sharp knife moving toward his tiny penis.

Though there were people crowded all around her eight-day-old brother, she could see everything clearly from the arms of her mother, who was standing in a corner of the room, alternately staring and wincing.

Danny lay on a pillow on the lap of his godfather, Uncle Saul—actually a distant cousin, but his father's closest male relative—whose strong but gentle hands were holding Danny's legs apart.

Then the *mohel*, a tall, gaunt man in white apron and prayer shawl, placed a clamp around her brother's penis and a bell-shaped metal shield that covered the tip down to the foreskin. At the same moment his right hand raised what looked like a stiletto.

There was a silent gasp as the males present all dropped their hands instinctively to cover their own genitals.

After rapidly reciting a prayer, the *mohel* pierced the baby's foreskin and in a single motion, swiftly sliced the tissue all around the rim of the shield. Little Danny wailed.

An instant later, the ritual surgeon held up the foreskin for everyone to see, then dropped it into a silver bowl.

Rav Luria intoned the prayer in a mighty voice, "Blessed art Thou, O ruler of the world, Who has commanded us to make our sons enter into the covenant of Abraham our father."

There was a sigh of relief, followed by a cheer.

A whimpering Danny was returned to his beaming father.

Rav Luria then called out to everyone to eat, drink, sing, and dance.

Since the Code of Law demands it, the men and women were separated by a partition, but even from her mother's side, Deborah could hear her father's voice above all the others.

When she was old enough to speak full sentences, one of the first things Deborah asked her mother was whether there had been a similar celebration when *she* was born.

"No, darling," Rachel answered gently. "But that doesn't mean we don't love you just as much."

"But why not?" Deborah persisted.

"I don't know," her mother answered. "That's the way the Father of the Universe ordained it."

As time passed, Deborah Luria learned what else the Father of the Universe had ordained for Jewish women.

In the men's morning prayers, there were benedictions to the Lord for every conceivable gift:

*Blessed art Thou Who hast enabled the
   rooster to distinguish between day and
   night.*

*Blessed art Thou Who hast not made me a
   heathen.*

*Blessed art Thou Who hast not made me a
   female.*

While the men were giving thanks for their masculinity, the girls had to be content with:

Blessed art Thou Who hast made me according to Thy Will.

Deborah was enrolled in a traditional "Beis Yakov" school, whose sole purpose was to prepare Jewish girls to be Jewish wives. There, they read the

Code of Law—or at least a specially abridged version compiled for women in the nineteenth century.

Their teacher, Mrs. Brenner, constantly reminded the girls that they were privileged to help their husbands fulfill God's injunction to Adam to "be fruitful, and multiply, and replenish the earth."

Is that all we are, Deborah thought to herself, baby machines? She did not dare ask it aloud, but rather waited impatiently for Mrs. Brenner to provide an explanation. The best her teacher could offer was that since women were created from one of man's ribs, they are therefore only part of what men are.

Pious though she was, Deborah could not accept this folklore as fact. And yet, she did not dare give voice to her skepticism.

By chance, years later when he was in high school, Danny showed her a passage from the Talmud that she had never been allowed to read during her own education.

It explained why, during intercourse, a man must face down and a woman upward: a man looks at the earth, the place whence he came, a woman at the place where *she* was created—the man's rib.

The more Deborah learned, the more she became resentful. Not only because she was regarded as inferior, but because the sophistry of the teachers tried to convince the girls that this was not really the case—even while explaining that a woman who gives birth to a boy must wait forty days before she becomes "pure" again, whereas one who gives birth to a girl must wait eighty days.

And why, when a tenth man was lacking to make a quorum needed for prayers, could no Jewish woman be counted as a substitute, although the tenth place could be filled by a six-year-old boy!

When in synagogue, she dared to peek over the curtain fringing the balcony where she sat with her mother and the rest of the women. She would look at the parade of old men and teenage boys called up to read the Torah and ask, "Mama, how come nobody up here ever gets a chance to read?"

And the pious Rachel could only answer, "Ask your father."

She did. At lunch that Sabbath. And the Rav replied indulgently.

"My darling, the Talmud tells us that a woman should not read a Torah portion out of respect for the congregation."

"But what does that mean?" Deborah persisted, genuinely confused.

Her father answered, "Ask your mother."

The only person she could rely on for straight answers was her brother, Danny.

"They told us that if women stood in front of the male worshipers it would confound their minds."

"I don't get it, Danny. Could you give me a for instance?"

"Well," her brother responded uneasily,

"y'know. Like Eve when she gave Adam . . . you know . . ."

"Yes." Deborah was becoming impatient. "That I *do* know. She made him eat the apple. So what?"

"Well, that sort of gave Adam ideas."

"What kind of ideas?"

"Hey, Deb," Danny apologized, "they haven't told us that yet." To which he added, "But when they do, I promise I'll tell you."

Ever since she could remember, Deborah Luria had wanted the privileges bestowed upon her brother at his circumcision. But as she grew up she was obliged to face the painful fact that she could never serve God to the fullest . . . because she had not been born a man.

PART I

1

Daniel

When I was four years old, my father called me into his study and lifted me onto his huge lap. I can still remember the sagging wooden bookshelves filled with tall leather volumes of the Talmud.

"All right," he said gently. "Let's start at the beginning."

"What's that?" I inquired.

"Well, naturally,"—my father beamed—"God is the beginning—as well as the unending. But you're still too young to delve into mystical concepts. For today, Daniel, we'll just start with *aleph*."

"Aleph?"

"Well pronounced," my father said with pride. "You now know one letter of Hebrew."

He pointed to the second symbol on the page.

"And what comes next is *bet*. So now you can see we are learning the Hebrew *aleph-bet.*"

And so we continued for the remaining twenty letters.

Curiously, I don't remember having to struggle with a single thing my father taught me. It all went straight to my heart and mind from his, and burned there like the eternal light above the Holy Ark in synagogue.

The next thing I knew I was reading in Hebrew the first words of my life: "In the beginning, God created the heaven and the earth . . . ," which I duly rendered into Yiddish.

This German-Hebrew dialect, which first evolved in the medieval ghettos on the Rhine, was still the language of our everyday life. Hebrew was sacrosanct, reserved for reading holy texts and prayers. And thus I repeated the first words of Genesis, *"In Ershten hut Got gemacht Himmel un erd."*

My father stroked his gray-flecked beard and nodded. "Well done, my boy. Well done."

His praise was addictive. I studied even harder to earn more of it. At the same time, on my father's part there was a ceaseless upward spiral of increasing expectations.

Though he never said it, I knew that he assumed I would absorb this knowledge into the very fiber of my being. By some miracle I learned it all—the holy words, the sacred laws, the history, the customs, the intricate attempts of scholars through the ages to extract God's meaning from a wisp of commentary.

I only wish my father had been a little less proud, because the more I knew, the more I realized how much I still had to learn.

I know each morning Father thanked the Lord for his great gift. Not just a son but—as he always put it—*such* a son.

I, on the other hand, was in a constant state of anxiety, fearing I might disappoint him in some way.

Father towered over other rabbis, physically as well as spiritually. Needless to say, he also towered over me. He was a large man, well over six feet, with shining black eyes, and while both Deborah and I inherited his dark complexion, unhappily for her, *she* got his height.

Papa cast a long shadow over my life. Whenever I was chided in the classroom for some minor lapse, the teacher always tortured me with comparisons: "*This* from the son of the great Rav Luria?"

Unlike my fellow classmates, I never had the luxury of being able to be wrong. What was innocent for others somehow was regarded as unworthy when it came to me: "The future Silczer Rebbe trading baseball cards?"

And yet I think that was why my father didn't send me to our own school, on the same street as our house. There, I might have gotten special treatment. There, such sins as giggling at the teacher—

not to mention tossing chalk at him when he turned to the blackboard—might have gone unpunished.

Instead, I had to make the long—and sometimes perilous—journey from our house to the notoriously rigorous Etz Chaim Yeshiva ten blocks north, an institute of learning where the principal was known as the greatest rabbi of the century— the twelfth century.

Each school day, including Sundays, I rose at dawn to say morning prayers in the same room as my father, he wearing his phylacteries and prayer shawl, swaying as he faced east toward Jerusalem and praying for our people's restoration to Zion.

In retrospect, this puzzled me—especially since there was now a State of Israel. Yet I never questioned anything this great man did.

School began promptly at eight and we spent till noon on Hebrew subjects, mostly points of grammar and the Bible. In our early years we concentrated on the "story" parts—Noah's Ark, the Tower of Babel, and Joseph's multicolored coat. As we grew older and more mature—that is, at about eleven or twelve—we began to study the Talmud, the massive compendium of Jewish civil and religious law.

The first of its two parts merely sets forth the precepts codified by subject. These contain no fewer than four thousand rules and postulations.

I sometimes wondered how my father could retain so much of this inside his head. Indeed, he seemed to know by heart not only the precepts but the commentaries as well.

Talmud class was like a junior law school. We began with obligations concerning lost property, and by the end of the semester, I knew, if I happened to come across fruit spilled out on the ground, whether I could keep it or must turn it in.

At noon, we all went down to lunch where we could see across the room our female schoolmates, who were segregated for the Hebrew classes. After dessert, always little square bits of canned fruit salad, we sang grace, and the older boys had to rush upstairs to the synagogue to say afternoon prayers before our secular studies began.

From one o'clock till half past four, we lived in a completely different world. It was like any New York public school. We began, naturally, by saying the Pledge of Allegiance. At this point, the girls were with us. I suppose some modern sage had decreed that there was no harm in both sexes studying Civics, English, and Geography in the same room.

Except on Friday when we ended early for the Sabbath, it was almost always dark when we finally emerged.

Then I would wearily head home and, if I managed to arrive intact, I sat down and gobbled up whatever dinner Mama had prepared. Afterward I remained at the table doing my homework, both sacred and secular, until in my mother's estimation I was too exhausted to go on.

I spent very little of my childhood in bed. In fact, the only time I can recall being there more than a few hours was when I had the measles.

For all its near-sweatshop regime, I loved school. Our double day was like two banquets of knowledge for my hungry mind. But Saturday was my special Day of Judgment. For then I had to show my father what I had learned that week.

He was quite simply the Almighty Power in my life and—just as I imagined the Jewish God to be—incomprehensible, unknowable.

And capable of wrath.

2

Timothy

S t. Gregory's parish school was doubly religious. The boys and girls would begin each
school day with an affirmation of both Faiths:
Americanism and Catholicism.

Regardless of the weather, they would assemble
in the concrete playground, where Sister Mary
Immaculata would lead them first in the Pledge of
Allegiance and then the *Paternoster.* On cold winter days their words came out in little white
puffs, sometimes—symbolically enough—briefly
turning the school yard into a kind of terrestrial
cloud.

They would then file inside, respectfully silent—
for they feared Sister Mary Bernard's ruler no less
than hellfire and damnation.

There were occasional exceptions. Self-styled
tough guys like Ed McGee and Tim Hogan were

fearless enough to risk the next world for the sake
of pulling Isabel O'Brien's pigtails.

Indeed, there were moments of such rowdiness
that Sister actually despaired of the boys' salvation.
By the end of September she had begun to include
in her nightly prayers a special plea that Our Lady
send a speedy end to this semester. Let the incorrigible duo terrorize a stronger soul than hers.

At the door of every classroom there was a stoup
of holy water so that each child could dip his fingers
and bless himself, or—in the case of Tim and Ed—
flick drops on some hapless victim's neck.

The parochial school curriculum was like that of
ordinary public schools—Math, Civics, English,
and Geography, and the like—with one significant
addition. As early as kindergarten, the Sisters made
it clear that at St. Gregory's the most important
subject was Christian Doctrine—"To live and die a
good Catholic in this world in order to be happy
with God in the next."

Sister Mary Bernard was obsessed with the early
martyrs. She would often read to her class with
relish the gory details from Butler's *Lives of the
Saints.* Her already rubicund face would become
nearly crimson, perspiration fogging her thick
spectacles, which sometimes, as her fervor
mounted, would slide down to the end of her nose.

"The mad Emperor Nero was especially cruel,"
she expounded. "For he had our holy martyrs torn

to pieces by hungry dogs—or smeared with wax and then impaled with sharp stakes to be ignited and serve as torches."

Even at horrifying junctures like this, Ed McGee was not beyond whispering, "Sounds like fun, Timmo. Why don't we try it on O'Brien?"

When Sister Mary Bernard felt her audience was sufficiently mesmerized, she would close the book, wipe her brow, and come to the moral message.

"Now, boys and girls, you must remember this was a *privilege.* For if you are *not* a Christian, suffering all the fires of a thousand hells will not permit you to be called a martyr."

This modulated into another of her more frequent themes: the *others* in the outside world. The unbaptized. The heathen. The damned.

"You must refrain from—indeed, avoid at any cost—friendship with non-Catholics. For these are not people of the true Faith and they will go to Hell. It is easier to recognize the Jewish people by the way they look and dress. But the greatest danger is from Protestants—they're hard to spot and will often try to convince you they are Christians."

After learning how to avoid eternal damnation, they turned to their next priority—preparation for their first Holy Communion.

They began to learn the catechism.

Each week they were obliged to commit to

memory a certain number of questions and answers from this fundamental doctrine of the Catholic Church.

> *What are the chief punishments of Adam which we inherit through original sin?*
>
> The chief punishments of Adam which we inherit through original sin are: death, suffering, ignorance, and a strong inclination to sin.
>
> *What is the chief message of the New Testament?*
>
> The chief message of the New Testament is the joyful salvation through Jesus Christ.

Their textbook contained discussion questions with homespun examples.

"Isabel O'Brien." Sister Mary Bernard pointed to the red-haired girl sitting near the window.

"Yes, Sister?" Isabel asked, obediently rising to her feet.

"Isabel, if a girl loves her radio more than her rosary, is she going full speed toward Heaven?"

The little girl's pigtails whipped across her face, as she shook her head. "No, Sister. That would mean she's going full speed toward Hell."

"Very good, Isabel. Now, Ed McGee—"

The stocky boy slouched upward to an approximation of vertical.

"Yes, Sister?"

"Suppose a boy spends five hours a day playing ball and only five minutes praying. Is he doing all he can to love God?"

All eyes in the class were on Ed. They knew Sister had been saving this one especially for him.

"Well?" she demanded impatiently.

"Uh," Ed temporized, "that's a real tough question." Twenty-four pairs of little hands tried to stifle twenty-four high-pitched giggles.

"Come here immediately," ordered Sister Mary Bernard.

Ed ambled toward the front of the room, knowing full well what was in store. Before Sister even asked, he held out his palms. She glared at him, then sharply struck his outstretched hands, as Ed tried to maintain his smirk without wincing.

The teacher then admonished the entire class. "There'll be more of that for anyone who dares to act disrespectfully."

The class grinned in anticipation as she called on Timothy.

"Now, Tim Hogan—say the Apostles' Creed."

"By heart?"

"By heart—and from the heart," Sister Mary Bernard answered, tapping her ruler in readiness.

To Sister's utter astonishment, Tim recited every syllable without the slightest hesitation. Letter perfect.

"I believe in God, the Father Almighty, Creator

of heaven and earth; and in Jesus Christ, His only Son, Our Lord; Who was conceived by the Holy Ghost, born of the Virgin Mary . . ."

"That's good—very good," she felt obliged to concede.

Tim looked around the room and thought he saw disappointment in the eyes of his classmates.

Glowering, Ed McGee muttered, "Bookworm."

3

Deborah

Deborah loved the Sabbath. It was the holiest of all holidays, the only one mentioned in the original Ten Commandments.

Moreover, it was God's special gift to the Israelites. For countless millennia, ancient civilizations had reckoned time in years and months, but the notion of a seven-day *week* that culminated in a Sabbath was a Jewish invention.

It is a day of unadulterated joy. Even mourning for a parent or husband must cease during this twenty-four-hour dispensation from grief.

The Bible states that on the Sabbath the Almighty not only stopped work, but "renewed his soul."

And this was precisely what Deborah Luria experienced when she closed the door behind her on a Friday afternoon. She was not shutting herself in, but rather keeping the world out. The world of cars, stores, factories, worry, and toil. On Friday evening, something miraculous—a mixture of faith and joy—was reborn within her.

Perhaps, Deborah thought, that was why her mother was so transported when she stood motionless before the glowing silver candlesticks, as the Sabbath like a soft silk shawl fell gently upon her shoulders.

As the family watched in silence, Rachel would place her hands over her eyes and say the blessing in a voice so hushed that only God Himself could hear.

Every Friday afternoon, Deborah and her half sister Rena would join their mother cleaning, polishing, and cooking to ready the house for the invisible angels who would be their honored guests till three small stars could be seen in the Saturday evening sky.

Some time after darkness fell, Papa and Danny would come home from prayers, the smell of winter emanating from their coal black overcoats. The family would exchange greetings as if they were reuniting after months apart.

Rav Luria would place his large hands on Danny's head to bless him—and afterward do likewise for his daughters.

And then at last in his deep, husky voice he would sing to Mama the famous lines from Proverbs 31:

> *A woman of valor, who can find?*
> *For her price is far above rubies.*

As they stood around the white-clothed table lit by the glittering candles, Papa would raise his large silver cup and sing the blessings over the wine, and then over the bread—two loaves to commemorate God's sending a double portion of manna to the Israelites in the desert, so they would not have to gather food on the Sabbath.

The meal that followed was a banquet. Even in the poorest homes the family would sacrifice during the week so that Friday evening's dinner would be sumptuous—with, if possible, a fish *and* a meat course.

All through the evening Papa led everyone in a treasury of Sabbath songs and wordless Hasidic melodies—some from other lands and other centuries; some he had composed himself.

Deborah could survive all the other ordinary hours of the week merely by reminding herself that at the end were the precious moments when she could be free. When she could let her voice soar above all others. Her voice was exquisite—so clear and vibrant that Rachel often had to caution her to sing softly in the synagogue lest it distract the men.

Her mother's cheeks shone on the Sabbath, her eyes danced with the music. She seemed to radiate love. One day Deborah learned the special reason.

She was walking home from school with Molly Blumberg, a sixteen-year-old neighbor who was engaged to be married that summer. Molly was in a state of agitation, for she had just learned one of the most fundamental and least discussed rules of Jewish marriage.

It was a man's *duty* to make love to his wife on Friday night—a commandment based directly on Exodus 21:10. Moreover, this obligation could not be fulfilled in a perfunctory manner, for the Law demands that he "pleasure" her. A woman may even sue her husband if he does not.

This, Deborah noted, partially explains the reason for giving husbands a hearty meal. And the smile on a Jewish woman's face when she prepares it.

———

After the rest of the family had gone to bed, Deborah would remain alone in the only illuminated room in the entire household. And even *that* light wouldn't burn all night. Since the biblical injunction against work on the Sabbath had been construed by later sages to preclude even the turning on or off of electric lights, the Lurias, like most of their religious neighbors, had engaged a gentile to come and extinguish all lamps at eleven.

Deborah's text was always the Bible. And most often the Song of Songs. Completely absorbed, she would sometimes read aloud unwittingly:

> *By night on my bed I sought him whom my*
> *   soul loveth;*
> *I sought him, but I found him not. . . .*

Then she would softly close the Holy Book, kiss it, and go upstairs.

This was the happiest time in Deborah's childhood. For to her, *Shabbat* was synonymous with love.

4

Timothy

One Saturday morning in late May, Tim Hogan and his equally nervous classmates knelt in pews near the confessional, awaiting their turn to perform an all-important rite for the first time.

Since they all were seven, Sister had drilled them endlessly on how to confess, for only by purging himself of his sins could a Catholic be in a State of Grace—pure enough to receive Communion.

In direct defiance of Sister's long-standing order (based on the principle of divide and conquer), Ed McGee climbed across several of his classmates in the pew, shouldered his way into a space next to Timothy, and with a hard poke to his friend's ribs, tried to provoke him to break the silence. In truth, despite his outward behavior, Ed's bravado had abandoned him at the church door and he was almost prepared to admit that he was frightened.

Sensing the commotion, Sister Mary Bernard whirled around and fixed Ed with a glare powerful enough to send him straight to purgatory. As she took his sleeve and pulled him away, she admonished, "And another thing, Edward McGee. You can tell Father that you disobeyed me even in church."

Tim craned his neck to look at Ed as he left the confessional a few minutes later, but his friend's glance was fixed on the ground, as he walked toward the outside gate.

Well, it can't be so bad, he thought. McGee's all in one piece.

At this moment, a gentle tapping on his shoulder made him start. He stood up nervously, as Sister gestured which confessional box was to be his.

Head bowed, Tim walked slowly toward the cubicle thinking, This is gonna be a piece of cake. I know it all backwards and forwards . . . I hope.

Yet, as he entered the left compartment, drew the curtain behind him, and knelt, his heart began to pound.

Before him was a wooden panel. It slid open, and through the mesh screen he glimpsed the purple stole around the neck of his confessor, whose features he could not discern.

Suddenly, in one split second, the gravity—the great significance of all this—electrified him. He knew that for the first time he would have to open his heart completely.

"Bless me, Father, for I have sinned. This is my first confession."

He took a deep breath and then recited, "I was late for school three times last week. I tore the cover off Davy Murphy's notebook and threw it at him."

He paused. No lightning flashed. Nor did the earth open and swallow him. Perhaps the Lord was waiting for the graver sins.

"Last Thursday I flushed Kevin Callahan's hat down the toilet, and made him cry."

He waited, his heart fluttering.

A voice from the other side of the screen said gently, "This surely was a disrespect of property, my son. And you must remember that Our Lord said, 'Blessed are the meek.' Now for your penance. . . ."

That was Timothy's first confession.

But his *first* real confession did not come until five years later.

"I peeked through the keyhole when my older sister Bridget was taking a bath."

After a moment, there was a monosyllabic reply from the other side. "Yes?"

"Well," Tim protested, "that's it. I just looked." Then he forced himself to add, "And had impure thoughts."

There was another silence as if the confessor sensed that more remained unsaid. He was right, for Tim suddenly blurted out, "I have these awful feelings."

For a moment, there was no reaction from the other side of the screen. Then he heard, "You mean of sexual matters, my son?"

"I've already told you about those."

"Then what are these other 'feelings'?"

Tim hesitated, took a deep breath, and confessed, "I hate my father."

There was a slight but audible "Oh" from the other side of the screen. Then the priest said, "Our Savior taught that God is love. Why do you . . . feel otherwise about your father?"

"Because I don't know who he is."

There was a solemn silence. Tim whispered, "That's all."

"The thoughts you had were most unchristian," his confessor said. "We must always fight the temptation to disobey any commandment in thought, word, or deed. Now for your penance. Say three Hail Marys and make a good Act of Contrition."

The priest then murmured the words of absolution, *in nomine patris et filii et spiritus sancti,* adding, "Go in peace."

Timothy left. But not in peace.

————

Reluctantly, Tim tried to accept that he would never meet his earthly father. But he could not quell the longing for his mother—nor come to terms with the painful knowledge that he was separated from her by a mere two hours' bus ride.

He had tried for his own sake to believe Tuck's lurid descriptions of a raving lunatic too mad to recognize him. To acknowledge that the terrible sight of her would cause him even more pain. But his visions were too strong to alter.

At night his imagination would conjure up a pure, golden-haired woman in flowing white robes, a kind of madonna who, though physically too weak to care for him, nonetheless reciprocated his longings and prayed for his visit.

Sometimes he would daydream that when he grew up and had a home of his own he would be able to take her in and care for her. He wanted her to know this. To reassure her.

Which is why he had to see her.

For his twelfth birthday, he pleaded for a special present: would they take him to the asylum to see her. Just look at her from afar even. But Tuck and Cassie refused.

Six months later he made the same request and was put off even more brusquely.

"Go for all I care," Cassie had screamed with exasperation. "Take a look at my demented sister and see what you have for a mother. You'll rue the day."

Tuck summed it up with his characteristically sardonic humor: "The present we're givin' you is not takin' you." He added, "Now let that be an end to it."

And it was an end. At least to *discussing* it. Now

Tim had no choice but to take matters into his own hands.

Early one Saturday morning, he casually told his aunt that he and some of the guys were going to watch the Knicks play at Madison Square Garden. She merely nodded, glad to be rid of him for the day. She did not even notice he was wearing his confirmation suit.

Tim raced to the subway and took the express into Manhattan, to the Port Authority bus terminal on Eighth Avenue and Forty-first Street. He approached the ticket window apprehensively and asked for a round-trip ticket to Westbrook, New York. The gum-chewing clerk took the five-dollar bill, moist and crumpled, from the boy's nervous palm and pressed two buttons with her crimson-nailed finger. Her machine spewed out a card.

Tim looked at it. "No, no," he said, his voice breaking. "This is a child's fare. I'm over twelve."

The woman stared at him. "Hey, kid, do me a favor," she complained. "Make like it's Christmas so I don't hafta rebalance my till sheet. Besides, you must be a little nuts to be so honest."

A little nuts. The words were chilling for a boy on his way to his mother in an insane asylum.

The next bus left at 10:50 A.M. Tim bought two Baby Ruth bars, which were intended to serve as lunch. But his anxiety had made him inordinately hungry, and he consumed them both more than a half hour before the bus took on its passengers.

Feverish with anticipation and desperate to distract himself from thoughts of where he was going, he went downstairs again and bought a Captain Marvel comic.

At last, the platform clock reached 10:45 and the driver, balding and bespectacled in a creased Greyhound uniform, announced that boarding would commence.

There were not many people heading for upstate New York in the inclement January weather, so it was only a few seconds later that Tim was climbing aboard. Just as he was handing his ticket to the driver, a large paw grabbed him firmly by the shoulder.

"Okay, buster, the game's over."

He whirled around. It was a huge, barrel-chested black man, wearing a revolver and the intimidating blue of the New York police force.

"Your name Hogan?" the officer growled.

"What's it to you? I haven't done anything wrong."

"Well, I don't know about that," the policeman replied. "You sure fit the description I've got of a runaway named Hogan."

"I'm not running anywhere," Tim persisted bravely.

The bus driver interrupted. "Hey, officer. I've got a schedule, y'know."

"Yeah, okay, okay." The big man nodded and,

keeping a firm grip on Tim's arm, said, "We won't be making any joyrides today."

The moment captor and captive descended, the bus door hissed closed and the vehicle pulled away from the curb, heading for a destination Tim now knew he would never reach.

The cruelty of this encounter—the fleeting, tantalizing seconds that had robbed him of a lifelong goal—now evoked in him a feeling of sadness so profound that he began to sob.

"Hey, take it easy, kid," the police officer murmured in a more kindly voice. "What'd you try the escape act for, anyway? Did you misbehave or something?"

Tim shook his head. Now he really did want to run away and never see the Delaneys again.

Unfortunately, he saw his uncle all too soon. He had waited less than a half hour in the terminal's police headquarters when Tuck appeared.

"So, you little twerp," he saluted Tim. "Thought you could pull a fast one on me, didja? Boy, are you dumb—you didn't even look in the papers to see if the Knicks were playing in town."

He looked at the arresting officer. "Thanks for nabbing him, pal. Have you got a room where I can talk to the kid alone?"

The black man nodded, indicating a small door in the rear. Tuck grabbed Tim by the elbow and started to pull him, but this time the boy protested.

"No! No! I didn't do anything—I didn't."

"*I'll* be the judge of that. Now you gotta take what's coming to ya."

As they disappeared into the room, the police-man lit a cigarette and began to flick through the *Daily News*. Moments later he winced at sounds he recognized: the repeated slaps of a belt against bare buttocks, followed by a muffled groan as the truant child attempted manfully to deny the pain.

———

On the subway home, Tim stood and gritted his teeth. He glared at his uncle and swore inwardly, I'll kill you some day.

5

Daniel

As I walked along the snowy sidewalk, Bible in hand, I could distinguish shadows of the faithful coming home from morning Mass.

It was Christmas morning. And I was doing what my ancestors had always done on this day— deliberately ignoring it. Which is why I was going to school. And the rest of my father's followers had all gone to work. This unfestive action was meant as a lesson in itself: Remember, this is not *your* holiday.

During the twilight of the year, our yeshivas and high schools also gave their students two weeks' holiday—which they pointedly designated as merely "winter vacation." To accentuate even further the difference between us and our gentile neighbors, school reopened for one day on December twenty-fifth. It was a gesture of defiance.

Our teacher, Rabbi Schumann, dressed in his customary black suit and homburg hat, watched solemnly as we filed in and took our seats. He was an austere and demanding tyrant who often berated us when we made even the tiniest error.

Like many of our other teachers, he had spent several years in a concentration camp, and pallor seemed ingrained in his features. In retrospect, I think his severity with us was a personal way of disguising the grief, and perhaps the guilt, he felt at having survived the Holocaust when so many had not.

The Bible passages he had chosen that day all emphasized the otherness of our religion, and as the morning progressed, Rabbi Schumann grew increasingly upset. Finally, he closed his book and with a deep sigh, rose and transfixed us with his hollow, dark-ringed eyes.

"This day, this awful, awful day is when *they* found the fuel for the torches that would burn us everywhere. In the centuries since our expulsion from the Holy Land, has there ever been a country that has not persecuted us in *his* name? And our own age has witnessed the ultimate horror—the Nazis with their ruthless efficiency— *Six million of us.*"

He pulled out his handkerchief and tried to staunch the tears. "Women, little children," he went on with anguish. "They all turned into wisps of smoke from the ovens." His voice grew hoarse.

"I saw this, boys. I saw them kill my wife and children. They wouldn't even do me the kindness of exterminating me. They left me living on the rack of memory."

No one in the classroom breathed. We were overwhelmed by his speech, not merely for its content but because Rabbi Schumann, normally a stern taskmaster, was now sobbing helplessly.

Then, still weeping, he continued. "Listen—we are sitting here today to show the Christians that we're still alive. We were here before them, and we shall endure until the Messiah comes."

He paused, regained his breath, and some of his composure.

"Now let us rise."

I always dreaded this moment when we had to sing the slender verses chanted by so many of our brethren as they entered the gas chambers:

> *I believe with all my heart*
> *In the coming of The Messiah,*
> *And though He may tarry on the way*
> *I nonetheless believe. I still believe.*

The afternoon sky was a gray shroud as I walked home, shaken. Once again, I passed all the Christmas lights. But this time what I saw in them were the shining, indestructible atoms of six million souls.

6

Timothy

On a hot afternoon in the summer of 1963, fourteen-year-old Tim, Ed McGee, and their perpetual cheering section, Jared Fitzpatrick, were passing through alien territory—the neighborhood adjacent to St. Gregory's, which was the center of the *B'nai Simcha* community.

When they passed the home of Rav Moses Luria, Ed sneered, "Look, that's where the head Hebe lives. Why don't we ring his doorbell or something?"

"Good idea," Tim agreed, but Fitzpatrick had qualms.

"Suppose he answers? He might put a curse on us. . . ."

"Aw, c'mon, Fitzy," McGee jibed. "You're just a lily-livered chicken."

"The hell I am," he protested. "It's just that

ringin' bells is kids' stuff. Couldn't we do something more interesting?"

"Like what?" Ed countered. "We ain't got a hand grenade."

"How about a rock through his window?" Tim suggested, pointing to a Con Edison excavation a few dozen feet down the road. The workmen had gone for the day, leaving potential missiles of all sizes.

Fitzy rushed over to the site and selected a stone slab roughly the size of a baseball.

"Okay, guys," Ed challenged, "who's gonna be the first-string pitcher?" He fixed Tim with a stare. "I'd do it for sure, but I've still got a kinda sprain in my arm from beating up those niggers last Thursday."

Before Tim had time to protest, Ed and Fitzy had elected him. "C'mon, chickenshit, throw the goddamn thing!"

In one furious motion he snatched it from Ed's hand, cocked his arm, and hurled the stone at the rabbi's largest window.

The noise was deafening. Tim turned toward his companions.

They were already halfway down the street.

———

Three hours later, the Lurias' doorbell rang.

Deborah answered, still in a state of shock, and was now further taken aback at the sight of the two callers. She immediately went to inform her father.

The Rav had been deeply engrossed in a difficult passage of a legal *midrash* when the enemy missile had pierced the sanctuary of his household.

Ever since that moment he had been standing immobile, staring through the few angry slices of glass still clinging to the window frame, his mind tortured by images of pogroms and goose-stepping storm troopers.

"Papa," Deborah said haltingly, "there's a policeman at the door . . . he's got a boy with him."

"Ah," he murmured, "perhaps we might receive some justice this time. Ask them to come in."

Moments later they appeared.

"Good afternoon, Reverend," the policeman said as he removed his cap. "I'm Officer Delaney. Sorry to disturb you, but I'm here about the damage to your window."

"Yes," the Rav acknowledged somberly, "damage *has* been done."

"Well, here's the malefactor," the policeman answered, pulling at the young boy's collar as if to hoist him like a trapped animal. "I'm ashamed to say that Tim Hogan here's my ungrateful nephew. We took him in after his poor mother Margaret fell sick."

"Oh," said the Rav. "So this is Margaret Hogan's son. I should have recognized the eyes."

"You knew my mother?" Tim asked.

"In a distant way. When my wife died, Sexton Isaacs hired her to come in now and then to keep my house in order."

"More's the disgrace." Tuck glared at Tim. "Now say it. Tell the rabbi what I told you."

Timothy screwed up his face as if tasting a bitter pill and mumbled, "I'm—"

"Louder, boy," the policeman growled. "This is a man of the cloth you're talking to."

"I—I'm sorry for what I did, Your Reverence," Timothy responded, and continued by rote, "I take full responsibility for my actions and I intend to pay for the damage."

Rav Luria looked quizzically at the young man for a moment, then said, "Sit down, Timothy."

Tim perched himself obediently on the edge of a chair facing the rabbi's book-strewn desk, but he could not keep himself from squirming nervously as he watched the bearded Jewish man pace back and forth along the sagging wooden shelves, his hands clasped behind his back.

"Timothy," the rabbi began slowly, "can you tell me what induced you to perform such a hostile act?"

"I—I didn't know it was your house, sir."

"But you knew it was a Jewish home, yes?"

Tim lowered his head. "Yes, sir."

"Do you feel any special . . . animosity toward our people?"

"I . . . well, some of my friends . . . I mean, we've been told . . ."

He could say no more. By this point his uncle was also beginning to sweat.

"But do you think it's true?" the Rav said quietly. "I mean, does this house look in any way different from your friends' homes?"

Tim looked around for a moment, before responding candidly, "Well, there are an awful lot of books . . ."

"Yes," the rabbi continued. "But otherwise, do I or any of my family look like demons?"

"No, sir."

"Then I hope that this unhappy incident gave you a chance to see that Jews are just like other people . . . with perhaps a few more books."

He turned to the policeman. "Thank you for giving me the opportunity to converse with your nephew."

"But we haven't discussed compensation yet. A big window like that must have cost a pretty penny. And since Tim won't rat on his accomplices, he'll have to pay you by himself."

"But Uncle Tuck—"

The Rav intervened. "How old are you, Timothy?"

"Just turned fourteen, sir."

"What do you think you can do to earn money?"

Tuck answered for his nephew. "He can run errands or carry groceries for the neighbors and they'll give him a little something."

"How little?"

"Oh, a nickel or a dime."

"But at that rate it would take years to repay the cost of my window."

The officer merely looked at the rabbi and stated, "I don't care if it takes a century. He'll pay you something every week."

Rav Luria put his hands to his forehead as if grasping for some elusive idea, then raised his head and spoke.

"I think I have a solution that may be of help to both parties," he declared. "Officer Delaney," the rabbi went on, "I can see your nephew is basically a good boy. How late is Timothy allowed to stay up?"

"School days till ten."

"And Friday nights?" asked the Rav.

"Ten-thirty, eleven. If there's a night game on TV, I let him watch till it's over."

"Good." A smile had taken over the rabbi's face. Turning to the boy, he announced, "I may have a job for you. . . ."

"He'll take it," his uncle said quickly.

"I'd rather he made up his own mind," said the Rav gently. "It's a post of great responsibility. Do you know what a *Shabbes goy* is?"

Again Officer Delaney interrupted. "Begging your pardon, Rabbi, but isn't '*goy*' what you people call Christians?"

"Yes," Rav Luria answered. "But the word simply means 'gentile.' A *Shabbes goy* is a non-Jew of impeccable morals who comes in on Friday evenings after our Sabbath has begun and performs the functions that are prohibited to us—like lowering the heat, putting out lights, and so forth. The individual in question," he explained, "usually runs additional errands for us during the week so he can learn something of our laws, since it is a sin for us to *tell* him to do anything once the Sabbath has begun." He turned to Timothy.

"It so happens that Lawrence Conroy is about to leave for the College of the Holy Cross to study Medicine. For the past three years he has been assisting us, the Kagans, Mr. Wasserstein, and both Shapiro brothers. Every month each household gives him some money and each Friday they leave out a portion of whatever dessert they're having that night. If you're interested, it would take you only a few months to pay your debt."

Several minutes later, as they were walking homeward, Patrolman Delaney offered his final comment on the unpleasant matter.

"Hear me, Timmy," he said, "and hear me good. Next time you break some Jew window, make sure it isn't some important rabbi's."

7

Deborah

When Deborah was barely fourteen years old, she witnessed a mighty—if unequal—battle between her half sister and her father.

"I won't marry him—I won't!"

"Rena, you're over seventeen," her father murmured, and then alluded to her older sister. "Malka was married by then. And you're not even betrothed. Tell me again what's so bad about Rebbe Epstein's boy?"

"He's fat," Rena said.

Rav Luria addressed his wife. "Did you hear that, Racheleh? Suddenly matchmaking has become a beauty contest! Our daughter believes this fine scholar from a respectable family is unworthy because he's a little overweight."

"More than a little," Rena muttered.

"Rena," the rabbi pleaded, "he's a pious boy and

he'll make you a fine husband. Why are you being so obstinate?"

"Because I just don't want to."

Good for you, Rena, Deborah thought to herself.

"Don't want to?" asked the rabbi in a tone of melodramatic astonishment. "How can 'I don't want to' be a valid reason?"

Danny suddenly leapt to Rena's aid.

"But Father," he interjected. "What about the Code of Law? Even Ha Ezer 42:12. Doesn't it say that a marriage must have the woman's consent?"

Had this come from anyone but his adored son and heir, Moses Luria would have fumed at having any of his statements questioned. Instead, he could not help but smile with pride. His little boy, not yet *bar mitzvah,* was not afraid to lock scriptural horns with the Silczer Rebbe. For the moment, the discussion was ended.

In the days that followed there was constant tension in the Luria household and whispered phone calls late into the night.

After concluding a particularly lengthy conversation, the Rav marched slowly and deliberately into the living room, where the rest of the family was seated.

He looked at his wife and said wearily, "Epstein's starting to push. He claims he's gotten an offer from the Belzer for one of *his* daughters." The Rav sighed histrionically. "Ah, what a pity to lose such a fine scholar." He glanced at Rena. "Of course, I wouldn't dream of forcing you to do anything you don't want to, my darling," he said gently. "It's still completely up to you."

In the silence that followed, Deborah could sense the closing of an emotional vise on her sister's will.

"All right, Papa," Rena sighed weakly, "I'll marry him."

The Rav exploded with joy. "Wonderful! This is wonderful news. Is two weeks enough to have the betrothal ceremony?"

He turned to his wife and asked, "What do you think, Racheleh?"

"It's fine by me. Will you arrange it with Rebbe Epstein?"

The Rav grinned. "I already have."

Deborah gritted her teeth and vowed that she would never let them manipulate her this way. She could not keep from wondering—would he be so overbearing with his beloved Danny?

———

Later, Danny vaguely remembered Rebbe Epstein's visit to his father's office to iron out the arrangements for the marriage, among them Rena's dowry and, most important, the date and place of the wedding.

The next part echoed in Danny's memory forever. To symbolize the sealing of the bargain, tradition made the parents break a plate. Sometimes—and this was the case that day—several women came with crockery, and when the agreement was announced, there was a loud cacophony of dishes crashing on the kitchen floor amid effusive shouts. *"Mazel tov, mazel tov!"*

"Why are they all going crazy breaking plates?" Danny asked his father.

"Well, my son." The Rav beamed. "There are several explanations. Some say just as a broken glass cannot be fixed, so the agreement between bride and groom cannot be allowed to shatter. There's also a more colorful tradition. The noise is supposed to scare away the evil spirits that might put a curse on Rena's marriage."

Even Deborah, who had been sulking at the prospect of her sister's unwilling marriage, took part in this and joined the universal laughter that preceded the betrothal feast.

On the Sabbath before the wedding, the rotund Avrom Epstein was honored as groom-to-be by receiving an invitation to the pulpit to read the week's selection from the Prophets.

As he mounted the podium, a bombardment of tiny missiles suddenly descended all about him. These were raisins, almonds, nuts, and sweet candies thrown from the ladies' gallery as a gesture of good luck. Most of the women carelessly tossed their handfuls, but Deborah made her own quiet statement, aiming as many nuts as she could at the head of her future brother-in-law.

———

It remained for Rachel to explain the special Jewish "facts of life" to her stepdaughter. Deborah should not have been present, but she wanted very much to hear, and neither Rachel nor Rena objected.

The essence of her mother's lecture was a woman's purity. Or, put another way, *impurity.* The Rav had been scrupulous in consulting with Rachel to determine Rena's menstrual cycle, so that on her wedding day she would be ritually pure. Now, in minute detail, Rachel explained to Rena how to examine herself every month to determine the onset of her period and its conclusion. Thereafter she would be required to change her underclothes and bed linen daily, and seven days later sexual intercourse would finally be permitted again.

During the fortnight of her spiritual "pollution," a wife might not touch her husband in any way. Even their twin beds had to be well separated. The rules were so stringent that a husband could not eat food left over from his wife, unless it had been transferred to another dish.

"Do you understand everything, Rena?" Rachel asked.

Her stepdaughter merely nodded.

Rachel reached over and patted her hand. "I know how you must feel, darling. I also wish it was your own mother telling you all this."

Rena nodded again and said, "Thank you."

Deborah could not restrain her feelings of

resentment at the notion that some day she, too, would be considered "unclean" in her husband's eyes. For half a month she would be impure, besmirched, *untouchable.*

Six weeks later, Rachel took Rena to the *mikva,* the ritual bath, for her first purification. Deborah remained at home to fantasize.

She knew what would be happening, for Mama had described it all beforehand. Her sister would have to go into a bathroom where she would remove all her clothing, watch, rings—even the Band-Aid covering the cut on her finger.

She would then have to wash, brush her teeth, comb all the hairs of her body, cut and scrub her fingernails. Finally, under the severe scrutiny of the matron in attendance, Rena would walk naked down a few stone steps into a large cistern filled with running water and immerse herself completely.

The diligent attendant had to be satisfied that every strand of hair was submerged. If a single hair remained above the water, the procedure would be invalid.

Rena would have to do this every month for the rest of her childbearing years, which could mean a quarter of a century.

For the next forty-eight hours, Rena was taciturn and nervous. Several times, Deborah even thought she heard her weeping softly in her room. Once, hearing a muffled sob, she knocked, but evidently Rena did not want to share her feelings.

"Look, it's normal," her mother explained to both girls. "Getting married is the most important event in a woman's life. But it's also a terrible wrench—leaving your parents' house, going to live with someone. . . ." She stopped herself.

"Someone you hardly know at all," Deborah bitterly finished the thought.

Rachel shrugged uneasily. "Well, there's that aspect, too. But do you know something, Deborah? Arranged marriages sometimes work out better than so-called romantic ones. Compared to others, the divorce rate among the Orthodox is like a little grain of sand—it hardly happens."

Yes, Deborah thought. Because it's almost impossible to *get* a divorce.

"Rena darling," Rachel whispered to her stepdaughter tenderly, "I'll share a very private truth with you. When my father came to me to propose Rav Luria—I mean Moses—as my potential husband, I was . . . to be honest . . . not that enthusiastic."

She paused, and then, to reassure herself that her confession would not travel, added, "Remember, you can't tell this to a soul."

Rena nodded and placed a hand affectionately on Rachel's.

Rachel continued. "I mean, after all, I was even

younger than you. Moses seemed to me more like a parent than what I had dreamed of as a husband. He was older, he had children . . . and he was the legendary Silczer Rav."

She closed her eyes as she reminisced. "But then we met alone. And from the first, I knew that he could read my mind. He understood exactly all the qualms I was feeling. And so he told me a simple story. It was one of the Jewish legends of the mystics—that when the soul descends from Heaven it has two parts, one male, the other female. They separate and enter different bodies. But if these people then lead righteous lives, the Father of the Universe will reunite them as a couple.

"I stopped being upset about marrying some-body twice my age, and began to think of it as my soul finding its other half. From that moment, I fell in love with him. And," she concluded, "I hope you agree that we have a marriage like an oak tree and a vine."

All three women stared at one another, speech-less: Rachel, astounded by her own unexpected candor; Rena, comforted.

And Deborah, confused and slightly frightened that she knew so little of the outside world.

———

On the morning of the wedding Rena did not come downstairs, for the Law bids bride and groom fast all day until the ceremonies are over. When Deb-orah inquired solicitously how her sister felt, she merely answered, "It's okay. I'm not hungry anyway."

The relatives and other celebrants were already gathered in the courtyard of the synagogue, when Avrom Epstein, wearing a prayer shawl over the bridegroom's traditional white costume, appeared at the door and was led by the women to the living room, where Rena waited.

Dancing at his heels was a trio of young, bearded *kletzmer* musicians—fiddler, clarinetist, and tambourine man—all looking like fugitives from a painting by Chagall as they played merrily. The bride stood to greet her future husband.

Avrom gazed at her and whispered, "It's going to be all right, Rena. We'll be good to each other."

He took her veil, placed it over her face, and then left, followed again by his mini-parade of musicians.

Scarcely an hour later, as they faced one another under the wedding canopy set up in the courtyard of the synagogue, Avrom placed the ring on Rena's index finger and said, "Be thou consecrated unto me as my wife according to the Law of Moses and Israel."

Then, in keeping with the magnitude of the occasion, each of the seven ritual blessings was pronounced by a different distinguished rabbi, some of whom had come from out of the state for the ceremony.

Yakov Ever, the famous cantor (and recording

artist) who had come all the way from Manhattan, chanted blessings over the wine. Finally, the traditional glass was placed on the ground next to the large black shoes of Avrom Epstein.

When he lifted his foot, smashing the glass, the gathered throng all shouted "*Mazel tov, mazel tov!*" and the musicians, now augmented by a double bass and a full set of cymbals and drums, struck up, as the psalm says, "a joyful noise unto the Lord."

The feast was splendid and, as was customary, segregated, with men and women seated at tables on opposite sides of the room. Only the children had a passport to toddle across the frontiers of gender, and they did so frequently and noisily.

Deborah always seemed to find one or two of Malka's five children on her lap. She later recalled these as the best parts of the evening.

The young musicians' enthusiasm was so infectious that Cantor Ever fairly bounded to the microphone to give a vibrant rendition of the most important song at any Hasidic wedding—"All the World's a Narrow Bridge," a reminder to the newlyweds that, even at this happy moment in their lives, they are perilously bounded by sadness on either side.

When at last the long meal ended and the benedictions for the couple were complete, tables and chairs were pushed to the sides and the room was transformed into an immense ballroom.

To the strains of "A Lucky Star, a Lucky Sign,"

the two mothers-in-law, Rachel and the full-bosomed Rebbitsin Epstein, began the dance, followed by the newlyweds themselves.

This was a unique moment in the festivities—the only time when a man and a woman would dance together.

The others danced on their respective sides of the room, and long after the ladies had returned weary and sweating to their chairs, the long-bearded men continued to dance energetically with one another, forming a huge ring by holding handkerchiefs between them.

It was at this point that the clarinetist gave his fellow musicians a sly wink. At that signal they launched into a special song whose lyrics were merely the syllables *"Biri biri bum biri bum."* It was the most famous of the melodies composed by Rav Moses Luria himself and had been printed in the two-volume *Great Book of Hasidic Tunes*.

At its conclusion there was ecstatic applause and cries of encouragement for Rav Luria to sing his own song. He happily complied, his foot tapping rhythmically and his eyes closed in concentration.

Danny tried to keep up with the older men, who—especially Papa—seemed indefatigable. Finally on the verge of exhaustion, he excused himself to get a drink. Unwisely, he quenched his thirst with wine instead of seltzer water, and was soon light-headed. And uninhibited enough to call out to his sister who was sitting pensively by herself.

"C'mon, Deb, don't just sit there. Get dancing!"

Reluctantly Deborah rose and rejoined the few women still holding hands and swaying to the music.

There was no way Danny could have known that her mood had just plummeted after hearing her ebullient Uncle Saul boom, "Deborah—just think, you're next!"

8

Daniel

This time I really thought he was going to kill me.

Was this my reward for taking extra lessons in Torah?

It was the year of my *bar mitzvah*, and Papa had arranged for me to stay an extra hour every afternoon to study with Rebbe Schumann the portion of the Prophets I was to read on that momentous day. My journey home was therefore even darker and more perilous than before.

I do not know what destiny brought the murderous Ed McGee into my path that night. Perhaps he had been lying in wait, since he seemed to derive some special joy from assaulting me.

I was caught in a kind of cross fire. The other kids at school resented me because I was the son of such a renowned and pious man. Their jealousy aroused, they would hurl abuse at me. But McGee—for almost the same reasons—would hurl fists.

This time there were no spectators—which frightened me. Who would restrain him should he go berserk? It was so icy cold that the rare pedestrian who passed us had his collar drawn up and hat down, barely leaving room enough for his eyes to see where he was going. And the wind was so loud it all but drowned my groans. My only arsenal was defensive—my shield of holy books, which I held up as quickly as I could.

Then suddenly Ed crossed the border of all precedent. His right fist smashed the cover of my Talmud, shattering its binding and knocking it from my hand onto the ground. I do not know whether the shock or the sacrilege caused me greater pain.

"Now, you little kike," he sneered, "you don't have your precious Jew books to hide behind. Stand and fight me like a man."

He lowered his fists, stuck out his chin, and boasted, "I'll even give ya the first punch free."

I had never hit anyone in my life, but suddenly my fear transmuted into rage, and I lashed out at his solar plexus. I heard a sudden whoosh, like air being expelled from a huge balloon.

Ed doubled over in pain and stumbled backward, trying his best not to fall. Though I knew this was my opportunity to run, I stood there paralyzed as my attacker continued to stagger, gasping for breath.

Why didn't I escape when I could? Shock, for one thing. I couldn't believe what I'd just done. And how effective it had been.

And, for some strange reason, I felt guilty. Guilty for having caused harm to another human being.

He was quickly in control again, and fire seemed to erupt from his mouth.

"Now," he growled. "Now I'm gonna kill you."

Suddenly there was a shout.

"Leave him alone, McGee, you stupid shit!"

We both looked up, startled. It was Tim Hogan running toward us.

"Stay out of this," Ed countered. "This kike and I are having a private fight."

"Just leave him alone," Timothy repeated. "He's a rabbi's son." He turned to me and ordered, "Go home, Danny."

"What are you, Hogan, his bodyguard or something?" McGee sneered.

"No, Ed, I'm just his friend."

"You call this sissy Jew your friend?"

"Yeah," Tim replied with a calm that awed me. "Wanna make something out of it?"

"Are you serious?" McGee gasped.

"There's only one way you can find out," Tim replied, turning to me again and ordering, "Danny, go home. Right now!"

I must have looked as if I was bowing when I bent down, picked up my injured books, and began to retreat. Out of the corner of my eye I could see the two of them standing toe-to-toe like gladiators. As I started down the street, I could hear the sound of fighting. Punches exchanged, parried, landed. I did not dare look back. And then I heard the unmistakable sound of someone falling to the pavement. It was followed by the soft-spoken words of Tim Hogan.

"Sorry, Ed. But you had it coming."

9

Timothy

Though her husband did not suspect it, Cassie Delaney had stopped pooling her salary with his each week. That is, she no longer contributed her entire share.

All through her childhood, her blue-eyed sister Margaret had been the "pretty one," and she—in their very own mother's words—the "scarecrow." They remained the same even as adults.

Nothing her husband could say dissuaded Cassie from believing she was inherently unattractive. She sensed that he daydreamed of a sexier wife.

She suddenly found an opportunity to change all that. Her department received an order of exquisite black French silk negligees, garments seductive enough to make any woman look like Brigitte Bardot.

She had to have one of them. But where would

she find the eighty-six dollars? Even with her employee's discount, she would never be able to afford such a luxury.

By a stroke of luck, Macy's unexpectedly raised her salary by $4.68 a week. She withheld this information from Tuck and began stockpiling the cash.

When she was certain that the household was asleep, she would creep into the kitchen, mount a stepladder, and place four dollars in an empty box of Kellogg's corn flakes.

The weeks passed slowly, but gradually her treasure grew. At last breathless count she had reached sixty-eight dollars.

One Saturday evening, she arrived home to find a note from her husband that he had taken all the kids out for a pizza. Tired as she was, she felt a tingle of delight as she climbed the stepladder to add four more dollars to her riches.

But there was something funny about the box. It did not seem as full as it had been. Counting the money bill by bill, she discovered to her horror that there were only fifty-two dollars.

She felt simultaneously sick and furious.

"Goddammit, there's a bloody thief among us."

Nor did she have to look far to find a likely culprit.

She stormed upstairs and began to ransack Timothy's room. In a pair of his sneakers, she found *money*—far more than he ever could have saved from his weekly twenty-five-cents allowance. And there was only one place he could have gotten it.

"That's the limit!" she exploded to Tuck. "We've got to send him away. I'm going to speak to Father Hanrahan tomorrow."

Voices easily passed through the plywood barriers of the Delaney house. Upstairs in his room Tim heard everything.

"Oh Jesus!" he whispered to himself, suddenly feeling a terrible emptiness in his chest. What could he do? Where could he turn?

———

It was a Sunday afternoon. Rachel had gone with Danny and Deborah to visit her mother in Queens. As usual, the Rav stayed home in his study. There was always so much work to do.

He was absorbed in a particularly complex case appearing before his religious court involving an abandoned woman—an *agunah*—who was applying for permission to marry again, when he was interrupted by a voice.

"Excuse me, Rabbi."

He looked up, startled. "Oh, it's you, Timothy." He smiled with relief. "I sometimes forget you have a key."

He reached into the top drawer of his desk. "I've got your month's wages right here."

As he offered Tim the envelope, Rav Luria suddenly sensed that the boy's visit was not merely to collect his salary.

"Sit down," he said, motioning to the chair opposite his desk and then, offering a plate, added, "Have a homemade macaroon."

Tim shook his head—but only in reference to the cookies. He seemed to welcome the invitation to remain, yet was afraid to speak.

Rav Luria took the initiative. "I want to tell you again, Timothy, how much the families appreciate how well you're doing your job."

"Thanks," Tim answered uneasily, "but I don't think I'll be able to do it much longer."

"Oh—? Is anything the matter?"

"Uh, no," Tim replied stoically. "It's just that I'll probably be going away to boarding school."

"Well," said the rabbi. "I suppose I should congratulate you, but quite selfishly, I'm a little sad."

"To tell the truth, sir, I'm not all that happy myself."

The silence that followed made it clear that both of them now understood the real topic of conversation.

"So who's forcing you to go?" the rabbi asked.

"My aunt and uncle," Tim began hesitantly. Then apologizing: "I really shouldn't be wasting your time. . . ."

"No, no, please," the rabbi gestured. "Go on."

Tim mustered his courage and replied. "It's the stolen money."

"You stole money?"

"No, that's just it," Timothy agonized, "some-body robbed my aunt's savings, and when she found the money I earned from you—"

"You didn't explain?"

He shook his head. "My uncle said she wouldn't like it."

"Well, Tim,"—the Rav frowned—"you have to tell her now."

"It's too late. She's seeing Father Hanrahan to-night about sending me away."

There was another silence, and then almost in-voluntarily Tim blurted out, "Would you help me, Rabbi?"

"How might *I* be of assistance in these circum-stances?"

"You could speak to Father Hanrahan," Tim pleaded. "I know he would believe you."

The rabbi could not suppress a bitter laugh. "That is, one might say, a rather large leap of faith."

"Well," Tim argued, "you're both men of the cloth, aren't you?"

Rav Luria nodded. "Yes—but very different fabrics. Still, I'll call him and see if he's willing to talk."

Tim stood up. "Thanks. I really appreciate it."

"Timothy—excuse my intrusion," Rav Luria inquired cautiously, "but even if you can't convince them you're innocent, isn't there any way you can make your aunt and uncle forgive you?"

"No, Rabbi," Tim answered painfully. "I guess

you don't understand." He paused and, holding back the tears, burst out, "You see, they hate me."

With that, he turned and left the room without looking back.

Rav Luria stood there for a moment and thought to himself, *Now* I understand why he broke windows.

———

Rav Moses Luria had stared down the gun barrels of angry Czech policemen; he had fearlessly confronted half a dozen hooligans daubing swastikas on his synagogue. But calling up a priest was something altogether different.

Finally, he took a thoughtful puff on his pipe, asked the operator for the number of the church, and dialed. The phone was answered on the second ring.

"Good evening. This is Father Joe."

"Good evening, Father Hanrahan. My name is Rabbi Moses Luria."

"Oh," the priest replied. "The Silczer Rebbe himself?"

How did Hanrahan know such things? the Rav wondered.

"How can I help you, Rabbi?"

"Well, I was wondering if you could spare the time for a conversation?"

"Of course. Would you like to come for tea tomorrow?"

"Well, actually, it would be best if we could meet outside."

"You mean, in neutral territory, so to speak?"

"Well, yes," the rabbi replied candidly.

"Do you play chess, by any chance?" the priest inquired.

"A bit," the rabbi answered. "I don't really have much time for games."

"Well, then," the priest suggested, "why don't we meet at the outdoor chess tables in the park? We could have a relaxing game while we chat."

"Fine," the rabbi concurred. "Shall we say eleven o'clock tomorrow?"

"Eleven it is," replied the priest. To which he added a cheery "*Shalom.*"

The next afternoon the two clergymen sat at a concrete table, a chessboard embedded in its surface. The rabbi opened by moving his king's pawn forward two squares.

"How can I help, Rabbi?" asked the priest affably, countering with the identical move.

"It's about one of your parishioners—"

"And who might that be?"

In a series of symmetrical moves, both players began to develop their knights and bishops.

"A young boy named Timothy Hogan."

"Oh dear." The priest sighed as he edged his queen in front of his king. "Has he broken another window?"

"No, no. This is something completely different."

The Rav paused, castled on his king's side, and then continued in slightly apologetic tones. "I really shouldn't be interfering, Father. But it has come to my attention that this boy is in some difficulty . . . about some stolen money."

The priest nodded. "He's such a bright lad, but he seems to have a talent for getting into trouble."

In an even exchange on the eleventh move, both players lost a knight.

"He is bright. I'm glad you agree," the rabbi responded, as he used a pawn to take one of the priest's bishops. "That's why it would be so unfortunate if he were sent away."

Father Hanrahan looked quizzically at the Rav. "How do you come to know about all this, may I ask?"

"Well, many years ago the boy's mother worked briefly for me. And the lad is currently in my employ . . . as a kind of Sabbath helper."

"You mean a *Shabbes goy*?" the priest inquired with a knowing grin. "I'm not unacquainted with your religious practices."

"Then you know that it's a position of trust and responsibility, which through the years has been held by such distinguished gentiles as the great Russian playwright, Maxim Gorky—"

"—not to mention James Cagney, the great Irish-American actor," Hanrahan added, as he suddenly moved his queen directly in front of the Rav's king, amicably pronouncing, "Check!"

Trying to avoid being distracted by his dilemma on the chessboard, the rabbi stated categorically, "I don't know this Mr. Cagney—but I do know that the Hogan boy is innocent."

Father Hanrahan looked up at the rabbi and replied enigmatically, "I believe you're right."

"Then why can't you do something?"

"This is difficult to explain, Rabbi," the priest said, moving his knight forward, apparently absentmindedly. "But I'm party to certain information that the seal of confession forbids me to disclose."

The Rav persisted. "Still, isn't there any way of saving the boy?"

Father Joe pondered for a moment, and then remarked, "Perhaps I can speak to the lad—get him involved more in the church. That might give me some ground for dissuading Cassie."

"So it's mainly the aunt?"

Hanrahan looked at his watch. "It's getting late. I must go. I hope you'll excuse me."

The Rav rose, but Hanrahan's voice stopped him.

"Oh, just one more thing, Rabbi Luria."

"Yes?"

Leaning over the board, the priest brought his remaining bishop straight down the diagonal, taking one of the rabbi's pawns. There was no way of saving the Jewish king. The Catholic then tipped his hat in a gesture of jaunty respect and started off.

Rav Luria stood in the windy park and thought to himself, He outplayed me.

But the important thing is that I *won*!

———

Before meeting with Timothy, Father Joe studied what his policemen parishioners might have called the boy's "rap sheet."

There was an extraordinary amount to read. Yet what struck him was that every one of Tim's teachers had been obliged to reduce his grades because of his misbehavior, despite the fact that he was by far the smartest in their classes.

"He's a clever little devil," Sister Mary Bernard had written. "If only his considerable talents could be marshaled for the good, we would all be blessed."

There was a knock at the door.

"Come in," the priest called.

The door opened slowly and Timothy Hogan, face nearly as white as his shirt, peeked anxiously inside.

At first, all he saw were endless rows of books set from floor to ceiling on wood and cinder-block shelves. It reminded him of a tidier version of Rav Luria's study. Then he focused on the gray-haired cleric, nearly dwarfed behind his huge mahogany desk.

"You wanted to see me, Father?" he asked diffidently.

"That I did. Sit down, my boy."

Before making the slightest move, Tim blurted, "I didn't steal the money, Father Hanrahan. I swear to God I didn't!"

The priest leaned across his desk and confided softly, "I believe you."

"You do?"

Hanrahan pressed his palms together and addressed the boy again. "Lad, it doesn't matter whether you're in the right this time, you've got a record for rowdiness as long as my arm."

Tim tried to read the old man's thoughts. "It's Aunt Cassie, isn't it? She hates me—"

Father silenced him with an upraised hand. "Come now, she's a pious woman and means well." He again leaned across the large desk and said in softer tones, "You must admit that you've given her a lot of trouble through the years."

"I guess so," Tim replied, then asked impatiently, "Where are you sending me?"

"I'd like to send you home to the Delaneys," the priest said slowly, "but no one wants a wild tornado in his house. Tim, you're a very bright young man. Why do you act the way you do?"

Tim shrugged.

"Is it because you think nobody cares?"

The boy nodded.

"You're wrong," Father Joe whispered. "To begin with, God cares."

"Yes, sir," Tim answered. And then added almost reflexively: "1 John 4:8, 'He that loveth not, knoweth not God.' "

The priest was astonished. "How much of the Scriptures do you know by heart?"

Tim shrugged. "I guess I know whatever stuff we've read."

Father Joe swiveled in his chair, pulled out a large Bible, and leafed through the pages. " 'If a man say, I love God, and hateth his brother, he is a liar: for he that loveth not his brother whom he hath seen, how can he love God whom he hath not seen?' " He glanced at Tim and asked, "Recognize that?"

"Yes—same chapter, verse twenty."

"Extraordinary," Hanrahan muttered. He slapped the Bible closed on his desk and shouted with exasperation, "Then why in heaven's name do you go around throwing punches at your fellow man?"

"I don't know," Tim confessed.

The priest stared at him for a moment and then said with fervor, "Timothy, I do believe the Lord ordains each move we make. And all that's gone before today was just to bring the two of us together. It has suddenly come clear to me that you were born to serve our Lord."

"How?" Tim asked uncertainly.

"Well, as an altar boy to start with. No—you're a

little old for that. You'll share the task of thurifer with Marty North. He's younger than you, but knows the ropes."

"But what happens if I don't want to be your spice boy?" Tim asked, his old defiance reemerging.

"Well," the priest replied, still jovial, "then you can hold a candle." Quickly he added: "Or you can go to St. Joseph's School for Boys in Pennsylvania."

Hanrahan's bluntness caught Tim off guard. He looked at the priest. "I don't mind getting up early," Tim said matter-of-factly.

The priest began to laugh. "I'm very glad, Tim. And I know you're on the right road now."

"What's so funny?"

"I'm just happy," Father Hanrahan replied. "After all, there's more delight in finding one lost sheep than the ninety-nine already in the fold."

To which Timothy replied, "Matthew 18:13— sort of abridged."

The priest beamed and inquired, "Same thought's also in Luke. Don't you remember?"

"To be honest, I don't," Tim replied.

"*Deo gratias*—there's at least something I can still teach you. Now go home. And be here at six-thirty in the morning."

———

If he was not converted by the churchman, Tim was definitely transformed by the ceremonies themselves. It was one thing to kneel and pray, it was another to *serve,* to feel a part of the prayer.

When he took off his jacket to don the garments of worship, he sensed that he was somehow removing a layer of sin. The simple black cassock and a white surplice made him feel *pure.*

And in stark contrast to the vestments of the priests, his own garb never changed. The priests altered the color of their garments according to the seasons.

The green worn on ordinary Sundays symbolized growth and hope, while the violet during Lent and Advent signified penance, and the rose on special Sundays during those same periods indicated joy. Most important was the white for Christmas, Easter, special Saints' Days, and holy occasions like the Feast of the Circumcision.

Tim would sometimes appear in school still emanating traces of incense.

"Hey, what's with you, Hogan?" Ed McGee taunted. "You wearing perfume or something?"

"Mind your own business," Tim replied.

"Jesus, Mary, and Joseph, you look so good in a skirt."

Tim felt his temper rising. "Cut it out, McGee, or—"

"Or *what,* altar boy?"

Tim thought for a split second. What was the proper response—turning the other cheek, or breaking the other's jaw?

He compromised by walking away.

———

They had reached the age when adolescents suddenly discover the opposite sex—though of course it was not considered manly to admit it.

In Tim's case, his female classmates had long whispered among themselves about the color of his deep blue eyes and sighed at his indifference. And, since he did not seem to notice them, they began to take the initiative.

One evening, as he emerged from a Latin tutorial session with Father Hanrahan, Tim was surprised to find Isabel O'Brien, her hair cut shorter and her figure grown fuller, waiting for him.

"It's dark, Tim," she said in a soft, nervous voice. "Would you mind walking me home?"

He was slightly disoriented, not merely by her request but by the way she was looking at him. He was sure she had some special purpose.

As they walked the first few blocks, it seemed she only wanted to report on his status among the girls in school. But she could not sense how uneasy it made him to hear that the girls thought he was "cute" and one or two actually found him "gorgeous."

Tim did not know how to respond, so after a moment Isabel persisted.

"Who do you like best?" she asked. "I mean, out of all of us?"

"I . . . I don't know. I never really sort of thought about it."

"Oh," said Isabel.

Tim was considerably relieved when they reached her front steps. Though it was cold and windy, Isabel did not dash up to the warmth of her home.

Instead, she startled Tim by saying, "It's okay if you want to kiss me. I mean, I won't tell anybody."

Tim lost his breath. He had often fantasized about what it would be like to . . . touch some of the girls in class. Yet he was afraid of making a fool of himself. Because he did not know what to do.

Without warning she showed him, pulling down his head and pressing her lips against his.

It was a nice feeling, he admitted to himself. Although she was forcing her warm mouth against his so strongly, she was stirring thoughts in him. Like wanting to see what her breasts felt like. Some of the guys had already boasted of accomplishing such things.

But then he did not want to offend Isabel. After a moment he stepped away and said, "I guess I'll see you in class tomorrow, huh?"

"I guess," she murmured coyly. "Will you walk me home again?"

"Uh . . . sure. Maybe next week some time."

———

Tim's new demeanor affected everyone around him. Even his aunt and cousins could sense—with a certain awe—that his once-demonic energy had been rechanneled.

"I don't know what it is," Tuck complained to

Cassie, "but something's happened to the kid. He's become such a goody-goody."

Part of the explanation was that serving publicly now gave him the chance to pray more often, without having to be furtive about his devotion to the Virgin.

Within six months he had advanced in rank and was swinging the thurible itself in the Mass procession.

They had already started Latin in class, and Timothy could easily translate such passages as the beginning of the Gospel of John:

> *In principio erat Verbum,*
> *et Verbum erat apud Deum,*
> *et Deus erat Verbum.*
>
> *In the beginning was the Word,*
> *and the Word was with God,*
> *and the Word was God.*

But his mind was too hungry to be satisfied with a diet of simple scriptural sentences, and Father Joe was more than happy to advance his knowledge of the holy language of Catholic Scripture.

Once again, he marveled at Timothy's prodigious memory, as well as the intensity of his desire to learn.

"Tim," Father Hanrahan remarked one day with

undisguised pride, "I can only say to you what Our Lord said to Nicodemus in John 3:3." He smiled conspiratorially. "I don't have to quote it for you, do I?"

No, Timothy shook his head, and recited the passage: "*Nisi quis natus fuerit desuper, non potest videre regnum Dei.* 'Except a man be born again, he cannot see the kingdom of God.' Yes, Father, I do feel reborn."

Tim believed with unswerving faith that next year when Tommy Ronan went off to seminary, he would be chosen to lead the procession as bearer of the Cross.

But Providence had more immediate plans.

On a wintry day, while playing hockey on roller skates in the street, Tommy Ronan slipped and broke his ankle, leaving Father Hanrahan the task of choosing someone else to carry the Crucifix.

There was the matter of seniority, of course. Many of the older boys had been in service for five years or more. And yet the handbook emphasizes that the youth who bears the heavy Cross must be distinguished by his height and strength. On these grounds, the mighty Crucifix was passed to Tim.

Both priest and server saw in it the hand of God.

10

Deborah

For years Deborah had lived in dread of this day.

The subject was first broached one evening after dinner. Danny, as usual, was upstairs doing homework. Mama and Papa sat alone with Deborah, waiting for the tea to cool.

"My child," Rav Luria began, "it's time—"

"I don't want to get married!" Deborah burst out.

"*Ever?*" her mother asked.

"Sure, some time, Mama. But not yet. Not now. There are still so many things I want to do."

"Could you maybe give me a for instance?" the Rav asked.

"Well, I'd like to go to college."

" 'College?' " her father echoed with amazement. "For what purpose should you want to go to college? Did your mother go? Did either of your sisters?"

"Times have changed," Deborah answered with quiet determination.

The Rav pondered for a moment, then reached over and patted his daughter's hand affectionately. "You're very special, Deborah. You of all my daughters . . . are the brightest and most pious."

Deborah lowered her head, hoping to mask some of the delight this compliment had given her.

"So," the Rav continued, "we won't restrict our search for a good husband just to Brooklyn—or New York City even. I assure you, there are many worthy candidates in Philadelphia, Boston, or Chicago."

"What makes you so sure?"

"Well,"—her father smiled—"I have already taken the liberty of making inquiries."

He leaned over, kissed his daughter on the cheek, then patting Rachel's shoulder whispered, "I'm working on a difficult ruling. Don't wait up."

When he had left the room, Rachel took her daughter's hand in hers. "Don't worry, it'll be all right. He'll never force you."

Deborah merely nodded, thinking, He didn't "force" Rena either. Father had a way of creating a tidal wave, drop by drop.

"Mama, is it written in stone that a girl has to get married when she's so young? I mean, God didn't mention this to Moses on Mount Sinai, did He?"

"Darling,"—Rachel smiled indulgently—"it's our tradition to get married early. Besides, nobody's rushing. I'm sure I could convince your father to let you wait a year or maybe even two."

"I'd still be only eighteen," she answered plaintively. "I can't imagine myself at that age having to cut off my hair and put on a wig."

Deborah looked at her mother and her *sheitel* of synthetic hair and wished that she could disappear. Rachel's smile reassured her.

"Want to know a little secret?" she began. "It isn't the end of the world. I hear lots of fancy socialites wear wigs."

"Not to make them unattractive," her daughter countered.

Rachel sighed with exasperation. "Listen, Deborah, hold your horses for a minute. Why not wait and see what kind of prospects your father comes up with? Maybe he'll find someone with the strength of Samson and the mind of Solomon."

"Oh, sure," said Deborah with a tiny laugh. "And we'll be married by Elijah the Prophet."

To which her mother responded, "Amen."

———

Rachel Luria did not exaggerate her husband's resourcefulness.

In April of Deborah's seventeenth year, he came home from evening prayer waving a manila envelope.

"Aha, I knew it," he declared. "I knew Chicago was the place to look."

He turned to Deborah with a flourish and announced, "My darling, in here is your future husband."

"Then he can't be very big," she joked weakly.

"But this boy is Rebbe Kaplan's son. He has all the virtues anyone could want. You've heard the expression tall, dark, and handsome?"

"Don't tell me," said Deborah facetiously. "It's Gary Cooper."

"I never heard of any Cooper boy," her father said blankly. "I was discussing Asher Kaplan—a tip-top candidate. Not only is your future husband steeped in piety and Torah, he's six foot five and plays basketball for the University of Chicago. Under special dispensation, of course."

"With or without his skullcap?" she asked sarcastically.

"With, naturally," her father countered. "That's what makes him so unusual. And he never plays on Saturdays, unless the game's after *Shabbes*."

"Wow!" Danny interposed in awe. "Like Sandy Koufax of the Dodgers. He never pitches on Jewish holidays."

"This Koufax boy I also never heard of. But Kaplan—"

"I don't know," said Deborah, hoping levity would dismiss the topic. "He sounds too athletic for me."

"Will you at least meet him?"

"Do I have a choice?"

"Of course, my darling." Her father smiled. "It can be any time you want."

Deborah sighed, defeated.

———

After an enthusiastic exchange of letters between the two fathers, Asher Kaplan was dispatched to Brooklyn on his chivalrous quest. He lodged with cousins two blocks distant from the Lurias.

Deborah got her first glimpse of him in synagogue that Saturday morning, when she peeked over the white curtain which protected the women from men's lustful gazes.

There was no room to doubt that he was six feet five inches tall. And he lived up to the "handsome" part as well, with his shock of auburn hair and chiseled features. Moreover, he was unbearded, and though his sideburns were of the required length, they did not spiral into curls on either side.

When her father honored Asher as a visitor by calling him up to read the Torah, he not only chanted the initial blessings by heart, but went on to demonstrate that he could sing the music of the text itself with complete fluency.

Moreover, he was chosen to come last and recite the portion from the Prophets. Those were practically the same prenuptial honors granted to her sister's husband. Deborah half-joked to herself that maybe Mama would be taking her that evening to the *mikva*. She had to admit that, had she not been under such pressure, she might have found him appealing.

Mama, who was sitting next to her, could not keep from whispering how impressed she was with Asher Kaplan's singing.

"What a golden voice," she gushed.

C'mon, Mama, Deborah thought to herself. Do *you* have to be on his side too?

After the service, while her father with Danny in tow was introducing their Chicago visitor to various important worshipers, Deborah and her mother hurried home to remove the cholent from the tin stand covering the burner on the stove which had been warming it all night.

By the time the men arrived, it was clear to Deborah that even Danny had given the candidate his seal of approval. His admiring eyes kept gazing up at Asher as if his head were in the stratosphere. Clearly, if there was going to be a battle, she would be vastly outnumbered.

All through the meal, Rav Luria's face was flushed with self-congratulation. He was certain that he had found the special bridegroom for his special daughter.

He even let Asher lead the after-dinner discussion, and the Chicagoan's explication of the Torah portion was yet another demonstration of his fitness to be the Silczer Rebbe's son-in-law.

Asher scarcely looked at Deborah. Outside of

"Nice to meet you," in Yiddish, he had not addressed a single word to her.

They spoke of Jeremiah's warnings to the sinners, whose misdeeds were "written with a pen of iron, and with the point of a diamond."

At which point Deborah interrupted and recited the next verse. "It is graven upon the tablet of their heart. . . ."

All faces suddenly fixed upon her, wide-eyed with astonishment.

She had done some preparation too.

At long last the great moment arrived. The entire family went for a stroll in nearby Prospect Park. Rabbi and Mrs. Luria kept a careful and discreet ten paces behind "so the children can get to know each other."

Asher was desperate to make a good impression on Deborah. Not only because Chicago was counting on him, but because he genuinely liked her.

At first sight he had been taken by her large brown eyes and sultry aspect. He had genuinely admired her voice when they had sung the Grace After Meals, and the pluck with which she had entered the men's conversation.

"They didn't exaggerate," he remarked.

"I beg your pardon?"

"My parents told me all these wonderful things about you and your family. For once it wasn't false advertising."

He paused, hoping she would reciprocate.

She sensed this, and finally said, "And you—you're just as tall as they told me."

Is that all? thought Asher to himself.

"I hear you're a real *eshes chayil,*" he said, tossing her the ultimate accolade for a Jewish girl.

"In other words, 'good wife material,'" Deborah replied tartly. "Actually, it depends how you translate the Hebrew term. I mean, if *gibor chayil* means a hero in battle, why couldn't *eshes chayil* mean a *woman* in battle?"

Asher wrinkled his forehead and shook his head, inwardly deliberating whether it would be wise to engage his bride-to-be in a semantic quibble. He decided it was best to placate.

"Can we change the subject?" he pleaded.

"I don't know anything about basketball," she replied.

"Well then, do you want to know about my prospects?"

Deborah merely shrugged.

They walked along for several minutes, each pretending to admire the foliage.

Then Asher spoke again. "Well, just in case you're interested, I'm not going to be a rabbi."

"Oh?" she replied. "Is your father upset?"

"Not really. I've got two older brothers who're already leading congregations of their own. Anyway, I just thought you might like to know that I'm going to be a doctor. What do you think of that?"

"I think that's wonderful," she answered sincerely and then after a moment added, "Do you know what I want to be?"

"A wife, I hope."

"Oh, I will eventually," she replied. "But I'd like to be something else as well."

"What else is there?" he asked.

"I'd like to be a scholar."

"But you're a woman."

"So I'll be a woman scholar," she replied.

Exasperated, and feeling the clock running down, Asher put on a full-court press.

"Deborah, do you mind if I ask you a simple question?"

"Not at all."

"Do you like me?"

"Yes," she replied uneasily.

"Well, do you want to marry me or not?"

"A simple yes or no answer?" she said.

"Yes," he replied.

Deborah looked up into his hazel eyes, and uttered, "No."

11

Deborah

It was a few minutes before eleven on Friday evening. Deborah Luria sat alone in the living room reading her Bible. As always, she had left the Song of Songs for last.

She was so engrossed that she barely heard the key turn in the front door lock. Even then, her reverie was broken only when the new arrival murmured shyly, "Good *Shabbes,* Miss."

She looked up. It was the gentile boy her family and the neighbors had engaged to extinguish the lights.

Aware that it was improper even to be in the same room with him, Deborah nodded her head and began to rise to her feet.

"Oh, I'm sorry," she apologized. "I must be holding you up."

"That's all right. Actually, I'm a little early. I can go take care of the Shapiros and come back."

"No, no," Deborah protested. "I'll stop reading."

She closed the book, placed it carefully on the table, and left the room.

"Good night," the young man whispered. But she seemed not to hear.

When Timothy Hogan had first begun to work for the Lurias, he had barely noticed Deborah, who was then a shy, gawky adolescent with dark, curly hair. Yet with the passing of time he had fallen under the spell of her exotic beauty.

He knew it was wrong, yet in moments of weakness he would pray that when he arrived to perform his Friday duties he might catch a glimpse of her.

He watched her dissolve into the shadowed hallway and realized he had behaved improperly. These girls were not supposed to talk to *any* boys—much less Irish Catholics. Though she had spoken only a few words, the echo of her lovely voice lingered in the room.

Curiosity impelled him to overstep the boundary once again. He leaned forward to see what she had been reading and was struck by the fact that this pensive rabbi's daughter had been sitting all alone with the Holy Bible.

Upstairs, Deborah undressed in the darkness of her room, but as she lay on her pillow and the onset of sleep relaxed her thoughts, she could still see the blue light of Timothy Hogan's eyes.

I must tell my father, part of her said. But then of course Papa would fire him, and I would never see him again.

But I was wrong to answer him. Why *did* I?

Suddenly it dawned on her.

Tim Hogan had been speaking Yiddish.

———

Although she made a solemn oath to go to bed earlier the following Friday, she was still downstairs when Timothy arrived at the unprecedented hour of ten-thirty.

"Please don't let me disturb you," he said, a slight tremor in his voice.

She pretended to ignore him. But she did not rise and leave as she had the previous week.

After another moment, Tim asked softly, "Would you like me to come back later?"

She sat up and said almost involuntarily, "How come you know Yiddish?"

"Well, it's been four years since I started working for the families, so I've had a lot of time to pick it up. Anyway, it's sure a lot easier to speak than to read."

"You can *read*—?"

"Only very slowly," Timothy answered. "You know Mr. Wasserstein is almost blind. After I started helping him on Friday nights, he persuaded me to come in a couple of afternoons a week so he could teach me to read the *Daily Forward* to him."

Deborah was touched at the thought of their eighty-year-old neighbor reaching into the semi-darkness of his memory to explain Hebrew letters to this young Catholic boy.

"But how can he teach you if he can't see the page?"

"Oh, he's worked out a very interesting system. He knows the Psalms by heart, so he makes me turn to the one that begins with whatever letter we're learning. For example, 'The Lord is my Shepherd' begins with *aleph*, 'When Israel left Egypt' begins with *bet*. And so forth."

"That's very clever," Deborah said with admiration. "And very generous on your part."

"Oh, it's the least I can do. Mr. Wasserstein is so lonely—except for me, his only contact with the outside world is *shul*."

Suddenly, he suppressed a laugh.

"What's so funny?" Deborah asked.

"He keeps joking that I'd make a good rabbi. Sometimes I actually think he's serious."

"Jews don't proselytize," Deborah stated, herself puzzled that she should be so dogmatic at this moment.

"I'm not worried." Tim smiled, and Deborah suddenly felt uneasy. His expression was so . . .

angelic. "Actually, if Father Hanrahan finds a place for me, I'll be going to seminary where knowing Hebrew letters will be a real advantage for the Old Testament classes."

"You mean you're going away?" she asked, almost involuntarily.

"If I'm found suitable for the priesthood."

"What do you mean?"

"Well, like Our Saviour, I'd have to be impervious to the temptations of the world, the flesh, and the devil."

"Oh," she remarked, not knowing what else to say, inwardly hoping she had not betrayed her disappointment at the prospect of not seeing him.

"Actually, I'm not worried about the devil—" he joked lightly, "but I'm still working on the other two."

Suddenly Deborah began to panic. What was he talking about? Why had she allowed herself to begin this conversation? She mustered all her inner strength and said nervously, "I'm sorry, I've got to go to sleep."

She forced herself to turn and start up the dark stairs.

His glance followed her long after she had disappeared. He was now more than curious. He was desperate to see exactly what text she had been reading.

He picked up her book, the Soncino Bible with Hebrew and English translation. His eyes fell upon the words, "Behold, thou art fair, my love . . . thine eyes are as doves."

He was now convinced that some greater power had intended him to read these words.

And, he thought, maybe Mr. Wasserstein is still awake and will help me learn this in Hebrew tonight.

———

Deborah was at once excited, confused . . . and frightened. She had to speak to someone, and the only person she could trust was her younger brother.

"For gosh sake," Danny said sleepily as she knocked softly and entered his room. "It's nearly midnight."

"*Please,* Danny. I've got to talk to you."

Sensing her urgency, he sat up. "Okay," he said, suppressing a yawn. "Now what's the big deal?"

"It's about—you know the *Shabbes goy?*"

"Yeah, Tim," Danny responded. "Good guy, isn't he?"

"Uh, I don't know," Deborah stammered.

"Hey, Deb," Danny whined, "what the heck is this conversation about?"

"Did you know he speaks Yiddish?"

"Sure. I've had a few talks with him. For this you woke me up on the only night I can get some sleep?"

"Well, don't you think that's weird?" Deborah persisted.

"Not really. Tim's an unusual guy."

"In what way?" she asked, eager to learn whatever she could about the young man who now held her imagination captive.

"Once when that *shaygetz* Ed McGee was trying to murder me, Tim came by and punched him out. He's a terrific fighter. Actually, I've never even thanked him. I just ran for my life." He paused for a moment and then looked at his sister, who was nervously biting her lip. "Now what was it you wanted to tell me?"

Deborah sensed that even confiding in her brother would be too great a risk. "Nothing," she answered. "I'm sorry I bothered you."

As she started out, Danny whispered, "Hey, Deb—"

"Yeah?"

"Has he—you know—tried anything?"

"I don't know what you mean."

"You darn well do. Has he?"

"Don't be stupid."

"No, Deb. Don't *you* be stupid."

———

All through the week, Deborah looked forward to the Sabbath—albeit not for the usual religious reasons. Yet she had a special reason, which both excited and troubled her.

This time he appeared even earlier—in fact, scarcely ten minutes after the rest of her family had gone upstairs.

"It's only ten-fifteen," she complained in an anxious whisper.

"I was watching from the street," Tim confessed. "When I saw you were alone, I thought it would be all right—"

"Well, it isn't," she retorted. "I mean, you can turn off the light and go. I shouldn't be talking to you. Don't you know that?"

"And I shouldn't be talking to *you*. Don't you know *that*?"

There was a pause. Finally, Deborah asked in a quiet voice, "Why?"

"They teach us in school not to consort with non-Catholics. Lately they've been telling us that Jewish girls are Jezebels."

"Jezebel wasn't Jewish," Deborah objected. "But I guess your school thinks anybody who's evil must be."

"That's unfair."

"Well, tell me one decent thing they've ever taught you," she demanded.

"Christ said 'Do unto others as you would have them do unto you.' "

"Our sage Hillel said the exact same thing."

"Who came first?"

"Well," Deborah said, "Hillel lived in the early part of the first century."

"So did Jesus."

They sat and glared at one another.

"Why are we having this argument, anyway?" Deborah asked after a moment.

"Because it's the only way you'll let yourself talk to me."

"Who said I wanted to talk to you, anyway?"

"Well, *I'd* like to speak to you," he said gently.

"Why?" she asked, instantly unable to understand why she had asked that question.

"Because I like you," Tim replied. "Are you offended by that?"

However innocuous they might have seemed in the outside world, these were the most intimate words that a man had ever said to her. Yet she could not stop the momentum of her emotions.

"I'm not offended. I just wonder what I've ever done to make you . . . feel that way."

Tim smiled. "Nothing, really. But I guess you can't help being pretty."

Part of Deborah was shocked. Even the vainglorious Asher Kaplan would not have been so familiar. But this first compliment ever paid to her as a woman was intoxicating. However much she did not believe his words, she wanted to hear more of them.

"Could we change the subject," she asserted.

"Sure. Fine."

There was an awkward silence, finally broken by Tim's seemingly irrelevant question. "Have you ever been to a movie?"

"No. We're not allowed to. It's too complicated to explain. What makes you ask?"

"Well, I just wondered if I were a Jewish boy, whether I could have invited you to one. Some of your people go, don't they?"

"Not the Orthodox," she replied. "I mean—"

Just then the clock began to chime, awakening both of them to the reality that what was separating them was not just a coffee table, but a bridgeless chasm between two faiths.

"I've got a surprise for you," Tim whispered.

"What is it?" she asked uneasily.

He cleared his throat softly and said apologetically, "I hope my accent isn't too terrible." And then he quoted: " 'Then the people of the Lord went down to the gates. Awake, awake, Deborah; Awake, awake, utter a song. . . .' " Eyes gleaming with pride, he looked at her and said, "Judges 5:12."

She was touched. " 'The Song of Deborah.' Oh, my goodness." She smiled. "I don't know whether to be flattered or embarrassed."

"Please be flattered," Tim answered earnestly.

And then he was sitting next to her. It had happened so swiftly that she had no time to grow frightened.

"I want to kiss you," he murmured.

She turned her head and looked into the ocean of his eyes.

"But you mustn't."

Yet her tone was not protesting.

Tim's words began to cascade as if racing the end of time. "Deborah. I've got to say this now because I know I'll never have the courage to again. I . . . I . . . With all my heart, I really . . . like you."

She closed her eyes but still did not move away. She felt a strange sensation at the nape of her neck. It was his hand barely touching her, and then the warmth of his lips brushed hers.

For Tim it was like nothing he had ever felt before.

Deborah was too frightened to respond but she wanted this electric moment to endure forever.

At that very moment Rav Moses Luria entered the room.

Tim instantly leapt to his feet.

There was only a single lamp still burning—the one that Timothy was hired to extinguish.

For an agonizing moment the Rav looked at them, then spoke with a preternatural calm.

"*Nu,* so what is this, children?"

"It was my fault, Papa," Deborah quickly insisted.

"No, Rav Luria," Tim contradicted, "it's *mine*—completely mine. It was my idea to read Hebrew to her."

Eyebrows raised, the rabbi asked, still softly, "Hebrew?"

"Tim's been taking lessons from Mr. Wasserstein."

Rav Luria pondered for a moment and then, still miraculously restraining his temper, spoke. "It's admirable that a Christian wants to read the Bible in the original. But for what exact purpose, I ask myself. And why did he choose Deborah as an audience? I would gladly have arranged for someone on my yeshiva staff to tutor him. And so finally I ask myself, 'What is really going on?' "

Timothy's self-castigating conscience made him speak again. "Rav Luria," he said bravely. "I started everything. I'm totally to blame. Please don't pour out your wrath on Deborah."

"*Wrath?* Young man, this situation calls for more than wrath." He paused, and then added, "So if you'll just leave your keys, we can say good night. And good-bye."

In a state of shock, Timothy withdrew a key ring from his pocket and placed it on the table. The metallic jangle seemed to desecrate the Sabbath silence. He glanced at Deborah.

"I'm sorry, Deborah. But I'm sure your father will believe that you were . . ."

"Good night," the Rav said emphatically.

Now father and daughter were alone. She stood barely illumined by the glow of the single lamp. He remained in a darkness so deep that he was almost as invisible as God.

She was terrified, sensing the fire that raged in him. She was certain he would lash out—if not physically, at least verbally.

He surprised her.

"Deborah," he said gently, "I was wrong to be angry at you. I should blame myself. I know that you're a good girl, and there was temptation. That is how the Evil Inclination entices us to sin."

"I didn't sin," she whispered.

The Rav looked heavenward with a gesture of his palms. Then, he peered at his daughter and said quietly, "Go to bed, Deborah. We'll discuss this when the Sabbath's over."

She nodded mutely and walked up the stairs. They always creaked, but tonight the groaning floorboards seemed like tiny voices all accusing her.

She went to her room, and slumped fully clothed onto her bed. She had no illusions about her father's seeming lack of anger. She knew when three stars shone tomorrow night, he would excoriate her. After all, she deserved it.

She had desecrated her parents' home, profaned the Sabbath, and disgraced her family.

But there was more. Counterbalancing all the sin was a kind of physical reverberation of the excitement she had felt when Timothy had touched her.

———

As he drank his morning coffee, Rav Luria revealed no trace of anger at the previous night's events. He and Danny left early for *shul,* leaving the women to follow in half an hour. Deborah dreaded the thought of what her mother might say when they were alone. From Rachel's expression and the timbre of her voice, Deborah could tell that Father had reported everything. But Rachel did not say a word.

At last the day was finally extinguished. From where she had taken refuge in her bedroom, Deborah heard the door slam downstairs. She did not have to wait much longer. She got up, splashed cold water on her face, and descended.

The Rav performed *havdalah,* the rite that marks the end of Sabbath. The sacred and the profane were severed. The angels of the Sabbath had departed. And the world, with all its imperfections, reappeared.

From force of habit, Deborah immediately followed her mother into the kitchen to start all the mundane washing up—the last remnant of the Sabbath presence. She was certain that her father would come in and ask to speak with her alone. But he did not. Instead, he vanished into his study.

It was nearly an hour later when he emerged and called quietly, "Deborah, will you come in please."

She was not unprepared. She had spent the last twenty-four hours desperately searching for a way to expiate her sin and assuage her father's anger. Yet she well knew that it would have to be a sacrificial gesture.

The instant she entered the study, she blurted out, "Papa, I'll marry Asher Kaplan—"

Her father calmly waved her to sit down. "No, my

darling. Under the circumstances, I would not ask Rav Kaplan to consider such a match."

Deborah sat mute, growing increasingly colder and light-headed.

"My child," the Rav continued slowly and deliberately, "this is all my fault. Foolishly, I always thought you'd be upstairs when he came by."

He paused and then murmured, "I think it best that you should go away."

Deborah was stricken. "Where . . . where do you want me to go?"

"My darling," he said, looking at her sadly, "I'm not talking of Siberia. I mean the Holy Land. 'Jerusalem the Golden.' After all, but a few months ago, did not the Almighty choose to reunite the City of David—and in only six days, no doubt so the Israeli soldiers could rest on the seventh? I think you should look forward with happiness to your new life there."

New life? Deborah thought to herself. Is he exiling me *forever?* She sat still for a moment, then asked hesitantly, "What would I be doing?"

"Rav Lazar Schiffman, who runs our yeshiva in Jerusalem, has agreed to find a family for you to live with. You'll finish school."

Her father leaned forward on his desk and looked at her.

"Listen to me, Deborah. I love you with all my heart. Do you think I want you half a world away from me? It pains me, but I'm doing this for your own good."

There was another silence.

Finally she asked, "What do you want me to say, Papa?"

"You can tell me you'll forget this Christian. That you'll breathe the holiness of the Jerusalem air and purify your soul from this unfortunate event."

He sighed again and then concluded, "Better go help Mama now."

"We've finished all the dishes."

"No, I mean help pack your things."

"When am I going?" she asked, feeling weightless as a leaf in a gust of wind.

"Tomorrow night, God willing."

12

Daniel

Once when I was very small, my father imparted to me a special kind of practical wisdom. Having escaped the Holocaust by scarcely a few dozen paces of the jackboot, he offered the following definitions: A sensible Jew is someone who always has a passport for himself and every member of his family. A *really* intelligent Jew is someone who carries his passport with him at all times.

Thus it was that, before any of us reached our first birthdays, we all possessed valid travel documents. It was a rite second in importance only to my circumcision, the first being a covenant with God, the second with Customs and Immigration. But never in my wildest dreams did I imagine this precaution would serve to accelerate my own sister's exile.

Deborah's last evening in Brooklyn marked the

end of both our childhoods. We spent every moment together, not just to console, but to assuage our pain at the prospect of not seeing each other for months, perhaps years.

I felt helpless, wanting desperately to *do* something. And I was glad when Deborah finally whispered to me in such mournful tones, "Hey, Danny, can you do me a really big favor? I mean, it might even be dangerous."

I was scared, but determined to help her. "Sure. What is it?"

"I'd like to write Tim a letter, but I don't know how to get it to him."

"Write it, Deb," I answered. "I'll mail it on the way to school."

"But there's more chance his family will see it—"

"Okay, okay," I interrupted. "I'll try and sneak it over there tonight."

She threw her arms around me and held me for a long time. "Oh, Danny, I love you," she murmured.

This gave me the courage to ask, "Do you love him too?"

She hesitated for a moment and then said, "I don't know."

———

It was a little after two A.M. I had waited till I was absolutely sure that everyone, even Deborah, was asleep, laced up my sneakers, and dashed into the empty darkness.

It was an eerie feeling, running along those foggy, deserted streets, lit only by lampposts casting a kind of vapory light.

I was right in the heart of Catholic territory, and even the windows of the houses seemed to stare angrily down at me. I wanted to get out of there fast.

I reached the Delaneys' house as quickly as I could, hurried onto the porch, and slipped the letter under their front door. Deborah had assured me Tim would be the first one up, since he had something to do with early morning Mass.

Then I sprinted with all my might till I reached our house. After I caught my breath, I quietly opened the front door and tiptoed in.

I was surprised—and frightened—to hear a noise coming from Father's study. It sounded like a wail, a cry of pain.

As I moved closer, I realized that he was reciting from the Bible. It was from Lamentations: "And gone is from the daughter of Zion all her splendor."

Even from another room I could *feel* his anguish.

The door was slightly ajar. I knocked quietly, but he did not seem to hear, so I pushed it open a little further.

He was at his desk, cradling his forehead with both hands, reading the wounded words of Jeremiah.

For a moment, I was afraid to talk, certain my

father would not want me to witness him in this condition.

He sensed my presence and looked up.

"Danny," he muttered. "Come sit and talk to me."

I sat. But talk did not come easy. I feared that whatever I might say would somehow hurt him even more.

At last he cupped my cheeks in his hands, his entire face a mask of sorrow, and said, "Danny, promise me—don't ever do a thing like this to your father."

I was struck dumb.

And yet I could not bring myself to say the words that would relieve his suffering.

PART II

13

Deborah

To the faithful of all religions, Jerusalem has existed since the beginning of time. Through the centuries, its venerable streets have been trod by pharaohs and emperors, caliphs and crusaders, Christians, Moslems, and Jews.

It was here, atop Mount Moriah, that Abraham, as a supreme act of faith, brought his son Isaac to offer him up as a sacrifice.

King David made Jerusalem his capital, bringing there the Holy Ark, for which his son Solomon built the first great Temple in 955 B.C.

Ten centuries later, David's descendant Jesus entered the city in triumph five days before His Crucifixion. Here, the many churches—including Ethiopian and Coptic—sanctify His death and resurrection.

For the ultraorthodox Jews the most important

area after the Wailing Wall is the quarter called Mea Shearim. It is a self-made ghetto for the devout—with the significant exception that its barriers are not to keep Jews *in,* but to keep the heathen *out.*

Yiddish is the *lingua franca,* Hebrew used exclusively for prayers. Women in their *sheitels* dress in modest clothes, long sleeves and dresses with high necks. Even on the hottest days of summer, men continue to wear heavy black garb and fur hats—and, of course, a *gartl* circling the stomach to bisect the sacred and profane parts of the body.

Some of the many Orthodox sects did recognize the State of Israel when it was born in 1948. Some even sent their sons (though not their daughters, as did secular Israelis) into the Army, where they were accommodated in special religious units, so they could study Torah when they were not fighting.

There are also a goodly number of fanatical extremists like the *Neturei Karta*—"Guardians of the City"—who do not acknowledge the nation's existence. Though they live in the heart of the Holy City, they still regard themselves as "exiles." To them the present Jewish State is a *sin* which has delayed the coming of the Messiah.

But all the factions of Mea Shearim agree on one thing: the sanctity of the Sabbath. Woe to the motorist who passes through one of their streets on Saturday—if indeed, the entrance is not already chained. He will be greeted by a violent hail of rocks. For some inexplicable reason, their spiritual leaders do not regard this action as a violation of the Sabbath peace.

It was to this fortress of holiness that Deborah Luria was exiled.

There had been a tearful parting at the airport in New York, though unlike her mother and brother, her father wept only within. As she walked among the jostling crowd through the El Al airplane hatch, Deborah recited the appropriate prayer for those traveling by plane:

If I ascend up into heaven, Thou art there . . .
If I take the wings of the morning,
And dwell in the uttermost parts of the sea;
Even there would Thy hand lead me,
And Thy right hand would hold me.

At first she let her thoughts be diverted by the flight attendants' efforts to cajole the colorful, chaotic passengers—especially when some of them had declared that very moment as a time for prayers.

But these distractions were short-lived, and all her thoughts returned to bereavement: loss of mother, father, family.

And Timothy.

She could not understand the strange feelings he had aroused in her. Had theirs not been an innocent relationship? Indeed, one could scarcely have called it a "relationship."

She wondered what God's purpose might have been in bringing them together—or at least into such proximity—only to tear them brutally apart. Was it perhaps some way of testing her?

When the lights dimmed to let the passengers sleep, she could still hear the cries of babies, the murmuring of prayers, and the humming of the aircraft engines. Darkness cloaked her tears— the other noises drowned her sobs.

At last she drifted off. She did not even waken when the plane stopped in London to squeeze on still more passengers.

The next thing she heard was the cheerful voice of the stewardess.

"Ladies and gentlemen, you can now see the shores of Israel. We will be landing in ten minutes."

As the loudspeaker system filled with song, "We bring peace unto you," Deborah felt a sudden thrill.

This was the Holy Land. The birthplace of her religion. In a spiritual sense, she was coming home after countless centuries of exile.

As she filed slowly through the door, down the steps to the tarmac shimmering from the summer heat, she noticed soldiers everywhere. This was a country under siege.

What struck her next was that, though she knew everyone *was* Jewish, not many of the multitude of faces looked like her coreligionists back home.

Some of the soldiers were darker than the Puerto Ricans she had seen in Brooklyn. Inside the terminal, the passport cubicles were manned by women, some black-eyed and olive-skinned, others red-haired and freckled. Some were even blond as Scandinavians. It was only when she was ungallantly jostled out into the stifling night that she saw faces she could recognize.

At the end of the fenced-off corridor of people shouting greetings in a carnival of languages stood a middle-aged woman. She wore a dark, long-sleeved dress and kerchief and held up a sign that read *Luria*. As Deborah neared, the woman called out in Yiddish, *"Bist du der Rebbes Tochter?"*

"Yes," she answered, sweating and out of breath, "I'm Deborah. . . ."

"I'm Leah," said the woman curtly, "Rebbe Schiffman's wife. The car is over there."

She turned and walked off quickly, with Deborah one weary step behind, carrying her own luggage.

It had been a shock to see Leah Schiffman up close. What had seemed from afar like a middle-aged woman was in fact a tired-looking girl in her twenties with lifeless eyes and a pallid face.

After a hundred or so paces, they reached the car. Deborah had expected it to be a run-down antique. Instead, to her surprise she saw a stretch Mercedes diesel crowned by a plastic tiara that read "Taxi."

While the driver put Deborah's luggage on the roof rack, Leah introduced the other passengers—

her sister, Bracha, a woman attired like herself holding an infant, and Bracha's husband, Mendel, a bearded, studious-looking young man.

"Shalom," the couple said together, the first words of welcome she had heard.

She could not help but notice that the husband conspicuously turned his glance away from her. He would not risk the Evil Inclination bewitching him unawares.

How much did they know? she wondered. Had they been told about her sin?

In any case, to survive in this environment she would have to win them over. Or else she would only see their backs, as she now saw that of Mendel, who was engaged in an animated conversation with the driver.

Halfway to Jerusalem, Bracha's infant cried out, and the mother began to sing him a lullaby that Deborah recalled from her own childhood. In its way it only intensified her estrangement. But she tried to be polite.

"That's a lovely baby," she offered. "Boy or girl?"

"A boy, thank God," the woman answered. "I have already three girls."

The taxi windows were open and the scent of pine filled the air. Less than an hour later the shadows of the Judean hills were broken by an oasis of light shining high before them. Though Deborah wondered how the other passengers could remain stonily silent as the holy city of Jerusalem came into sight, no one said a word.

They reached the narrow streets of Mea Shearim in the dead of night. Here and there a solitary lamp in a window revealed a scholar still rapt in the study of some holy text.

The taxi pulled up near the corner of Shmuel Salant Street and they got out.

Mrs. Schiffman fumbled with some keys, the door creaked open, and they entered, Deborah bringing up the rear.

A corpulent man with a gray-flecked beard was seated at a table. Its oilcloth cover suggested that it was the dining room by day.

He rose and looked at Deborah. "Ah, so you're the daughter of Rav Moses. You seem a healthy girl. God shield you from the evil eye."

Physically tired, jet-lagged, and emotionally exhausted, Deborah did not know what she should say. The best she could offer was, "Thank you, Rebbe Schiffman—I mean, thanks for having me."

"It's late," her host replied, turning to his wife. "Show her where she sleeps."

Leah eyed Deborah, nodded, and then started to the back of the house where several doors led off a narrow corridor.

She opened one of them and said, "In here. I gave you the bed by the window."

It was only then that Deborah heard the sounds. There were other people in this little room, sleeping soundly and breathing audibly. In the dim light from the hallway she could barely discern three narrow beds crowded into the room. Two of them were occupied by small forms huddled under grayish-looking blankets.

"Maybe it's best you use the bathroom to change clothes. We shouldn't wake the children, they have school tomorrow."

Deborah nodded mutely. She opened her valise, pulled out a bathrobe, and left her bags inside what she could now see was a very crowded room. Relieved at the thought of being alone, albeit for only a minute, she went down the hall to the bathroom.

As she scrubbed her face, she glanced in the streaky mirror. It reflected the pale image of the young girl she once had known, a girl who was now totally transformed. Dark rings circled her eyes, which seemed dim and lifeless.

Didn't you used to be Deborah Luria? she asked her reflection.

And the exhausted face said, Yes—I used to be.

14

Timothy

In the month that followed Deborah's departure, Timothy was torn between guilt and anger. He could not forgive himself for being the cause of Deborah's banishment. He had even dared to write to the Rav reasserting his responsibility for the incident and insisting that whatever punishment it involved should be meted out to him.

And yet he could not bear the strictures of his confessor. For the priest continually reminded him of what the Lord said in the Sermon on the Mount: that anyone who even looks at a woman lustfully has committed adultery in his heart.

He was wounded by the implication that his feelings for Deborah Luria could be described as in any way impure.

And he missed her terribly.

Yet he reluctantly accepted that if he was to

become a priest he had to do penance. Among the texts and prayers assigned for him to memorize were the words of the Apostle Paul:

I am persuaded, that neither death, nor life, nor angels . . . shall be able to separate us from the love of God, which is in Christ Jesus our Lord.

But no matter how often he recited the passage, it could not obliterate the verses from the Song of Songs, which he had read because he knew how much they meant to Deborah: "Love is strong as death."

He tried to drown himself in prayer. For three weeks in succession he even went off to a *cursillo,* an intensive Jesuit-organized retreat tailored for people like himself. It offered him a chance to look inward and confront himself, and then upward to discover what God meant to him.

Unbeknownst to his family, he fasted. On many weeknights he meditated in church for several hours.

This extraordinary behavior could not go unnoticed—especially in so small a parish. Late one evening Father Hanrahan came up to him as he was kneeling, head in hands, and whispered, "Timothy, Bishop Mulroney wants to see you at eleven tomorrow."

Tim was thunderstruck, certain this was a call to judgment.

Surely, despite the seal of confession, word of his offenses had somehow reached the prelate's ear.

He spent a sleepless night. And then, dressed in his only suit, he walked the two miles from St. Gregory's to diocesan headquarters just to slow his racing heart.

His legs were unsteady as he mounted the steps of the large brownstone which served as the bishop's chancery.

"Hogan, I've heard a great deal about you," Bishop Mulroney said cryptically as Timothy kissed his ring. A corpulent man, he was imposing in his black suit and large pectoral cross. "Sit down, my son," he continued, "we've things to talk about."

Timothy poised himself on the edge of a chair, while the churchman returned to his desk. In a corner, his secretary, a young, scholarly looking priest, sat inconspicuously, pencil and notepad in hand.

"You know," His Excellency reflected, "I do believe that God watches over some of us with special diligence. He probes our hearts. He reads the language of our souls. . . ."

Tim was certain now of what was to come—an avenging thunderbolt for all his evil thoughts.

He was wrong.

"Your activities are not unknown to me," the bishop continued. "Your zeal in the *cursillos,* your general demeanor, display a piety that is—especially these days—extraordinary. Father Hanrahan and I both believe that you have a true vocation. . . ."

Timothy listened silently, wanting to believe this was God's way of telling him how to resolve his painful dilemma.

"Am I right about your feelings?" Bishop Mulroney asked.

"Yes, Your Excellency," he answered with alacrity. "If you think I'm worthy, I want to dedicate my life to serving God."

The prelate smiled. "I'm pleased. My instinct told me Father Joe was right. So I've gone ahead and made some arrangements for you. St. Athanasius' Seminary has a place right now. So you could either finish out the school year at St. Gregory's and start this summer, or—"

"No, no," Tim interrupted anxiously, "I'd like to go as soon as possible."

The bishop laughed. "My goodness, you're the most devoted lad I've ever come across. Why don't you take a day or two to think about it, talk it over with your family?"

"I have no family."

"I mean, of course, your uncle and your aunt," the bishop answered.

Tim thought to himself, I wonder how much more this man knows about me.

He left the diocesan office more upset than when he had arrived. He knew that what the bishop called his "devoutness" was in reality a frantic desperation. He wanted to escape, renounce the world, and thereby exorcise all thoughts of Deborah Luria.

He stopped by a lamppost at a busy intersection. He reached into his jacket pocket and withdrew a folded piece of paper, already frayed from many readings.

Dear Timothy,

I know it's dangerous, but this is my last chance of contacting you.

They're sending me to Israel tomorrow. To be honest, I feel guilty for disobeying my religion and my parents. But I feel even worse for what I have done to you.

You acted with such friendship and pure heart, I hope you don't get into any trouble on account of me.

I am sad to think we will probably never see each other again. But I only hope that I will remain somewhere in your thoughts.

Yours,
D

P.S. I'm told that the YMCA in Jerusalem holds letters for people who are traveling around. If you can, please write me there. That is, if you want to.

A sudden feeling seized him that this was the most important moment of his life, the crossroads of two paths, both leading to a point of no return.

He sensed that, through his bishop, God was giving him a sign—forsake the world.

Did he really have a choice?

He began to tear up the letter.

As he scattered the fragments in a nearby bin, he burst into tears.

15

Deborah

Deborah could have slept forever. Indeed, that first morning in Rebbe Schiffman's house, she wished she had never awakened.

At five-thirty in the morning the five-year-old in the next bed began to wail loudly for her mother.

After a few minutes, Leah entered sleepily in a faded bathrobe, eyed Deborah, and complained, "Couldn't you keep her quiet?"

Deborah was astounded. "I don't even know her name."

The rabbi's wife stared at the little girl. "What is it with you, Rivkah?" she demanded.

"I wet my bed," the child murmured fearfully.

"Again? Sheets don't grow on trees, you know. Get up and wash."

Shamefaced, the little girl docilely obeyed and headed for the door.

"And be sure to give your clothes to Deborah," her mother called after her.

Me? Deborah thought to herself. What am *I* supposed to do with a kid's wet pajamas?

She soon found out.

"Let her bed air after you strip it," Mrs. Schiffman commanded matter-of-factly. "And be sure to rinse the sheets before you wash them. But don't turn on the machine till we have enough to fill it. Electricity costs."

Deborah had naturally intended to pitch in with the household duties. This was starting to look like more than "pitching."

As she sleepily removed the dirty bedclothes, another roommate—a girl who looked about three and a half—awoke and asked casually in Yiddish, "Who are you?"

"My name is Deborah. I've come from New York."

"Oh," replied the little girl, unimpressed with Deborah's transatlantic credentials. The Schiffmans often had visitors from all over the world.

Shivering and unsteady, Deborah put on her bathrobe, gathered the sheets, and carried them to an alcove at the back of the hallway, where an ancient washing machine was crammed under a louvered window. She filled the small nearby sink, put the laundry in to soak, and retreated toward the bathroom. It was no warmer than the night before, and she began to wonder if the Schiffmans had any heating at all.

The bathroom was already occupied, and two young boys were waiting in line outside the door.

The Schiffman sons—pale with dark, deep-set eyes—looked even more tired than their sisters. She bade them "Good morning," but they seemed not to notice her.

By the time her turn arrived, the hot water was gone, so she washed with cold as best she could, then quickly dressed and headed for the dining area.

The Schiffman family was already seated, father studying the morning paper, the various children eating—or loudly refusing to eat—their toasted white bread smeared with jam. Leah had yet another child on her lap.

Rebbe Schiffman nodded a silent "Good morning" and, in what Deborah optimistically construed as cordial tones, said, "Help yourself. There's coffee in the kitchen."

She attempted a smile, took a slice of bread and, quickly uttering the blessing, wolfed it down.

As she cut and buttered two more pieces, Rebbitsin Schiffman admonished, "Don't be such a *chazer.* Leave some for other people."

"Sorry, sorry," Deborah answered meekly. Then, trying to initiate a dialogue, said to no one in particular, "It was a really long flight."

"So?" said the rabbi's wife. "You didn't have to drive the plane, did you?"

Deborah could only interpret their frosty attitude as proof that her infamy had preceded her. Both parents were warm and affectionate to their children, hugging and kissing them before they left for school.

"You let them go by themselves?" Deborah observed with surprise.

"This is something special?" asked the Rebbe.

"Well, back home young kids aren't allowed . . ."

She was jarred by her own utterance of the word "home." She had left America with the distinct impression that she no longer had one.

"Things here are not like by you in America," the patriarch explained. "We are a community. We look after one another. All the children are our children."

Deborah continued to sip her coffee in silence, hoping to learn what had been arranged for her own education, but Rebbe Schiffman was too absorbed reading an article about the day's most burning issue.

"The *chutzpah* of these people!" he fulminated. "They want to open the Jerusalem cinemas on Friday nights!"

"Outrageous," Leah agreed, clucking her tongue in disapproval. "I hear they already have some in Tel Aviv—but they're *goyim,* anyway."

Deborah, who came from a background where

movie theaters were open for the nonobservant on the Sabbath, saw no wrong in this. Besides, there were no cinemas in Mea Shearim, anyway. But she kept her peace.

Until she ventured to inquire, "Rebbe Schiffman?"

"Yes, Deborah?"

"What about *my* school?"

"What about it?"

"Where is it? What time do I go?"

"It's in America and you already went," he answered curtly.

Deborah protested, "But I thought I was—"

"You're sixteen, no?" Mrs. Schiffman asked.

"Nearly seventeen."

"Well, the law of this so-called State only requires education till sixteen years. You've had enough."

Deborah was taken aback. "Don't the sages say . . ."

"What kind of talk is this?" Leah scolded. "What does a young girl have to do with sages? You know your Abridged Code of Laws, right?"

"A lot of it. But there's so much more I want to learn."

"Listen, Deborah," Rebbe Schiffman interposed with polite finality. "You know what is expected of a wife. More than that is not the business of a woman."

"I can see already why she got herself into such trouble," Leah remarked to her husband.

Deborah felt both hurt and relieved. Now at least she knew they had been told of her transgression.

Still, she would not go down without a fight.

"My father told me I'd be finishing my education here," she protested as politely as she could.

"Education can mean many things," Rebbe Schiffman answered. "Your father asked me to— how can I put it?"

"Set me on the right track?" Deborah offered.

The rabbi nodded. "Yes, that's more or less the concept. He trusts me to treat you like my own daughter. And, believe me, come sixteen for my little Rivkah, she'll be married like a shot. That way we won't have *tsores* and *skandal*."

Trouble and scandal, Deborah thought to herself. What on earth do they think I *did*?

"Well, if I'm not going to school, what am I supposed to do all day?" she asked, a sinking feeling in her stomach.

"Tell me, child," Rebbe Schiffman answered, "have you looked around the house? Is it the Hilton here? Don't you think my wife could use a little help?"

Until that moment, Deborah merely had felt lost, disoriented, and tired from the change of time. Now she could find room for anger.

"This isn't what I want to do, Rebbe Schiffman," she said firmly.

The rabbi raised an eyebrow, stared at her, and then spoke slowly. "Listen, Madam Luria, I'm the head of the household here. What I say goes."

Heartsick, Deborah sat silently at the center of the table, as husband and wife glared at her from either side.

"Now what?" she asked.

"Now we clear the dishes," answered Leah.

And that was that.

16

Deborah

To Deborah, the days and the nights were a
monochrome gray. Curiously, the only burst
of color was not the Sabbath itself—for though she
was permitted to go to the synagogue, she was
denied access to Rebbe Schiffman's afternoon
study group—but the three hours she spent with
Leah each Friday morning shopping in *Machaneh
Yehudah,* the noisy, bustling outdoor market off the
Jaffa Road.

Her eyes, glazed by the mist of melancholy,
would react to the sight of a huge pile of oranges as
if sunlight were dazzling her.

Even the normally phlegmatic Leah sprang to
life, cheerfully bargaining with merchants for delicacies her family could afford only on this special
night.

To Deborah, this little taste of liberty made her

long for more. It did not escape her attention that the street that gave the Mea Shearim quarter its name ran only one way—*in.*

It was here in the market on a bright April Friday that she had what she first thought was a hallucination. No more than ten yards away, she caught sight of a girl about her own age—wearing a *sheitel,* but an attractive one—handing packages to a tall, athletic, red-haired man in a skullcap.

He saw her and called out, "Deborah! Deborah Luria, is it really you?"

She waved in recognition just as Leah whirled around and asked suspiciously, "What's going on? This is somebody you know?"

"Oh, yes. It's Asher Kaplan."

"Never heard of him." Leah frowned. "He isn't one of us."

"He's from Chicago," Deborah began to explain, just as Asher approached.

"Hello." He smiled. "Small world, isn't it?"

"Yes," she replied, thinking, Asher, you've just enlarged mine more than you know.

"What are you doing here?" he asked.

"I'm staying with some friends," she answered. Then introducing Leah, continued, "This is Rebbitsin Schiffman. We live in Mea Shearim."

" 'We'? You mean you're married to her son?"

"What are you saying?" Leah replied with annoyance. "My oldest boy is not even *bar mitzvah.*"

She did not like this brash American. True, he

was wearing a skullcap, but he was also sporting a T-shirt that said, in Hebrew, *Koka-Kola*.

"What are you doing here, Asher?"

"I'm on my honeymoon," he replied with a touch of shyness.

Trying to muster the appropriate enthusiasm, Deborah responded, "*Mazel tov.*"

"Thank you," Asher replied. "So you must be studying at the university, huh? I remember you had big academic plans. Mount Scopus is so beautiful—Channah's father is a professor at the Medical School."

Just then his wife caught up with them. She was attractive even in her wig—tanned, with sparkling brown eyes.

"*More* friends, Asher?" she playfully chided. Addressing the two women, she explained, "We've been here only three days and he must have run into two hundred people he knows."

"Come on, Channah," he retorted, "lots of my father's congregation emigrated here."

Suddenly it occurred to Leah.

"You don't mean *the* Rav Kaplan from Chicago?"

"Yes," Channah responded proudly.

Asher addressed Deborah with a sheepish smile. "Now do you see why I'm going to be a doctor? At least the first question out of a sick patient's mouth won't be 'Are you Rav Kaplan's son?' But you still haven't told me what you're doing here."

Deborah glanced nervously at Leah. "Uh, my

father wanted me to . . . you know . . . live a little in the Holy City."

Asher turned to Mrs. Schiffman and politely asked, "May we invite Deborah to lunch with our family at the King David on Saturday? Channah and her mother could come by and walk with her. It's within the *Shabbat* limit."

Deborah looked at Leah, her eyes pleading.

"Well, if your mother-in-law is coming, I don't think my husband would object. But why don't you call me this afternoon before *Shabbes*?"

"Fine," said Asher. And then to Deborah, "We look forward to it."

The encounter made Leah more animated than usual. As they lugged their packages past Hacherut Square, she remarked to Deborah, "How do you know this boy?"

"It was a match my father tried to make," she answered blankly.

"So what happened?" Leah asked, eyebrow raised.

"I turned him down."

"Are you *meshugge* in the head?"

"Yes," Deborah replied, overcome with melancholy.

———

Deborah had never seen anything as opulent as the dining room at the King David Hotel, with its lofty ceilings buttressed by huge, square, roseate marble pillars. Its *Shabbat* noon buffet was legendary.

There were endless tables laden with gefilte fish and herrings in a half-dozen sauces, chopped liver, enough cold cuts to feed a cavalry, and multicolored salads of fruits and vegetables, plus a dozen different varieties of eggplant.

And those were only the hors d'oeuvres. Then there was the hot food—cholent, boiled beef, baked chicken, *kasha varnishkes,* stuffed veal, and *kishkes.*

Dessert filled two whole tables—cakes and pies, chocolate mousse, rainbows of sherbets and ice cream—all nondairy, of course.

Deborah felt like a prisoner on parole.

While Channah's parents did not ask why their son-in-law had invited this attractive stranger, Channah knew. As the two young women stood marveling at the dessert table, she whispered, "I feel as if I should thank you, Deborah."

"What for?"

"Not marrying Asher. I don't know why you turned him down, but I'm glad you did."

They had coffee on the hotel terrace. The banquet had been long, and it was nearly four o'clock.

"Why don't you stay till sundown?" Channah suggested. "Then we could take you home in a taxi."

"Thanks," Deborah answered, "I'd like that very much."

In fact, she had an ulterior motive. Directly across the street from the King David Hotel was the large, pastel stone YMCA building. Deborah saw it as a chance—perhaps her only one—to discover if Timothy had written.

The moment three stars shone in the Jerusalem sky, she telephoned to explain her absence and received grudging approval from Leah.

"Just don't be too late," she cautioned. "We have a lot of dishes to wash."

As she hung up, Deborah could already note the post-Sabbath activity, store lights being switched on, a louder hum of conversation in the lobby, and the noise of traffic in the street which twenty minutes earlier had been silent and deserted.

"Well," Deborah said to the newlyweds. "This was really nice, but I think I'd better grab a bus and go home."

"You can't," Asher retorted.

"What do you mean?"

"Well, first of all, I know you're not carrying any money on *Shabbes*. And besides, we promised the Schiffmans we'd take you in a cab. If you girls wait here, I'll get my wallet."

Now there was just one obstacle standing between Deborah and a possible message from Timothy.

"Channah, do you mind if I dash over to the Y? I want to leave a note for some friends of mine who are coming next week."

"I'll go with you," she insisted amiably.

"No . . . thanks. You wait for Asher and I'll be back in a sec."

She sprinted across King David Street, down the corridor of high, thin cypress trees that led to the steps, and finally into the large hall of the YMCA.

She pushed through crowds of polyglot students to the reception desk and asked, breathless, "Is this the place where I could get a letter—I mean, if someone wrote to me?"

"What's the name?" the pasty-faced clerk responded blandly.

"Luria," she replied, "Deborah Luria."

He turned to an overflowing stack of mail in a tray marked "Hold For Arrival," and began desultorily to sort the multicolored pieces of correspondence.

"I'm in a big rush," Deborah said nervously.

"I know," the clerk replied. "Everybody is."

He went back to searching in what seemed like slow motion and at last said phlegmatically, "I have just one for 'Deborah Luria.' Do you have any identification?"

She was stymied. "I'm really sorry," she stuttered, "I forgot."

"Then come back tomorrow with your passport."

"I can't. I, uh . . . work tomorrow."

"We're open in the evening."

Less than three feet away was perhaps the most important message of her life, and she could not get her hands on it.

Her eyes brimmed with tears. "*Please* believe I'm Deborah Luria. Who else could want to be me?"

"All right," he capitulated. "I shouldn't do this, but I'll take your word for it."

He handed her the letter.

She tore it open as she rushed outside. There was just enough time to see it was indeed from Tim before the Kaplans arrived.

"Take care of everything?" Asher inquired.

Stuffing the letter into her pocket and trying to disguise her great excitement, Deborah answered, "Yes, it's all fine. I mean—everything's okay."

"Good. Now, let's get you home before the Schiffmans think we've kidnapped you."

———

"How was it?" Leah inquired.

"What?" Deborah asked, as the two women struggled through the huge accumulation of Sabbath dishes.

"The meal, Deborah," Leah persisted. "My husband sometimes meets philanthropists from overseas in the King David. He comes back raving about the food."

"Well, there was certainly a lot, and it was nice," Deborah allowed. "But I think you're a better cook."

Paradoxically, this outrageous bit of flattery won Leah's heart. Suddenly she almost liked her American servant, and she burst into a torrent of girlish chatter. Deborah could not wait to escape into the refuge of her bedroom.

As usual, the electricity was off, not merely for economy's sake, but because there was always at least one child sleeping. Groping in the darkened room, she pulled her valise out from under her bed and withdrew what had become her most treasured possession—the tiny flashlight she used to read herself to sleep. Hands shaking, she trained its slender beam on the letter.

Dear Deborah,

I pray this reaches you some day. I share the sentiments you expressed in your letter, and also feel indescribably guilty that I was the cause of your being sent away.

As it is, I, too, am leaving Brooklyn to study at St. Athanasius', a seminary in upper New York State.

Unlike your journey, this was not a punishment, but rather a reward for my scholarly diligence—a fact that makes me feel all the more guilty, since among the things I will be doing is what you always dreamed of—studying the Old Testament in Hebrew.

I tried everything to see your father and explain. But when I called, your mother always said he wasn't there. And when I camped for hours outside his office at the synagogue, Reb Isaacs, the sexton, refused to let me in. I also wrote to him, but he didn't answer.

I'm trying to convince myself that what we had between us was a little spark that has been blown out by the winter wind. I'm hoping to take Holy Orders, and it would be naive to think we'll ever see each other again. And this impossibility gives me courage to say what I never could have otherwise.

I think that what I felt for you was *love*— whatever earthly love may be. I know that it was tenderness, a longing to be with you and protect you.

I wish you well, Deborah, and I, too, hope that you will let a bit of me live somewhere in your thoughts.

Let's pray for one another.

Yours affectionately,
Tim

To Deborah it mattered little how tentatively he had said it. There was no longer any doubt. They . . . loved each other.

And there was nothing on earth that they could do about it.

17

Timothy

The day at St. Athanasius' Seminary began before dawn. At five-forty-five a bell rang, and a
student caller would walk along the rows of beds in
the vast dormitory, rousing the young seminarians
with the exhortation, *"Benedicamus Domino"* —
Let us bless the Lord. To which they would each
reply, *"Deo gratias"* — Thanks be to God.

They had twenty minutes to shower, tidy their
beds, and get down to the chapel. They performed
these tasks without speaking to one another. In fact,
the entire time span between lights-out at nine-
thirty and breakfast was known as the Great Silence.

Then, wearing their black cassocks, they descended to the chapel for meditation. It was, as the
Fathers always reminded them, the time for looking
inward. To reflect on how to live better for the

coming day. And how better to establish a personal relationship with Christ.

After morning meditation, the seminarians would line up in the refectory, each holding a tray, waiting to pass a long, narrow hatch where they could help themselves to a bland but filling breakfast.

The opening was just wide enough for gloved hands to place the food out on the counter. For the only females allowed on the seminary grounds were those who worked in the kitchen, and a strict rule forbade hiring women under the age of forty-five, lest the young men be in any way exposed to what the Fathers referred to as "the temptations of the other sex."

But then almost everything reminded him of Deborah.

Although the Fathers did so frequently, there was little need to expound upon the evil influence of women, since the only females within the boundaries of the seminary existed as disembodied limbs behind the refectory hatch or in the boys' nocturnal fantasies.

Still, these were adolescents, ranging in age from fourteen to twenty-one, and even a churchman's word could not dam the surging tide of hormones. For the pious youths who fell victim to erotic urges, the most urgent order of the day was "hitting the box"—confessing and obtaining absolution.

Sex was everywhere, intensified precisely in proportion to the power of its prohibition.

In the winter, the classrooms were ill-heated—for a purpose, so they said. To teach them how to cope with hardships that would inculcate humility.

Yet however harsh the weather, after lunch they had to go outside for half an hour. A few indulged in sports, making use of a metal rim without a net for basketball, a set of rusty dumbbells, and some wooded paths for walking.

Here they could chat freely—although they were required to remain in threes, and were subject to the closest scrutiny. The priests continually emphasized the regimen of "custody of the eyes" and inveighed against what they called "particular" friendships. Loving thy neighbor was one thing—thy classmate another. The watchword was *numquam duo:* never in couples.

Every day's horarium was identical—meditation, prayer, study, thirty minutes' outdoor recreation. Except for the Sabbath.

On Sunday afternoons, the boys would remove their somber cassocks and don special garb—black suit, white shirt, black tie and shoes—for visiting the ordinary world.

They would march down to the village, led and followed by priestly chaperons. The purpose was not wholly clear to them, since they were not allowed to buy a newspaper, or even a chocolate bar. They simply paraded into town and back, under the curious gaze of the villagers, to whom, of course, they were forbidden to speak.

Toward the end of Timothy's first year, four boys in his dormitory were discovered in a serious breach of conduct.

It was a rule that all correspondence—in and out—had to go through the Rector's office. But Sean O'Meara had mailed a letter during one of the Sunday promenades. Three other seminarians had seen him, but had not reported his misdemeanor.

In the hearing presided over by the Rector, Sean bravely, though foolishly, tried to defend himself on the grounds that the letter had merely been to his old parish priest and spiritual adviser.

This did not mitigate his offense.

The punishment was harsh. O'Meara was banned from major orders for twelve months, during which time he was to study, pray, and do penance.

The conspirators were sentenced to stay at school in July and August, to work in the gardens—and to pray.

Timothy stayed on as well. The summer months provided an opportunity to receive daily tutorials in Hebrew and Greek and accelerate his journey toward ordination.

Besides, he had nowhere to go.

One hot July afternoon at the end of his daily tutorial, Tim excused himself so he could go to the library and commit to memory what had been taught that day.

Father Sheehan urged him to get some sun instead. "Those boys out there trimming rose bushes aren't really being punished," he said with a smile. "It's a joy to be in the fresh air—the summer sun is God's reward for suffering the winter."

And so, unwillingly at first, Tim went into the garden after lunch and joined the penitents in weeding plants.

It was the first occasion in nearly a year that Timothy found himself with others of his age beyond official supervision. At first they were hesitant, wary of each other no less than of him. But as the summer heat intensified, so did the need for fellowship. They began to talk.

All three "prisoners" were saddened by their punishment. It was not the work, for they enjoyed the beauty of the outdoor life. But they had been looking forward to returning to their families.

"What about you, Tim?" asked Jamie Mac-Naughton, the tallest, leanest, and most nervous of them. "Haven't you got any family—brothers, sisters—anybody that you miss?"

"No," he answered blankly.

"Parents not alive?"

He hesitated for a moment, unsure how to answer. Discretion was the wisest course.

"Not really . . . ," he said evasively, his voice trailing off.

"You're lucky in a way," said another of the trio. "Frankly, Hogan, I've always admired how self-sufficient you are. Now I can sort of understand. You don't miss the outside world because you don't have anybody in it."

"Yes," Tim replied.

And—as he had throughout that agonizing year—he tried to suppress all thought of Deborah Luria.

18
Daniel

Dear Deb,

Thanks for your last letter. I hope by now you've sort of settled in. I suspect your gloom is just the result of being so far away. I mean, nobody could be as wretched as you describe the Schiffmans.

I'm happy to report the continued broadening of my horizons. My journey across the Bridge to the Hebrew University of New York involved not just the crossing of a river separating Brooklyn and Manhattan. It was the spanning of two cultures. Our childhood was insular, hermetic, and safe. My new world is filled with all sorts of confusions and temptations.

There are twenty-six of us in the first year of the rabbinical program (as opposed to nearly one hundred future doctors).

More than half my classmates are married and commute from as far away as Staten Island. We share the same turf as Columbia and Union Theological Seminary, so the rents in our neighborhood are extortionate. And since some of the future rabbis' wives have already begun fulfilling the *mitzvah* to increase and multiply—the married couples have to live at their parents' homes and survive on the meager scholarships the seminary affords.

I, on the other hand, with my tuition paid by our community, can live the life of a carefree bachelor in the Hyam Solomon Dormitory for Men, where I have a room all to myself, with plenty of bookshelves for Talmudic volumes.

The competition is absolutely brutal. But at least I don't get teased for being a crown prince of the Silczer realm. Among my fellow students are the sons of other distinguished rabbis. The only trait we heirs apparent have in common is a fear that we will never be the men our fathers are.

Papa still calls me several times a week to ask how I'm doing. I keep telling him what a great adventure it all is—how Talmud classes are exciting mental duels, using the swords of Scripture to strike home and win a point.

And best of all, unlike most college students in these troubled times—with the war in Vietnam tearing generations apart—our religion makes me feel secure.

Now a few personal secrets I can only share with you.

Here, beyond paternal supervision, I can go out onto Broadway—okay, so it's only Upper Broadway, but it's still Broadway enough for me. I can go to a bar for a Coke—or even something stronger, though I haven't gone *that* far yet.

And near the campus is a movie theater called the Thalia, which shows all sorts of classic movies. You can't imagine how many of its West Side devotees know all the dialogue by heart.

Since I've been going there, I'm really hooked on films. They transport me to places I've never been—and probably never will be. I've watched—and practically lived through—the Russian Revolution as seen through the imaginative lens of Sergei Eisenstein.

But—and it's kind of embarrassing to confess this to my own sister—my favorite part of the evening is waiting in the lobby for the film to break—looking at the Barnard girls, and listening to their laughter.

So as you can tell, I'm getting an education.

Not just from books, but from what I see when I close them.

I'd like to hear what's happening inside you as well. Write soon.

Love,
Danny

19

Deborah

It was the Fast of Esther, the solemn day that precedes Purim, the merriest holiday on the Jewish calendar.

The festival of Purim celebrates the bravery of Queen Esther, who successfully petitioned her husband, King Ahasuerus, to revoke the death sentence he had imposed on all her fellow Jews in Persia. Since Esther spent the preceding day praying and fasting, religious Jews commemorate her piety by doing the same.

Despite the outward sadness of the Fast Day, Deborah always found it a heartening occasion, for no other holiday in her religion celebrated the noble actions of a woman.

To her growing resentment, not once in all the time she had been a captive in Jerusalem had the Schiffmans allowed her to visit the Wailing Wall.

So it was not surprising that Deborah chose to grieve over her own exile by praying there.

Perhaps she even hoped to put in a *kvitl*—one of the tiny slips of paper containing personal pleas to the Father of the Universe—which pilgrims traditionally left in the crevices of what some called "God's mailbox."

She knew that Rebbe Schiffman went to the Wailing Wall often, not merely to pray but to communicate with other religious leaders. Yet during all the time that Deborah had been with the Schiffmans, he had never once invited even his wife to come along.

"What's the point, anyway?" Leah rationalized to Deborah in a rare moment of conversation. "They squash us into a fenced-off corner, and the men pray so loud that you can't even concentrate."

"*I'll* concentrate," Deborah insisted.

Rebbe Schiffman capitulated. "All right, Leah. If she wants it so badly, go with her."

His wife frowned. Exhausted from her household duties, caring for their offspring (and carrying a new one), she did not relish the prospect of walking to the Old City—even for so sacred a purpose. She scowled and muttered, "Very well. I'll ask Mrs. Unger next door to keep an eye on the children."

An hour later, the two women were trudging along Hanevi'im Street. The narrow byways of Mea Shearim always seemed in perpetual shadow, and Deborah welcomed the early spring sunshine on her face.

As they entered the walls of the Old City at the Damascus Gate, and walked down the slender cobbled alleys, Deborah was almost dizzy with anticipation. She could feel the immanence of a million pilgrims who had left invisible atoms of their spirit reverberating like silent prayers in a thousand tongues.

They passed the Via Dolorosa, and reached the rampart above the wide expanse of courtyard that had been cleared by Israeli soldiers after the Six Day War.

As a military policeman checked Leah's purse, she grimaced at him and then remarked to Deborah in Yiddish, "Look at this bunch of storm troopers. Do I look like a terrorist bomber?"

Before Deborah could respond, one of the soldiers replied, also in Yiddish, "Do you think I like this job, Madam? But I'd have to do it even if you were my mother."

Leah glowered, and again commented to Deborah, "Did you hear how disrespectfully they talk?"

The soldier merely smiled indulgently and waved them through.

As they descended into the forecourt, they could see the multitude of black-garbed worshipers swaying fervently in front of the Wall. Their prayers soared into the air and resounded in a cacophony of melodies in accents as diverse as Damascus, Dresden, and Dallas.

A metal barrier set off a small area in the far right-hand corner for the use of women worshipers. As they headed in that direction, Leah tugged at Deborah's arm to keep her as far away from the men as possible.

"What are you doing?" Deborah whispered with annoyance. "I'm not disturbing them."

"Don't talk," Leah snapped. "Just do as I say."

The tiny area of their segregated sanctuary was crowded, but Deborah eagerly pushed her way through the press of other women to reach the front. And felt a shiver as she gently kissed the holy stones.

Without opening her book, she joined in the morning prayer. By the time they had reached *ashrey*—"Happy are they that dwell in Thy House"—Deborah's glorious voice had grown in volume and fervor, inspiring the others to follow her example.

> *Praise the Lord, O my soul:*
> *I will praise the Lord while I live:*
> *I will sing my praises unto my God*
> *While I have my being. . . .*

Then came the attack.

From across the barrier angry shouts began to bombard them: *"Shah! Zoll zein shah!"* Shut up! Keep your voices down!

But the women were so caught up in Deborah's zeal that they sang their prayers even more loudly—except for Leah Schiffman, who kept trying to quiet them.

The men continued to shout, and the women continued to chant. Suddenly, a wooden chair was hurled over the barrier, striking a grandmotherly woman and knocking her to the ground.

Then, as Deborah bent down to help her, a metal object was lobbed into the air. As it struck the ground, it split open, and began to hiss.

"My God—it's tear gas!"

Outraged beyond fear, she snatched up the canister and hurled it at the men with all her might. There was an outcry of indignation. As more missiles began to fly over the barrier, the women followed Deborah's lead and threw them back.

Deborah shouted frantically to the policemen ringing the area above, "Why the hell don't you do something?"

But the guards were uncertain how to act. They had strict orders not to interfere with the worshipers except by express permission of the Religious Ministry. (Who had thrown the tear gas was anybody's guess.)

Captain Yosef Nahum arrived at the only solution that would prevent further injury.

"Get the women out of here," he barked. "And try to keep the men away."

Some of the officers hurried to help the frightened women retreat. A dozen others locked arms to restrain the rioting male zealots from chasing after them.

Ten minutes later the women were allowed to regroup and finish their prayers elsewhere.

Though Deborah was in shock, the irony was not lost on her. They had been banished to the Dung Gate—the door of the Old City, which for thousands of years had been used to expel the garbage.

———

They reached home to find Rebbe Schiffman incensed.

"You mean you've heard about it already?" Leah asked her husband.

"In Mea Shearim you don't need newspapers to know what's happening."

Pointing an accusatory finger at Deborah, he growled, "It's all because of this devil. I knew we shouldn't have let her go to the Wall."

"Me?" Deborah asked in a stunned voice.

"Of course *you,*" the rabbi shouted. "Your father didn't tell me you were such a harlot."

"Harlot?"

"You sang," he shouted accusingly.

"I was *praying,*" Deborah protested angrily.

"But *loudly,*" snapped the rabbi. "The men could hear your voices. Don't you know the Talmud says 'the voice of a woman is a lascivious temptation'?"

He turned to his wife. "I tell you, Leah, I'm ashamed this girl is staying in our house. I've half a mind to ask Rav Luria to take her off our hands."

Oh, thought Deborah to herself, inwardly wounded and grieving, If he only would.

20

Daniel

O urs was a twentieth-century university.
Unlike some of the ultraorthodox seminaries that act as if Jewish scholarship has scarcely evolved since the Babylonian Talmud, Hebrew University was a "modern" institution. It believed in such liberal intellectual activities as secular philosophy, the arts, and nuclear physics. It even allowed an occasional lecture by conservative rabbis.

In keeping with this progressive outlook, we future rabbis were required to take courses for "distribution." That is, something outside the realm of our majors. This could be Math, Chemistry, English Literature, or any of a vast number of disciplines. But most of us were pragmatic enough to choose classes that somehow related to our future calling, and so opted for things like Philosophy.

While H.U. offered a splendid course in the History of Ideas from Plato to Sartre, we were not obliged to limit ourselves to the four walls of our own school. Thanks to a reciprocal arrangement with nearby Columbia University, we could choose from courses taught by that world-renowned institution's roster of academic giants. Simply leafing through the enormous Columbia catalog was like reading a vast menu for a banquet of knowledge.

But I think I knew what I would choose even before I perused the catalog.

There was a famous course on the Psychology of Religion, taught by an eminent maverick named Professor Aaron Beller, himself descended from a line of distinguished rabbis.

Beller was what we disparagingly call an *epikoros*—a learned Jew who has left the fold. The Orthodox believe that when the Messiah comes, such moral libertines will burn in Hell.

Why, then, did I deliberately elect to confront a serpent who might tempt me with the apple of apostasy?

Perhaps since I believed that throughout my life as a rabbi I would encounter ever stronger arguments against religion, and thought I might as well be armed. And what better way than hearing the devil himself—the most revolutionary, rebellious notions put forth by a brilliant rebel.

Every Tuesday and Thursday morning, I walked the eight blocks from my dorm to Columbia's Hamilton Hall, the largest lecture room on campus, which Aaron Beller filled to overflowing.

That first morning not many of my fellow seminarians were in evidence, although I did notice a small enclave of other skullcaps. Perhaps the rest were too scared, but Columbia students and dozens of faculty auditors flocked to Beller as moths to a flame—to see how close they could fly without setting fire to their own beliefs.

Scattered among the young, tweed-jacketed Columbia preppies and the scruffy graduate students were a number of middle-aged clean-shaven gentlemen with clerical collars—obviously visitors from Union Theological Seminary across the road.

There was a murmur in the classroom, and then a sudden hush as a tall, angular, silver-haired form glided through the door and up to the podium.

Professor Aaron Beller, M.D., Ph.D., eyed his potential victims with a Mephistophelian grin—especially those of us in the back row, those who by sitting as distant from him as possible had betrayed ourselves as the most afraid of his ideas.

"In order to avoid harming the more susceptible among you," he began, "perhaps I should explain the philosophy of the course. I think my course should carry a warning analogous to the one on a package of cigarettes. It can be dangerous to your mental health. My psychiatric training has confirmed my opinion that man created God—*not* vice versa."

He leaned forward on the podium and gave us all a conspiratorial glance.

"Now to the unspoken secret of all religions." He paused. "In one way or another, man reaches out to God through sexuality."

The class started to percolate.

"Even during the reign of King David," Beller continued, "a full five centuries after Moses received the Ten Commandments, Jews still worshiped an 'Earth Mother,' as well as Baal, her phallic consort. These were religions whose rites included sacred prostitution."

At this point the members of the small Orthodox platoon rose to their feet. I recognized their leader as my stocky, full-bearded classmate Wolf Lifshitz, who began to stamp angrily out of the room.

"Hold it!" Beller commanded.

They stopped in their tracks.

He addressed them calmly. "My aim is to inform, not offend. Can you tell me what I've said that you find so unacceptable?"

The students exchanged looks, each hoping the other would act as spokesman. Finally, Lifshitz inflated his barrel chest and replied, "You're blaspheming our religion."

"Am I?" Beller asked. "Does your religion regard truth as blasphemous?"

"What you're saying isn't true," Lifshitz protested.

"Can you be more specific?"

Wolf's whole face went crimson. "What you said about . . . sacred prostitution."

"I'm sure your Hebrew's far better than mine," Beller replied. "But would you translate the word *kodesh* for the benefit of some of the others present?"

Wolf answered warily. "It means . . . 'holiness,' 'sanctity.' It can even refer to the holy Temple."

"Very good," Beller commented. "And do you know what the obviously related words *kadesh* and *kedeshah* mean?"

A look of worry passed over Lifshitz's face. He murmured something to one of his companions, then turned back and answered, "Well, obviously, it's something to do with holiness."

"Indeed it is." Beller smiled triumphantly. "They are the Hebrew words for sacred prostitutes—male *and* female—in the worship of Baal and Astarte."

Rage flushed his face as Lifshitz again took the initiative. "Where do you find such words in the Bible?"

"Well," said Beller, "they are unambiguously

present in Deuteronomy 23:18. I can quote it verbatim if you'd like."

"I think I know the passage," Wolf rejoined. "But isn't the Bible saying these are things you *shouldn't do*?"

"Absolutely," agreed Beller. "But the fact remains that however abhorrent it may be to our current sense of morality, our ancestors were attracted by this practice, which was widespread in the ancient Near East. I refer you to the *Code of Hammurabi,*" he continued, "and the word *qadištu*—obviously cognate with *kedeshah*. In other words, like it or not, early Jewish priests had to put up with these practices. They were, I can imagine, quite an incentive to visit the Temple."

At this point the class broke into laughter.

I confess to being a bit upset myself. But I was also fascinated. Lifshitz and company stood rigidly in place as Beller expatiated.

"You see, the rabbis who wrote and codified the Laws were astute enough to recognize that the most potent driving force in man is *Yetzer Hara*—literally the 'evil inclination,' but nowadays commonly rendered, especially in psychoanalytic literature, as libido."

Beller eyed the dissenters, who were still closely huddled by the exit door, then turned again to us.

"As our departing scholars will confirm, Jewish Law requires a man to pleasure his wife on the Sabbath."

Quickly glancing at the opposition, he quoted the original Hebrew: "*Lesameach et ishto.* Am I correct, gentlemen?"

Wolf Lifshitz was not cowed. "You are talking about a *mitzvah,* Dr. Beller—a commandment from the Torah. We should all be proud of the fact that we treat marital relations with respect."

"Quite right," the professor acknowledged. "But do you also know what the *midrash* enjoins a man to do as he approaches orgasm?"

His adversary glowered angrily but did not answer.

Beller quoted the passage from Volume Four of the Abridged Code, chapter one-fifty: " 'When having intercourse, a man should think of some subject of the Torah or other sacred subject.' "

He then asked the rest of us, "Do we not find a contradiction here? If a pious Jew is enjoined to have sex, why is he commanded *not to think* about it when approaching his climax? Indeed, why is he specifically told that the sexual act is 'not to satisfy his personal desire'?"

The crowd murmured for a moment, as Beller turned to them and remarked, "There's nothing like sex to bring out the Armageddon of ambivalence in a man's psyche."

He waited for the laughter to subside before continuing.

"It doesn't matter whether the doctrine is 'Thou shalt have intercourse,' or 'Thou shalt *not* think about it.' The real significance is that *either way* sex is in the forefront."

He looked once again at his young antagonists and said without sarcasm, "I'm sorry if you find this offensive."

Wolf spoke once again on their behalf. "Professor Beller, I find *you* offensive."

With this, they all marched out of the room.

Beller turned back to us. "Well, now at least I know that whoever has stayed will keep an open mind."

He then surveyed religious practices of both East and West to demonstrate how in each one of them sex plays a central role.

"Many cults encourage pleasure without remorse. Hinduism, for example, sees the union of a man and woman as reflecting and reaffirming the coherence of the universe.

"In India today there are literally thousands of altars to the erect *linga,* the phallus, symbol of the god Shiva. In ancient Chinese Taoism, making love was a solemn action, a 'joyful necessity,' which brought paradise on earth. And early Christianity," he continued, "was anything but celibate. More than one holy man reached sanctity only after a detour of compulsive sexuality—St. Anthony and St. Jerome, for example, freely admit they were sexual libertines before espousing celibacy. And we recall the youthful St. Augustine's fervent plea to God: 'Give me chastity and self-control—but not too soon.' "

As laughter again rippled across the lecture room, I could not keep from glancing at the churchmen among us. Unlike the rebellious students, they were respectfully listening to Beller, some even nodding their heads—perhaps because most of them were older and knew he was merely marshaling evidence, not concocting it.

Beller's approach was that of the Freudian psychiatrist, dismissing blind faith as irrational, neurotic, or a sublimation of erotic impulse.

I actually read everything on the syllabus, plunging deep into the torrent of religious conflict and soon wondering if I would resurface with my faith intact.

The course had no final exam. The only requirement was a single five-thousand-word term paper. Since the class was too large for Beller to read the essays personally, four graduate assistants helped do the grading. But I was desperate to have *him* see my paper, and racked my brain to find a way to arrange it.

His lectures ended at one. Rather than sprinting back to the seminary to make lunch, I would grab a salad at the student cafeteria at John Jay Hall.

One Thursday after I had gone through the line and was looking for a place to sit, I spied Professor

Beller eating alone. He was leafing through some learned journal, and I wondered if I dared disturb him. But it was now or never.

"Excuse me, Professor Beller. Would you mind if I joined you?"

He looked up with a friendly smile. "I'd be happy to have company. Please call me Aaron."

"Thank you. My name is Luria—uh, Danny. I'm in your class."

"Really?" he remarked, visibly pleased, as he noted my skullcap and black attire. "I guess you're aptly named, Daniel. You were the only *frummer* brave enough to remain in the lion's den."

I wanted to tell him how much his course meant to me, but he kept asking all kinds of questions about my background. I was surprised and proud when he said he knew my father. That is, he knew of the Silczer Rebbe.

"The Silczers have a splendid tradition of scholarship. Do you intend to follow in his footsteps?" he inquired.

"Yes," I acknowledged, "although my feet aren't as big."

"That shows true Socratic humility," he remarked.

"Well, I'm no Socrates."

"And I'm no Plato," he rejoined. "But that doesn't keep us from pursuing all the elusive truths. Tell me—what good books have you read lately?"

I answered, cravenly seeking his approval, that I had bought a few of his—in hardback—and was intending to read them during the upcoming vacation.

"Please," he protested. "Don't waste your money. Buy Martin Buber or A. J. Heschel—*God in Search of Man*. They're original minds. I'm just a synthesizer." His eyes twinkled, and he added, "And professional troublemaker."

"On the contrary," I replied as bravely as I could. "You've lit fires in a lot of dark places. Certainly for me."

I could tell that he was genuinely touched.

"Thank you," he said warmly. "That's the nicest thing a teacher can hear. Perhaps you'll write something some day that'll bring me back to the fold."

This surprised me. "Do you actually want to believe?" I asked.

"Of course," he answered candidly. "Don't you know that agnostics are people who are really the most desperate to find proof that God's in Heaven? Perhaps you'll make the case for existential Judaism, Daniel."

Suddenly, he glanced at his watch and stood up.

"Excuse me, but I see my first patient at two. I enjoyed our little talk. Let's do it again some time."

I stared unblinking as he wandered off.

As I pondered our conversation, it dawned on me

that the most important thing he'd said was his farewell. That he was actually going out into the real world to treat anguished souls, no doubt people for whom faith was not enough.

And I began to think, Could I, too, be one of them?

21

Deborah

Now it was Rebbe Schiffman's turn to dine at the King David, and he dressed for the occasion—fresh white shirt, black suit and tie. His wife even brushed his best black hat.

But there was an air of mystery about the luncheon. His host was referred to only as "Philadelphia."

He had spent the morning reading a dog-eared manila file with cryptic markings, which to Deborah—who had dared to peek when he was out of the room—had looked like Japanese.

"Okay." He sighed, closed the file, and rose to go. Half to himself and half to Leah, as she was helping him on with his black coat, he said, "When it comes to 'Philadelphia,' the wife makes the decisions."

Leah squeezed her husband's hand. "Good luck, Lazar."

He smiled gratefully and left to catch the bus.

Deborah did her best to pry the secret out of the rebbitsin.

"This must be a very high-level meeting—what sort of business?"

"None of yours, so mind your own," Leah cut her off firmly. "Besides, Rav Luria—may his name be for a blessing—must do the same sort of thing."

Deborah was swimming in confusion. She could not recall an instance when her father had to attend a luncheon meeting at the Waldorf-Astoria with "Philadelphia" or any other city.

The rabbi returned just before evening prayers, flushed with excitement.

"So *nu*?" Leah asked impatiently.

"Thanks be to God," her husband answered, " 'Mrs. Philadelphia' liked the idea. They're in for half a million."

Deborah, who was beginning to fear that the Schiffmans were involved in some illegal practice, was eavesdropping intently but could hide no longer.

She entered the front room and asked ingenuously, "Did I hear someone say half a million dollars?"

And then an astonishing thing happened: Rebbe Schiffman did not get angry. Instead, he smiled broadly and replied, "This is a wonderful day. The Greenbaums from Philadelphia have given us the funds to build a dormitory for our yeshiva. Now we can take in more students."

"Wonderful," Deborah said. "That means you'll be able to afford a larger house." And a warmer one, she thought to herself. "Maybe with a garden so the children can get sun—"

The Rebbe scowled, cutting her off with a wave of his hand. "Bite your tongue. God forbid that I should use a penny of this money for myself. This isn't America, where congregations give their rabbis Cadillacs."

Her chagrin at Rebbe Schiffman's scolding was overwhelmed by a momentary respect for his altruism. But that did not prevent her from detesting him.

He was still allowing his own family to live in squalor, not to mention treating *her* as the pharaohs did her forebears when they were slaves in Egypt.

———

Deborah knew she had to break free. She could no longer bear the condescension of Rebbe Schiffman, or the tyranny of his wife, who regarded her as a mere extension of the washing machine.

Had her father really known where he was sending her? Could he have told Rebbe Schiffman to combine the penalty of exile with the rigors of a labor camp?

She could not know for certain, for he never wrote. Her mother did—to say that she was pressing Moses to be reasonable and set a limit to their daughter's punishment.

Moreover, as she had secretly promised, Rachel sent money with each letter. Clearly, she was sacrificing, for it was always at least ten dollars—and occasionally more.

Deborah kept the bills in an empty Elite coffee tin in the single drawer she was accorded in the girls' dormitory.

On the morning of her eighteenth birthday, there was no celebration. Not that she expected a fanfare or a cake. But what would it have cost the Schiffmans to offer congratulations, or at least a smile?

At least her mother had remembered. And her affectionate letter was accompanied by a lavish gift of money—a ten *and* a twenty!

Deborah's coffee can was full to overflowing, with nowhere to put her new largess. Leah had already advised her that, although there were—God forbid—no thieves in Mea Shearim, a person shouldn't leave that kind of money in a drawer. Why didn't she open a savings account?

It seemed a sensible idea. Early the next morning, Deborah left the house to walk to the Bank Discount on Hanevi'im Street.

Though it was the height of summer, the men wore heavy caftans and fur hats. Whenever she came close to any of them, they averted their gaze as if she were the Medusa.

She herself was overdressed for the season. Even

if she had not known from her upbringing to wear long sleeves and a closed neckline, she could not have missed the omnipresent posters exhorting women to sartorial modesty.

Still, she felt a modicum of happiness just to be free of the stifling Schiffman household.

A block from the bank, while waiting to cross the road, she glanced up at the sign and realized that she was on the corner of Rechov Devora Hanevia—the street of Deborah the Prophetess. It seemed amazing that the Orthodox male residents would countenance even the mention of a woman in public, yet here was a street sign honoring her biblical namesake: Deborah, the Jewish Joan of Arc who had led forth the army of Israelites to confront the nine hundred iron chariots of mighty Canaan.

Could Deborah Luria not muster a scintilla of the same courage? Here she stood on a Thursday morning, several hundred yards from her dungeon, with ninety dollars—*and her passport*—in her pocket!

Afraid of losing her nerve, she broke into a run, racing by startled pedestrians, past the bank, down the Jaffa Road, across Nordau into the Central Bus Station.

Deborah stopped, breathless but exhilarated. She had escaped—almost.

Now the only problem was—where to go?

The signboards offered her a dizzying array of destinations: Jericho—the oldest city in the world, Tel Aviv—the most gaudy and *nouveau.* Or the Galilee.

The last seemed most attractive, not only because of its fabled beauty, but because it was as far from the Schiffmans as she could get.

Suddenly she had second thoughts. I'm a woman. No, be honest—I'm a *girl.* I can't go traveling around on my own. I need . . . other people.

She paced the station anxiously, ransacking her mind for ideas and trying to bolster her faltering resolve.

Then she saw the little sign marked *Egged Tours.*

Two hours and fifty-six dollars later, she joined a busload of pilgrim-sightseers from Atlanta, Georgia, for a three-day guided trip through Haifa, Nazareth, and northward into the Galilee. She had seventy-two hours—and thirty-four dollars—to decide her fate.

They stopped for lunch in a tourist restaurant atop Mount Carmel in Haifa, and were seated at long tables by the picture window. Several hundred feet below, the shoreline looked like a huge sapphire on a white marble table.

As the tourists snapped photographs, Deborah went to the cashier and bought three tokens for the telephone.

She glanced at her watch as she began to dial. It had been nearly five hours since she had left for the bank. Had the Schiffmans begun to worry? Had they called the police?

Not likely, she assured herself. She was so insignificant they might not even have noticed she was gone.

"Hello?"

"Leah—it's me, Deborah."

"*Nu,* Madam Princess—where are you? I had to serve lunch all by myself."

The reference to her servitude only strengthened Deborah's resolve. "Listen, Leah, I'm not coming back. I can't stand it anymore."

"What craziness is this? Besides, who gave you permission?"

"I don't need it anymore. I know you didn't notice, but I've turned eighteen. That means I'm free to go anywhere I want."

Suddenly Leah shifted gears. "Listen, darling," she implored, her tone betraying panic. "I know you're upset. Just tell me where you are, and I'll get Mendel to drive and we'll pick you up."

"It's no business of yours anymore. But I'll make a deal with you."

"Anything—anything."

"Don't tell my father, and I'll call you in three days at this same time."

"From where, Deborah?"

"From wherever I am," she answered and hung up, herself wondering where that would be.

When she returned to the table, there was only a single empty seat. Her neighbor—a portly woman who introduced herself as Marge—clucked, "You've missed the soup, honey. You should tell the waiter."

"That's okay," Deborah answered blankly, reaching hungrily for the bread.

"No," her new friend insisted, "you paid for it. Waiter!"

As a bowl of soup was placed before her, Deborah was pleased that Marge had been a stickler for her "rights." With less than forty dollars in her pocket, she would need every calorie to which she was entitled.

Indeed, as they were getting up at the end of the meal, she took an apple from the center of the table and stuffed it into her pocket.

The bus then proceeded to Nazareth. Here, oblivious to the commercialism that seemed to Deborah to have paganized the city of Christ's childhood, the pilgrims prayed. They sat in the newly built Basilica of the Annunciation, gazing at the spectacular mosaics gathered from the four corners of the Christian world.

Much to their tour leader's irritation, they overstayed their schedule, and it was nine P.M. when they finally reached the Roman Villa

Hotel in Tiberias on the shores of the Sea of Galilee.

The hotel was merely a glorified four-storied concrete bunker, with no elevator or air conditioning. In the dining room, old-fashioned ceiling fans stirred the heavy air, keeping most of the flies at bay.

"I was really moved today," Marge sighed at the dinner table. "It was one of the great moments in my life. How about you, Debbie dear?"

Deborah replied simply, "Yes . . . it was fascinating."

"Are you here on your own?" Marge inquired.

"Sort of," Deborah temporized. "Uh, I'll be joining my parents later on."

The dining room was airless, and the prevarication only made her sweat more profusely.

"Why, I think that's wonderful," the older woman remarked. "Most young girls nowadays are hippies, travelin' with their boyfriends—if you know what I mean."

Unsure of how to respond, Deborah pretended to concentrate on their dessert of canned fruit salad— incongruous in this land of Jaffa oranges and abundant fruit trees.

"Aren't you hot in those long sleeves, dear?" Marge continued chattily.

"Yes," she replied. "In fact, I'm going to take them right off."

Even at the far end of the table, her fellow tourists were startled at the sound of Deborah ripping off first her right, then her left sleeve.

For Deborah, it was a double liberation. She was not only making herself more comfortable physically, she was also tearing away the past.

———

Though she would have preferred to be alone, Deborah could not spare the twenty-dollar surcharge for a single room.

Her roommate was a straitlaced teacher from a Baptist college in the South, who knelt by her bed for several minutes, palms together, looking upward.

She shot Deborah a disapproving look, and remarked, "I hope you won't think I'm impertinent, young lady, but this is the Holy Land. Don't you think you should say your prayers?"

"I did," said Deborah to avoid more conversation, "while you were—you know—down the hall."

The next morning, Deborah said a special inward prayer—blessing Israeli breakfasts, which offered not merely eggs and assorted breads, but yogurt, fruit, and salads.

This time, she appropriated two bananas.

Their tyrannical leader herded them into the bus at eight A.M. sharp to tour the ancient city and the Sea of Galilee—where St. Peter fished, Greeks raced in the stadium, and King Herod built a mint for the Roman emperors.

Afterward, they traveled past the city walls built by twelfth-century Crusaders, and proceeded to the final stop of their explorations: a visit to one of those idiosyncratic, altruistic communities known as a kibbutz.

This one was particularly radical—founded by European Jews of the *Ha-Shomer Ha-Tza'ir* movement, who had divorced themselves from religion to regain their kinship with the soil.

The pilgrims found Kfar Ha-Sharon interesting if, in Marge's words, "a teenie bit too communistic."

But Deborah was smitten. Here were Jews completely different from any she had ever known. If the Torah student was characterized by cadaverous pallor and stoop-shouldered frailty, the kibbutzniks were at the other extreme—bronzed and bursting with vitality.

Here, men in shorts, working side by side with women in still shorter shorts, tended orchards, planted vast fields of potatoes, and made honey from the hives in their enormous apiary.

The tour's host was none other than the kibbutz leader, a Falstaffian man named Boaz, who spoke to them in Hungarian-accented English.

"Nowadays, little kibbutzim like ours cannot survive from agriculture alone. If you glance up the hill, you'll see a building that looks like a small factory. Here we take the produce that we pick, then quickly freeze and pack it to be shipped to foreign markets."

He paused and then asked, "Would any of you ladies and gentlemen like to observe the freezing of a thinly sliced potato?"

The Americans demurred. They had not traveled five thousand miles to see what Birds Eye showed them nightly on television.

But what did impress them was the idealism of the place—that an entire community could work for mutual benefit and not be paid in money. Yet, as Boaz commented, each member was supplied with everything he or she needed—physically and spiritually.

"For example, when we know we'll need a doctor in, say, six or seven years' time, we send a clever boy or girl to university in Jerusalem or Tel Aviv."

To Deborah this was a revelation. Boaz had said, "We send a clever boy or *girl*. . . ." In the kibbutz, whether the fields were agricultural or academic, Jewish men and women were seen as equals.

And there was more. At almost every work site they visited, the young men *looked* at her—indeed, some even looked her over, and actually smiled.

During the early dinner that concluded the tour, Deborah determined to speak with Boaz. To her surprise, he had intended to do the same thing.

"Tell me," he asked, "what brings a girl like you

on a tour of Christians from the Bible Belt? Are you a convert maybe?"

Deborah smiled. "If I'd stayed another week in Mea Shearim, maybe I would have been."

Boaz raised his eyebrows. "Mea Shearim—and you ate dinner at our table?"

"Was it pork?" Deborah asked, unable to conceal her distress.

"No," Boaz answered. "But that was real butter we served with the chicken, not margarine. You've mixed milk with meat. By any rebbe's standards, that's unkosher."

"Oh," said Deborah, feeling shocked and guilty. "I didn't even think of that. I just took it for granted that everybody in Israel was kosher."

"You *have* been spending too much time in Mea Shearim." Boaz smiled. "Now, tell me how you got on this crazy tour."

Deborah spilled out her story—that is, most of it. She did not feel it necessary to explain why she had been exiled from her father's house.

"So," Boaz concluded when she finished her narrative, "now you're homeless in the homeland of your own people."

"That's about it," Deborah shrugged. "So when my money runs out . . ." She stopped.

In truth, she had been afraid to give serious thought to what she would do when her remaining dollars were exhausted. She knew only that she would not go back to the Schiffmans'.

Boaz sensed the words that would most comfort her. "Why don't you stay here on the kibbutz for, say, a month while you think things over? Of course, you'd have to work like everybody else."

"Don't worry, I'm used to hard work," she responded eagerly, then diffidently asked, "Could it be outdoors?"

"Outdoors, indoors—in the fields, in the kitchen, with the chickens, with the children. Everybody here does a little bit of everything."

"Then I'll do a little bit of everything," she affirmed with a tiny smile—and for the first time since she had left America felt the stirrings of happiness. "When do I begin?"

"Well, officially, tomorrow morning—unofficially, right now. I'll have my wife find you a bed in one of the girls' dormitories, and," he added with a smile, "get you something to wear besides that *shmatta* you've got on. Meanwhile, I'll go explain things to your tour leader."

"Will he be upset?" Deborah asked uneasily.

"No," Boaz answered, with a hearty laugh, "we pay him a commission on every recruit he brings us."

———

The next day she made her final call to Mea Shearim to announce that she intended to stay at "a kibbutz up north."

Leah's first questions were not unexpected. "Are they Orthodox? Is the food kosher?"

"No," Deborah replied, "but the people are."

"Will you at least give us your address? We have to call your father. Please, Deborah, out of respect for—"

"No." She cut Leah off. "I'll call my parents myself—when I'm ready."

After a moment she added, "Thank you for your hospitality."

In other words, thank God it's over.

———

For all her bravado with Leah, Deborah did not call her parents immediately. It took her several more days—and many bitten fingernails—to work up the courage.

Surprisingly, her father did not lose his temper.

"Deborah," he murmured sympathetically, "you must be under enormous stress."

"On the contrary, Papa. I feel calmer than I've ever been in my life."

"But a kibbutz is no place for a girl like you— certainly not one of the *Ha-Shomer Ha-Tza'ir.* They're immoral people."

"That's not true," she retorted, hurt and angry. "Besides, I don't care what you say, I admire them."

She was deliberately goading him now, venting the rage that had accumulated since he had cast her off, but the Rav simply answered softly.

"Listen to me, Deborah," he said. "I have no time for squabbling. Tomorrow they will come to take you home."

"Papa, this is my home now. Anyway, who do you mean by 'they'?"

"Some of our people . . . from Jerusalem."

"You make them sound like the Mafia."

"Deborah," her father cautioned, "you're trying my patience. Now you will do what I say, or—"

"Or what? I'm eighteen, Papa. I'm officially an adult. And if any of your 'people' try to drag me from this place, they'll have to deal with two hundred kibbutzniks."

For a moment there was silence. Then she heard her exasperated father remark, "Rachel, you try and talk some sense to her."

Now her mother was on the phone.

"Deborah, how can you do this to your father? You're breaking his heart."

"I'm sorry, Mama," she answered, "but I've made up my mind."

The tone in Deborah's voice convinced Rachel that she was immovable.

"You'll write at least?" her mother pleaded in capitulation. "Even a postcard—just to let us know you're well."

Deborah tried to speak, but her throat tightened. She was saddened for her mother, trapped in a Brooklyn ghetto in a medieval marriage and a Dark Age mentality.

At last, despite the tears that almost choked her, she responded.

"Yes, Mama. I would never hurt you. Please give my love to everyone." She stopped, took a breath, and then added softly, "Including Papa."

22

Timothy

By the summer of Tim's twenty-first birthday, he had completed three full years at St. Athanasius'.

All that time, he had remained in school during the holiday breaks and taken ever more intensive private tutorials, not only with Father Sheehan, but with Father Costello, who had a doctorate in ancient languages from the Pontifical Oriental Institute in Rome.

In recent times the number of candidates for the priesthood in America had declined alarmingly. Yet suddenly as if from nowhere, there had appeared in this barren desert the dazzling figure of Timothy Hogan, strikingly handsome, charismatic, and brilliant.

His teachers were in awe. Tim had not only completely mastered the Bible tongues—Latin, Greek, and Hebrew—but even Aramaic, the everyday language spoken in the Holy Land at the time of Jesus.

Tim was unique in yet another way: he did not seem to have a single friend. Some speculated that his very brilliance intimidated the other students, but the more acute minds on the faculty realized that he shunned all relationships—with anyone but God. Whatever time he did not devote to study he spent in the chapel praying.

Thus it followed that unlike the rest of his classmates who saw the summer as their only chance to laze—and perhaps furtively gaze—on a crowded beach, Tim had no intention of spending these precious months in frivolity. On the last official day of school, he bade farewell to his classmates and, despite the seductive sunshine, headed into the library.

He was so immersed in comparing St. Jerome's two versions of the Psalms that he barely felt the gentle tap on his shoulder or heard the soft voice of Brother Thomas, one of the newly ordained deacons.

"They want to see you in the Rector's office."

Tim looked up, puzzled. "Who?" he asked.

"I wasn't told. I only know they arrived in the longest car I've ever seen."

Could it be someone to inform him that his uncle or his aunt had died? That was the only thing that he could imagine, since he had no other ties with the outside world.

He knocked diffidently and then heard Father Sheehan's friendly voice call out, "Come right in, Timothy."

Tim opened the door and was somewhat taken aback to see—in addition to the Rector—five imposing visitors. All were elegantly clad, only one in clerical dress—Bishop Mulroney, his hair now fully gray.

"Your Excellency. . . ."

"Good to see you, Tim. I've heard some absolutely splendid things about your studies. I'm extremely proud."

Tim glanced at the Rector, who nodded, beaming.

"Yes, Timothy. I've been in constant touch with the diocese."

"Oh," was all that Tim could manage, hesitant to express his pleasure, lest it be deemed sinful pride. "I'm glad that I didn't . . . disappoint Your Excellency."

"On the contrary," the Bishop replied. "In fact, you're the purpose of our journey."

Tim glanced at the other visitors and thought he recognized at least two of them. For even in the "edited" newspapers the seminarians were allowed to read, he'd seen pictures of John O'Dwyer, Junior Senator from Massachusetts. And he was fairly certain that the man in the dark gray three-piece suit was the current Ambassador to the United Nations, Daniel Carroll.

But they were never formally introduced.

Each merely offered Tim a friendly smile, as the Bishop motioned him to sit, and then offered a partial explanation.

"These gentlemen are all important businessmen and public servants, as well as devout and committed Catholics. . . . Tim, the record you've set at St. Athanasius' has drawn us here like a lodestone."

Tim lowered his head, not knowing whether it would be proper even to say, "I'm flattered."

"Tell me, Timothy," the senator politely interrupted, "what are your future plans?"

He looked up in mild surprise. *Plans?* "I—I hope to be ordained in two or three years."

"We know that," Ambassador Carroll acknowledged. "Our real question is your future plans within the Church."

"Do you have any particular aspirations?" one of the other men inquired.

Aspirations? Another term that struck Tim as incongruous in an ecclesiastical context. "Not really, sir. I only want to serve the Lord in whatever capacity I might be useful." He hesitated, then confessed, "As Father Sheehan may have told you, I've been doing a lot of work in Scripture. Someday, I'd like to teach."

The others present nodded at one another, exchanging knowing glances. Senator O'Dwyer even whispered audibly to the Bishop, "There's no question in my mind." He then looked at the Rector, who addressed the young seminarian.

"Tim," Father Sheehan began, "there are two roads to Rome. . . ."

Rome?

"The first is that on which you've already embarked—the pursuit of sacred learning. The other is what we might call—for lack of a better word—'leadership.' "

"I don't believe I understand," Tim murmured uneasily.

The bishop took up the discussion.

"Tim, as pastors of the Church, our primary purpose is of course to do God's work. But we are also an earthly institution. The Vatican needs gifted administrators. And the American Church needs to have its interests represented at the Holy See."

During the pause that ensued, Tim tried to read the compass of the conversation. Where were they heading?

At last, the senator spoke on behalf of his colleagues. "We would like to send you to Rome to complete your studies."

Overcome, Tim barely managed to say, "I feel honored . . . very honored. Does that mean I'd be going to the North American College?"

The bishop leaned back in his chair, and smiled. "In due course. Naturally, you'd have to get a degree in Canon Law. But first we would be happy if you spent a semester at the University in Perugia studying Italian."

"Italian?" Timothy inquired.

"Of course," Bishop Mulroney responded. "It's the *lingua franca* of the Vatican and of those who serve there—from the Swiss Guards to the Holy Father himself."

Timothy was too astonished to say anything.

"You're leaving on July fifth," the bishop continued, in a matter-of-fact tone. "That gives you two weeks to visit your family and come to Fordham University to meet the rest of the group."

"Sir?" Tim inquired.

"Yes," explained one of the industrialists. "We're sponsoring four young men as gifted as yourself. Good Catholic boys."

The senator from Massachusetts added, "*Irish* Catholics."

———

Tim was sad at the prospect of leaving St. Athanasius'—the only real home he had ever known. Moreover, he was reluctant even for appearance's sake to pay a farewell visit to his family.

And, worst of all, to return to the scene of his crime.

The Delaneys were glad to see him—though the feeling was not mutual. And Aunt Cassie had an unfortunate way of expressing it.

"If only your poor mother were sane enough. . . ."

Tuck exploited the occasion as a festival worthy of expansive toasting.

"They don't send just any priest to Rome—

especially when he's not even got the collar. God's chosen you, Tim, believe me. And I love you for it."

It did not escape Timothy's attention that this was the single time in their entire relationship that his uncle had employed this phrase.

———

Tim blessed the dawn of his departure.

It seemed to him that he had barely taken a breath during all the time he had spent in Brooklyn. Naturally, he went regularly to Mass and met with some of his old teachers, but for the most part he remained in the house, reading. He could not even bring himself to walk on Nostrand Avenue for fear of meeting any of the families he had once served—especially the Lurias.

He rose at six, dressed quickly in his formal clothes, embraced Aunt Cassie, endured his uncle's hug, and left to walk the three blocks to the subway, just as the bells of St. Gregory's began to toll for early Mass.

He had nearly made it to the stairway of the IRT, when he thought he saw someone waving from afar, calling his name.

It was Danny Luria, running with a heavy briefcase.

Tim's heart began to beat frantically. Although he had not spoken to Danny since that fateful night so long ago, he assumed he was still anathema to all the Lurias.

Seconds later, Danny reached him.

"Nice to see you back," he puffed, as they shook hands. "How long are you staying?"

To Tim's immense relief, he spoke in what seemed a friendly voice.

"Well, actually, I'm just leaving."

"Going to Manhattan?" Danny asked.

"Well yes, but then a long way afterward."

"Come on," said Danny, "we can talk about it on the train."

As they descended into the depths of Brooklyn, Tim could not help thinking, Look at us, two future men of God—a Catholic and a Jew—dressed like twins. The only difference was that Danny's black attire was augmented by a hat.

They bought their tokens, carried their respective bags through the turnstiles, and waited on the long, empty platform.

"Are you a priest yet?" Danny asked.

"I've a few more years to go," Tim answered, wondering which of them would be the first to mention Deborah, and yet hoping neither would. "Are you a rabbi yet?"

"I also have a ways to go—a lot of it inside my head."

Just then the train roared into the station. The doors snapped open, swallowing them both. The car was virtually deserted, and they sat side by side in a corner.

"So, *nu,* what's this long way you're going?"

"Rome—to study for the priesthood."

"Gosh, you must be very excited."

"Yes," Timothy answered, growing increasingly anxious as he thought to himself, Why doesn't he make some mention of . . . the scandal?

"How are your parents?" Tim asked tentatively.

"Both fine, thank you," Danny replied. Almost as an afterthought, he remarked, "Deborah's still in Israel."

"Oh," said Timothy. "Is she happy?" The unasked question being, Is she married?

"That's kind of hard to say. Her letters read like travelogues. I mean, there aren't any *people* in them."

Timothy took this to mean that she was still single. Yet he had been certain that the day she arrived in Jerusalem, her father would have had a husband waiting for her.

They rode for a few minutes, their silence broken only by the raucous scraping and lurching of the subway cars.

Danny could tell by Tim's expression that he was still ill at ease.

"This may sound silly after such a long time. But I'm sorry about what happened," he said quietly. "I mean, from what Deborah told me—which wasn't much—it was a terrible misunderstanding."

"Yes," said Tim gratefully and thought, There was *no* misunderstanding.

"Is she studying?" he inquired, hoping that the question was within the parameters of politeness.

"Not really, she's sort of just learning the language."

Danny saw no reason to suppress the details of his sister's daring act of independence, and so told Tim of her servitude in Mea Shearim and her escape to Kfar Ha-Sharon.

"What's that?"

"A kibbutz in the Galilee. She's been there for more than a year now."

"Lovely name," said Tim and immediately recited in Hebrew, " 'I am the rose of Sharon, and the lily of the valleys . . .' Song of Songs, chapter two, verses one and two."

"Hey," Danny remarked, "your Hebrew's better than some of my classmates'."

"Thanks," Tim responded shyly, "I've been studying it for several years now. Trying to see what the Lord actually said to Moses."

"Do you believe that God spoke to Moses in Hebrew?"

"I've never doubted it," Tim replied, puzzled by the question.

"Well, it isn't specified anywhere in the Bible. For all we know, they could have spoken in Egyptian—or in Chinese for that matter."

"Isn't that a bit irreverent?" Tim chuckled.

"No," Danny replied. "College has taught me to

keep an open mind. After all, Moses lived after the Tower of Babel. There were hundreds of languages in the world by then. They could have talked in Akkadian, Ugaritic—"

Tim nodded, and began to feel a warmth emanating from Danny. He seemed so grown up now, so *open*.

"Well then," Tim responded lightheartedly, "what proof do we have that Moses *didn't* speak Chinese?"

Danny looked at him and answered wryly, "If he had, we Jews would have been eating a lot better food."

Finally, the train reached 116th Street. Danny rose to leave and Tim followed. It was only when they were on the platform that Danny realized.

"Hey, weren't you supposed to get off at Seventy-second?"

"That's okay," Tim replied, "I've still got time, and I was enjoying our conversation."

"Same here," said Danny, offering his hand. "Good luck in Rome—and keep in touch. You know where to find me now."

"You too," Tim responded amicably. And then, as Danny Luria walked away, repeated to himself, I am the rose of Sharon, and the lily of the valleys . . .

Kfar Ha-Sharon.

And now I know how to find *Deborah*.

———

When Timothy met his traveling companions at Fordham, he was even more amazed at having been chosen for this journey.

He had assumed that they would be scholars—and indeed they were. But two of the four other young seminarians being sponsored by the mysterious "committee" had already published articles. Perhaps even more significant, each in his own way generated a kind of animal magnetism. Charisma was too pale a description.

Why me? Timothy puzzled.

Later that night, as he lay in bed in the luxury of a small room all to himself, he wondered what he had in common with these imposing young seminarians. The only link he could find was superficial. They were all about his own age—and Irish Catholics.

By two A.M., he realized that it was not the enigma of his selection that was keeping him awake, but all the feelings that had resurfaced when he'd talked with Danny Luria. He knew now that he had to see Deborah one more time. Not to pursue their relationship, but to bring it to a proper end.

On their flight the next evening, the quintet was chaperoned by Father Lloyd Devlin, a spry sexagenarian who unfortunately was terrified of flying. All across the ocean he fortified himself with a rosary in one hand and a glass in the other.

After the cabin darkened to show the movie, Timothy pretended to be leafing aimlessly through the Alitalia magazine, hoping that no one would notice him studying a map of the airline's routes.

Yes, they regularly flew from Rome to Israel. But how could he possibly arrange it?

He tried to imagine what would happen if he ever saw Deborah face to face, thousands of miles from the authorities who had ordained their separation. What might she say to him? How would he feel?

He could not conjure up the answers. But he knew he had to find them.

23

Daniel

It was the most traumatic night of my life.

I was brain-weary from studying *Solomon's Wisdom*, the famous work on the different tractates of the Talmud written by Rav Solomon ben Jehiel Luria in the mid-sixteenth century—a fact that may explain the effort I had expended on it.

I was about to take off my shoes and flop into bed, when a guy from down the corridor knocked on my door to say I had a phone call.

At this hour?

It was my mother—and she was frantic.

"What's the matter?" I asked, my heart beginning to pound uncontrollably. "Is something wrong with Papa?"

"No," she answered, her voice quavering, "it's Rena. . . ." She took a deep sobbing breath, and blurted out, "She's possessed! She's hallucinating—in a kind of trance—and groaning in a strange voice. Your father thinks it must be a *dybbuk*."

"A *dybbuk*?" I nearly shouted, fear and disbelief commingled. "For God's sake, Mama, this is the twentieth century. Demons don't enter other people's bodies. You should get a doctor."

"We did," my mother said softly. "Dr. Cohen's talking to your father right now."

"Well, what did he say?"

Her voice dropped to a fearful whisper. "That we should call . . . an exorcist."

"Surely Papa wouldn't agree to *that*."

"Danny, he's already found one."

My incredulity gave way to fright. I didn't even know there *were* such people. "Mama, are you telling me Papa believes a so-called demon is actually inside Rena, talking through her?"

"Yes," my mother replied. "I heard it myself."

"Well, who . . . who does it claim to be?"

She hesitated for a minute. "It's Chava. . . ."

"Papa's first wife?"

My mother could only repeat, "Chava says she's taken over Rena's soul and won't leave till she receives justice. Please, Danny," she implored, "get here as quickly as you can."

I dashed back to my room, grabbed a windbreaker, and hurried toward the subway. Then it occurred to me—What the hell could I do? I mean,

I didn't believe in *dybbuks*. For God's sake, dead people are dead.

But suddenly I realized that I couldn't go alone.

Though ashamed, I forced myself to dial Professor Beller's number. A sleepy voice answered.

"Yes?"

I was shivering with cold and fright as the black wind sliced through the crevices of the phone booth.

"It's Danny Luria, Professor—you know, the *frummer* in your lecture course. I'm incredibly sorry for calling you this late, but it's something very serious—"

"That's all right, Danny," Beller replied in a calming tone. I guess it was his psychiatric training. "What seems to be the matter?"

"Professor," I begged. "Please hear me out before you think I'm crazy and hang up. I don't know what to do. My mother just called to say my half sister's possessed by a *dybbuk*."

"That's superstitious nonsense," he answered without raising his voice.

"I know, but Rena's raving and hallucinating—"

"Of that I have no doubt," Beller replied. "But whatever your sister's saying—even if her voice has changed—has got to be coming from her own psyche. I'll call one of my colleagues in Brooklyn—"

"No, please! You see, my father's already called an exorcist."

"Not the Silczer Rav," Beller responded, half under his breath. Then he asked quickly, "Where are you now, Danny?"

"Outside the Hundred-and-sixteenth Street IRT."

"I'll get dressed and meet you. Give me ten minutes."

———

Throughout the excruciatingly slow subway ride to Brooklyn, Professor Beller tried to explain what he knew about the ceremony he was hoping to prevent. "If she's had a mental breakdown—which I clearly think she has," he said, "this sort of medieval voodoo is bound to make it worse."

We got to the synagogue at about one-thirty in the morning. It was dark except for the lights in front near the Holy Ark.

Half a dozen men were gathered in a circle around my father, who was seated, wringing his hands. Among them were my Uncle Saul, my brother-in-law Dovid—a yeshiva teacher who was married to my older half sister, Malka—and Rena's husband, Avrom, pale and quivering.

Reb Isaacs, the sexton, was scurrying back and forth between them and a far corner where the women—my half sister and my mother—were taking turns trying to soothe Rena, who was groaning unintelligibly.

Dr. Cohen, obviously with Papa's dispensation,

stood in the segregated women's section and shrugged his shoulders.

As we drew nearer, I suddenly realized that Beller did not have a skullcap. Luckily I always carry a spare, which I offered to him, half-afraid he would refuse to wear it. He simply nodded and placed it on his head.

As we joined the men, I saw a bizarre figure hovering close to my father—a wizened, bearded old man in a long caftan and wide-brimmed hat. He seemed to be whispering to all present, punctuating his words with emphatic gesticulations.

Standing respectfully a few paces behind him was a tall, cadaverous youth, obviously some kind of assistant.

At this moment, Father saw us. His face was gray as a tombstone. In all my life I had never seen him so distressed. His shirt collar was open and his prayer shawl draped over a wrinkled jacket. He hastened toward us and motioned me aside.

"Danny," he confided hoarsely, "I'm glad you're here. I really need your support."

Him need *me*? That was an unsettling reversal of roles.

When I asked who the strange old man was, he looked at me with pain and helplessness.

"He's Rebbe Gershon from the Williamsburg *Talmidey Kabbala*. I asked him to come. You know that our ancestors were mystics, but I myself never believed in this sort of black magic. And now it's right in front of my eyes."

He paused and added mournfully, "What else could I do? Anyway, we have another problem. We don't have ten men. I could only ask people we could trust. So there's Rebbe Saul, the two sons-in-law, Reb Isaacs, Rebbe Gershon and his apprentice, Dr. Cohen—and now you make the ninth. We still need one more."

He looked at my companion and asked, "Is this gentleman—"

"This is Professor Beller, Papa—" I interrupted.

"Oh," my father responded. "Are you Jewish, Professor?"

"I'm an atheist," he replied. "Why don't you ask one of those women to make the quorum?"

Father ignored him and demanded urgently, "Will you just stand with us? That's all the Law requires."

"Very well," Beller conceded.

A sudden piercing shriek came from the front of the synagogue and echoed from the rafters.

The men had now moved Rena to the front of the pulpit and surrounded her. This time, despite the hysteria in her voice, I could hear the words.

"I am Chava Luria, and I cannot be admitted into the life of the world-to-come until the man who murdered me does penance."

Beller and I exchanged glances.

"Does that sound like your sister?" he asked.

"No," I answered, my heart pounding. "I've never heard that voice before in my life."

As we neared the circle, I could see Rena writhing on a chair, her face contorted. She had pulled off her *sheitel* and looked so grotesque I could barely recognize her. Her heavy-jowled husband, Avrom, stood by her, looking helpless and terrified.

I went to her, bent down, and said as gently as I could, "It's me. Danny. Tell me what's wrong."

She moved her lips and yet another unearthly sound emerged. "I am Chava. I have attached myself to Rena's soul, and I will remain until I have revenge."

I froze. Like the other onlookers, I was petrified.

Only Beller reacted. To Rebbe Gershon's visible annoyance, he stepped forward, knelt next to my sister, and simply spoke to the voice as if conversing with my father's long-dead wife.

"Chava," he said quietly, "I'm Dr. Beller. What is this revenge you're talking about? Whom do you think has wronged you?"

The reply spewed out like lava from a volcano. "He *killed* me. Rav Moses Luria killed me!"

Nine pairs of eyes suddenly fixed on Papa, as Professor Beller turned to him and asked, "Do you have any idea what she's talking about?"

My father shook his head emphatically, and added in a whisper, "I never did anything to hurt her."

"You killed me," howled the voice. "You let me die."

"No, Chava, no," my father protested. "I begged the doctors to do everything to save you."

"But you made them wait. You wanted to have your son—"

"No!" Father's face had gone chalk white.

"You have my blood on your hands, Rav Moses Luria."

My father lowered his head to avoid the startled gazes of the onlookers and murmured in agony, "It's not true. It's not true." He then addressed the exorcist in suppliant tones. "What shall we do, Rebbe Gershon?"

"Open up the Holy Ark and we will pray to chase this evil spirit out of your daughter."

I bounded onto the pulpit, opened the doors, and pulled apart the curtains. There, row by row, stood the sacred scrolls, clothed in their gold-fringed silk and crowned with silver ornaments. They seemed to shine more brightly than ever on this night of supernatural blackness.

Rebbe Gershon turned to the others. "We will surround this woman and recite the Ninety-first Psalm."

We quickly turned to the appropriate page, and awaited his instructions.

He signaled us to begin.

Normally, our prayers were torrents of words moving at different speeds across the text, creating a sacred cacophony. But this time we all spoke in unison, as if the Lord had sent a metronome into our midst.

We had studied this psalm in one of my classes, where we learned that in ancient times superstitious Jews regarded it as having antidemonic powers, since its first two verses invoke God by four completely different names.

> *Oh Thou that dwellest in the covert of the Most High,*
> *And abidest in the shadow of the Almighty;*
> *I will say of the Lord, who is my refuge and my fortress,*
> *My God, in whom I trust,*
> *That He will deliver thee. . . .*

I looked over my shoulder and saw my mother and half sister praying intensely. I glanced at all the frightened faces of the worshipers—except my father's. I could not bear to look at him.

As we recited, Rena's head slumped forward. She shook as if locked in mortal combat with the spirit who had captured her. Then suddenly she fell into a faint. Professor Beller dropped down beside her and began to take her pulse.

We all ceased praying. There was total silence. I could hear the angry winds blowing outside.

My father asked anxiously, "Are you all right now, Rena?"

His daughter looked up, eyes pleading. From within, the demon howled once again, "I will never leave until you beg forgiveness from the Almighty!"

Papa had his head in his hands, lost for what to do. I wanted to go to him, to comfort him. But before I could move to his side Rebbe Gershon commanded him, "Rav Luria, you must confess."

Father stared at him. "But it isn't true!"

"I beg of you, Rav Luria. Do not question the Lord of the Universe. If He finds you guilty, then you must confess."

Papa was adamant. "But I told the doctors that *her* life was more important. You know I would have—it's the law of our religion. I am innocent!"

After a dreadful silence, once again Rebbe Gershon murmured, "We sometimes do not realize what we do. But He who sits on High can only be placated if we ask forgiveness for the sins we might have committed."

"All right!" my father shouted.

He sank to his knees before the Holy Ark and, sobbing, chanted the *Al chet,* the "Great Confession of Sins," which we recite nine times on the Day of Atonement.

Without a sign or signal, all of us said in unison the congregational response to the prayer, "Forgive us, have mercy on us, pardon us."

When our voices finally ceased to echo in the empty synagogue, my professor spoke.

"Rav Luria, I think your daughter should be seen by a psychiatrist as soon as possible."

Father's head snapped up. He riveted Beller with his eyes. "You keep out of this."

"All right, have it your way—for the time being. But remember, as a doctor I have the authority to insist that she be taken to a hospital."

The others in the *minyan* glared at him. They would, I'm sure, have chased him out had we not needed him as a tenth man. Then they all turned to my father.

"What should we do, Rav Luria?" one of them inquired.

"Ask Rebbe Gershon," Father answered weakly. He had clearly abdicated all authority.

"There's no alternative," the elderly rabbi declared. "We must perform the entire ceremony of excommunication—rams' horns, Torahs, lights—everything. These are dire circumstances and one must take the ultimate measures. Are you in agreement, Rav Luria?"

"Just tell me what you need," Father said softly.

"First, we all put on *kittels*." The exorcist motioned impatiently to his assistant. "Ephraim—quickly."

The young man rummaged through a large suitcase, and withdrew the white garments Jews wear on Holy Days—and as a burial shroud.

Rebbe Gershon turned back to my father. "We

will use seven rams' horns and seven black candles."

"Black candles?" said my father in disbelief.

"I brought everything," Rebbe Gershon murmured. "I left the bag in your office."

Papa nodded. "Danny, hurry and get it—please."

I charged up the stairs and entered the little office on the second floor. It looked as though it had been vandalized. Open books strewn everywhere. Tracts on mysticism and demonology. Several on the mystical theories of the sixteenth-century "Divine Rabbi," Isaac Luria. I never knew he had such works. Or perhaps the exorcist had brought them.

Near the desk was Rebbe Gershon's weathered valise. I stared at it for a moment, frightened by what else it might possibly contain, then picked it up and carried it gingerly down the stairs.

By the time I returned to the synagogue, the others, including Professor Beller, had put on the white shrouds.

The moment I gave the bag to Rebbe Gershon, my father pushed a *kittel* at me.

"Hurry, Danny. . . . Let's get this over with."

As I quickly dressed, I could hear Rena—or was it Chava?—moaning incoherently.

Rebbe Gershon now ordered seven of the men to take down Torahs from the Holy Ark. He then opened the valise and motioned me toward him.

"Here, boy, give these out."

One by one he handed to me seven of those sinister candles.

Father was pacing back and forth, every so often slapping his forehead as if it had been stabbed with needles.

Mama nervously approached the exorcist.

"Rebbe Gershon, we want to do something. May we at least hold candles? I mean, in the women's section, of course."

The old man waved her off. Then he pointed again to me. I understood, without the need of words, that he was commanding me to extinguish the other lights.

In a moment the vast synagogue was drowned in darkness, except for seven candle flames.

By their eerie flickering light, the exorcist then distributed among us seven rams' horns. I took one, but I wasn't sure I could produce a sound because my lips were numb.

At another of Rebbe Gershon's signals, we again surrounded Rena, still sitting, her shoulders hunched and eyes tightly closed.

He took a deep breath, stood in front of her, and declaimed, "Evil spirit, since you will not hear our prayer, we invoke the power of the Most High to expel you."

And then he commanded us, "Blow *tekiah*."

I had always been chilled by the sound of a single ram's horn on the High Holy Days. I imagined the great blast to be the seal of God's Supreme Judgment. But the sound of *seven* all at once was beyond description.

All eyes were fixed on Rena's face. She began to writhe again, and a voice clamored from within her, "Let go! Stop dragging me! I will not leave!"

Rena seemed to surrender. She fell back in her chair, completely limp.

Rebbe Gershon persisted, beads of sweat on his brow glowing in the candlelight.

"Since you will not heed the higher spirits, I now invoke the cruelest powers of the universe to tear you out."

He turned again to us and commanded, "Blow *shevarim*."

Three low, even notes came forth and filled the empty synagogue. We all bent closer to Rena. The demon was still within her, but noticeably weaker.

"All the powers of the universe are now against me," it wailed. "I am torn by spirits with no mercy—but despite the pain, I will not go!"

Rebbe Gershon now ordered brusquely, "Put the Torahs back and close the Ark."

The men obeyed as quickly as they could and, I am sure, wondered as I did what more the exorcist could do.

When we all once again encircled the *dybbuk*, the old man walked into the middle, looked straight at Rena, and roared like a lion: "Rise up, O Lord! Let thine enemies be dispersed and scattered . . . I,

Gershon ben Jacov, do sunder every thread that binds you to the body of this woman."

He paused, and then cried even louder, *"You are excommunicated by the Lord Almighty! "*

Signaling the horns again, he told us, *"Teruah."*

Driven by blind fear, we trumpeted a sound that transformed the atmosphere into primal chaos. Though we were nearly out of breath, he urged us to keep on blowing. Now the writhing of my sister's body was so violent, it almost lifted her above the chair.

Then, suddenly, she collapsed, unconscious.

Rebbe Gershon waved at us to stop. Papa was the first at her side. He lifted her face.

"Oh, Rena, my little girl, are you all right?"

She opened her eyes slightly, but said nothing.

"Talk to me, please, my child," he implored.

She was silent, her eyes unfocused.

Someone tapped me lightly on the shoulder. I turned. It was Beller. "Go to her," he whispered.

I nodded and took two or three steps toward my sister. By some miracle, she seemed to recognize me.

"Danny," she muttered. "Where am I? What's happening?"

"Everything's all right," I tried to reassure her. "Your husband's here. . . ."

I motioned to Avrom. He came forward, leaned down, and embraced his wife.

Reb Isaacs had put the lights back on as Rebbe

Gershon's assistant collected our extinguished candles.

Following his lead, the men took off their white garments, returning to their earthly clothing.

Beller was again checking Rena's pulse, and having borrowed a penlight from Dr. Cohen, was looking into her eyes. He stood up, evidently satisfied.

"Get her into bed and see she gets a lot of rest. I'm going to make sure somebody from the hospital comes to see her."

I waited for my father to object, but he said nothing. To my astonishment, he had also become Beller's patient.

"May I speak to you for a moment, Rav Luria?" he asked.

Papa merely nodded and walked a few steps away with the professor. They had a whispered dialogue, which I could not hear. For a moment they nodded at one another, then Papa returned to the rest of us.

Avrom had his arms around Rena. I was touched by his devotion.

Then Father addressed us all. "As you can see, the Lord of the Universe has heard our prayers. Thank you, Rebbe Gershon—and everybody." He added with surprising severity, "But I command you all to keep silent about what you have seen and heard tonight."

———

During our ride home I gathered my courage and asked Beller, "What did you and Papa talk about?"

"His first wife, Chava, how she died."

"Actually, I've never known. He's never really talked about it."

"What he told me was enough to put the pieces together. I pretty well sensed that she died of toxemia."

"What's that?" I asked.

"It's one of the great mystery diseases of pregnancy. A special form of blood poisoning. If you take the baby out, it stops immediately and the mother's fine. Of course, if the baby is extremely premature . . ." He sighed, then continued, "In Chava's case, it was probably too tough a call, and the doctor may have foolishly tried to save mother and child—and lost both. I'm sure the decision whether or not to act was out of your father's hands. But still he feels guilty. . . ."

"About what?"

"He wanted a son, Danny," Beller answered. "He feels responsible for Chava's death, and he thinks that losing the boy was his punishment."

We both rode silently for a few minutes. Then out of nowhere, he said quietly, "I'm surprised."

"What do you mean?"

He looked me in the eye and replied with compassion, "I'm amazed it wasn't *you* who suffered from the *dybbuk*."

———

That almost pagan ceremony marked a turning point in my life. I had seen my father, whom I had till then regarded as omniscient and omnipotent, grow helpless in the grip of atavistic superstition— diminished to a frail replica of his once titanic self.

I could no longer look at him with the same eyes.

And I wondered if I could believe in a God who lets evil spirits fly around the world and has to be propitiated by black candles, spells, and the bleating of rams' horns.

One thing became disturbingly clear.

If exorcisms and the like were ceremonies that the Silczer Rav believed in, I could not be his successor.

24

Deborah

Deborah's dark brown hair was streaked with copper—the natural result of working in the sunbaked fields of Kfar Ha-Sharon.

Boaz had arranged to give her as much time as possible outdoors, although he could not totally absolve her from serving and cleanup duties in the dining room.

During her first weeks on the kibbutz, her diet seemed to consist entirely of aspirin and orange juice—the first to bring relief to aching muscles, and the second to replace the perspiration she lost each day.

Despite all the physical discomfort, she was euphoric. And, for the first time since she had been in Israel, she began to make friends.

Boaz and his wife, Zipporah, were really more like parents. He, for all his brawny masculinity, was like a mother bird sheltering a wounded fledgling under her wing.

There were a hundred or so families on the kibbutz, each couple having a *srif*—a spartan wooden hut—to themselves. Meanwhile, their offspring joined the other children, who all lived in a separate dormitory.

Of the surprises Deborah had encountered, this segregation was the most radical. Yet the youngsters seemed to enjoy living with several dozen other "siblings," and accepted as completely natural the fact that their parents visited them only in the late afternoon. Their time together was brief, but passionate.

She herself shared a *srif* with four other female volunteers—a German, two Dutch girls, and a Swede, each of whom was there as a six-month visitor.

They were all dedicated Christians with varied and complex reasons for having come to Israel.

Almuth's father had been a captain in the German army, but had never talked about his war experiences. It was only when her parents were killed in an accident on the autobahn, and she and her brother Dieter were going through their personal effects, that she discovered documents and campaign medals showing that her father had served with distinction in Greece and Yugoslavia organizing the deportation of Jews. Like so many other young Germans, Almuth felt compelled to make some kind of gesture—if not of expiation, then at least conciliation.

The others had been inspired by various religious feelings—like wanting to learn Hebrew to read the Old Testament in the original. But all were unabashedly candid about their more terrestrial motives. The glorious sunshine not only warmed them, but turned the faces of attentive Israeli men to a more handsome bronze.

The kibbutz did observe the Sabbath in its fashion. They lit candles and sang songs—then, after dinner, screened a movie.

On Saturdays, instead of working, they would take a bus to picnic in the hills or at the seaside.

Sometimes they would visit an archaeological site, and as a change from laboring in the fields, would wield trowels and dig enthusiastically for antiquities, while the professionals watched with amusement.

At first Deborah faithfully obeyed the injunction against traveling on the Sabbath. But finally, when all the others were planning a trip to the Dead Sea, she could resist their blandishments no longer.

Early that Saturday morning, she packed a towel and bathing suit—which, though it was standard kibbutz issue, looked embarrassingly skimpy to her—and walked to their very own antique, a rickety all-purpose school bus.

It was then that she hesitated.

Boaz, who was herding a happy crew of

kibbutzniks into the bus, noticed her standing motionless by the open door. "Deborah," he said gently, "everybody in that bus has read the Bible too. But doesn't the Torah say that the Sabbath is for rest and joy?"

She nodded nervously, but still did not move. At last he put his arm around her and remarked, "Besides, if you believe the words of Zechariah, even if you sin a bit, God will refine you like gold or silver, and you can still go to Paradise in style."

She was swayed by the prophet's words.

As she sat down next to Yoni Barnea, the kibbutz physician's teenage son, she thought aloud, "If you guys are so unreligious, how come you all know the Bible by heart?"

Yoni grinned, his eyes brightening. "Ah, Deborah, you don't understand. For us the Bible's not a prayer book—it's a road map."

She smiled, then leaned back in her seat, trying to forget how many Sabbath prohibitions she was violating, and determined to enjoy the day of rest in a new way.

Deborah had never gone to summer camp. Such frivolous activities were frowned upon by her parents and their circle. Summer vacation had consisted of a week or two in an enclave of Spring Valley, where Brooklyn was transplanted from concrete and asphalt into grass and forest, the brownstones exchanged for tired wooden bungalows. But the faces stayed the same.

This bus ride was the first she had ever made simply for "fun." The very word was alien to her childhood experiences.

And throughout the dusty, bumpy journey the grown-up kindergartners sang and clapped to a repertoire that ranged from biblical songs to tunes from the Israeli hit parade (which sometimes coincided).

When the passengers were not themselves singing, the loudspeakers reverberated with the latest from the American Top 40—courtesy of Abie Nathan's "Voice of Peace," a pirate radio station broadcasting from a ship "anchored somewhere in the waters of the Middle East." Its renegade director believed that the magnetism of music could succeed where the diplomats failed—to draw Arab and Jew onto the same wavelength.

They stopped for Coca-Colas at Tall as-Sultān, location of the ancient ruins of Jericho, the oldest inhabited city in the world.

Most of the kibbutzniks carried dog-eared guidebooks, and everyone seemed to be an expert on one site or another. Here it was Rebecca Mendoza, an immigrant from Argentina, who read aloud, translating into Hebrew from her *Guía de la Tierra Santa*.

"Jericho was an important Crusader city, and there are still many Christian points of interest. The Monastery of the Temptation," she explained, "is built on the spot where Satan tempted Jesus to prove Himself by transforming stones into bread. And Jesus answered, 'It is written, Man shall not live by bread alone, but by every word that proceedeth out of the mouth of God.' This can be found in the Gospel of Matthew, Chapter Four—"

"You forgot to say something, señorita," one of the elder kibbutzniks heckled. "Jesus was quoting Moses—'Man doth not live by bread only, but by every thing that proceedeth out of the mouth of the Lord.' Deuteronomy eight, verse four."

"Wrong as usual, Yankel," another chiding voice piped up.

"What do you mean?" the old man retorted with histrionic indignation.

"It was verse *three*!"

———

As they returned to the bus, Deborah was already dog tired, her feet aching.

"Isn't this wonderful?" Boaz trumpeted, as he bounded aboard after rounding up the last straggler. "And the best is yet to come."

Gazing at the tireless sexagenarian, Deborah whispered to Almuth, "Where does he get the energy?"

The German girl shrugged. "Almost all the Israelis are like that. It's like six days a week they're plugged into an electrical generator, and on the seventh they just let it all zap out."

The bus ricocheted southward, passing Qumran,

where in 1947 a shepherd boy, chasing a stray lamb, wandered into one of the many mountain caves and chanced upon a cache of ancient papyrus scrolls, later to be known as the Dead Sea Scrolls. He traded them to a crafty antiquarian in Jerusalem for the extravagant price of a new pair of shoes. In the fullness of time, the youth's footwear had turned out to be worth more than five million dollars.

Less than an hour later, they were on the banks of the Dead Sea.

"Lowest point on earth," Boaz lectured. "A quarter of a mile below sea level."

"Hey," a young woman called out, "look at those people in the water."

"They're not *in* the water," Boaz corrected her, "they're *on* it."

All eyes turned toward the bathers, who were lounging on the surface as if on invisible mattresses. The high salt content had turned them into human corks.

In her excitement, Deborah temporarily forgot her anxieties about donning a bathing suit and swimming in mixed company. A few minutes later, she and her friends were bobbing up and down, giggling.

Something was transforming Deborah's whole outlook on life. Could it be the magic water, the balmy air? For a few fleeting moments, she thought she might even be happy.

Dear Danny,

I have an important announcement to make. In my small way, I've earned a special place in the annals of the Luria family.

Though we've produced centuries of scholars, biblical commentators, and philosophers—at least to my knowledge, we've not as yet produced a driver.

I, however, earned that distinction this afternoon a little before sunset, and the feeling of freedom it gives me is indescribable.

I now can take one of the communal Subarus and drive to Haifa two afternoons a week to start a B.A. in Hebrew Literature.

I'm even typing my term papers on a Hebrew typewriter—a skill I picked up during my stints in the kibbutz office.

The schedules at Israeli universities seem geared for working people, with a great many classes in the early evening. The stuff I'm learning is secular and fascinating (or perhaps it's fascinating because it's secular and *not* religious).

I've discovered the genius of some of our literary ancestors we never heard about in Brooklyn.

Like, for example, the incomparable Judah Halevi (eleventh-century Spain). He sings of earthly and celestial love with such passion:

*"I am racing toward the source of the life of
    truth,
Fleeing the life of lies and vanity.
If I could only hold His image fast in my heart,
My eyes would not look outward at the world."*

That just about epitomizes how I feel at the moment.

Please find time to write more about the old films you're seeing at the Thalia. You're making me jealous. All the kibbutz seems to get is Westerns.

Kiss Mama.

Love,
D

As she slipped the paper into an envelope and licked two colorful stamps, Deborah thought of the final verses of the poem she had quoted in her letter:

*If I could only hold His image fast in my
    heart,
My eyes would not look outward at the world.*

The world seemed filled with expressions of her love for Timothy.

25

Daniel

I had recently celebrated my eighteenth birthday, and I was living on borrowed time. The Law requires a man to marry when he reaches age eighteen. Do you know, there is no word for "bachelor" in the Old Testament? That's because the Jews couldn't even conceive of a man being unmarried. Marriage would be his only way of coping with the Evil Inclination. After all, eighteen is the age when the male sex drive is at its peak.

There was no question that my libido was in full flower, and I think I would have had erotic dreams even without having seen those exotic foreign films at the Thalia. Moreover, I was painfully aware that the Talmud regarded sinful thoughts as tantamount to the deeds themselves.

I concluded that if I was going to be punished just for thinking of sex, I might as well try the real thing. But of course I had absolutely no idea how to go about it.

Then, consciously or not, Beller afforded me the opportunity.

Toward the end of April, he invited me to a party at his home. It was mainly for his students at Columbia, but I knew I would also encounter girls from Barnard. Still, no one could accuse him of leading me into temptation. He merely opened the door. It was I who walked in of my own accord. Eagerly.

He never said it, but I knew that even my best Sabbath clothes would not fit the bill for such an occasion. And so I made a self-conscious expedition to Barney's, where I bought my first secular garment: a neat blue blazer.

Then came the moment of real soul-searching. Could I attend a New York cocktail party with curly sideburns rolling halfway down my cheeks? Admittedly, I had seen posters of some rock and roll performers whose coiffures were far longer and more stringy than my own. But since I couldn't sing or play guitar, I thought it best to make myself as inconspicuous as possible.

I therefore visited a barber (twenty blocks away from school) and asked him to trim my sideburns till they were just long enough to satisfy the biblical decree forbidding hair to be cut above the juncture of cheek and ear.

"What about the curls, mister?"

"Uh, sort of . . . shorten those too," I responded nervously.

"No way," he dissented. "You're not the first Orthodox kid I've had in my chair. You've gotta make up your mind—if it's short enough to be 'modern,' it won't be long enough to be kosher. Know what I mean?"

Alas, I knew all too well. I closed my eyes—a gesture he correctly interpreted as assent. His blades were swift and painless. My subsequent pangs of conscience were neither. I took to wearing a low-brimmed hat, a practice my fellow students assumed was one of deepened piety. More hypocrisy.

I tried to convince myself it would be worth it.

———

What first struck me was an orchestration of new sounds. The tinkle of ice against glass, the voice of Ray Charles (as I later learned) on a stereo, loud conversation rising above the music, everything blending into a buzz, which sounded like the whir of my mother's Mixmaster.

I stood on the stairs to Aaron Beller's sunken living room and gazed in disbelief.

There were men and women everywhere talking freely to one another. Some were even touching. It all looked . . . alien.

"Rabbi Luria, you aren't Moses on Mount Nebo. This is a promised land that you *can* enter."

It was the host himself, at his side an elegant blonde in her early forties.

"Come in, Daniel. There're lots of people I think you'd enjoy meeting. For a start, this is my wife, Nina. You know that silkscreen in my office you admired? She's the artist."

Mrs. Beller smiled. "Nice to meet you at last," she said. "Aaron's told me so much about you."

"Thank you," I replied, wondering what exactly Beller could have said. That I was a mixed-up Jew in the throes of an identity crisis?

Though Mrs. Beller herself was beautiful, I could not keep my glance from wandering past her. There were lots of women here, all exquisite.

"Aaron," she addressed her husband, "why don't you see to the punch, while I make the rounds with Danny?"

There were also many distinguished minds in the Bellers' salon, including a prize-winning poet who kept calling me "man"—perhaps because he'd forgotten my name—while soliciting my opinion on the relative merits of Walt Whitman and Allen Ginsberg.

To my chagrin, I had read neither *Leaves of Grass* nor *Howl.* Once, in a bookstore, my father had picked up the hippie poet's *Kaddish* and after only a few seconds cast it back as "blasphemous." I made a mental note to buy both books.

After half a dozen introductions, Nina left me to

fend for myself, advising, "Just walk up to anyone and say hello. You're among friends here."

I looked around, still feeling insecure, for I had never heard such uninhibited laughter—except perhaps at Purim parties.

Suddenly I felt a tap on my shoulder and heard a breathy female voice.

"Are you some kind of holy person?"

I turned and saw this . . . creature. She was blond and bare-shouldered in a skin-tight black dress. She was smoking a long, thin cigarette. Her smile was dizzying.

"I don't understand," I stammered.

"That's okay," she answered. "Actually, it was just an excuse to meet you. But I mean, that cap you're wearing makes you look just like the pope."

"Good joke," I rejoined, assuming she knew full well I was an Orthodox Jew.

Nevertheless, her quip made me self-conscious. As we continued talking, I removed my skullcap as inconspicuously as possible and stuffed it into my pocket.

Yes, I felt guilty . . . traitorous even. But I rationalized it as a gesture to preserve the good reputation of truly pious Jews. Why should my sins be ascribed to them?

"I'm a rabbinical student," I explained.

Her eyes widened. "Really? How fascinating! That means you must believe in God."

"Of course," I answered.

"Oh!" she exclaimed. "Do you know you're probably the only person in this entire room who does?"

Somehow I didn't think she was being completely facetious. There was a sense of—I don't know—pagan hedonism about this whole party. And this girl in particular.

"What do *you* do?" I inquired casually.

"Oh, I'm into lots of things," she replied. "Officially, I'm a graduate student in Art History at NYU. But I have all sorts of projects going. By the way, my name's Ariel."

"Do you know your name means 'Jerusalem' in the Bible?"

"Really?" she retorted. "I always thought it was the 'brave spirit' in Shakespeare's *Tempest.*"

"I'm sorry, I've never read *The Tempest.*"

"That's okay. I've never read the Bible, so that makes us even. Are you really sure about my name?"

"Absolutely," I replied, feeling comfortable for the first time. "It's Isaiah twenty-nine, verse one— 'Ariel, the city where David dwelt.' "

"That's fascinating. How much of the Good Book do you know?"

"A bit of it, I guess," I replied.

"I bet you're being modest—I bet you know the whole damn thing by heart. You could probably go on a quiz show. I expect you even know what they ate at the Last Supper."

"Right," I answered, managing a grin. "It was matzos."

"You mean those little balls you put in soup?"

"No, the Last Supper was a Passover seder, and that's when Jews eat only unleavened bread called matzos."

"Hey, that's right—Jesus *was* a Jew."

"But did you know he was also a rabbi?"

"You mean, like you're going to be?"

"Well, more or less," I equivocated.

For some reason she was interested in pursuing this line of questioning. "Tell me—do rabbis have to take a vow of chastity?"

I think I blushed. "No," I replied. "Only priests do."

"That's a relief," she commented. "Don't you think it's a little unnatural for people to deny that part of human nature?"

It took only a few more exchanges with this intoxicating blond Lilith to make me realize that the subtext of our conversation was not sexual abstinence but sexual indulgence. Hers . . . and mine.

At this moment, Nina Beller approached with a tray of assorted tidbits, none of which looked familiar to me.

"Well, I'm glad you two have gotten together," she smiled, offering the food to Ariel.

"Gosh, Nina," she enthused, "I'm a sucker for your pâté."

She took a cracker with her long, graceful fingers. Nina then offered the array to me. I thought I recognized little squares of smoked salmon and was just reaching for one when Ariel suggested, "Try those, they're one of my favorites."

"Which is that?" I asked warily.

She pointed to crescents of cantaloupe wrapped in some kind of unrecognizable meat.

"Actually," Nina said pointedly, "I think Danny would prefer the egg and olive."

Here the hostess was considerately steering me in the right direction, yet this woman deliberately tempted me to eat something that was manifestly unkosher.

"Go on," Ariel urged. "You'll really like it."

I had no illusions. This was a flagrant sin with no mitigating circumstances.

I reached for the melon. And—I'm ashamed to admit—my primary worry was not the wrath of Heaven, but the fear that I might gag on it.

At last, I closed my conscience, reached down, and opened my mouth. I swallowed the . . . item as quickly as I could.

By a supreme mental effort, I succeeded in numbing my taste buds so I would not recall what I had ingested.

"Well?" Ariel asked, grinning.

"You were right. It was very good," I lied. "What did you call it?"

"Prosciutto," she answered.

"Oh." I tried to sound casual. "I must remember that."

"Prosciutto's the Italian word for 'ham,' " Nina Beller said and glided off, leaving me in the hands of a woman who was clearly the quintessence of the Evil Inclination. And to whom my senses were completely prisoner.

With new, unblinded vision, I looked at Ariel and imagined I saw the sensual body scarcely hidden beneath her black silk dress.

Nothing was going to keep me from seducing this seductress.

———

As the party began to break up, I looked at my watch. It was nearly midnight. I had a class at nine the next morning, which meant I had to be up by seven so I could pray.

Yet I wasn't about to stop this side of Paradise.

"Ariel, it's been so nice talking to you. Could we continue this conversation somewhere else?"

Some secret part of me hoped she would say no.

"How about my place?" she quickly replied.

———

It took us about two minutes flat to zoom in Ariel's Italian sports car to her duplex apartment on the upper floors of an expensively furnished town house just off Central Park West.

On the way, she placed her hand on a part of my anatomy that heretofore had been touched only by my mother, myself, and the *mohel.*

That night I ecstatically experienced a second, more protracted ritual of manhood.

As I walked all the way home in the early dawn, I contemplated the number of transgressions I had committed within the past twelve hours.

I'd eaten unkosher food. I'd missed my morning prayers—and since I was planning to sleep, would miss class, showing disrespect to my teachers. And, worst of all, I'd surrendered to the Evil Inclination. I was riddled with sin.

And happier than I had ever been.

26

Deborah

Deborah sat on the steps of her *srif,* breathing the jasmine in the evening air. Inside, her roommates chattered, wrote letters to their parents and boyfriends, while Frank Sinatra was "doobie doobie dooing" on the "Voice of Peace."

Her gaze was fixed on the main hall, some three hundred yards down the hill, which sloped gently to the edge of the Sea of Galilee.

An unfamiliar male voice shattered her reverie. "You must be Deborah."

She turned quickly to see a short, wiry young man standing beside her, the glint of Air Force wings on the shoulders of his khaki shirt.

"I'm sorry if I startled you," he said in heavily

accented English. "But I know the kibbutz is voting on your membership tonight. My father said you'd be nervous, so I came to hold your hand. By the way, I'm Avi, Boaz and Zipporah's son."

"Election's not automatic, you know," Deborah declared to justify her anxiety.

"Of course I know," Avi conceded. "I'll only be a candidate when I finish my tour of duty."

He added with a smile, "Do you mind if I ask you a personal question?"

"That depends on how 'personal.' "

"Is Ulla still living here?"

Deborah sighed, thinking to herself, Typical Israeli Casanova, then she answered, "You're in luck. Ulla's inside. She doesn't leave till next week."

"Thanks," said Avi, as he mounted the steps. "And stop worrying."

Half an hour later, Deborah could hear chatter and the scrape of chairs from down the hill—noises of a large meeting breaking up.

Moments later Boaz was hauling his heavy frame up the hill, shining his flashlight in the direction of Deborah's hut. Though badly out of breath, he still managed to blurt out, "Deborah, it's official! You're a *chavera*."

As he hugged her tightly, lifting her off the ground, she thought: At last I really belong somewhere!

To celebrate her new equality, the next day Deborah was assigned to wash pots in the kitchen.

And what pots! They seemed more like aluminum barrels. By the time she and her co-workers had finished the first half-dozen, her right arm felt ready for a sling.

About an hour later, Avi appeared.

"See, I told you there'd be no problem," he said blithely. "Anyway, I missed breakfast. Can I steal a roll and coffee?"

" 'Steal' if it makes you feel good," Deborah answered. "It's all common property, anyway."

By this time, he had already opened the door of a huge refrigerator and pulled out a chunk of cheese. After pouring himself a cup of coffee, he sauntered back to Deborah.

"You don't have to work so hard anymore," he joked. "You're already in."

Deborah merely scowled and continued scrubbing.

He leaned against a counter, and as he munched on the cheese, said, "I still don't understand what made a Jewish-American princess want to become a kibbutznik."

"Did it ever occur to you that there might be a Jewish-American girl who wasn't a 'princess'?"

"Well, I've never met one. Aren't you filthy

rich and spoiled? What big business is your papa in?"

"He's a rabbi—the Silczer Rav if you must know."

"Really?" said Avi with surprise. "And how does he feel about his daughter working in an unkosher kitchen?"

"Why do you keep asking so many questions about me?" she demanded.

"Because you won't ask any about me."

"Okay," said Deborah, playing along. "Tell me about yourself."

"Well," Avi began. "I was born on the kibbutz, I went to school on the kibbutz, and when I finish flying around, I'll go to university, write a thesis, and then come back to the kibbutz."

"A thesis on what?" Deborah asked, genuinely intrigued.

"Not on the Talmud—it's more down to earth. In fact, it's *under* the earth. I'll be studying new forms of irrigation."

"And you'll really come back to live here?" Deborah asked.

"Unless you lead a movement to reject my application."

"That's wonderful," Deborah said sincerely. "They say lots of the kibbutzniks who go into the Army don't come back after they've seen the glitter of the outside world."

"Well," Avi answered, "not all kibbutzim are as nice as Kfar Ha-Sharon."

"You mean they haven't got such pretty Swedish volunteers."

She detected a glint of embarrassment in Avi's eyes.

"You won't believe me, Deborah," he replied. "But they're a very important aspect of our lives. Men almost never marry women from their own kibbutz. We're all brought up like brothers and sisters. It seems somehow incestuous."

"So you exploit the female volunteers as sexual objects."

He laughed. "It's funny to hear that feminist bullshit in a place like this. For your information, six volunteers—two of them men—have married kibbutzniks and are living here as *chaverim*. Maybe this summer when the new volunteers come in, you'll find a handsome Dutchman."

"Thanks, but no thanks," Deborah answered tartly. "Why does everybody always want to marry me off?"

"Why 'off'?" Avi asked. "I'd think people would just plain want to marry you. Anyway, why doesn't a *frum* girl like you have a husband already?"

Discomfited, Deborah retreated into scouring the huge pots.

"Did I touch a sore spot?" he asked sympathetically.

Deborah looked up, said, "Very," and went back to her scrubbing.

"Can I give you a hand?"

"Be my guest," she answered, handing him an extra scouring brush. "Now tell me what a pilot does all day."

"It's pretty boring actually," he said ingenuously. "I pull a few levers, I go up in the air. I push a few more levers, and suddenly my sonic boom is breaking people's windows."

"What's so boring about that?" Deborah asked.

"Well, you don't exactly get to see much of the world. At Mach Two you can go from one end of Israel to the other in about three minutes."

"That fast?" said Deborah, genuinely impressed.

"No," he answered wryly, "Israel's that small."

They were suddenly interrupted by an angry voice.

"Deborah—is this what you call work?"

It was the gargantuan Shauli, head cook and absolute monarch of the kitchen.

Deborah blushed.

Avi leaped to her defense. "I shouldn't have been talking to her."

"You," Shauli bellowed. "You aren't even *allowed* in here."

"Yes, sir," Avi responded with a salute. "May I just be permitted to ask *Chavera* Deborah a single question?"

"Only if it's short," the cook replied.

Avi quickly asked, "Have you any plans for after dinner—I mean after you wash up and everything?"

"No," Deborah answered, off balance, "not really."

"Why don't I get some wheels from the kibbutz car pool? The Aviv in Tiberias is showing *Butch Cassidy*—which is so great I've seen it four times."

"You mean a movie?" Deborah asked uneasily. How could she tell him that she still felt guilty watching television newscasts and had even avoided the Friday night films at the kibbutz.

But Avi quickly sensed the problem. "Listen, if you've got religious scruples, you could keep your eyes closed all the time."

He laughed. And she laughed.

And, as Avi bounded off, Deborah felt somehow unsettled. Simultaneously happy and curiously apprehensive.

I think I like him.

———

Deborah was not morally shaken after having seen the film. Indeed, she had found the advertisements that preceded it—especially those for bathing suits—far more risqué.

They had coffee and cake in a restaurant on the

Tayellet, a seaside promenade making a heroic effort to resemble the Riviera. When they climbed back into the car, Avi boasted, "I once made it from here to the kibbutz gate in seven minutes and thirteen seconds. Shall we try to break that record tonight?"

Recalling the many curves on the road, Deborah suggested, "Why don't we try to beat the record in slowness?"

Avi cast her a meaningful look.

"Fine." His eyes twinkled. "We'll go as slow as you like."

Twenty minutes later, he brought the car to a halt in a quiet corner near the orchards of Kfar Ha-Sharon. Below them the Sea of Galilee was a vast, pearl gray reflection of the moon.

He turned toward Deborah and touched her gently on the shoulder.

"Are you nervous?" he whispered.

"Why should I be?" she asked, trying to be nonchalant.

"A rabbi's daughter must have led a very sheltered life."

She looked at him for a moment, and then conceded, "You're right. I feel sort of . . . uncomfortable with you. Besides, didn't you yourself say that kibbutzniks are like brothers and sisters?"

"Yes, that's true," he said softly. "But I didn't grow up with you. To me, you're attractive as a woman."

Though Avi was unaware of their significance, his words struck her like lightning. In the nearly twenty years of her lifetime she had been variously referred to as a girl, a *shayne maidel,* and a sweet young thing—but never as a *woman.* And what was more astonishing, she felt like one.

She welcomed Avi's arm around her shoulder and tried to enjoy his kiss, but she was worried that he might try to go too far.

Yet it was his *questions* that became too intimate.

"Why did your parents send you to Israel?"

She hesitated, then replied unconvincingly, "The usual reasons."

"No, Deborah," he said firmly. "I've lived on this kibbutz long enough to tell a volunteer from an exile. Were you involved with someone?"

She lowered her head.

"And they didn't like him?"

This time, she nodded in the affirmative.

"Did it work?" Avi asked quietly.

"What?"

"Did the separation cure you?"

"I wasn't sick," she answered pointedly.

Avi was silent for a moment and then asked, "And are you still involved with him? I mean, in your heart?"

Her feelings had been pent up for so long that she wanted to shout: He's the only person in the world who's loved me for myself.

Yet the voice that answered Avi was barely audible. "I think so . . . yes."

His questions followed with a delicate persistence. "Do you write to each other?"

She shook her head. "I don't have his address."

"Does he have yours?"

Again, she shook her head.

A look of hope—or was it relief?—crossed Avi's face.

"Then it's just a question of time," he murmured. "Sooner or later, when you've mourned enough, you'll be free."

She shrugged. "I suppose so."

He held her by the shoulders, whispering, "And when you are, I hope I'll be right there."

Then, trying to raise her mood, he said jauntily, "I'd better get you home. I'm due back at the base by six."

As the motor revved, he shifted the gears and drove back to the road and into the parking lot.

"How are you going to get there?" she asked, as they walked to her new *srif.*

"I'll hitchhike, how else?"

"Isn't that dangerous?"

"No," he joked. "Thumbing a ride here is perfectly safe. It's only when you get *in* with an Israeli driver that you risk your life."

He squeezed her hand, kissed her on the cheek, turned, and headed down the gravel road, finally vanishing into the shadows.

Deborah stood there and watched him, suddenly having seen through his bravado and discovered the sensitivity it tried to camouflage—the constant fear of living a mere sixty-second scramble from mortality.

She only wished with all her heart that she could like him enough to forget Timothy.

27

Timothy

Tim's plane landed in the early morning at Rome's Leonardo da Vinci Airport, where a bus was waiting to transport the five seminarians through the ocher hills of Umbria to Perugia.

As they entered the city, Father Devlin expounded on the remnants of numerous cultures standing side by side—Etruscan, Roman, Carolingian, Early and Late Renaissance—reminding them that though civilizations rise and fall, the Faith abides forever.

"And perhaps most significant of all," Father Devlin waxed floridly, "Perugia is the home of the only sensual delight that isn't a mortal sin. I mean, of course, their chocolate."

The bus pulled up at the Ospizio San Cristoforo—only blocks from the eighteenth-century Palazzo Gallenga, the Italian University for Foreigners.

During their first few days in Perugia, Tim began to wonder if their group was not being deliberately subjected to an ordeal, some trial to measure their resistance to temptation.

Although the university arranged for special classes that included only seminarians, and half a dozen full-fledged priests who were being transferred to the Vatican from other countries, outside the classroom there was no way of concealing other students from the celibates' view.

Perugia in summer was a lodestone for American college girls, all vying for the maximum of masculine attention by wearing the minimum of clothing. They were there learning Italian, not as a foreign language, but as a *Romance* language.

"I can't believe it," remarked Patrick Grady, a member of Tim's group, shaking his head in bewilderment. "I've never seen girls like this in my life. I could never be a priest in *this* diocese."

They were walking back to the Ospizio for lunch, stifling in their cassocks, as a pair of Texan nymphs in the flimsiest of summer attire wafted across their path.

Grady's eyes bulged.

"Stay loose, Pat," Timothy remarked. "The strain will be over in a few more weeks."

"Do you mean you're actually impervious to all this, Hogan? How do you do it?"

Tim pretended not to understand, but Grady persisted.

"Look, we're normal men. In my hometown, most of the guys our age are already married—and just about all of them have lost their virginity in the back seat of a car. You can't make me believe that you don't at least—you know—sometimes . . . relieve your tensions."

Tim merely shrugged. How could he tell a fellow seminarian that he had thoughts far more passionate than his and hence was indifferent to the local temptations?

At mealtimes, each of them took turns saying grace and vied with one another in the sophistication and length of their prayers.

Tim was no match for the articulate Martin O'Connor, whose benedictions were often so long, it took several coughs from Father Devlin to remind him that the tagliatelle were growing cold.

Since there were no afternoon classes till the language labs at four, most of them had adopted the local practice of taking a postprandial siesta.

While the others slept, Tim would sit in a shady corner of the cortile, diligently memorizing the Italian irregular verbs.

One torrid July afternoon, as he was mastering the principal parts of *rispóndere,* out of the corner of his eye Tim noticed George Cavanagh walking furtively through the portico toward their rooms, a look of anxiety on his face.

"Are you all right, George?" Tim called out.

Cavanagh pulled up short, and then immediately demanded, "What makes you think anything's wrong?"

"I don't know," Tim answered ingenuously. "You seem distracted. Maybe it's just the heat."

"Yeah, yeah," Cavanagh allowed, walking toward him. "It's like a broiler out there."

He sat down, withdrew a cigarette, lit up, and inhaled deeply.

Tim sensed that Cavanagh wanted to confide in someone.

"Want to talk about it, George?" he offered.

After another moment's hesitation, Cavanagh said softly, "I don't know how I'm even going to be able to confess this."

"Come on," Tim reassured him. "Whatever it is will be forgiven."

"Yeah, but not forgotten," George murmured in pain. He looked at Tim with a pleading glance. "You promise you won't tell a soul?"

"Yeah, I swear."

Cavanagh blurted out—albeit still in a whisper—"I've been with a woman, a prostitute."

"What?"

"I've had sexual intercourse. Now do you see why I can't confess?"

"Look," Tim said, "you're not the first to give in to temptation. Think of St. Augustine. I know you'll find the courage—"

"But that's just it," Cavanagh agonized. "I'll never find the strength to keep away."

He put his head in his hands and rubbed his forehead in despair. "I guess you despise me for this, huh?"

"I don't make moral judgments," Tim responded. "Just don't surrender, George. Have a talk with your Spiritual Director and work out your feelings."

The anguished seminarian looked up into the innocent eyes of his classmate and muttered, "Thanks."

———

"Carissimi studenti, il nostro corso è finito. Spero che abbiate imparato non solo a parlare l'italiano ma anche ad asaporare la musicalità di nostra lingua."

The course had ended. Tim and his classmates rose to affirm, with their applause, that they had learned not only to speak Italian but also, as their professor had put it, to savor its music.

That afternoon as four of the five seminarians hauled their luggage to the back of the minibus, Father Devlin congratulated them effusively.

George Cavanagh was not there. For reasons he had confided only to Father Devlin, he was spending the weekend in nearby Assisi.

When apprised of this conspicuous display of devoutness, Martin O'Connor muttered audibly, "Showoff."

———

In Rome, they were in for a surprise.

The special summer courses at the North American College still had three weeks to run. And, since they could not yet be properly housed, the members of Tim's elite American group were offered the option of either spending the time on retreat in a monastery in the Dolomites, or—for the more adventurous—joining a group of young seminarians from Germany and Switzerland on a pilgrimage to the Holy Land.

The group was led by Father Johannes Bauer, a pious old man with a slight stammer and a complete ignorance of any language but German and Latin—which sounded identical when he spoke them.

Once again, Tim saw divine intervention in this undreamed-of opportunity. He quickly signed up for the tour, regretting only that George Cavanagh and Patrick Grady elected to do likewise. Ever since their intimate conversation in the Ospizio courtyard earlier that summer, George had been discernibly cool to him.

Tim had hoped that during these three weeks at least he would have been able to escape the saturnine glances of his classmate.

The moment George learned the group would be divided into pairs for lodging, he teamed up with Patrick, leaving Tim cast adrift on an untranslatable sea of German with a red-cheeked Bavarian named Christoph.

Yet in their very first half hour together on the

plane, Tim and Christoph discovered that they
could indeed communicate. Timothy had not forgotten his Brooklyn Yiddish, a language largely
derived from medieval High German. When he
suggested that their ability to converse would make
the tour a *gryse fargenign,* Christoph smiled.

"*Ja, ein sehr grosses Vergnügen.*" In either language, a mutually comprehensible pleasure.

It was late evening when they reached Tel Aviv's
Ben-Gurion Airport, where Israeli Immigration officers questioned them to be certain their motives in
visiting Israel were sacred and not subversive.

One of the seminarians lost his temper.

"You're only doing this to us because we're German, *ja?*"

An officer—a dark-haired woman in her late
twenties—replied sweetly, "*Ja.*"

Timothy and Christoph were the very last to be
interrogated. Paradoxically, the fact that the blond-
haired American seminarian spoke Hebrew made
him even more suspect than any of the Germans.
But once the senior Duty Officer had elicited from
Timothy that he had begun his career as a "*Shabbes
goy*" and could quote verbatim from the Old Testament, he broke into an effusive welcome, and as a
token of friendship, offered him half his bar of Elite
chocolate.

"*Baruch ha-ba,*" he remarked. "Blessed be your
arrival."

Then the two young men grabbed their suitcases

and started out into the heavy August night toward the bus, where the rest of the group was waiting with growing impatience.

Their energetic Israeli driver whisked them to Jerusalem at what seemed the same speed as the plane they had flown. As they passed the Judaean hills and were approaching the city itself, Timothy—unlike the others—was not gazing out the window.

Instead, with the help of a small flashlight, he was studying a map of the Holy City he had picked up while waiting in line at the airport, trying to memorize the route between Terra Sancta College, the Franciscan hostel where they would be lodging, and the YMCA on King David Street.

Yet, when the bus actually turned the final corner and he saw "Welcome to Jerusalem" illuminated in flowers on a bed of grass, his soul stirred. Looking out at the city of a stone so white it could even be seen in darkness, he whispered to himself, "Pray for the peace of Jerusalem: They shall prosper that love thee."

———

As he carried his bag into his tiny room, Tim overheard through the wall the irritated voices of George and Patrick.

"This may be the only chance I get to see the Holy Land, and if you think I'm going to waste it with a guide who can't speak a word of English, you're crazy."

"I agree, Cavanagh. But what can we do about it?"

"Why don't we just tell Father Bauer the truth?" George suggested. "We're grown men. I've got four guidebooks in English. Maybe he'll give us permission to travel on our own."

"Good idea," Grady replied. "Let's just pray he allows us to go."

Timothy said an inward amen.

To his great relief, Tim's classmates did not invite him along when they petitioned the German leader next morning. From their smiling faces as they sat down to breakfast, he could see that the request had been granted.

Now it was his turn.

In Tim's case, however, Father Bauer was more reluctant.

"But there are so many inscriptions in Greek and Hebrew you could help us translate," he protested in a German Tim could comprehend with great difficulty.

"That's just it," Tim pleaded in Latin. "I'd really like to spend some extra time in the places where Our Lord preached—especially in Capernaum."

"How could I deny such an admirable request," Father Bauer conceded. "Very well. *Placet.* Anyway, you have our itinerary, so you can rejoin us at any time you wish. Can I count on you to be back here by six P.M. precisely on fifteenth September?"

"Absolutely," Tim replied.

"Then off you go," Father Bauer smiled. "Join your American friends, and breathe deeply of the Holy Land."

Tim could barely constrain his joy as he turned to leave, rationalizing to himself that he had not actually lied to Father Bauer.

The German had not specified *which* American friends.

———

His first stop was the mail desk at the YMCA, where he inquired diffidently, "How long do you keep letters here if they're not picked up?"

"Forever," the clerk replied. "My boss is crazy. We've still got stuff from the fifties that's turned completely yellow."

Feeling his spine grow cold, Timothy asked, "Is there anything for Timothy Hogan?"

"I'll see," the clerk replied, picking up a brown carton labeled *H* and beginning to search. Finally, he looked up and said, "Sorry, nothing for Hogan."

Tim could barely breathe. He had only one slender hope. "Could I ask—is there anything for 'Deborah Luria'?"

The clerk riffled through the pile of *L*'s and replied, "Sorry. Nothing under that name either."

"Does that mean she might have picked up the letter?" Timothy asked with growing excitement.

Bemused by his anxiety, the young man smiled. "That's a pretty logical conclusion to make."

Tim dashed out of the building, down the wide front steps, along the cypress-lined path toward the Central Bus Station.

He soared on wings of hope.

Even before he had left Italy, Timothy had done sufficient research to know not only where Deborah's kibbutz was located, but what number bus would get him there from Jerusalem.

During the last tension-filled days in Rome, he had hoarded his pocket money to have more to spend on the journey.

Now his sacrifice was rewarded. For at eleven-forty that morning, he boarded a bus for Tiberias— one that would drop him within walking distance of kibbutz Kfar Ha-Sharon.

As they sped along, the driver's voice on the loudspeaker called their attention to scenes of the most dramatic events of the Bible.

Under ordinary circumstances, Timothy would have stared awestruck as the driver remarked: "On your right you can see ancient Bethany, the home of the sisters Mary and Martha, where Jesus raised their brother Lazarus from the dead." Instead, he spent most of the time gazing out the window with unfocused eyes. He was in a kind of hypnotic state, yet was not so numb that he could not feel the ache of fear. How would Deborah react? After all, she had read his letter and not left an answer.

Somewhere near Afula, Tim saw a road sign indicating *Nazareth* to the left.

How could he not feel moved?

Could his feelings for Deborah be even stronger than his love for Christ?

28

Deborah

"Deborah . . . Deborah!"

She was busy working in the fields when one of the ten-year-old boys came running toward her, shouting.

"Be careful, Motti," she warned. "We're not growing mashed potatoes here."

She wiped her brow with a handkerchief already grimy from a morning's sweat.

"Deborah," the boy cried once again, "Boaz wants to see you."

She straightened up and answered, "We break for lunch in half an hour. Can't it wait?"

"He told me 'right away.' "

Deborah sighed, stabbed her fork into a mound of earth, and began trudging toward the kibbutz headquarters.

Halfway up the hill, a thought struck her. Could someone in her family be sick—or worse? She grew apprehensive. Boaz would not call her from the field for something trivial. It had to be bad news.

Three elderly kibbutzniks were busy in the anteroom. There was a pair of gray-haired women tapping away at large typewriters, and eighty-two-year-old Jonah Friedman at the center desk manning the switchboard.

"Jonah," Deborah asked in frightened tones, "what's the big emergency?"

The old man shrugged. "What do I know? I'm just a receptionist. Shall I tell Boaz you're here—or do you want to freshen up?"

"Why would I need to 'freshen up'?" she asked impatiently.

"Well," he answered with an apologetic smile, "you're a little *shmutzik* here and there. . . ."

"I've been picking potatoes—how else do you expect me to look?"

"All right already. Just go the way you are."

She knocked softly.

"It's okay, Deborah," Boaz said solemnly. "Take a deep breath and come right in."

A breath? She was about to faint. Slowly she opened the door.

Standing before her, looking incongruous in his ill-fitting sports clothes and lobster-red from the Israeli sun, was a man whose face she had carried in her thoughts for three long years. Someone she had never dreamed she would see again.

At first, she was totally paralyzed.

Timothy, no less confused, could manage only, "Hello, Deborah. It's good to see you."

The room was silent except for the steady hum of Boaz's air conditioner.

At last Tim spoke. "You look wonderful," he said softly. "I mean, I've never seen you with a tan. . . ." His voice trailed off.

Suddenly, she was embarrassed.

Though long accustomed to the casual attire of the kibbutzniks, now standing in front of Tim in her shorts, she somehow felt undressed.

Boaz tried to ease the strain.

"Listen, Deborah, I can see you two have things to talk about. Go to the kitchen and get some sandwiches. Have a picnic." Then, adding with mock severity, "Only be back in the fields at four o'clock sharp."

He rose and marched out of the office, leaving them too stunned to know how to behave.

They looked at each other. Neither moved.

Tim asked her hesitantly, "How are you feeling?"

"Cold," she smiled, rubbing her suntanned arms. "The air conditioner—"

"Me too," he replied, already feeling more at ease. "Let's go somewhere warmer."

———

They put pita bread, cheese, and fruit in a wire mesh basket, and were about to leave, when the master of the kitchen called out, "Wait a minute."

They stopped and turned. In his beefy hands, Shauli was holding out an opened bottle of red wine.

"Take this, children—" he offered in broken English. "It's on the roof."

———

They sat beside the lake, watching the little boats bob in the distance.

"So this is where St. Peter fished," Tim murmured.

"And where Christ walked on the water," Deborah added.

Tim's eyes widened. "Don't tell me you've accepted Jesus."

"No," she smiled, "but He spent so much time in this area, He's almost a member of the kibbutz. Have you seen Bethlehem?"

"Not yet."

"Well, I drive now—maybe I can take you."

"Oh," he said, somewhat surprised, not at the nature of her suggestion, but that she could think of anything beyond the reality of this one distilled moment.

The present was difficult enough, the future too fraught with a thousand unanswerable questions. Indeed, all they could discuss with any equanimity was the past.

"How did you ever track me down?" she asked.

"My guide was Jeremiah 23:13—'And ye shall seek me, and find me, when ye shall search for me with all your heart.' "

Deborah was moved. "Your Hebrew's beautiful, Tim," she said softly.

"Well," he replied with a touch of embarrassment, "I've been really working on it. I guess I've learned a great deal since we saw each other last."

So have I, thought Deborah to herself. And then said aloud, "No, seriously, how did you really find out where I was?"

"I would have started in the Sinai and searched right up to the Golan Heights—except by sheer coincidence I ran into Danny on the subway."

"Oh."

"I saw it as the hand of fate," he insisted.

Deborah averted her eyes and nervously plucked at blades of grass. At last she spoke.

"I've really been through a lot since . . . that night."

She told him about her servitude in Mea Shearim and her flight to freedom.

"You were very brave," he murmured.

"My father didn't exactly see it that way."

"I'll bet," he acknowledged. "He's a very strong-willed person."

"So am I. I'm his daughter after all," she said. "Besides, I've done a lot of growing up. I'm nearly twenty now."

"Yes," he responded, gazing at her face, "and very beautiful."

"That's not what I meant," she said shyly.

"I know. I was just changing the subject to something more important."

"Don't you want to know the rest of my story?" she asked uneasily.

"Some other time." He moved to within an arm's length of her, still not touching.

"I'd like to hear about how it was in the seminary," she said.

"No, you wouldn't," he whispered. "Not this minute anyway."

"What makes you so sure?"

"Deborah," he persisted, "I can read your thoughts. You're feeling scared and guilty."

She lowered her head, clenched her fists, and said, "Yes, you're right—I am. But it's natural to be scared. I just don't know why I feel so guilty."

He held out his hand and raised her face to look at his. "You're afraid it's wrong," he murmured. "But it isn't, Deborah. Believe me, there's nothing wrong with the way we feel about each other."

His hand was moving gently down to her shoulder.

"Tim, what's going to happen to us?"

"Today? Tomorrow? Next week? I don't know, Deborah, and I don't care. I just know I'm with you now. I love you, and I won't let you go."

Their faces were inches apart. It was as if she had been holding on to the edge of a precipice for the three aching years they had been separated.

And then suddenly Deborah let go.

She put her arms around his neck and kissed him.

She remembered how it had been with Avi.

And now she knew the difference.

As they held each other tightly, Tim whispered, "Deborah, I can't believe this is a sin."

She nodded wordlessly as they embraced.

Both were nervous, yet neither was afraid. Though completely innocent, they intuitively knew the intricacies of the act of love.

It was yet another sign that what they were doing was meant to be.

And so, in a wooded corner near the Sea of Galilee, the future priest and the rabbi's daughter consummated the passion that had begun one Sabbath eve so long ago.

———

Deborah referred to him simply as Tim. That night at dinner in the hall, she introduced her friends to her American visitor. Tactfully, they all refrained from asking what he did at home. Their only question was to them the most essential: "How long will you be staying?"

Tim looked at Deborah, hoping that her eyes would tell him how to answer, but all he read in them was, That's what *I'm* wondering too.

"Don't think we're just being nosy," Boaz explained. "We are, of course, but we have rules—anyone who visits the kibbutz for more than two nights is obliged to do his share of work."

Tim answered instantly, "What would you like me to do?"

"Are you any good with cows?"

"I'm afraid not," he apologized. "But back in America I did some gardening. I'd be happy to work in the fields."

"That's fine," said Boaz. "Only wear a broad-brimmed hat and *shmeer* yourself with lotion. Otherwise you'll get red as a tomato, and they'll pick you by mistake."

Tim was assigned to a bungalow with two Australian volunteers. But everyone knew that this was just pro forma.

Deborah had been sharing her new *srif* with Hannah Yavetz, who, by happy coincidence, was off doing her annual thirty-day stint in the Signal Corps. For their brief time together, the lovers had a private place to call their own.

Each day they worked side by side in the fields—
the first opportunity they had to talk and get to
know each other without the pressure of a clock
racing toward twelve on a Sabbath eve.

With each night they spent in each other's arms,
the notion that their lovemaking could possibly be
sinful vanished like the early morning haze upon
the lake.

They were already married in a way no earthly
force could ever separate. Why could they not remain this way forever?

Indeed, that was the real question burning in
Deborah's mind.

Could she ask *him* to stay?

Would he ask *her* to go?

———

Deborah wanted to share every one of Tim's feelings. Overriding his objection that the only thing
that mattered was being together for these precious
days, she obtained permission to take him to see the
holy sites of his religion.

Supported by a month's advance in Deborah's
pocket money, they planned to set forth like pious
pilgrims to trace the footsteps of Timothy's Messiah.

By unspoken agreement, they did not—dared
not—talk about the future. They lived merely from
day to day. But each circle of the sun brought them
inexorably nearer to the moment when difficult decisions could no longer be avoided.

Yet were they not in a land where Joshua had commanded the sun to stand still—and had it not obeyed him?

———

Late one afternoon, Deborah was walking along the lake shore, asking herself a million answerless questions, when she came upon Boaz, who was reading quietly on a grassy bank.

She knew that he sometimes went there to escape the burden of his leadership ("Two hundred kibbutzniks—two hundred opinions") and intended to leave him in peace. But even from afar, he could sense her need to talk and beckoned to her.

He dispensed with cordiality and went to the heart of the matter. "How much longer?"

"I don't know." Deborah shrugged.

"Of course you do," he said paternally. "You know to the very hour—the very minute maybe."

"We're leaving to drive around the country tomorrow," she offered.

"But you're not going like Moses for forty years in the desert," he answered. "He has to be back in Jerusalem—when?"

"On the fifteenth," she replied tonelessly.

"Well," he said quietly, "that gives you five days."

"You mean for one of us to make up his mind?" she asked hopefully.

"No, Deborah," Boaz replied as gently as he could. "Neither of you can change what you are. The five days are for you to get used to the idea."

———

The next morning Deborah and Tim climbed into a beat-up sedan for what they both knew—but neither said—would be a journey of separation.

Deborah took one last look at the *srif,* as Tim put his suitcase into the trunk. He was taking all his belongings. Everything. There was nothing left of him she could come back to.

———

The next few days were all a blur. Long sun-filled expeditions with guidebooks in Nazareth, Caesarea, Megiddo, Hebron, Bethlehem.

Then in the evenings, they would check uneasily into modest hotels, feeling self-conscious— although dozens of other young couples were doing the same.

Finally, there was Jerusalem, a city fraught with passion for them both. Not merely for their faiths, but for their lives.

They did their best to stave off sadness. Deborah even joked that their inn was a mere ten minutes from Mea Shearim, and playfully threatened to take Timothy to meet the Schiffmans.

They walked everywhere—visiting the Old City, now united physically yet still divided into tiny spiritual fragments.

As they passed through the narrow streets, they rubbed shoulders with priests from the Armenian, Greek Orthodox, and Ethiopian churches, mullahs from the Arab mosques—and *frummers* who seemed carbon copies of Deborah's neighbors back in Brooklyn.

At last Deborah brought Timothy to the ridge atop the Wailing Wall, pointing out where her "sinful voice" had caused a riot.

"I don't believe it," Tim declared. "They look too pious. They're so rapt in prayer."

"I promise you, some of them would still recognize me, so I couldn't even pray in the fenced-off area. But you—my blond, Irish friend—would be embraced with open arms."

She whispered something in his ear.

"No," he protested, smiling, "that'd be a sacrilege."

"Not unless you make it one," she countered.

"But I don't have a skullcap."

"Don't worry, my darling, just give them a quick burst of Yiddish and watch how fast you get the accoutrements."

Tim shrugged, and reverently started toward the crowd of worshipers.

Suddenly, a handful of young men began to point to him.

"Look, look," they called in Yiddish, "here comes a soul to save."

They rushed forward, surrounding him with bonhomie.

"Do you speak Yiddish?" one inquired.

"*Yo, a bissel,*" Timothy replied.

Their excitement mounted, as they continued in their catechism.

"Do you know how to *daven*?"

"Well, I know some prayers."

"Come, we'll help you."

Almost magically a skullcap appeared on Tim's head as they affectionately led him to the front, where he could touch the holy stones.

Timothy was immensely moved and they could see it.

"Pray," one of them urged, thrusting a book into his hand. "You can read Hebrew, can't you?"

"A little."

Another began to leaf through the Psalms.

"Can I choose my own?" asked Tim.

"Of course," their leader said enthusiastically. "Which one?"

"The very last—one hundred and fifty," Tim answered.

"Wonderful," they all responded joyfully.

Timothy recited what he had been taught was the "grandest symphony of praise to God ever composed on earth," a song which began and ended with Hallelujah ("Praise ye the Lord") and had the selfsame word in every line.

The spiritual recruiters were overwhelmed. "Why don't you come with us to meet our rebbe?" they urged.

For a moment, Tim was lost. For these young men, unlike the joyless fundamentalists Deborah had described to him, were passionately infused with the love of God.

Suddenly, he thought of the only logical excuse.

"I'm sorry," he apologized in Yiddish, "I already have a spiritual leader."

Then he rejoined the rabbi's daughter and began to follow the fourteen Stations of the Cross.

The last five stations—which included the site of the Crucifixion at Calvary and Christ's Tomb— were enshrined in the Church of the Holy Sepulchre, a solemn place shared by six sects, the Greek Orthodox faith, the Roman Catholics, as well as the Copts, Armenians, Syrians, and Abyssinians.

As Tim stared speechless at this stark memorial of his Savior's Passion, Deborah sensed that he was not even aware of her presence.

He was silent for nearly half an hour, and even then had difficulty speaking.

"What would you like to do now?" she asked hesitantly.

"Deborah," he answered, his voice quavering slightly, "would you mind if we took a walk?"

"No, of course not."

"On second thought, it's pretty far. We can take a bus."

"No, no," she insisted. "We'll walk wherever you want to go."

"I want to see Bethlehem one more time."

She nodded, and took his hand as they turned to begin the long hike.

It was late afternoon when, parched and covered with dust, they entered the Church of the Nativity, built more than a thousand years earlier, above the place where Christ was born.

They emerged from a passageway into the Catholic Church of St. Catherine, where Timothy knelt in the last pew and began to pray. Deborah stood beside him, unsure of what to do.

Suddenly she heard him gasp. "Oh my God." And then in a furious whisper he ordered, "Kneel down, Deborah. *Kneel!*"

Sensing his terror, she quickly obeyed.

He whispered another command. "Lower your head—and *pray.*"

Moments later, two worshipers from the front pew rose, moved to the aisle, genuflected and crossed themselves, then turned to leave. They were wearing black jackets and white shirts, open at the neck.

As they approached, Tim could see what he had suspected from afar—that they were indeed George Cavanagh and Patrick Grady.

"Are you sure they didn't notice you?" Deborah asked later as they stood in the shadows waiting for the bus to Jerusalem.

"I don't know," he answered, unable to control his panic. "They might have and just didn't say anything."

"If they did, do you think they'd tell anyone?" she asked, fully sharing his anxiety.

"I'm pretty sure Cavanagh would," he said bitterly.

"But how will you ever know—?"

"That's just it," he cut her off, shaking his head in anguish. "I never will."

———

They sat on a low stone wall at the top of the Mount of Olives. Neither spoke. In less than an hour, Deborah would leave him to return to the kibbutz.

A part of his life would be over.

They gazed at the valley below and the Old City beyond it almost in silhouette, reflecting occasional sparkles of gold from the setting sun.

Finally, Tim broke what was almost a monastic silence.

"We could live here," he said softly.

"What do you mean?"

"Here, this city—Jerusalem. If you look at it, you can almost see all religions come together— the spirit of God sort of hovering in concentric circles above the Old City. This is everybody's home."

"Spiritual home," she corrected him.

"I mean it, Deborah. This is a place where we both could live. Together."

"Tim," she said in desperation, "you want to be a priest. All your life you've wanted to serve God—"

"I could still do that without taking Holy Orders," he replied, trying to convince himself as well. "I'm sure one of the Christian schools would let me teach. . . ." His voice trailed off.

He looked at her. She knew full well the implications of his words and loved him too much to pretend otherwise.

"Timothy," she began, "in my heart of hearts, we're already married. But, in the real world, it would never work."

"Why not?"

"Because I can't forget my religion—and neither can you. Nothing—not all the holy water in the world—could wash away the essence of what we are."

"You mean you're still afraid of your father?" he demanded.

"No, I don't feel I owe him anything. I meant the Father of the Universe."

"But don't we all serve Him in the end?"

"Yes, Timothy. But we serve Him each in our own way *until* the end."

"But when the Messiah comes again—"

He did not have to finish his sentence.

Although they both believed with perfect faith that the Messiah would ultimately appear, they also knew the world they lived in was far too flawed to receive Him.

The Messiah would not come—not in their life-time anyway.

29

Timothy

They parted at the Jerusalem bus station. As Deborah climbed onto the first step, he impulsively pulled her back for one last embrace.

He could not let her go. He loved her with a fire so intense it would have burned all his resolve had Deborah allowed it.

"We shouldn't do this," she protested weakly. "Your friends, I mean the ones who saw us—"

"I don't care—I don't care about anything but you."

"That's not true—"

"I swear to God, I love you more."

"No, Tim, you really don't know how you feel."

"What makes you so sure?"

"Because I don't know myself."

She tried to break away, not only because his priesthood was at risk but because, for her own sake, she had to leave now or never. And she did not want him to remember her face streaming with tears.

Yet as they stood in one another's arms, she could feel the sobs he, too, was struggling to suppress.

Their parting words were the very same—and spoken almost in unison. Each told the other, "God bless you." And turned away.

————

When he reached Terra Sancta College, the two other Americans were already there.

"We were dog tired from the heat," Patrick Grady explained. "Besides, no one can spend too much time here in Jerusalem."

His colleague Cavanagh agreed, "It'd probably take a lifetime to see it all."

Neither gave the slightest indication of whether he had seen the lovers in Bethlehem. That was yet another cross Tim had to bear. He would now be living in perpetual anxiety, wondering what his two classmates knew. Whether they would somehow use it to discredit him. And *when*.

"I confess, Hogan," George said in a more amicable tone, "we're sorry we didn't ask you to come along. We would have had a much better time."

"Oh?" Tim asked.

"I mean, my Latin's good enough, but most of the inscriptions seemed to be in Greek. You would have really come in handy."

"Thanks," Tim answered dourly. "I'm flattered."

Just as promised, *pünktlich* to the minute, Father Bauer and the German seminarians returned. All were exhausted, dusty, roasted by the late-summer sun.

Tim gave a retroactive shiver. It was a minor miracle that he and Deborah had not run into them as well.

———

The next morning, flying thirty thousand feet above the earth, and that much closer to the heavens, Timothy read his breviary, trying to flood his mind with pious thoughts. As their plane circled the city, awaiting permission to land, they passed over the Vatican. With Michelangelo's rounded basilica opening out into Bernini's many-columned piazza, St. Peter's looked like a giant keyhole.

Lest the metaphor be lost on any of his sleepy charges, Father Bauer commented, "That is the true gate to Paradise, my brothers. And it is for us to earn the keys to the Kingdom of God."

Timothy gazed down, and wondered if those gates were not shut to him forever.

PART III

30

Timothy

"**B** less me, Father, for I have sinned. . . ."
      How can I begin, Tim agonized as he knelt in a stifling confessional in the chapel of the North American College. How could he describe what had occurred in the Holy Land?

That he fell in love with a woman? But that was such an inadequate expression of his feelings.

That he had had sexual intercourse? He, a seminarian, already committed to chastity, who in barely two years would take a vow of eternal celibacy?

"*Sì, figlio mio?* "

It was some consolation that his confessor spoke Italian. The gravity of his words could perhaps be diffused through the filter of a foreign tongue.

"*Ho peccato, Padre,* I have sinned," he repeated.

"How may I help you?" whispered the voice behind the screen.

"I have loved a woman, Father."

There was a pause. The pastor rephrased it, "You mean you have *made* love. . . ."

"There's no difference," Tim asserted, almost indignantly.

The confessor coughed.

"We made love because we cared for each other's souls. When our bodies touched, our souls met."

"But your bodies . . . touched," the confessor replied.

He doesn't understand, Tim thought. How in God's name can I confess to someone who doesn't know what earthly love is?

He tried to tell the story coherently, but for all his urgent desire to confess in full, he wanted to protect Deborah. He would not name her. Nor would he say that her father was a man of God.

The dialogue took a long time. The priest had so many questions. Where? How many times?

"Why do you have to know all this?" Tim pleaded desperately. "Isn't it enough that I did what I did?"

He tried to rationalize that perhaps this probing was intended to be a part of his penance. To excise carnality from his soul and lay it like a cancer on a surgeon's tray, malignant, apart from him.

Finally the ordeal was over. He had confided as much as he was able. For what remained, he thought, God knows what I did and how I feel. Let Him pass judgment on me.

He was sweating and out of breath as he waited for the priest's comments.

"There still are questions left unanswered . . ." was all his confessor vouchsafed. He fell silent, waiting to measure Timothy's contrition.

"I know, I know. I'm a seminarian. I should have been more resolute. I love God—and I want to serve Him. That's why I'm here." He paused, then added, "That's why I was able to come back."

"Are you certain of your new resolve?"

"I'm a human being, Father. I can only know my own intentions."

"Will you, of your own accord, discuss your future with your Spiritual Director?"

Tim nodded and whispered, "Yes, Father. I'll do whatever's necessary to be worthy of the priesthood."

At last his confessor delivered his judgment.

"We are all of us but flesh. Even saints have battled with the same demons. Need I but mention St. Augustine—and St. Jerome, both now Doctors of the Church? It is their example you must follow. And for your penance, for the next thirty days say all three chaplets of the rosary every day. Meditate on each of the Joyful, Sorrowful, and Glorious mysteries, asking Our Lady to intercede for you with Our Lord to grant you grace. Also, recite Psalm fifty-one at morning and at evening prayers."

"Yes, Father."

Through the screen Tim glimpsed the movements

of his confessor's right hand making the sign of the cross as the priest absolved him in the name of the Father, and of the Son, and of the Holy Spirit.

"*Va in pace,*" murmured the priest, "*e pregha per me.*" Go in peace, and pray for me.

———

Rome, the fabled "City of the Seven Hills," has an eighth: the Janiculum, situated across the Tiber, on the right bank. Here in the third century A.D., the Emperor Aurelian built what he thought would be an impregnable wall, twenty feet high and twelve miles long, to protect all of Rome from barbarian attacks.

It was on the Janiculum in 1953 that Pope Pius XII himself, in the company of Francis Cardinal Spellman of New York (the prime mover in the fund-raising appeal), dedicated the new North American College—a seven-story structure of tan pastel brick—a magnificent gesture of fealty on the part of the faithful in the New World.

The porticoes of its airy courtyard are lined with insignia celebrating the generosity of various dioceses in the United States. The graceful fountain at its center spouts a jet of pure water from a rock spangled with stars representing each state of the Union.

Various public rooms bear the Coat of Arms with the college's motto, "*Firmum est cor meum,*" My heart is steadfast. For a significant portion of its one hundred and thirty inhabitants, mostly American candidates for ordination, the motto hides an invisible question: Is my heart strong enough?

It was here that Timothy and his four colleagues would lodge while they continued their studies. A few of the classes like Canon Law were still given in Latin, but most were in Italian, the tongue they had supposedly mastered during their intense summer in Perugia. Since they were not all linguists, Mondadori Italian-English dictionaries were clutched as earnestly as if they were breviaries.

During his month of penance, Timothy had twice daily addressed God in the words of the Fifty-first Psalm, asking Him to "wash me thoroughly from mine iniquity, and cleanse me from my sin." And he was confident, in the words of the psalmist, that the Almighty had created in him a clean heart and renewed a "right spirit."

He knelt before the altar and swore an oath that he would never communicate with Deborah again.

Yet even as he uttered his vow, a light was kindled in a distant corner of his despair. It illumined in his thoughts a flickering question. Might God have ordained that we meet again?

He was drenched with sweat as he left the chapel, but it was not from the windless warmth of the October Roman night. A desperate thought had suddenly breached the wall of his defenses.

I will live in hope of seeing Deborah.

For the rest of my life.

31

Deborah

It was a shock, but not a surprise.

Since Deborah and Tim had spent nearly three weeks together, it would have been surprising had she *not* been pregnant, but in truth, an irrational part of her had longed for the "misfortune" that confronted her scarcely four weeks after she and Timothy had parted.

She heard the test results from Dr. Barnea, the kibbutz physician. He at least was not ambivalent, for he smiled warmly. "*Mazel tov.*"

She sat silent for a moment. "I don't know what to do," she murmured.

"Don't worry," said the doctor reassuringly. "I can tell you everything you need to know. Besides, there's always someone pregnant on the kibbutz. You can get better information from them than from any of my textbooks."

Was it that simple? she asked herself. Was she just going to sit and watch her stomach grow? Would she not be a laughingstock or, worse, overwhelmed by a tidal wave of communal pity?

"Dr. Barnea, this . . . baby that I'm carrying . . ."

He waited patiently for her to find the courage to continue.

At last she remarked, "There's no way in the world I could . . . marry the father. I couldn't even tell him."

The physician smiled reassuringly. "So who's asking? On the kibbutz, the arrival of a baby is always an occasion for rejoicing. And your child will grow up in the most wonderful circumstances in the world. By the way, you're not the only single parent on the premises. Haven't you noticed?"

"No," she replied.

"Aha," said the doctor, waving his finger in rhetorical triumph. "That's exactly my point. You haven't noticed because all children are treated the same."

"But what if this baby . . . asks about its father?"

"Well," he smiled, "unless it's extremely precocious, it won't be doing that for quite some time. By then, your situation may have changed."

No, Deborah thought to herself, it won't change. This is Timothy's baby, and no one else's.

The doctor mistook her introspection for discomfiture and added, "Listen, Deborah, it's a sad fact of life that sometimes our young husbands go off to the Army and . . . don't come back. I am sorry to say we have two widows even younger than you with five children between them."

He leaned over and slammed his hand on his desk. "But the kids are fine! The community gives them all the love they need. Right now, it's more important that you watch your diet, take your vitamins, and think happy thoughts."

Deborah knew his prescription was impossible to follow. She would walk out of the clinic into the real world and be alone—yet not alone. And having resolved never to love anyone else, she was prepared to be a mother without ever having been a wife.

By now the doctor was aware that she had other anxieties.

"Are you worried about your parents?" he asked solicitously.

"Yes," she confessed. "My father seems to have a way of finding these things out."

Dr. Barnea understood only too well.

"Deborah, do you want to know my definition of an adult? It's someone who wakes up one morning and says to himself, 'I no longer care what my parents think.' To me that's the real psychological *bar mitzvah*."

She nodded, rose, and slowly left the clinic. The searing midday sun reminded her how long she had been inside—for it had been cool when she'd arrived to hear the news.

As she walked slowly to her *srif,* a thousand warring thoughts swept her mind and shook her like a sandstorm in the desert.

She was reasonably sure that she no longer cared what Moses Luria would think.

But the only thing she yearned for was impossible.

She wanted Tim to know.

32

Daniel

As my lust intensified and my faith diminished, I realized why I was so attracted to Ariel: In one stunning package, she was the incarnation of everything considered taboo by my religion.

She had told me she was studying Art History at NYU, and seemed to be going about it in a big way. The walls of her apartment were hung with impressive works of modern art, including an authentic Utrillo oil, a Braque, and several Picasso drawings. The living room shelves were packed with what must have been hundreds of illustrated books on the works of contemporary masters.

I'd never seen a place quite like hers before—and certainly not a grad student's.

To begin with it was huge and furnished entirely in white. The only exceptions were silver serving dishes, yet even they were filled—I kid you not—with white chocolate.

Her Frigidaire was stocked with champagne, caviar—and Birds Eye frozen dinners.

I should have guessed by the fact that she could never see me on Tuesday, Wednesday, and Thursday nights. Sure, I knew it was possible to have evening classes, but when once or twice I proposed coming over around midnight, she laughed.

I finally caught on one Friday night (yes, I was besotted enough to violate the Sabbath) when she accidentally poured red wine over me, and light-heartedly offered to lick it off as "penance." She undressed me and shoved me into the fancy multi-spigoted shower in her bathroom.

When I stepped out, she handed me not only an extra bathrobe, but a man's shirt and pants as well.

I tried to rationalize the presence of these masculine garments by thinking that they had belonged to some previous lover—or even a husband.

But somehow the pants were too neatly pressed, the shirt too freshly laundered. And when I looked at its diamond-shaped monogrammed initials *CM,* curiosity overcame me.

"Who belongs to this?" I asked, trying to sound casual.

"A friend," she answered offhandedly, and beckoned me to come and play.

But even during the preliminary embraces, I persisted.

"What kind of friend?"

"Nobody important. Leave it, huh?"

"He's obviously important enough to hang his clothes in your closet."

Finally she lost patience. "For Christ's sake, Danny. Are you that far out of touch with the world? Isn't it obvious that I'm a kept woman?"

I was, to tell the truth, knocked off balance—and very hurt. "It wasn't obvious to me," I murmured. "You mean this is his apartment?"

"No, it's mine, but he pays the rent. Is that too heavy a trip, little Rabbi?"

"No," I lied. "It's just that where I come from this sort of thing is—"

"Lover, where you come from is another planet."

"You're right," I replied, feeling embarrassed for having the vestiges of conventional values. "There's just one thing I don't understand."

"Yes?"

"What the hell about me attracts you?"

She answered unabashedly, "Your innocence."

She smiled broadly. "And aren't I like a whole salad of forbidden fruit to you?"

I nodded and grabbed her hungrily.

As she grew pliant in my arms, she murmured throatily, "You won't be able to go back to nice Jewish girls after this."

———

On many of those muggy nights I spent cramming for courses I would only begin in the fall, part of me was grateful that her boyfriend had invited Ariel to join him on the Riviera. I was living at home for the summer and it would have been impossible to speak to her without going to a pay phone.

My father's Puritanism was so all-pervasive I tried my best not even to *think* about her, lest he be able to read my thoughts.

The house seemed strange without Deborah. She had scrawled only a few lines to Mama saying that "all was well," but the kind of letters we exchanged were far more candid. I was waiting on tenterhooks to hear the next installment of her romance—as I hoped it would be—with Avi the pilot.

Every so often I called my dorm to see if there was any mail. But all I got was the occasional picture postcard from my seductress. Anyway, I immersed myself in study, mightily attempting to efface Ariel from my thoughts.

Sometimes Papa would knock gently on the door. Then, after saying that he hoped he was not disturbing me, would sit down and try to help me find a topic for the thesis I had to write as part of the requirement for graduation.

Most of his suggestions involved mysticism, for which there was a "Lurianic" tradition dating back to the Middle Ages. Though some of the most important books on the subject, like the *Zohar,* were, by custom, if not formal legislation, forbidden to be read by any man beneath the age of forty, my father was convinced that he could persuade the dean that mine were "special circumstances."

I would merely nod and offer him some of the peanut butter crackers and ginger ale that Mama saw to it were always on my desk. I did my best to camouflage the truth that I already knew what I would like to write about, and whom I wanted to be my supervisor.

At summer's end I went to see the dean to engage in special pleading. As usual, he welcomed me heartily. As usual, I assumed it was merely because of my father's eminence.

"I'd like to do a thesis under Dr. Beller," I said, trying not to squirm.

"A truly erudite man," the dean remarked. "But I never knew you had an interest in archaeology—"

"Oh no," I interrupted. "I don't mean *Rabbi* Beller. I mean his brother at Columbia."

"Ah." Suddenly he was less enthusiastic. He stroked his beard, uttering sounds like "Mmmm" in several different octaves.

At last he spoke distinguishable syllables. "That Aaron Beller's such an *epikoros*, such a wicked genius. And yet what honest scholar can deny he has the greatest mind his brilliant family has produced in generations. . . ."

"Yes, sir," I responded. "That's why I picked his course. You can see from my record that I got an

A." I waited anxiously as the dean reverted to more interrogatory grunts.

At long last, to my surprise, he leaned across the desk and smiled.

"You know something, Danny? Maybe if Beller takes you on, he might just find your piety contagious. You might actually win him back to the fold. Don't worry, I'll make a few phone calls and arrange it."

"Thank you." Elated, I stood to go.

"But I warn you," the dean called after me. "This man has a gift for mischief. Don't let his personality bewitch you."

"No, sir," I answered.

"But then, the son of the Silczer Rebbe won't let his faith be shaken," the dean said, with a confidence that disquieted me.

———

The topic Beller and I had settled on was "Sexual Sublimation as a Factor in Religious Faith," a title whose first word we agreed to omit when we presented the topic for approval to the University Degree Committee.

. The obvious point of departure was Freud's heretical monograph "Future of an Illusion," in which he sees the origin of religion in the suppression, or at least rechanneling, of that primary driving force in life—libido. I could, after all, testify firsthand to the power of the Evil Inclination.

My research, ranging from Plato to Freud and

beyond, brought me ever closer to Beller's essential view that "religion" arose from the guilt-inspired need to invent a patriarchal Supreme Being.

I guess I got carried away, since the curriculum required ten thousand words and I gave Beller nearly twenty.

I also became a regular guest at his apartment—with Ariel, of course—still, I was in a state of high anxiety when we met a week after I gave him my first draft. Fortunately, he put me out of my misery as soon as he could.

"It's first rate, Danny. Quite frankly, I think you've got the nucleus of a book here. But I've made some marginal notes where you can cut out the more controversial ideas so that this draft can be certified 'kosher' by the dean."

It was good advice, for my paper as it stood was riddled with heresy.

———

Late one evening when we were sharing the last of a bottle of white wine, I asked tentatively, "Aaron, can we talk?"

"Sure, Danny," he replied. I think he sensed what was coming.

"Knowing what I know—I mean, the things I learned from you—I can't go through with it. I mean . . . ordination."

I waited nervously for his reaction.

"Daniel," he said slowly. "I'm glad you've initiated this, since now I feel ethically justified in speaking freely."

He paused and then said gently, "I've always thought that you had qualms about becoming a rabbi—especially when it came to succeeding your father. I can't see you spending the rest of your life sitting in Brooklyn, writing *Responsa* on medieval quibbles. To me it would be a waste of a good mind."

I was embarrassed at the way he could read my thoughts. And yet, I felt a kind of incredible relief.

I realized that his course had been a pretext for my excavating my deepest feelings, which had all my life oscillated between fear and resentment of my father.

The most frightening discovery was that not only did I not want to be the next Silczer Rebbe, I wasn't even sure I could become a rabbi at all.

"I don't know what to do," I said in desperation.

"It was all said by Hillel two thousand years ago: 'If I am not for me, who is?' Danny, it's *your* life." He paused, reflecting, then frowned.

"Still, who am I to give you advice?" he said finally. "I confess to having occasional spasms of doubt. I mean, my own father and two brothers are all rabbis. Maybe they're right and I'm wrong. They're able to accept that 'our' God had some inscrutable purpose in allowing six million of our people to perish. But I ask what kind of unspeakable sins could those Jews have committed to deserve complete annihilation? Martin Buber tries to explain it by saying that God went into 'eclipse.' But that's where faith and I part company."

His face had grown flushed, and it was clear he had said more than he had first intended.

"Sorry," he remarked. "I think I was riding my hobbyhorse over the speed limit."

"No," I assured him. "You're putting into words exactly how I feel. Only what do you tell your patients when they discover the truth about themselves and it's almost impossible to bear?"

Aaron smiled and answered quietly, "I say—see you at our next session."

33

Deborah

After thinking she would die, Deborah had finally survived the debilitating bouts of morning sickness that had plagued her during her first trimester of pregnancy.

She now felt well enough to contemplate the realities of motherhood with a touch of equanimity. And even a scintilla of happiness. She was carrying Tim's child—something of him that no force on earth could take away.

Then the tragedy occurred.

The news came as they were starting their evening meal in the dining hall. A tight-lipped, solemn-looking Air Force colonel appeared and asked to speak privately with Zipporah and Boaz. Both of them went chalk white as they followed him into a far corner.

Though the officer was speaking too softly to be

heard, everyone in the dining room already knew what message he was bearing. Their fears were confirmed when they heard Zipporah's shriek of anguish.

She continued to howl, so completely out of control that when Boaz tried to embrace her, she flailed her arms to keep her husband away.

Dr. Barnea was already at their side. With another member, he helped walk Zipporah to the clinic.

The rest of them sat immobile, as if turned to stone.

Deborah whispered to Hannah Yavetz, "Avi?"

She nodded somberly. "There was an air strike on a guerrilla base in Sidon. I heard it on the radio. One of our planes was hit by antiaircraft."

Oh God, thought Deborah, dizzy with shock.

They sat in silence. In a matter of seconds, they had been transformed from communal farmers into a congregation mourning without words.

Twenty minutes later the doctor reappeared, himself on the verge of tears. All crowded around to hear the report he delivered in hoarse and halting tones.

"Avi was hit and wounded badly. Yet he didn't eject even when he got back over the border. He wanted to land the plane . . . ," his voice now broke, "so someone else could fly it."

Many of the kibbutzniks, men and women who had known Avi since birth and grown up with him, covered their eyes and wept softly.

"He didn't have to go," Hannah murmured bitterly.

"What do you mean?" Deborah asked.

"He was an only son. In the Israeli Defense Forces, only sons are never put on the front lines. Avi had to get special permission."

Deborah nodded mutely.

"I know he wasn't scared to die," Hannah continued. "But he's destroyed his parents too. Now they have nothing."

———

The kibbutz literally cared for its members from cradle to grave. At the antipodes from the children's quarters, in the distant southwest corner, was the cemetery.

Here in the presence of his extended family—augmented by his wing commander and fellow pilots—Avi Ben-Ami, aged twenty-five, was laid to rest. A volley of rifle shots was fired, as a simple coffin draped in the Star of David was lowered into the earth. There was no rabbi. And except for a brief eulogy from his Commanding Officer, the service was perfunctory. The grief was real.

A pall was cast over the kibbutz for weeks. Deborah felt the urgent need to unburden her thoughts to someone beyond the closed community.

And so she sat down at her small wooden desk and began another long letter to Danny, this time recounting how the death of a single soldier could sadden not only a community but an entire nation.

For the whole country had seen Avi's picture on television that evening. And in a real way they shared the Ben-Amis' sorrow.

She had been writing for about fifteen minutes when there was a knock at her already opened door. She was not surprised to see Boaz and Zipporah. Since the death of their only child, the couple had established a routine to enable them to face each long night. At nine-thirty—right after the television news—they would walk the kibbutz grounds until they had exhausted themselves enough to sleep.

"Anyone home?" Boaz asked, trying to sound lighthearted.

"Come in," said Deborah, herself trying to sound casual.

"No, no," he answered. "Besides, there isn't room in there for all of us. Come and take a stroll. It will do your little one good to get some fresh air."

She nodded and rose. Standing up was growing a bit more difficult now, but she went out with them.

Deborah knew she had not been invited merely to make casual conversation. In the past weeks, Boaz and Zipporah had become near-recluses.

"Deborah," Boaz began, "we've been working up the courage to speak to you. . . ."

" 'Courage'?" she interrupted.

"Well, yes," Boaz continued awkwardly. "But if you examine our situation and yours, I think we could be of help to one another."

Deborah forced a smile. "At this point, I can use all the help I can get."

"The way I see it," Boaz continued, "your baby will never have a father—and Zipporah and I will never have a grandchild. If we could somehow put the two broken pieces together, we might make all of us whole again." He paused and added, "As far as possible."

"What . . . ," she began hesitantly. "What would you like me to do?"

"Would you consider giving the child our name? I mean, we wouldn't ask you to call it Avi or Aviva. Could you just let him be a 'Ben-Ami'? Then we two can be Grandma and Grandpa."

Zipporah added almost apologetically, "That would actually be good for the baby. . . ."

Deborah threw her arms around them both. "Thank you," she murmured, tears welling in her eyes.

"No," Zipporah protested. "Thank *you*."

———

Early one May morning, Deborah went into labor. Since there was no phone in the *srif,* her roommate, Hannah, rushed to wake Dr. Barnea, who muttered sleepily, "Wait till the contractions are three minutes apart and then bring her to the surgery. I'll get the nurse."

In the last three months of Deborah's pregnancy, Hannah had gone with her to the natural childbirth classes so she would be able to help her control her breathing.

The pain was worse than Deborah had imagined. Each time the spasms came, she clenched her teeth and tried—vainly—to avoid uttering imprecations. In one of her ever-decreasing moments of remission she gasped to Hannah, "Goddamn Eve—look what she did when she ate that apple!"

The kibbutz had a small but well-equipped operating room, so Dr. Barnea and his two part-time nurses could perform emergency procedures like appendectomies and set broken bones. And, of course, deliver babies.

At 8:15 the doctor deemed the crucial moment to be at hand. The nurses wheeled Deborah in, with Hannah at her side offering words of encouragement.

At 8:27 the crown of the baby's head emerged, and moments later Hannah called out excitedly, "It's a boy, Deborah. You've got a lovely blond boy."

The medical staff called out almost in unison, "*Mazel tov!* "

Deborah was euphoric.

Later in the day, she and grandparents Boaz and Zipporah shed tears together.

"What are you going to call him?" Zipporah asked.

Deborah had given it much thought and had decided that if it were a girl she would call her Chava, after her father's first wife. She could not fathom her own motivation, but had an inkling that she might still be trying to please him.

There was no question, however, that if it were a boy she would give it the closest Hebrew equivalent to Timothy, which meant "honoring God." The choice came down to Elimelech—"My God is King"—and Elisha—"God is my Salvation." Deborah settled on the latter.

On May 22, 1971, Elisha Ben-Ami was circumcised and entered the covenant between God and His people. His last name commemorated a dead man who was not his father. His first honored one still living who would never know Eli was his son.

Deborah oscillated between elation and helplessness. There were times even in those first intoxicating days when she would sit mutely, awestruck at what she had done.

For while Eli had been inside her she had survived moments of self-doubt by thinking, "Everything will be all right as soon as my child is born." His living presence turned rosy fantasy into a yowling reality.

Naturally, all the kibbutzniks were supportive and congratulatory. But, to everyone except Boaz, Zipporah, and Deborah herself, Eli was just another of the many babies who were always welcomed with affection.

The tidal wave of love that Deborah felt was something that she longed to share with her real family, her mother at the very least, and Danny, to whom she had at several moments during her pregnancy come close to confiding her secret.

And yes, she admitted to herself, there was an irrational part of her that still yearned to tell her father. Though she believed she had severed all emotional ties, the little girl in her still wanted Papa's approval.

But would he ever welcome the prodigal daughter into his fold again?

34

Daniel

I was the last of the candidates to fall by the
wayside.

That was my only distinction. In our first year,
Label Kantrowitz had had some kind of nervous collapse. It was especially tragic, since
he had a wife and two children. Word had it he
was teaching back home in a Baltimore yeshiva
and still suffering from migraines and high blood
pressure. But I was pretty sure there was more to it
than that.

There were two more dropouts near the end of
our third year, when we still had more than twelve
months to go toward ordination. About these our
teachers were silent, vouchsafing merely that they
had some "inner difficulties."

Unlike Kantrowitz, the two late defectors were
not sons of rabbis, and Label's father was merely

the principal of a small yeshiva, not the leader of a community.

None of them was heir apparent to the Silczer Rebbe. None of them would break a "golden chain"—and his father's heart.

I wondered what Papa would do. He had led so meritorious a life and prayed so long for a successor. Why should this pain be visited upon him from on High?

There, I stopped myself. How could I dare to presume that my loss of faith had been caused by some unearthly power? I was not a modern Job who had failed the test. I was a human being who no longer could believe in the dictates of his religion.

Yet how could I face my father knowing that he regarded my forthcoming ordination as a perpetuation of his own life and dedication? How could I pronounce the words that would destroy him?

I was grateful when Beller appeared unannounced at my dormitory to give me courage.

"Why am I doing this?" I agonized.

Beller looked at me and, in what I presumed to be his therapeutic tone of voice, softly asked, "Exactly whom do you think you're doing it *to*?"

I cast down my eyes, confessing, "To my father." I paused and then repeated, "I am doing this to hurt my father."

I looked up and asked in anguish, "Why, Aaron, why should I want to do that?"

"Only you can find the answer," he whispered softly.

"Do I hate him?"

"Do you?"

How could I answer such a terrible question—except with the truth.

"Yes," I murmured. "Something in me wants to punish him. Look at the way he treated my sister."

"Is it only Deborah?" Beller interposed.

"No, you're right. It's what he's doing to me. Why should I have to be a rabbi? Why should I just allow him to slam my life down on an anvil and forge it into whatever shape he wants? Suppose I'd never been born?"

"It's too late for that," said Beller with a glint of humor. "Retreating to the womb won't help you now."

I tried to reciprocate with a smile but couldn't quite manage.

"When are you going to tell him?" he asked.

"As soon as I can buy a bulletproof vest," I jested weakly, then confessed, "Aaron, I don't know how to do it."

"Simply tell him the truth. That's the honorable thing."

"I know. But I just can't say it straight out. It'll kill him."

Beller shook his head. "Danny, he's already suffered worse catastrophes in his lifetime—the

Holocaust, Chava's death, and the loss of his first son. I guarantee you. This may hurt your father, but it won't kill him."

"You don't know him," I protested softly. "You don't know the man."

He did not respond.

———

All during my subway ride to Brooklyn, I agonized over how I would do "the honorable thing." I had thought of a million subterfuges, lame excuses, delaying tactics—"I'd like to take an extra year in Jerusalem. . . ." But Beller had convinced me that these would be unnecessarily cruel to both of us.

By the time the train reached Wall Street, I had formulated my text so I could have the rest of the journey to rehearse it.

The late spring evening had been muggy, and even in the relative coolness of the night I was pouring sweat.

It was nearly midnight as I walked slowly down our street, past the silent, darkened synagogue, and up the steps to our house. My mother would have long since gone to bed. A craven part of me hoped that perhaps my father would have taken an early night as well.

I was deluding myself. While the whole world slumbered, he was always working at his desk. I can even recall moments in my childhood when he came to breakfast having spent the entire night completing his opinion on a difficult doctrinal question.

My hand trembled as I put my key into the lock. The door creaked. Would this wake my mother? Perhaps unconsciously I wanted her to be present, to help Father absorb some of the shock, maybe even act as mediator or comforter. For both of us.

A stream of light from the half-open door to Father's study spilled across my path. I heard him call affectionately, "Daniel, is that you?"

I answered, "Yes, Papa," but my voice was so imprisoned in my throat that he left his desk and came to peek out the office door.

He was beaming.

"Well, almost-Rebbe Luria, what a nice surprise. Did you finish your exams early?"

I did not reply. I stood in darkness, hesitant to enter even the slenderest rays of light.

Unable to see my expression, he continued cheerfully, "Come in, come in. I'd like you to hear what I've written on proper conversion for marriage. At this hour I could use a fresh Talmudic mind."

I walked forward slowly, my head bowed. He put his arm around my shoulders and led me inside. I shivered, not merely from the tension, but because his office was the only air-conditioned room in the house—cooled not for his personal comfort, but rather to protect the great tomes of Law. These treasured leather-bound volumes, some—like the Vilna Talmud—more than a hundred years old, had been rescued from Hitler's clutches at great risk and were now the only "living" testament from the dust and ashes of the town of Silcz.

"Sit down, sit down," he gestured affably. "Do you want a cold drink? Iced tea? A glass of seltzer maybe?"

"No, thank you, Papa. I'm not thirsty."

In truth, my throat and mouth were parched. My lips were almost cracking.

He leaned across his desk, peered over his reading glasses, and stared at me.

"Daniel," he remarked. "You're looking pale. It must be the examinations, eh?"

I merely shrugged.

"You've probably had very little sleep these past few weeks."

I nodded, guilty and shamed to be so tired in his presence. Among the many qualities of his I lacked was that enormous energy which enabled him to thrive with a bare minimum of sleep.

He leaned back in his chair. "So, *nu*." He smiled. "How did they go?"

"What?"

"The examinations. Did you find them difficult?"

I began a sentence, but still lacked courage to complete it. "I didn't . . ."

"That's good," my father beamed.

"I beg your pardon?"

"You were going to say you didn't find them difficult. That means you studied well."

"No, no," I said quickly—and my voice quivered slightly.

"Daniel," he said in a worried tone. "You're not coming to tell me that you . . . didn't pass, are you?"

"No, Papa."

"That's a relief. It doesn't matter what grade you got. The important thing is that you passed."

God in Heaven, after all these years of wanting me to be the best, he suddenly was willing to accept me as an average—maybe even mediocre—scholar. The irony fueled my growing frenzy.

Now I had to get out what I had to say before my heart would beat so quickly that I couldn't talk at all.

"Father . . . ," I began, and was further unsettled by the tremor in my voice.

He took his glasses off, and in a tone still solicitous he murmured, "Danny, something's wrong. I can see it on your face. Out with it. Don't be afraid. Remember, I'm your father."

Yes, I am all too painfully aware who you are.

"I didn't take any of my exams," I said feebly, and then waited for the thunderbolt to strike. It did not. Once again, Father surprised me.

"Daniel," he said gently. "You're not the first to have an inner crisis at a time like this. I think what you need now is rest. Examinations can be taken any time."

With a mere nod of his head, he signaled his permission to depart. I couldn't. I knew that I could never face the sunlight till I told him everything.

"Father?"

"Yes, Daniel?"

"I don't want to be a rabbi."

For a moment he did not speak. Perhaps no words existed to respond to such a statement.

"You don't *want* to? You don't want to follow in the footsteps of your father and of his father before him?" He paused and asked almost pleadingly, "*Why,* Danny, just tell me why?"

I had come this far—I had to say it all.

"Because . . . I've lost my faith."

There was an apocalyptic silence.

"This is impossible," he muttered, shaken and disoriented. "What the Romans couldn't do, the Greeks, Hitler . . ."

He did not have to complete his sentence. We both knew that he was accusing me of murder, of killing off the line of Silczer Rebbes.

At last he whispered hoarsely, "Daniel, I think that you should see a doctor. First thing tomorrow we'll call—"

"No," I cut him off. "I may be sick, but it's incurable. My brain is full of demons, Father. No doctor—" And then I added pointedly, "And no Rebbe Gershon . . . could exorcise my pain."

It was so quiet I could almost hear the clouds moving across the blackened sky.

Curiously, my father now seemed in total control.

"Daniel," he began slowly, "I think you should move out of the house. As soon as possible."

I nodded in submission.

"Take everything you want and leave your key. Because when you leave this room, I never want to see you again."

I had anticipated all this on the train to Brooklyn. I'd even made a mental list of what I'd pack in my room. But I was not prepared for what came next.

"As far as I am concerned," my father said, "I have no son. I'll say *Kaddish* for eleven months, and then you'll vanish from my thoughts forever."

He rose and walked out of the room.

A moment later, I heard the door close softly. I knew where he was going. To *shul* to say the prayer of mourning.

For his only son was dead.

35

Daniel

I spent the next forty-five minutes frantically packing. Along with all sorts of memorabilia, I grabbed some clothes and half a dozen books. Fortunately, my real library was back at school.

Mama, who had been awakened by the sound of our voices, stood there in her robe, looking strange without her *sheitel,* talking to me—babbling really—as if her words could somehow blot out the sorrow of what she was watching. The scene was reminiscent of another played out five years earlier. A drama called The Banishment of Deborah. Only this time Mama was utterly desolate.

"I can't bear it," she wept. "He's sent away both my children. Where will you go, Danny? When will I see you again?"

All I could do was shrug. I was afraid to talk,

fearing I would burst into tears and throw myself into her arms for the comfort I so badly needed.

But she had asked a valid question. Where *was* I going to go? I'd probably get a night or two in the dorm before they kicked me out for being a traitor—and then what?

"What will you do, Danny?" Mama sobbed.

"I don't know," I muttered. "Maybe I'll go to graduate school next fall."

"And study what?"

"I don't know. I'm much too confused right now."

I didn't say I was tending toward Psychology, not wanting to incriminate Beller.

The reins with which I had held back my anger now slipped, and I vented all my rage on my poor mother.

"Do you think this is easy for me?" I shouted. "Do you actually think I wanted to hurt you—or even Papa? I'm upset. I'm very . . ."

She put her arms around me and wept so copiously that her tears stained my shirt.

"Danny, we're your parents," she implored. "Don't just leave like this."

I could not stand any more.

"He's thrown me out," I shouted. "To him I'm not a person—I'm just a link in his goddamn 'golden chain.' "

"He loves you," my mother pleaded. "He'll get over it."

I challenged her. "Do you honestly believe that?"

Mama did not move. She was torn into shreds of conflicting emotions and felt more lost than I.

I looked at her with sadness and compassion. After all, she had to remain in this house of perpetual mourning.

I kissed her on the forehead, took my suitcase, and ran down the stairs into the street.

I reached the corner, turned around, and took one final glance at the neighborhood where I was born and grew to manhood, the familiar homes of the people who had formed my childhood, the synagogue where I had prayed since I was old enough to read. The eternal flame would burn above the ark, but I knew it would never light my face again.

My punishment had begun.

———

I got back to the dorm and walked into my room, which—like my emotions—was in total disarray. Open books were spread out on the bed and the radiator, all remnants of my previous chaotic existence.

With unconscious irreverence I pushed several books to the floor and sat on my bed. Late as it was I felt a desperate need to talk to someone—on the telephone at least. But I couldn't muster the guts to wake up Beller. And I knew Ariel couldn't provide the spiritual consolation I needed.

There was no one. So I just sat there motionless as my entire universe ossified into sadness.

I can't recall how long it was except that during the time I was grieving the first dawn of my banishment had turned into day.

When I heard a knock at my door I thought for a moment it was one of the deans—or maybe two—come to kick me out . . . or put me in front of a firing squad.

It turned out, however, to be one of my former classmates from down the hall.

"Hey, Luria," he said in a tone of annoyance, his excursion to my room having taken him away from his studies, "there's a call for you."

I shuffled to the pay phone and picked up the dangling receiver.

It was my mother.

"Danny," she said, voice like a zombie, "your father's had a stroke."

36
Deborah

After her Modern Hebrew Poetry class, Deborah's instructor, Zev Morgenstern—a tall, sinewy Canadian immigrant in his midthirties—stood at the doorway waiting to invite her discreetly for a cup of coffee.

She was flattered. Moments later they were sitting in an outdoor café—Zev trying to enjoy what looked like plastic cheesecake, and Deborah eating the sandwiches that would have been her dinner, since on Tuesdays and Thursdays she would arrive back at the kibbutz after the dining room had closed.

Zev had just concluded the seminar with a brilliant explication of Yehuda Amichai's poem, "Half the people in the world," evoking comparisons with the Roman poet Catullus, as well as Shakespeare and Baudelaire.

Half the people love,
Half the people hate.
And where is my place between these halves
that are so well matched?

"It's exhilarating," Deborah enthused. "Back in Brooklyn they never even told us there was any Hebrew literature outside the Bible. I think you're right to rank him among the greats."

"I'm glad you think so," Zev responded. "By the way, he lives about three blocks from me. I could take you to meet him some time, if you'd like. I think he's as good as Yeats, don't you?"

Deborah's smile narrowed. "I'm embarrassed to say my acquaintance with English Lit sort of stopped at *Julius Caesar.*"

Zev smiled. "Well, if you'll allow me to lead you across the Rubicon, I'd gladly give you a one-man tutorial in Modern English Poetry. Can you stay for dinner after next week's class?"

She was torn. Inexplicably trying to deny herself the pleasure of this man's company, she replied, "I've got a thirteen-month-old baby, and I should really be back at the kibbutz before he goes to bed. But I could come an hour earlier, if that's okay with you."

Zev could not suppress a monosyllabic expression of surprise. "Oh."

"What?"

"I didn't know you were married. I mean, you aren't wearing a ring."

Deborah shifted uncomfortably in her chair. "Well, actually I'm not. I mean . . ."

She had never actually told the elaborate lie to which her fellow kibbutzniks were accomplices, believing that it shamelessly exploited the tragedy of Avi's death, but now she allowed herself to continue.

"He was a pilot," she began slowly. She did not have to say any more.

"I'm sorry," Zev said sympathetically. "When was it?"

"Over a year ago," she answered. "Lebanon."

"And so he never saw his son."

Deborah shook her head. "No," she answered softly. "His father never saw him."

"Well," he commented at last, "you have the kibbutz. I'm sure they give you lots of moral support."

She nodded, then glanced nervously at her watch. "I think I'd better be going. I hate driving on those narrow roads at night."

She stood up. Zev rose as well.

"Don't forget next week. I'll bring the books."

Deborah smiled. "I'm looking forward to it."

In the year since Eli had been born, she had given no thought to seeking a relationship with any man. After all, she told herself with bitter irony, she was a woman who had never married but had been widowed twice.

She wondered why Zev had singled her out. There were far prettier girls in the seminar, and yet he had always given her a special smile when she entered the classroom. And whenever he read poetry out loud, it seemed as if he was reciting it just for her.

She had to admit to herself that she had found him attractive. Before they even said good-bye, she was looking forward to seeing him again. The thought both pleased and confused her.

The sun was setting, and atop Mount Carmel Deborah could feel a cooling breeze from the sea.

Ninety minutes later, when she pushed open the door to her *srif,* she was astonished to find a cloud of cigarette smoke. Sitting behind it was Boaz Ben-Ami.

Deborah took one look at his expression and let her books slide to the floor.

"All right," she demanded, her heart pounding. "Tell me."

37
Daniel

They had taken Papa to Brooklyn Jewish Hospital and rushed him into Intensive Care.

When I arrived, my half sisters were clustered protectively around Mama, both of them ashen-faced as if already sitting *shiva*—mourning my father's memory.

They glared at me as if I were a murderer.

"How is he?" I asked.

They refused to answer.

The drab waiting room was silent, except for the quiet echoes of my mother's sobs. I knelt down beside her as her head lay buried in her hands.

"Mama, is he . . . alive?"

Her nod was barely perceptible. Then I heard the muffled words, "He's still unconscious."

I looked up at my sisters and demanded, "What do the doctors say?"

Rena took pity on my desperation and whispered, "He'll live. But tests they did say he'll have some paralysis." She paused, and added, "It's pretty likely that his speech will be . . . slurred."

Malka, the eldest, hissed at me, "*You* did this to him. Let this be on your conscience."

I didn't need *her* castigation. "C'mon, where is it written that obedience demands you automatically enter your father's profession?"

I turned my attention back to Mama. "Has anyone called Deborah?"

She nodded.

Rena explained, "I phoned the kibbutz. She's coming—"

"Wonderful," Malka muttered. "She can finish the job her brother started."

Suddenly my mother stood and shouted, "*Shtil, kinder!* Stop this bickering. You are all his children—all of you. Now, Danny, you go Sunday and meet your sister at the airport. . . ."

I nodded.

"And you'll stay at the house tonight."

"No!" Malka objected.

Mama looked at her sternly. "Excuse me, while Moses is . . . ill, *I* make the rules," she said.

———

They arranged for my mother to sleep at the hospital. My sisters and their husbands could walk there after morning services.

Both couples left before night fell, so they could at least ride home on the bus.

I waited with my mother, shared a partly defrosted kosher dinner provided by the hospital through which we barely spoke, and finally, when she had been given a sedative, left for home.

As I wandered through the darkened streets, something in me prayed I would be mugged.

Because I wanted to be physically assaulted for the unspeakable crime I had committed.

————

Though she was exhausted from the flight, and fraught with worry, Deborah looked healthier and prettier than I had ever seen her. Tanned and slender, she was totally unlike the pale, slightly overweight teenager I remembered.

We hugged each other tightly, in a moment of both joy and sadness. I had been at the hospital earlier and could reassure her that Papa had regained consciousness at six A.M., spoken briefly with Mama, and then gone to sleep.

"When can I see him?" she asked urgently.

"So far they're only allowing Mama to go in. They may let him have more visitors this evening."

"Danny, what exactly happened?"

I told her of my Great Betrayal and Malka's accusation of attempted patricide.

"Listen, Danny," she said affectionately, "no law says we have to live out our parents' fantasies."

I looked at her. A lot more had changed than her appearance.

———

Understandably, Deborah felt pretty grimy from the plane trip and wanted to wash and change. While she was showering, I sat on the bed, happy to be in her room again.

A small overnight case was flipped open, and underneath two paperbacks I noticed a photograph of a radiant woman holding a handsome blond baby. The background clearly was the kibbutz.

The woman was Deborah.

And it did not look like someone else's child.

———

I was in such mental disarray that I couldn't find the words to broach the subject with Deborah on our ride to the hospital. The focus of all my anxiety was my father's health.

When we arrived my half sisters and their husbands were all crowded around Papa's door, keeping impatient vigil.

Naturally, Malka greeted me with another reproach. "You didn't come to services yesterday."

I protested that what I did with my life was none of her business. I did not feel I owed her the whole truth, which was that I had felt too guilty to appear in public. I had spent the entire morning up in my room praying on my own. But she continued haranguing me, arguing that if I had come to *shul* they could have called me to the Torah and then said a special prayer for Father's recovery.

I retorted that if she felt so strongly, *she* could have gone to Beth El, the new Reform synagogue on Ocean Parkway, where women are called to the Torah.

"They're not real Jews," Malka retorted. "They have organ music—like a church."

"They had all kinds of music in the Holy Temple," Deborah said. "Read Jeremiah 33:11, and you'll find an allusion to Psalm One hundred being performed by the Levitical chorus and orchestra."

This stupid debate would have become even more acrimonious had Mama not appeared from inside the room. None of us dared ask how he was. We merely gazed at her.

"He talks—a little fuzzy, but he talks," she began quietly. "The doctor said the girls can see him one at a time—"

"Thank God," Malka muttered and started to go in.

"No." My mother stopped her. "He wants to see Deborah first."

My eldest sister froze in her tracks. "Why?"

"Because that's what he wants," Mama asserted.

I could see that Deborah was herself unsettled by this curious disregard of family hierarchy. Scarcely daring to breathe, she tentatively opened the door and entered.

She was in with him for about ten minutes, after which he spoke with the other sisters. As we stood outside, I asked Deborah how he was. She shrugged "Okay"—and had to bite her lip to keep from crying.

"What's wrong? Is he still angry with you?"

She shook her head. "He . . . he asked me to forgive him."

In the ensuing moments, I allowed myself a scintilla of hope. Perhaps he and I might also have a miraculous reconciliation.

When she came out, Malka answered the question before I could even pose it. "He doesn't want to see you, Daniel—not at all."

"But why?" I pleaded.

"He says his son must become a rabbi. The Master of the Universe demands it."

At that moment, Deborah—bless her—gripped my arm and squeezed it hard. It kept my heart from stopping.

———

It was strange. During the bus ride home from the hospital Deborah and I scarcely exchanged a word. I assumed she was silent out of concern for Father. I later discovered she had been thinking the same about me. And yet we had so many things to share. So many thoughts that could only be our secret property. Despite the distance and the lapses in communication, we knew that we were still the best friends that we had or would ever have.

By the time we got home, I could no longer bear the suspense. I made us both some lemon tea and sat down across from her.

"Deb," I started tentatively, "can we have one of those heart-to-hearts we used to have when we were kids?"

"I'd like that too."

I then asked her straight out, "Deborah, do you have a child?"

She answered without blinking, "Yes."

"How come you didn't tell me you were married?"

She hesitated for a moment and then said, "Because I'm not."

I was too shocked to say any more and assumed she would interpret my silence as a subtle question mark, a delicate demand for more information. But she vouchsafed none.

"Hey look," I remarked at last, "I'm not making a moral judgment . . ."

Her mouth was closed so tightly that her lips were white.

"Okay," I said in defeat, "if you don't want to tell me—"

"No, no," she cut me off. "I do, I want to. But it's just so hard."

"Fine," I answered, "drink your tea. I'm in no hurry." In truth I was burning with curiosity and could not keep myself from asking, "Was he somebody from the kibbutz?"

She held back for a moment, then answered softly. "Yes, someone at the kibbutz."

"Oh, I guess those stories about 'free love' aren't apocryphal."

What an unthinking *shmuck* I was. That really hurt her.

"It wasn't just an affair," she protested, tears welling in her eyes. "He was in the Air Force." She added softly, "He was killed."

"Oh, God," I said, desperately groping for words. "That's terrible. I'm so sorry."

I put my arms around her. We held each other tightly for a moment, then wept together.

Ironically, she tried to comfort me. "Danny, Danny, it's okay. The baby's got grandparents on the kibbutz—and about a dozen brothers and sisters."

"Does Papa know?"

She shook her head.

"Mama?"

She shook her head again.

"But why? It would still bring them some joy to know about the baby. By the way, is it my nephew or my niece?"

"A boy," she answered tonelessly. "His name's Elisha."

"Elisha—'God is my Salvation,' " I translated as a reflex. "That's lovely. What made you choose it?"

For some reason she was unable to answer this straightforward question.

"Hey, Deb," I said as cheerfully as possible. "This is still something we should celebrate. *Mazel tov*. He looks like a sweet kid. I wish you'd brought him along."

I couldn't keep from adding, "He might even have consoled Papa for my premature death."

"C'mon, Danny," came her rejoinder, "don't talk that way. You two will work it out."

"No," I shook my head. "He swore he'd never speak to me again unless I'm Rabbi Luria. And that means never."

"I still don't understand why you couldn't go through with it," she said. "What difference would a few more weeks have made? That might have pacified him—and bought you time."

"That's just it," I answered, growing angry. "I wanted to stand up to him, to show him that he couldn't push me around anymore." Her face seemed frozen as I murmured, "Yes, I know I'll burn in Hell for this."

"I thought we Jews didn't believe in Hell," she said.

"Sorry, Deb," I pedantically corrected her. "We do—it's called *Gehinnom*. So if you want my future address, better write on asbestos."

She looked at me quizzically. "I don't get it. You

believe in Hell. You believe in the Day of Judgment. Do you believe in God?"

"Yes."

"Then why can't you be a rabbi?"

"Because," I answered, pain wrenching me, "I don't believe in myself."

38

Deborah

All the world will come and greet Thee
And praise Thy glorious name. . . .

The congregation sang the concluding hymn loudly and fervently. Then, as they bowed their heads, their spiritual leader raised his hands in benediction.

May the Lord bless you and keep you,
May He cause the light of His countenance
to shine upon you and be gracious unto you,
May He lift his spirit toward you
and grant you peace.

As the huge organ pipes began to sound forth with the solemn notes of Albinoni's "Adagio in G minor," Rabbi Stephen Goldman, dressed in black robes and a hat that, except for its color, looked like a cardinal's biretta, strode energetically down the center aisle of Temple Beth El. He stood at the exit, personally extending Sabbath greetings to his congregants as they left.

Though the Tabernacle was air-conditioned, their numbers were few on this hot June evening. After some three dozen handshakes, the crowd had thinned enough for Rabbi Goldman to notice the deeply tanned young woman standing nervously in the center of a distant pew.

He caught her eye with a smile and bade her exchange Sabbath greetings. "*Shabbat Shalom,*" said the rabbi, as he shook her hand. "You're new, aren't you?"

"Actually, I'm only here for a few days."

"Oh," he responded. "And your name?"

"Deborah," she replied. Then, self-consciously added, "Deborah Luria."

"Not one of *the* Lurias?" he asked in genuine awe.

"Yes," she answered hesitantly.

"What on earth brought you to worship here? Don't you people regard us as pagans?"

"I'm not exactly one of them anymore. I live on a kibbutz."

"Wonderful," he reacted enthusiastically. "Which one?"

"Kfar Ha-Sharon. Do you know it?"

"Indeed I do. Several of my classmates in the seminary spent summers there. Don't you can tomatoes or something?"

"Not exactly," Deborah smiled. "We freeze potatoes."

"Well, at least I knew it was vegetables," he joked. "Can you wait a minute while I shake a few more hands? I'd like to chat."

She nodded.

In a matter of moments, Deborah and the young rabbi were seated in adjacent pews, sharing Israeli reminiscences.

"I enjoyed your sermon, Rabbi."

"Thank you," he replied. "Korah's rebellion against Moses lends itself to a host of modern analogies—including the Board of Trustees of a Temple."

"Will you be speaking again tomorrow morning?" she inquired.

"Yes, on the special Isaiah portion."

"I recall chapter sixty-six," Deborah said. "I love the image of Jerusalem as a woman in labor. The metaphors are striking."

"You certainly know your stuff," the rabbi commented. "But I would expect no less from the daughter of the Rav. How long will you be here?"

"I can't really say. My father's had a stroke. He's still in the hospital."

"I'm sorry to hear that. How serious is it?"

"Pretty bad," she replied. "But we hope he'll come through with a minimum of damage."

"With your permission, I'd like to say a prayer for his recovery tomorrow morning. Will you be here?"

"That's very kind of you. Yes, of course I'll come."

"Fine," he answered. "Then we'll call you up to read the Torah."

Until this instant, Deborah had regarded herself as liberated. Now, she suddenly realized she was not.

"Oh, no—no, I can't do that," she stammered.

"I don't see why not," Rabbi Goldman countered. "I'm sure you read Hebrew better than I do. And, besides, all you'll need to say are the blessings, which—"

"I know the blessings," she stopped him. "It's just the way I was brought up."

"You don't have to spell it out," he replied sympathetically. "But are you bold enough to defy tradition and taste a little equality?"

She hesitated. But only for a millisecond. Come on, Deborah, she thought, you've waited your whole life for this.

"Yes," she answered bravely. "I'd be honored to read the blessings."

"Good," Rabbi Goldman said. "The honor is mutual. I'll see you tomorrow morning."

"Thank you, Rabbi," she said hastily, and darted off.

Deborah was giddy with a mixture of excitement and fear.

Tomorrow—except for the day Eli was born—would be the most important moment of her life.

As Danny had at age thirteen, she would perform the rite of passage marking her full acceptance as an adult in the Jewish world.

———

It was a beautiful June morning.

Perfect beach weather, Deborah thought to herself. With luck, no one will show up in Temple.

She was not far off the mark. Of the few dozen worshipers sitting in the vast sanctuary, most were senior citizens.

Deborah sat in the back—but on the aisle so she could get up the instant her name was called. During the early prayers she nervously twisted her handkerchief, hoping Rabbi Goldman would acknowledge her signals of desperation. But from where he sat on the pulpit, he merely smiled reassuringly.

Finally, at twenty minutes past eleven, the congregation rose. The Holy Ark was opened, and the rabbi and his cantor withdrew the Sacred Scrolls, holding them as lovingly as parents would a precious child.

The choir—accompanied by the organ—sang the words of Proverbs, which exquisitely describe the most beautiful rhapsody of the Torah:

> *It is a tree of life for them that hold fast to it, and its supporters are happy. Its ways are ways of pleasantness, and all its paths are peace.*

Two congregants—one male, one female—
helped to remove the breastplate and other finery
that decked the Scroll they were to read from,
spreading it open to the passage for the day.

Earlier, as he had entered the sanctuary before
the service and passed her row, the rabbi had whispered, "Good morning, Deborah. You're number
four."

Now she waited nervously as the cantor sang out
successively in Hebrew, "Let the first reader arise.
Let the second . . . Let the third . . ."

Deborah sat holding her breath, afraid she would
not hear her number, or would stand too soon.

At last she heard—or thought she heard, "Let
the *fourth* . . ."

She took a deep breath. Suddenly, miraculously,
she found herself in total command.

Walking straight-backed, she mounted the car-
peted steps to a point less than ten feet from Rabbi
Goldman, and even closer to the Torah.

This was the nearest she had ever been to the
sacred parchment.

Just as she reached the holy words the cantor
placed the silken prayer shawl on her shoulders. She
shivered.

This was the garment traditionally worn exclusively by men. Yet now it graced *her* shoulders,
befitting the honor about to be bestowed on her.

With silver pointer the cantor indicated where her
text was to begin. She took the fringes of her prayer

shawl, placed them on the lettering, and then kissed the shawl as she must have seen men do in her father's synagogue ten thousand times.

Almost clandestinely, the cantor then slipped a large white index card into her line of sight on the lectern. She glanced downward. They were the Hebrew prayers for the Torah, written out phonetically in English letters.

But Deborah Luria knew it all by heart:

Blessed art Thou, O Lord, King of the
  Universe,
Who chose us from among the nations
and honored us with the gift of the Torah . . .

She tried to follow the silver pointer, as the cantor sang out her portion, but her eyes were blurred with tears.

Then it was over, except for her closing prayer of thanksgiving. This time, she sang in a strong voice that acknowledged the momentous significance of the occasion.

The cantor began to chant the special prayer that was the traditional reward for one who has been called up.

Again, Deborah could almost have said it with him.

"May He Who blesses our Fathers—Abraham, Isaac, and Jacob . . ."

Then she was startled to hear something new. For

the cantor continued, ". . . and our *Mothers*—
Sarah, Rebecca, Rachel, and Leah—may He
bless . . ."

Leaning over to Deborah, he asked her Hebrew
name.

She whispered it.

". . . Deborah, daughter of Rav Moses and
Rachel, and may He send a full recovery to her
honored father. . . ."

In her short lifetime, Deborah had known mighty
and apocalyptic moments. But this transcended all
of them. It was as if lightning had struck her soul,
setting it ablaze.

She had performed her filial duty. And believed
with all her heart that God had heard the prayer for
her father.

As she walked down the aisle, various congregants showered her with "Congratulations" and
"More power to you."

It was almost too much to bear, and she would
have continued out of the synagogue had she not
spied a figure peering from behind a pillar.

"Congratulations, Deb."

Danny had come to celebrate her *bat mitzvah.*

39

Deborah

"Deborah. Telephone for you."

"Who is it, Mama?"

"I should know," Rachel shrugged. "He said his name was Steve." She quickly added the all-important question, "Is he Jewish?"

Deborah could not keep from laughing. "If it's who I think it is, he's a rabbi, Mama."

"What kind of rabbi calls himself 'Steve'? He can't be one of ours. Still, if he's . . . suitable, invite him for *Shabbes*."

"He's married, Mama," Deborah casually remarked, as she went to the phone.

"Oh," said Rachel, her enthusiasm rapidly evanescing. "Since when does my daughter come to be telephoned by married rabbis?" Looking heavenward, she added, "Father of the Universe, why must You concentrate Your tribulations on *my* children?"

"Hi, Deborah. I actually watched till I saw *four* stars in the sky to make absolutely sure it was after *Shabbat*."

"That's fine, Rabbi," she replied.

"Please," he insisted. "The only people who address me as 'Rabbi' are the congregants who object to the content of my sermons. Anyway, my wife and I were wondering if you could come to brunch tomorrow. Just bagels and lox—and a little proselytizing."

"What do you mean?" she asked with surprise.

"I'll tell you after you have your bagel," the rabbi answered good-humoredly. He gave her his address and hung up.

"What was all that about, may I ask?" Rachel eyed her sharply as Deborah strolled back into the living room.

"Nothing," Deborah replied breezily. "Only bagels."

The moment Esther Goldman opened the apartment door, Deborah felt a sharp pang, for she and her husband were each holding a baby—twins.

Deborah suddenly missed her son desperately.

Steve Goldman thought he could read the emotion on Deborah's face. "Babies are not all joy, I assure you," he explained, as he led her into the dining room. "They're wonderful, but not in the middle of the night." He pointed to a well-laden table and commanded, "Have a bagel."

As promised, the rabbi did not engage in serious conversation until Deborah had nearly finished her second bagel.

"I'm curious about something—and please tell me if this is none of my business. But I find you quite an enigma. . . ."

"Well, I've been called a lot of things but 'enigmatic' is a first. What mystifies you?"

"I'm sure you know," Steve answered amiably. "I mean, the Silczer Rebbe's daughter lives on a kibbutz so vehemently secular that they work the fields on High Holy Days. Then she comes back to Brooklyn and attends what her family surely would regard as a heathen service." He paused to let his prefatory remarks sink in and then said, "I can only conclude that you're searching for something. . . ."

"You're right," she conceded, "and I hope this doesn't sound pretentious. But I think what I'm looking for is a better relationship with God."

"That's what our movement's all about," Esther spoke up, "and not everything we do is newfangled. Calling women to the Torah used to be common practice back in Talmudic times. It was the *frummers* themselves who 'reformed' it."

"Frankly it offends me that your people look down on me because I won't accept the idiosyncratic ways they've interpreted the Bible." Fervor mounting, Steve slapped the table and said, "But the Torah belongs to every Jew. God gave it to Moses on Mount Sinai, not to some rebbe in

Brooklyn who thinks he has the franchise on holiness."

Deborah nodded. "Steve, a lot of the things you've just said sound exactly like my brother, Danny. He's just dropped out of the seminary. It looks as if my father's going to be the last of the line."

"I'm sorry," Steve remarked. "Are you upset?"

"For Papa yes, for Danny no. And, to be brutally frank, I'm not sure we need a Silczer Rebbe in a world where Silcz no longer exists."

"But that doesn't mean the line of Luria rabbis has to die out as well," Steve interposed dramatically. "Have you ever thought of becoming one? My seminary has already started ordaining women."

Deborah was caught off balance. She could only reply, "My father could probably give you a thousand doctrinal reasons why females can't become rabbis."

"And with due respect," Steve replied, "I could give him a thousand and one why they *can*. Have you got time for a lecture?"

"I'm listening." Deborah smiled.

"To begin with," he enumerated, "for centuries rabbis have insisted that the Bible's use of the masculine pronoun in phrases like 'Man doth not live by bread alone' implicitly suggests that God's laws are a kind of male prerogative. But a more accurate translation of the word 'man' in this case is 'human being' or 'person.'

"In fact, as we sit here, there's an interfaith team updating the Revised Standard Version of the Bible. They still use 'He' to refer to Jesus and God, but they render sayings like Deuteronomy 8:3 as '*One does not live by bread alone. . . .*' "

Deborah's eyes lit up. She quickly quoted the words that had been a lifelong thorn in her side. "Don't you remember Rabbi Eliezer's famous objection to letting girls learn Torah?"

"What about Ben Azzai?" Steve countered. "A sage who was just as much a heavyweight. He said that a man is *required* to teach Bible to his daughter. In fact—and I'll bet anything you didn't hear this at school—the Talmud says that God actually endowed women with greater understanding than men."

"You're right," she said with a wry smile. "They never told us that."

"It's in *Tractate Niddah* 45G," Esther interjected. "In case you want to look it up."

As Deborah marveled at his wife's learning, Steve continued enthusiastically, "You, Deborah, of all people, a descendant of Miriam Spira—"

"Who?"

"Let me show it to you in black and white."

He spun around to a bookshelf and pulled out a volume of the *Encyclopaedia Judaica,* quickly leafing through it.

"Would you mind reading that aloud, please,

Deborah?" he asked, indicating a spot on the page.

" '*Luria*—well-known family, traceable to the fourteenth century.' "

He pointed to the paragraphs below. "Continue, please."

" 'It is related that the founder's daughter Miriam—circa 1350—taught Jewish law from behind a curtain in the yeshiva.' " Deborah looked up in amazement.

"You see," Esther smiled. "You wouldn't even be the first."

After another second to let it all sink in, her husband asked, "Now don't you think it's about time that the Luria women came out from behind the curtain?"

There was a moment of uneasy silence. At last Deborah murmured, "But I have no college degree."

"Did Moses?" the rabbi grinned. "Did Christ? Did Buddha? The entrance test for Hebrew Union College is in Torah, Talmud, and the Hebrew language. I bet you could pass it now."

Deborah hesitated for a moment. "This really throws me for a loop. I don't know what to say."

"Just promise you'll give it serious thought."

"I can certainly promise that," Deborah conceded.

"Fair enough," Steve responded. "Now it's time

for cosmic things. Wait till you taste Esther's strudel."

As the rabbi's wife began to cut the pastry, Deborah felt embarrassed at having addressed so few words to her. So she came up with the polite query, "Tell me, Esther, how does it feel to be married to a modern rabbi?"

"You should ask me that question," Steve interrupted.

"Why?" Deborah asked.

"Because Esther's a rabbi too."

———

Danny was the only person she could turn to.

"Hey, I'm really sorry to burden you at a time like this."

"C'mon, Deb. If a crisis came when we expected it, it wouldn't be a crisis. I mean, just because I'm screwed up myself doesn't mean I can't be objective about you." He paused, then added warmly, "And proud as hell."

"But, Danny, let's suppose I do get accepted. Are the *B'nai Simcha* going to pay my tuition the way they paid yours?"

Danny's enthusiasm was not dampened. "Well, maybe you'll do so well in your exams, they'll give you a scholarship."

"Okay, let's say they're crazy and they do. Now tell me under which tree in Prospect Park your nephew and I are gonna pitch our tent."

Danny was silent for a moment, thumb and index

finger on his forehead, as if he were squeezing his brain.

"Be honest, Deb," he said in a tone that suggested he was convincing himself. "You know how desperate Mama and Papa are to have you back. And the prospect of having a new grandson—in his own house—would really give Papa the will to live."

"But what about when he finds out what I'm doing?"

"Who says you have to give him a detailed job description? 'Rabbi' means teacher. Just say you're studying to be a teacher. It isn't a lie—it's just not the complete truth."

Danny folded his arms and beamed with satisfaction. "Now, you can solve all *my* problems," he joked.

But Deborah remained solemn.

"Hey," her brother chided. "What's the matter now?"

"I can't lie anymore," she said softly.

"About being a teacher? I told you—"

"That's not it, Danny!" she shouted. "And when you hear what I've been hiding, *you'll* probably wish I were dead too. I'm going to explode if I don't tell somebody."

She paused, waiting for Danny's signal to open the floodgates.

"Go on, Deb. I'm listening."

"Eli isn't Avi's son. That's just a story I cooked up

to hide the truth. Somehow at the beginning it seemed so simple. . . ."

"Deb," her brother responded. "Who cares who the kid's father is? You obviously loved him. Whatever you did won't change the way I feel about you or Eli."

"Yes, it will." She took a deep breath, stared at Danny, and blurted, "It's Timothy Hogan."

For a moment he sat frozen with disbelief.

Not shocked. Not outraged. Totally numb.

The next moments passed in slow motion—even the tears that trickled down her cheek seemed to be scarcely moving.

Finally he murmured, "I thought he was a priest by now. I mean, that he was studying in Rome. . . ."

"Danny," she said. "Rome is only three hours away from Israel."

Then she told him everything.

———

"Does Timothy know any of this?"

Deborah shook her head, and even as she did, conjured up an image of her child's father the last time they had made love, his blue eyes gazing at her with ineffable tenderness.

Long ago she had sought comfort in believing that she had spared Timothy the pain. In truth, she had also denied him the joy. Now, with unmistakable regret, she said to her brother, "He'll never meet his son. He'll never even know he has one. Oh God, Danny, what can I do?"

"Well, for starters," he said, trying to cheer her, "you'll have a drink. Where does Papa keep his booze?"

"I couldn't—"

"C'mon, Deb, remember Ecclesiastes: 'Wine maketh glad the life. . . .' "

"Okay," she acquiesced, wiping her cheeks. "I could use a little gladness right now."

Rav Moses Luria's liquor cabinet was modest to say the least: a few bottles of sacramental wine, some schnapps, and—eureka! "Slivovitz?" Deborah exclaimed, as Danny withdrew their father's special Passover decanter of plum brandy. "I hear that stuff's a bomb in a bottle."

"Well," said Danny, eyeing the label. "It's a hundred proof. If it were any stronger, you could drive your car with it."

He set down two small cut-glass tumblers and filled them with the potent, almond-smelling liquid. A mere whiff made Deborah blanch.

"I think this occasion deserves a blessing," said Danny as he raised his glass and spoke in Hebrew, his voice trembling with emotion. "Blessed art Thou, Oh Lord our God, King of the Universe, Who hast kept us alive, sustained us, and brought us to this wondrous moment." He added, "If I had a ram's horn, I'd blow it too," and, looking with affection at his sister, he began a toast. "To you, Deborah—long life, health, and good luck to Eli—"

His vocal cords were suddenly paralyzed.

"My son has a real last name," she pleaded.

Danny hesitated for a moment. And then confessed, "I know. But I just can't say it."

40

Daniel

I waited in vain for a dramatic bedside call from my father. But it never came.

By now, the term had ended. The rabbis—all but those who'd fallen by the wayside—were anointed. I had to come to terms with the fact that by not taking my finals, I not only failed to receive the laying on of hands, but also didn't get a Bachelor's Degree—which can spell the difference between owning a limo and having to drive one.

Fortunately, I still had a few friends. Two, to be exact. Beller—who offered me the study in his apartment. And Ariel—at whose place half my wardrobe was already stashed. She agreed to let me and my books move in with her. She even invited me to stay for the summer while she accompanied her "keeper"—as I mockingly referred to him— on another European spree.

How I would eat, after consuming all the delicacies in her refrigerator, was another matter.

Beller also proposed the guest cottage at his place in Truro—the psychiatrists' summer refuge on the Cape. But I had to stay in the city and help Deborah prepare for the special entrance exams the seminary had arranged for her.

After lending her money for books, I concluded that the two hundred and sixty-one dollars left in my checking account would probably last all of six weeks—provided I only ate one meal a day.

I didn't confide my impending bankruptcy to Ariel. Yet before she left, this strangely amoral creature sat me down for a heart-to-heart. Apparently, as a change from the Riviera, Charlie Meister had this year rented them a villa and yacht on the Caspian, where presumably they could cruise the world's largest lake and get caviar and sturgeon at the source.

"I'm worrying about you being here all alone, Danny," she said. "I wish you'd go and stay with Aaron. At least you'd have all those analysts to talk to."

"Shrinks don't talk," I countered. "They only listen. Besides, I'll be tutoring my sister. And this is a perfect place for her to concentrate. I'll be fine."

"C'mon, Danny," she said in a surprisingly maternal tone. "You don't have to put up a front for me. What are you going to do for money?"

I was searching for some quip when I saw the

concern in her beautiful eyes and was totally disarmed.

"I don't know, Ariel," I confessed. "As soon as Deborah's set I'll have to get some kind of job."

"Would it dent your masculine pride if I offered you a loan?"

How to respond to this—that I had no pride? Or, more candidly, that I had no money? I just shrugged.

"Okay," she said, leaning toward me. "Give me your account number, and I'll have the funds transferred tomorrow—"

"As long as it's a loan," I protested. "I mean, I'll pay you back."

"Agreed." She nodded so vigorously that some of her blond locks fell across her face. "Anyway, there's no rush. I don't really need the five thousand."

"Five thousand?" I was knocked off balance. "What the hell makes you think I'll need that much?"

"I just want you to have a good time while I'm away. Besides, maybe you could invest that money wisely and be a rich man next time I see you."

"But I don't know the first thing—"

"Well, perhaps I can help. Charles is a kind of genius in wheeling and dealing. Sometimes I overhear little things. . . ." She suddenly broke off and thought for a moment before continuing in conspiratorial tones. "Danny, I shouldn't be telling you, but this summer, the biggest bread will be made out of wheat. Think about it."

The only sense I could make out of Ariel's generous words was a concern for my health and a warning to avoid bleached flour. I vowed to give it more thought when I got over the initial shock of my sudden wealth.

The next morning Charlie's Rolls stopped in front of the house to pick Ariel up. I was tempted to go downstairs with her and wave good-bye.

But I could not bring myself to see his face.

———

My sadness at losing her—something told me that we had parted without saying so—was somewhat mitigated when, at 9:30 A.M., my bank called (a first!) to inform me that my account was now healthier, thanks to a transfusion of a full five thousand dollars. I think the clerk was even more impressed than I was.

Flushed with this largess, I went out to Zabar's and bought mountains of whitefish, Nova Scotia salmon, whole wheat bread, and a few other delicacies, so I could feed my plucky sister when she showed up for her first lesson. As it turned out, we also celebrated my father's release from the hospital.

Deborah worked like a maniac. Years of academic frustration had built up a head of steam that drove her tirelessly. Not only did we study together from early morning to early evening, but God knows how long she stayed up each night to memorize the stuff we had gone through. In any case, she always knew it cold the next day.

My prediction about Papa proved totally correct. His brush with death mellowed him, and he encouraged Deborah's decision to become a "Hebrew teacher" and did not question her choice of academy. Of course, the time would come when she would have to break the news about his unknown grandson. But this could wait till he was a little stronger.

On her first visit to Ariel's pleasure dome, Deborah could not help asking just how the hell I, who had been kicked out of our own Eden, had landed in this one. So while we were drinking coffee at the end of the afternoon, I told her everything.

Despite all she had been through, she still retained a kind of innocence. Though she had had a baby out of wedlock—with a Roman Catholic seminarian, yet—none of this seemed to have affected her spiritual purity. She'd loved Tim with her soul and felt no sense of sin.

I could see she was shocked by my confession, but she suspended judgment, merely commenting, "Hey, Danny. This doesn't sound very kosher to me, but who am I to make judgments?"

Yet I also felt it was my duty to look after *her* emotional well-being.

I knew instinctively how much affection she could lavish on her son, but even in my screwed-up state I was aware that adults need the raw material of *being* loved to metabolize into love for children.

Avi Ben-Ami had always been a myth. Timothy, though real enough, would—I believed—gradually fade from memory like a figure on an aging tapestry.

I knew that her life was filled to the brim with anxiety about exams at the moment. But this would only be a short-lived anodyne for the enduring pain of loneliness. How could she sing nursery rhymes like " 'Bye, Baby Bunting, Daddy's Gone A-Hunting," knowing all the while that as far as Eli was concerned there was no daddy?

Deborah argued that her life was full, but when I pressed her for the cast of characters back in Israel who supposedly filled it, she volunteered no personal information.

Still I was able to detect a clue.

One of the special topics she was offering for the entrance exam was modern Hebrew verse, about which I knew nothing, since my seminary reserved judgment on a poet's worth until he had been dead at least a hundred years.

After a little subtle probing, I discovered that she'd taken courses with a guy called Zev, who, if he had not—as Ariel might have put it—lit her fire, at least had kindled something more than love of words.

Of course, she was defensive.

"What makes you think he's even interested in me?"

"Hey, come on, Deb. College instructors don't go offering extra tutorials unless they've got an ulterior motive. Are you gonna call him when you're back in Israel?"

She temporized, "Only if I do well on the test."

Okay, I told myself. I only hope that Zev's not married or some kind of Jewish monk.

———

Deborah took the entrance examinations on June 27 and 28, 1972. Twelve hours of written tests on Torah, Talmud, History, and Language, followed by an oral—which I knew she'd pass with flying colors.

Before she left to return to the kibbutz—and her son—Deborah had the awesome task of confronting our parents with the secret of her motherhood.

She waited till the eve of the first Sabbath Papa was home and once again comfortable in his seat at the head of the table. After dinner, with our sisters, their husbands, and children all in attendance—a kind of Greek chorus to react to the drama—she told her story.

They cried for Avi Ben-Ami, and my father pledged to say a month of Psalms in memory of his heroic son-in-law—a response which made Deborah even more ashamed. Everyone agreed it was a blessing that Avi still lived on in their son.

My mother did not hide her joy as she looked forward to the sound of a child's laughter echoing in the house once more. And, perhaps most important, my noble sister would help to heal my ailing father's broken spirit.

With my psychoanalytic bent—acquired from Beller—I concluded that my father viewed young Eli as a replacement for me, thereby consigning me not only to oblivion but to nonexistence.

But Deborah's departure on Thursday, June 29, left me wholly unprepared to confront the person I had so conscientiously avoided during the frenzy of her preparations: myself. And at this of all times, the July Fourth holiday weekend. The Festival of Independence.

It was—to be poetic—at this sunset of what would be a dark night of the soul that I received the call that altered the course of my life.

41

Daniel

It was Ariel calling from the banks of the Caspian Sea in reddest Russia. The connection was terrible to begin with, but she did not help matters by whispering.

"Can't you talk louder?"

"No," she murmured, even more quietly. "They may be tapping our line."

"Who's 'they'?"

"I don't know. The KGB or one of Charlie's competitors. The only secure phone is on the yacht, and he's out there using it now."

Egotistically, I hoped this furtive conversation might be some kind of declaration of eternal love. I was wrong.

"How much wheat have you bought?"

"I don't know, I'm sort of averaging about a loaf a day."

"Danny, this is no time for jokes," she scolded, urgency in her voice. "Charlie's been brokering for Brezhnev all summer, and the Department of Agriculture's about to announce a huge sale of wheat to Russia."

"Really?" I said, wondering what all this had to do with me.

"Why else do you think he'd take me to this godforsaken dump?" she replied. "I mean, how much borscht and vodka can you drink, anyway? Get into wheat futures as heavily as you can. And you know my little Utrillo?"

"You mean the snow scene?" I asked, my head now really spinning. "What about it?"

"It's yours. I mean it. I want you to have it."

"Be serious, Ariel. What could I possibly do besides hang it where it is now?"

She paused and then replied portentously, "Take it to the Fat Man."

"What?" Things were getting surrealistic.

But Ariel explained: While poor people get into hock for necessities, rich people just as regularly get into hock for frivolities. Naturally, they do not hot-foot it up to Harlem in their minks.

Though he dwelt, in Ariel's words, "on the shady side of discreet," the Fat Man conducted a legitimate business from his inconspicuous brownstone in the Upper 80s. The exquisite paintings hanging on his walls gave testimony to the quality of the Park Avenue matrons for whom his loans had provided the wherewithal to maintain their lifestyles.

Despite my uneasiness about her generosity, Ariel at last persuaded me that this would make her as happy as it would me. As I furiously scribbled notes, she explained the slightly Byzantine method of approaching the mysterious broker.

Almost on cue, at the very moment she completed her instructions, there was a sudden silence. I did not know if Ariel had been cut off by the KGB or merely the telephone company.

The next morning, with much trepidation, I dialed the number of the gentleman called, by his customers at least, "Laurence de'Medici." He answered on the first ring.

"Good morning." His English-accented voice resonated like a Stradivarius.

"Good morning, sir. My name is Daniel—uh—Lurie." For some irrational reason I transmuted my last name, perhaps out of fear of dishonoring my family. "I'm a friend of Ariel Greenough—"

"Ah, how is Ms. Greenough? It's been a long time."

"Fine, fine. Uh, could I possibly make an appointment to discuss a painting she's just given me?"

"Certainly, Mr. Lurie," he said affably. "Let me consult my diary." A moment later he was back on the phone. "I have a one-thirty luncheon at

Lutèce, but if you could possibly make it here by twelve?"

"That's fine," I answered hastily, gratified that I would not be subjected to the strain of anticipation. "I can be there in half an hour."

"Splendid," he replied, adding matter-of-factly, "Which is it to be this time—the Braque or the Utrillo?"

"The Utrillo," I said, amazed that he knew so much.

"Lovely," Mr. de'Medici commented. "It's not a masterpiece, but for what it is, it's quite a nice little picture."

———

For once, the image matched the telephone voice precisely.

The Fat Man was, indeed, extremely portly, and his every mannerism seemed to be a studied replica of Sidney Greenstreet, as I had come to know the stout actor in those movies at the Thalia.

"Has Ms. Greenough explained my terms?" he asked, trying to pretend he was glancing casually at the painting rather than verifying its authenticity.

"Yes, I believe so."

"And you're aware that my rates are higher than those of other lending institutions? Not out of greed, of course, but—as you can see for yourself—I have nearly thirty million dollars' worth of art on these walls and the insurance companies are absolutely Shylockian."

"I understand, sir."

"Lovely. Then I've got some splendid news. This *petite toile* has gone up considerably in the last few months." He patted the frame of the Utrillo affectionately. "It's just exceeded the one-hundred-thousand barrier."

I had a retrospective *frisson* at the thought of having lived in blithe proximity to such expensive art.

"That means I can let you have thirty thousand dollars," the Fat Man said.

"What?" I stammered.

"Thirty-five, then. I'm afraid I can't go any higher."

"Yes, of course," I answered sympathetically. "Your insurance premiums."

He then dispensed with the formalities as quickly as possible, bidding me peruse his standard contract, according to which he was lending me thirty-five thousand dollars for sixty days at the mind-boggling rate of sixteen percent. After I scribbled my (new) name in the appropriate place, the Fat Man opened a magnificent escritoire, withdrew what looked like rubber-banded, green paper bricks and began to pile up hundred-dollar bills.

"Cash?" I gasped.

"Yes," he sighed with histrionic nostalgia. "In this barbarous plastic age one rarely gets to see it. But I'm hopelessly old-fashioned."

Quickly placing the money in a slightly torn

manila envelope, he gave it to me, and we shook hands.

"Thank you, sir," I said politely.

"*À votre service, Monsieur.*"

I thought it was a good omen that the only two words I knew in French were fortuitously appropriate at this moment.

"*Bon appétit.*"

———

On my way home, I stopped in a bookstore and searched the business section for material on commodities trading. To my chagrin, every text I scanned carried the same warning:

> Although dabbling in futures seems seductive—since a few pennies can sometimes "leverage" a buy of many dollars— beginners can go bankrupt overnight.

Still, my philosophical mind deduced the unwritten corollary: If you can go bust in a day, the reverse must also be true.

I bought a couple of "How to" volumes as well as the *Chicago Commodities Booklet,* which contained the rules of the game. And I spent a lonely but productive weekend absorbing all I could about the trading of futures.

According to *The New York Times,* wheat for delivery in September had closed on Friday at $1.50 a bushel. Since you could buy a contract for five thousand bushels for only $375, if I merely used a bit of my "summer allowance" to top up the Utrillo money, I could start my career on July 5 with precisely one hundred contracts.

But there was a further problem, as my manuals cautioned:

> Margin levels can change at any moment, which means that purchasers of futures may have to put up additional funds to maintain their holdings.

That, alas, was the chaff in the potential wheat caper. By rights, in order to buy on credit, I would have to prove my ability to sustain a fall in fortune. Since this would involve something closely resembling mendacity, I could not take my business to a large, reputable brokerage firm, but rather had to find one small and hungry enough to look me over with myopic eyes.

I studied the Yellow Pages and hit upon McIntyre & Alleyn, who did business from what was practically a cubbyhole in a large Wall Street building. A blond, conservatively dressed receptionist seemed almost amazed to hear that I wanted to become a client. She quickly took my name and disappeared behind a glass partition, reemerging with a guy about my age. He had obviously been clothed by Brooks Brothers since he wore the uniform: a no-pocket, pink button-down shirt, bow tie, and red suspenders.

He introduced himself as Pete McIntyre, grandson of the founder. Inviting me back to his desk, he inquired if I wanted refreshment. I gratefully declined coffee, tea, and Jack Daniel's and got straight to the point.

When I explained the intention of my visit he remarked, "Very risky business, futures. Especially wheat—which is already played out. Wouldn't touch it with a ten-foot pole."

"Well, Pete," I persisted, "could you see yourself clear to touching it on my behalf?" At this point, I withdrew a banker's check for thirty-seven thousand five hundred bucks and placed it on his desk.

His interest perked. Somewhere along the line, he had taken my particulars—address (thank you, Ariel, for living in such a good neighborhood), phone and social security numbers.

We then got to the sticky question of how I would cover any potential shortfall.

"What exactly is your net worth, Dan?"

"Well,"—I retreated into sophistry—"doesn't that remind you of the Psalm—you know, 'What is man that Thou are mindful of him?' "

"Uh, in a way." He was slightly flummoxed but recovered himself enough to assert, "Actually, in this business we tend to be a bit more pragmatic, Dan. After all, you've just committed yourself to spending seven hundred and fifty thousand bucks—before commissions."

"Well, the way I look at it," I prevaricated, "that's just a half dozen or so Utrillos."

"Oh, are you a collector?" Pete inquired, temporarily sidetracked.

"Yes," I said, and, letting my imagination run riot, added, "Naturally, I've loaned the biggest pieces to museums. But why don't you put in that little purchase order and then we'll grab some sandwiches and I'll show you my collection."

"Let's save it for some evening," Pete responded enthusiastically. "Then I could bring my wife along. Meanwhile, I'll have Gladys take care of the buy—and lunch is on *me*."

A week later the price of wheat had gone up three cents a bushel, giving me the leverage to acquire thirty more contracts. Pete took the order over the phone without question. I declined lunch.

Wheat continued to rise and on July 19 was worth $1.57 a bushel, enabling me to buy sixty more contracts. Pete again invited me to lunch. I declined.

And my investment rose.

———

On the night of August 2, 1972, when I was holding two hundred and fifty contracts, wheat was nudging $1.60 a bushel, and I was pondering whether I should cash in my chips. I received another breathless phone call from Ariel.

"Sell every picture—sell the wallpaper, even—but buy as much wheat as you can!"

"More?" I asked in disbelief.

"Yeah, I can hardly believe it either. But Leonid and Charlie are downing vodka in the next room, so I guess we're gonna see something spectacular."

I left her collection intact, but true to her prediction, the following day wheat shot up by a full seven cents. Pete McIntyre hysterically tried to take a little profit. I now stood to lose thousands for every penny drop in price. But I was adamant. I even increased my position.

Twenty-four hours later, the amber waves of grain had risen yet another five cents. My net worth was no longer fictive. I was really worth more than a quarter of a million bucks.

"Sell, Danny, sell!" McIntyre shouted as if cheering his beloved Notre Dame football team.

"No, Pete," I said coolly, totally intoxicated with a sense of infallibility. "Now I can leverage another two hundred and fifty contracts. . . ."

"No, Danny, no!"

"Yes, Pete, yes!"

And so it went for another two weeks, with rumors of a possible Chinese buy fueling the price still further. At last, on August 23, I calmly told Pete to sell my entire position, which now consisted of thirteen hundred contracts. By now, he was so bedazzled he was almost disappointed.

After deducting their commission, McIntyre & Alleyn transferred $1,095,625 to my bank account.

So there I was, a genuine millionaire. But with whom could I share this triumph? Even if we were on speaking terms, had I called my father, he probably would have quoted the Hebrew proverb, "Who is rich? He who is content with his lot."

I did fire off a telegram to Deborah, euphorically but enigmatically informing her that I had arranged a full scholarship for her rabbinical studies.

But that was it. I had no other way to celebrate.

I sat up alone, reading, of all things, Ecclesiastes.

The next morning I took the subway to the Bronx, found a *shtibel,* a kind of Hasidic mini-synagogue, and was honored, as is the custom for strangers, with a call to the Torah. It was the only way I knew how to thank God.

As the Reader was blessing me I said an inward prayer to the Almighty, offering a deal I hoped He would not refuse: Deduct Deborah's tuition and my family's doctor bills, throw in a college scholarship for Eli, and please, God, *take the rest and give me back my father's love.*

———

Several days later, Ariel called again. This time the connection was crystal clear. I could tell she was smashed to the gills.

"Too much vodka?" I joked.

Before I could unleash my cannonade of gratitude, she interrupted. "Danny, I'm in Vegas. I'm calling to say good-bye. I'm really sorry. . . ."

I anticipated the rest of her announcement. "Then he's going to marry you? Hey, I'm really glad."

"No," she slurred. "I guess you don't know what today is."

I allowed that I knew the date, but not its significance.

"It's my birthday," she said mournfully. "My goddamn thirtieth birthday."

"So what?" I retorted, "You're Ariel, the 'brave spirit'—"

"No, Danny," she cut me off. "Thirty is a kind of statute of limitations for Charlie."

"You mean he dumped you?"

"Well, sort of. But he was totally honest up-front. And besides, he hasn't exactly left me destitute."

"Hell," I assured her. "That wouldn't matter. You can bet I'll take care of you. In fact, I'll—"

"No," she said adamantly. "You're too nice a guy to have a screwed-up wife like me. Besides, I'm only good when I'm illicit. Anyway," she went on, "Charlie's bought me a house in Bel Air and a record company. I'm in Vegas trying to sign up talent. With any luck, I'm hoping to lure Tom Jones into my stable."

"I'm sure you will," I said as fondly as I could, thinking how sad this blithe creature really was.

390

"Oh, yeah, Danny, I almost forgot. Charlie said could you please move out by Labor Day?"

"Hell, I'll move to the Pierre tomorrow. Will you promise to keep in touch?"

"No," she said emphatically. "You deserve somebody better than me."

"Can you at least tell me where to send the Utrillo?"

"Hey," she said softly, "it doesn't matter anymore. Sell it and give the money to an orphanage."

I knew that for the rest of my life I would always wonder if there was any deeper meaning to her final words.

42

Deborah

It was a terrible wrench when, on August 30, 1972, Deborah bade good-bye to the place she would always regard as home, and the people she would always look upon as family.

During her last days at Kfar Ha-Sharon, wherever she walked, friends would stop what they were doing to chat. And every conversation ended with an embrace.

Counterbalancing the sorrow of leave-taking was the inexhaustible joy in her growing son, and the prospect of actually living with him in the same household.

When Steve Goldman phoned her with the news that she had been accepted by the seminary, she was jubilant, regarding it as another small step in the battle for the equality of Jewish women.

It seemed as though half the kibbutz had boarded

the old bus to accompany her to the airport. Deborah sat holding Eli in her lap, unable to look back at the azure waters of the Galilee lest she burst into tears.

Not even the magniloquent Boaz could convince Security to let the entire group enter the terminal. He and Zipporah alone were allowed to see her off.

"Now, Deborah," Boaz admonished sternly. "I have your solemn promise you'll come back to visit us next summer?"

"I'll come back *every* summer, I swear."

"Let's take them one at a time," he replied philosophically. "But just between the two of us I'll make a special deal with you. You'll only have to work in the fields *half* a day, so you can study the rest of the time."

Eli could sense the sadness of the occasion and began to cry.

"Shush, darling," Deborah murmured, "you've got to be a big boy. Now kiss Grandpa and Grandma good-bye."

The little boy obeyed and said in a quavering voice, "*Shalom sabta.*"

———

Eli was too restless to sit still, so Deborah spent most of the flight as a human pillow. Her only respite came when a kindly stewardess offered to hold "the little sweetie"—not a word that Deborah would have used at the time—while Mama freshened up in the bathroom.

Though exhausting, her son's insomnia kept her mind from other, far more awesome thoughts.

Like the prospect of going to the university and still managing to be a good mother to her son. And most of all, living once again in her father's home.

She had left as a naughty girl being punished. Now she was returning as a woman who had suffered pain and tasted the most fundamental joys of life.

Would her father accept her change of status? Would he acknowledge her as an adult? Even if he didn't, there was no alternative. Not until she found the means to be independent.

This worried her even more than the classes at the seminary, for she was excited at the prospect of studying Talmud, Torah, and history with the men. She did not think beyond classes to her actual ordination as a rabbi. That was still so many years away, she could not take it seriously enough to be frightened. She already had enough challenges on her hands.

———

The reality of his sister's baby only fully struck Danny at the Arrivals area. He rushed to embrace the warm little human being. Deeply moved, he looked at Eli and, keeping his gaze riveted, remarked softly, "He's got his father's eyes."

"Yes," Deborah whispered.

Sleepy and frightened, Eli began to wail. "C'mon, kid, this is your Uncle Danny," he cajoled and then asked Deborah, "What does he speak? Hebrew? English?"

"Half and half," Deborah replied.

Suddenly Eli grew calm. He placed a warm, dimpled hand on Danny's neck.

Nodding to the porter, his uncle ordered, "Follow us through here. My jalopy is waiting."

The waiting limousine was so long it looked more like a railroad car.

A blue-uniformed chauffeur held open the door. After making certain that Deborah and Eli were comfortable, he went around to see to the luggage.

As her brother slid in and closed the door, Deborah protested, "Danny, are you crazy? This must be costing you a fortune."

"Nothing's too good for my sister," he replied affectionately. "And as far as money is concerned, my only problem is what to do with it."

As concisely as possible, he told her of his sudden rise from rabbinate to riches.

To Deborah, her brother's worldly success and outwardly euphoric manner were very troubling. He seemed to be trying too hard to convince her that he was happy.

"Do Mama and Papa know anything about this?"

He shook his head. "No, I can't find the courage to pick up the phone. I mean, Papa's a lot better, but he very seldom leaves the house except to go to *shul.*"

His facial muscles had now tired of maintaining a

smile. His eyes were downcast, and he said softly, "I wish I could help them, Deb. Especially Mama. I'd love to take her to Saks Fifth Avenue and let her buy out the store. But I know he'd despise what I've done and wouldn't let her go. I only wish there was a way . . ." His voice trailed off.

"Tell me," she said affectionately.

He took her hand. "Deb, if you could find out anything they possibly might need—for the house, for the school, anything—just let me know. I want to do something, you know—helpful—useful. . . ."

To Deborah's astonishment, just as they approached the Brooklyn Queens Expressway their driver pulled over to the shoulder where a second limousine was waiting.

"What's going on?"

"I'm afraid this is where the prodigal son has to get off. I can't show my face in Father's territory. I feel like Spinoza being excommunicated."

She grasped her brother's hand with both of hers. "Listen, Danny," she whispered fervently, "I'll make things better, I swear I will. Now, will you keep in touch?"

"You're gonna have to do that too," he replied. "I'm at the Pierre Hotel."

He fumbled in his pockets and produced a black silken book of matches. "The number's here. Call me whenever the coast is clear. May I at least take my nephew out sometime and buy him a few million toys?"

"Yes," Deborah laughed, as they kissed each other on the cheek. As Danny embraced little Eli, he whispered, "Take care of your mother, okay?"

In an instant, he was gone.

As her own limousine drove off, Deborah watched through the back window as Danny climbed sadly into the other car.

43

Deborah

She who had left in silence and disgrace returned now as glorious as Queen Esther.

Deborah and Eli were greeted not only by her parents and sisters, but by dozens of relatives, all of whom wanted to see the child they now eagerly proclaimed to be even more beautiful than his pictures.

When all were assembled, Rav Luria commanded them to silence. In addition to having some residual stiffness in his right side, he still looked pale and somewhat fragile as he raised a toast to the arrival of the newest member of the Luria family . . . Eli Ben-Ami.

Deborah could tell that her father had carefully choreographed the entire occasion, for no one mentioned her brother's name.

Had he been killed by a truck instead of exiled,

they would at least have referred to him as "Danny, of blessed memory."

But nothing was said. Nothing.

There was no way she could ascertain whether any of them knew about his golden metamorphosis.

Yet, when the celebration was at its height, Deborah caught sight of her mother sitting in a quiet corner, weeping inwardly for her only son.

No sooner had the last guest departed than the resident Lurias sat down to a late supper.

The Rav smiled at his blue-eyed grandson and, even while the youngster persistently dropped his spoon on the floor to make Deborah retrieve it, said, "*Nu,* my boy, let's speak a little *mamaloshen.*"

Deborah bristled at her father's proposal that her son chat in Yiddish. In some ways the old man still lived in the ghetto of Silcz, and the phrase "mother tongue" was reminiscent of an age when Yiddish was the language of second-class citizens—the mothers who were not privileged to learn Hebrew.

She, on the contrary, had just come from a land where Hebrew was the language not only of blessings, but of asking for the nearest bus stop.

Though he was far from being like the abominable Rabbi Schiffman, her father was no longer Deborah's idea of a modern Jew. Yet he was still her father. She would have to learn to separate ideology and affection.

One of her great consolations in taking her son away from Israel had been that at the very least he would learn English. Now she realized that while she was at school all day, Eli would be hearing less English in Brooklyn than he had on the kibbutz. And she did not want him growing up to read the words of Shakespeare or Thomas Jefferson as a foreign tongue.

———

Dean Victor Ashkenazy—a broad-shouldered man who looked more like a football coach—stepped up to the podium.

He smiled down at his audience, which consisted of perhaps a dozen men and half as many women, then uttered words that Deborah Luria had never dreamed she would hear spoken to rabbinical students:

"Ladies and gentlemen . . ."

What a long and arduous road she had traveled to reach this moment.

"Before it became an honorific title," the dean continued, "the word *rabbi* simply meant 'teacher.' Interestingly enough, it only took on its modern meaning during the age of Hillel, which was of course contemporaneous with the ministry of Christ. . . ."

Yet another word Deborah never imagined she would hear in a Jewish seminary.

"In the Gospel of Mark, when Peter sees a vision of Jesus talking with Elijah and Moses, he addresses his leader as 'rabbi.' And historically speaking, the other two Jewish worthies could not claim the same title." The dean paused, scanning the faces before him.

"A rabbi has no priestly privileges. He is not an intermediary between God and Man. He cannot grant absolution—that is only in the hands of the Almighty. He can command no one. But he must command respect. For he is first and foremost a teacher. And it is his awesome duty to act as a paragon of earthly behavior and of reverence for the Divine.

"Permit me to repeat a very old joke, which is as painfully true today as it was when I heard it as a child.

"Several matrons are sitting on the beach in Florida bragging about their children's accomplishments. One says proudly that her son is a surgeon. Another boasts that hers is a successful lawyer, and so on.

"Finally, they get to Mrs. Greenberg. 'So, *nu*— what about your children?' they ask. And she replies, 'Well, my son is a rabbi.'

"At which all the women groan, and one commiserates, '*Oy vey*, what a terrible job for a nice Jewish boy.' "

His audience smiled, sharing this uncomfortable truth.

"Of course," the dean quickly added, "today it's also a terrible job for a nice Jewish *girl*. And I'm afraid that the designation 'job' is all too appropriate.

"The near-impossible task of a rabbi is to try to keep his or her fellow Jews from giving in to the exhaustion of maintaining an identity in a non-Jewish world, of being a minority that wishes to remain one. Not to mention the sheer pressure of trying to do good in a world in which evil not only exists, but as God tells Isaiah in chapter forty-five, verse seven, He Himself created it."

He walked to the front of the lectern to be closer to his listeners, and spoke in softer, almost confidential tones.

"That goes to the heart of the matter, doesn't it?

"For the rest of your lives, no single day will pass when you are not approached by someone—Jew or gentile—and asked the most challenging existential question a man or woman of God will ever confront: 'Why did our loving, righteous, merciful God also create evil?'

"This is the problem that Job could not comprehend. Nor can the victims of the Holocaust—or its survivors. Our task as rabbis then is to teach men and women how to live in this imperfect world.

"Your studies for the rabbinate will be twofold. One—looking back and assimilating the heritage of millennia of sages, and passing it like a torch in an ancient relay race to the younger generation.

"The second, perhaps more important, is the pastoral function of a modern clergyman—counseling, comforting. Above all, showing the way—in the words of Micah, 'To do justly, and to love mercy, and to walk humbly with thy God.'

"I offer you my blessings and good wishes."

———

Deborah spent the morning with Moses and the afternoon with Jonah.

Though she had been familiar with the texts from her independent reading, this was the first time she could freely discuss them with a professor and her fellow students.

Their lecturer in Old Testament, Professor Schoenbaum, was an acknowledged hard-liner who had voted against the ordination of women and was known for such gratuitous barbs as, "Even a woman could understand this concept."

Yet when on the first day it became apparent that Deborah's knowledge and insight far exceeded her classmates', and Schoenbaum concluded the day's proceedings with, "I think you could all benefit from following the scholarly example of Miss Luria, who thinks like a real yeshiva *bocher.*"

In other words, a *man.*

As she left the building to go home that first day, she was greeted by her faithful mentor.

"What a nice surprise," she exclaimed, rushing to embrace him.

"I just wanted to be sure everything went okay," her brother replied.

"Oh, Danny, I love it. I mean I've spent my whole

life reading Torah by candlelight. Now, all of a sudden, I'm in the bright sunshine with people who share the same values."

"Was it tough?" he asked, as he took her heavy book bag and flung it over his shoulder.

"Compared to a slave driver like you, Professor Schoenbaum is a pussycat."

"Well," Danny said with mock humility. "That was all part of my plan—to harden you for the real battle. Got time for a cup of coffee?"

"Just a quick one," she replied.

They sat at an outdoor café and drank cappuccinos, as the reluctant prodigy of Wall Street meekly inquired, "Have you had a chance to talk to him? Papa, I mean."

"No, not yet. I don't want to hurry things."

"Yeah, yeah," said Danny, trying to mask his disappointment. "I guess that's the right strategy. It's just that I'd like to know if he . . . needs anything."

"To be frank," she replied, "I think what he really needs is time. But I'll work on it, I promise you."

"And Mama?" he persisted. "Did you find out if there's anything I could get her?"

"Well,"—Deborah smiled—"I think she daydreams about a toaster oven. But it might look awfully suspicious if it suddenly appeared in the kitchen. Why don't we wait till her birthday and we can give it to her as a present?"

"Okay . . . good . . . sure," said Danny, who seemed edgy and nervous. "But I wanted to do more. What I really wanted was to buy them that bungalow we always rented in Spring Valley. You know, so they could use it whenever they want." He paused and then confessed, "As a matter of fact, I've already bought it."

Deborah took his hand. "Danny," she said softly, "try to be patient. I don't think you can buy Father's love."

"Yeah," her brother replied bitterly. "That's what I was afraid of."

"Tell me," she asked, trying to lift his mood, "what do you do with yourself all day?"

"Well," he replied, "my admirers at McIntyre & Alleyn have set me up with my own desk and secretary, and they're sponsoring me so I can take the official broker's test at the Institute of Finance."

"Ah," smiled Deborah. "So you're a student again?"

"Yeah, I'm enjoying that part. Unfortunately, they're all treating me like the Delphic Oracle— waiting religiously for my next prediction. Hopefully I'll learn enough to know what I'm doing. In any case, I've bought a computer—I need all the intelligence I can get."

"You must be very busy."

"I'm not," he answered morosely. "I don't enjoy just watching my money earn interest. I've got a six-bedroom apartment on Fifth Avenue—and five of them are empty. For some reason I can't even buy friends."

"Have you seen Beller?"

"Yeah, I took them to dinner the other night. He fixed me up with a shrink. . . ."

"And?"

"Instead of exploring my psyche, the guy kept asking me for stock tips."

"Is that a joke?" she asked.

"Am I laughing?"

He studied her with a wan smile and asked, "It's such a schlep from here to Brooklyn. Won't you and Eli come and live with me in Manhattan? I mean, I'd hire a housekeeper—or anything you wanted."

Deborah wanted very much to say yes, but she needed time to think about leaving the parental embrace she had just regained.

"Danny . . . Eli's in a nice play group run by two Israeli girls. I don't want to uproot him again. I'd like to live at home a little while longer."

Danny's tone became more assertive. "Hey, big sister, can't you manage to break your newfound umbilical cord? You don't really think I believe it's Eli's play group that's keeping you at home, do you?"

"No," she said, lowering her eyes. "I'm kind of embarrassed to admit it, but something in me still hungers for Papa's approval."

Danny nodded and confessed in a whisper, "I understand. That makes two of us." Suddenly self-conscious, he glanced at his watch. "Hey, it's getting late. I'll walk you to your car."

"I don't have one," she replied.

"Oh yes, you do." He took her arm as they left the café.

Deborah sensed extravagance in the air. "No," she pleaded, "not another of your block-long limos."

Danny smiled. "I only wish it were. But I don't want them to know that we're even seeing each other. That would create too much tension at home. So I've made a compromise. He's called Moe."

"What?"

From afar she could see a yellow cab parked near the corner, with its corpulent driver, in a flat leather cap, leaning against it.

"Getta move on, youse guys. We're gonna hit all the traffic at the tunnel."

"Who's that?" Deborah inquired.

"That's Moe, your friendly driver—and believe me I interviewed plenty before I chose him. He'll pick you up after school every day and take you home—so you don't have to hang from a strap, and you can either study or rest."

Deborah was touched. "Danny, you don't have to spoil me."

"But I'm dying to do *something* for you, Deb. At least let me give you Moe."

Deborah hugged her brother affectionately and whispered, "Thank you, Dan."

"Hey, c'mon," Moe urged. "Another five minutes, we'll need a helicopter."

He held the door open and tipped his hat. As Deborah stepped inside, she thought to herself, If Danny had only heard Dean Ashkenazy's speech, he'd know that he was acting as a paragon himself—of goodness, generosity, and love.

Deborah would think about her brother standing alone on his balcony, watching the carnival of activities in Central Park—lovers sitting on the grassy meadows, old people strolling, young people jogging, middle-aged people moving at a gait somewhere between the two—and being a part of none of them.

Why was he so lonely? she wondered. Surely, a boy—she could not think of him as a full-grown man—who had once had such *joie de vivre* could have found friends if he really wanted to. Why had he exiled himself from normal life?

44

Daniel

As wise as he is, even my father cannot make history repeat itself.

For two years I had been pleading with Deborah to live on her own in Manhattan. During this time I had made a number of lucky calls in the market, predicting thc devaluation of the dollar in '73 and the rise in orange juice futures in '74, and I was now so wretchedly rich that I had a twelve-room duplex to house my loneliness.

I had even proposed to Deborah that I divide my apartment so that we could be at once close but independent. Still, she stubbornly chose to remain in Brooklyn and commute to HUC each day.

But an incident one Sunday finally forced her to confront the conflicts she felt about living as a grown woman in her parents' home.

She had been upstairs working on a term paper

and was on her way to retrieve a book from Papa's immense Talmudic library, when just outside his study she heard the sound of a young boy reciting, *"In Ershten hut Got gemacht Himmel un erd."*

It was my father teaching his grandson the immortal words of Genesis in the medieval language of Yiddish.

Deborah peeked in, at once touched and dismayed to see her own son seated on Papa's knees—as I had once been—learning Torah.

For a moment she was gratified that her son was enjoying a privilege that she had never had. Then she suddenly realized that our father was obsessed with having Eli relive Papa's experience with me.

The moment Papa left for his usual Sunday tour of the yeshiva classes and she was sure she could not be overheard, Deborah called me to say she would be moving into my place that night—at least until she could find something of her own.

She was more gratified than surprised when I told her that—out of folly, or more likely optimism—I had already requested permission for the construction work that would create apartment 1505-A from the "rib" of my own place.

Since, I informed her happily, she would no longer have the assistance of my mother as cook and babysitter (something I subsequently made her see as yet another prolonged adolescent attachment), she was pleased to learn that I had also found her a suitable housekeeper. The matronly Mrs. Lucille Lamont, though a native of Birmingham, Alabama, had been cooking kosher for nearly forty years. From a gastronomic point of view, Eli would endure no cultural shock.

As she told it to me that night, both Papa and Mama were upset at her sudden decision to leave and took small consolation in her promise to spend as many Sabbaths with them as she could.

The sadness in my father's eyes had evoked a feeling of guilt that almost broke her resolve. In the end, thank Heaven, my sister's instinct for survival buttressed her will. At three P.M. Moe arrived with his taxi to help her move out lock, stock, and tricycle.

A surprising thing occurred as Deborah was packing her last textbooks. Mama appeared, ostensibly to help, but, as it turned out, to support her decision.

"Believe me, my child," she said. "No one will miss little Eli more than I. But this is the right thing for you. How else are you ever going to—" She hesitated.

"Going to . . . what, Mama?" Deborah demanded.

"You know," my mother stammered, flustered and embarrassed, "live a normal life."

"And what I'm living now isn't normal?"

"No," she answered. "You're not married."

Although my father had stubbornly refused to ask her where she was going, both of them knew full well. Mama even gave Deborah a message for me.

"Be sure Danny wears a warm coat."

PART IV

45

Timothy

The men, twenty-six of them, lay prostrate on the cold stone floor of St. John Lateran. Dressed identically in snow white albs, they looked from above like a cluster of linen cocoons. Though they were on a carpet, the stones beneath still afforded some palliative for their burning cheeks, which had been heated by the Roman summer and stoked by the ardor of the crowds.

It was June 29, 1974, the Feast of Saints Peter and Paul, one of the holiest on the ecclesiastical calendar. Henceforth, it would have an additional significance for all of them. This was the awesome day on which they would distance themselves from earth-bound mortals and wed their souls to the eternal Church.

Among the twenty-six were four of the five Irish-American candidates (George Cavanagh had been ordained the previous year). Relatives had traveled from as near as Naples and as far as the Philippines to see this ceremony. Yet among the large contingent of American families gathered to bask in their sons' and nephews' glory, there was no one present to take personal pride in Tim.

In a way, he preferred to experience this moment on his own. For that was how he would face the rest of his life. Publicly his bride would be the Church. Privately he would know her by her true name: loneliness.

All in red, on a throne three steps above them, sat the principal celebrant, Emilio Cardinal Auletta, Prefect of the Congregation for Catholic Education. It was a special honor for these young men, one which signaled that they were especially cherished by the aristocracy of the Holy See.

After the Gospel of the Ordination Mass, the candidates were presented to the cardinal and for the final time were asked about their dedication and readiness.

Then they knelt, heads bowed, as in gravelly, stentorian tones Father John Hennessy, rector of the North American College and today's *Cerimoniere*—Master of Ceremonies—read out their names, and turned to His Eminence. "Holy Mother Church asks you to ordain these men, our brothers, for service as priests."

"Do you judge them to be worthy?" the cardinal asked.

"After inquiry among the people of Christ and upon recommendation of those concerned with their training, I testify that they have been found worthy."

As Tim knelt, the cardinal placed his hands gently upon his head. In the ensuing silence, something deep inside him began to stir, and gradually to crescendo, as each of the other officiating priests in turn blessed him with the laying on of hands.

Paradoxically, it was the most physical and the most spiritual moment of the day. Those who had themselves already been touched by the hand of God now passed that sacred honor on to Tim. It was a way of saying, We are all brothers now.

After Cardinal Auletta sang the Prayer of Consecration, the assisting priests quickly vested the candidates with red stoles and chasubles. They who had begun the morning prostrate, white as chrysalises, had risen like newly born butterflies in the crimson of the Church.

Now they were privileged to stand on either side of the cardinal and concelebrate the Mass.

As he walked in the final procession down the central aisle and saw the guests, relatives, and friends all in tears, despite his determination Tim asked himself, Who is crying for me?

———

If the ceremony had been solemn, the postlude was anything but staid. At the North American College, corks and flashbulbs popped as Asti

Spumante poured with such gusto that many a cup ran over.

Among the American prelates who had made a special journey for the ordination was Tim's patron, Francis Mulroney, the former Bishop of Brooklyn, who had recently been elevated not only to the Archbishopric of Boston but had also been honored with the red hat of a cardinal.

As Tim tried to proffer congratulations, His Eminence replied, "Not a bit of it, my boy. It's you who deserve the praise. And I'm delighted you've decided to move downtown and continue your studies."

Tim smiled. "I'm sure Your Eminence used a little influence to arrange the generous burse I received."

"It was the least I could do. You'll love it at the Gregorian, Tim. I don't have to tell you that the institution has produced more cardinals and popes than Harvard has senators and presidents. By the way, do you know how our European colleagues refer to the *Pontificia Universitas Gregoriana*?"

"Yes, Your Eminence. They call it 'the Pug.' That's very amusing to the American ear."

"Yes," Mulroney chuckled in assent, "especially the Brooklyn ear."

"You're not by any chance referring to my early career as a hoodlum, are you?" Tim joked.

"No, of course not," the Cardinal responded. "Although Father Hanrahan was wont to speak of your left hook with something bordering perilously on adulation."

Once again Tim was driven to think, They seem to know everything about me, *everything*.

The newly ordained Father Timothy Hogan walked out in the gardens of the North American College, high above the Eternal City. And on what should have been the most joyous day of his life, looked to Heaven and asked with an aching heart, O Lord, how long must I serve Thee before I learn the truth of who I really am?

46

Timothy

"**D**omine Hogan, *surge*."

"*Adsum*," Timothy responded as he rose to his feet. By now he had become accustomed to the Latin language not only for lectures but for classroom dialogue.

Five mornings a week for the past two years, Tim had climbed the left-hand marble staircase of the main building of the Gregorian to the lecture hall on the *primo piano*. Here, from 8:30 to 12:30, he and nearly a hundred classmates, all seated at small wooden desks, had attended the required courses for the Licentiate in Canon Law.

A few of his courses dealt with philosophy, theology, and history of Canon Law. But essentially their focus was on a laborious word-by-word, sentence-by-sentence, section-by-section examination of the massive *"Textus,"* officially known as the *Codex Iuris Canonici.*

"Domine Hogan."

Tim looked up at Professor Patrizio di Crescenza, S.J.

"Dic nobis, Domine," the lecturer continued, *"Habenturne impedimenta matrimonii catholicorum cum acatholicis baptizatis in codice nostro? "* Does our Code specify any obstacles to the marriage of a Catholic and a baptized non-Catholic?

Tim answered without hesitation, *"Itaque, Domine. Codex noster valet pro omnibus baptizatis et impedimenta matrimonii sunt pluria."* Yes, Father. Our Code applies to everyone who is baptized, and the obstacles to such a marriage are numerous.

"Optime," Father di Crescenza exclaimed, as he turned his gaze elsewhere to select another student to enumerate some of the specific impediments to the marriage of true minds but differing churches. Tim could not help wondering why the Roman Catholic hierarchy took for granted that it had jurisdiction over *all* Christians.

None of it was easy going. On more than one occasion, when Tim was memorizing the nuances of an Apostolic Constitution, he thought, Sometimes I wish we had an exciting case like a fox who ate somebody's chickens. Anything remotely *relevant* to everyday life.

It reminded him of a long-ago conversation he'd had with Danny Luria, as the two were riding in the subway from Brooklyn to Manhattan. The young rabbinical student had offered some examples of the quibbling legislation in certain portions of the Talmud.

The text Tim held in his hand was nearly a thousand pages long, setting forth two thousand four hundred and fourteen Canons—some on the most arcane matters—all of which he would be required to know inside out by the time of his written and oral exams for the Licentiate.

Some were rules that every priest must learn in order to serve a parish. For example, the subject of annulments for nonconsummation of a marriage.

And yet in committing these to memory, Timothy wondered about the hypothetical opposite— consummation *without* marriage. Or at least without ceremony.

Could God sanctify a marriage consecrated merely by love?

———

"*De impedimentis matrimonii clericorum,* 'On the problem of priestly marriage'—an excellent if dangerous thesis topic, Father Hogan. But if anyone can do it justice, it is a mind like yours," Professor di Crescenza pronounced, speaking Italian now, since Tim had come to see him during his office hours.

One of the elderly scholar's greatest satisfactions

was that he had been permitted to teach beyond the age of seventy, which meant that he could still enjoy the stimulation of contact with bright young minds—in Tim's case, he had decided, a brilliant one.

"It's a territory that, after Vatican II, needs quite a bit of recharting. I know you'll produce something very valuable, Father Hogan."

Suddenly, from behind, Tim heard the irascible voice of an antiquated man addressing Father di Crescenza.

"Patrizio, *habesne istas aspirinas americanas? Dolet caput mihi terribiliter.*"

Tim turned and immediately recognized the wizened face peeking through the doorway. Father Paolo Ascarelli, S.J., was the official Latin Scribe, one of the highest-ranking members of the papal household.

Again the professor answered in Italian. "I'm terribly sorry, Paolo, all I've got is the ordinary Italian aspirin. I gave you my last miracle pill on Monday."

"Oh, the devil's work," the old man responded, wincing as he held his aching head. "I have a cerebral agony that only something like Excedrin can cure. Do you think maybe we might call the American Embassy?"

As his professor smiled indulgently, Tim interrupted. "I've got some Bufferin, Father, if that'll help?"

"Ah," the priest exclaimed, "you have been sent from Heaven, young man. What is your name?"

"Timothy Hogan, Father. Unfortunately, the bottle's in my room."

"Where are you lodging?" asked the old man.

"On the Via dell'Umiltà."

"Ah . . . 'the street of humility.' Well then, if you're as fit as you look, it probably won't take you more than a few minutes to hurry there and back. Thank you in advance."

Father di Crescenza shot a quick glance at his pupil, trying to telegraph the message: You don't really have to indulge this hypochondriac.

But Timothy answered, "Of course, Father Ascarelli. I can do it in no time."

"Splendid, splendid," God's suffering servant replied. He called after Tim, who by now was halfway out the door, "And should you perchance come across a bottle of San Pellegrino on the way back . . ."

Less than ten minutes later, a breathless Timothy Hogan laid a small plastic jar of Bufferin and a large bottle of mineral water on the seminar table.

The professor himself had already left. It was his nightly routine to walk the considerable distance from the Gregorian University to the far periphery of St. Peter's and number five Borgo Santo Spirito, the Jesuit headquarters.

"Sit down, sit down, Father Hogan," Father

Ascarelli commanded, as he went through the ritual of taking his headache remedy. "I want to know you better. In the short space you were absent, your professor never ceased to sing your praises. I rarely listen to Patrizio—he's getting on in years, you know—but he stopped chattering long enough to show me some of your written work. It's outstanding."

"Thank you, Father," said Tim, both embarrassed and pleased.

"Of course you've got a way to go before you're a Doctor of Canon Law," Ascarelli cautioned. "But your Latin is absolutely splendid. I dare say if you hadn't been trained in America you'd be nearly up to my standard by now. Forgive an old man's arrogance, but I don't think you can truly learn the language of Cicero anywhere but within echoing distance of the Roman Forum."

He sighed histrionically. "What a pity about Vatican II. It all but made my once-honored position obsolete. Thank God they still issue papal bulls, encyclicals, and letters of appointment in Latin, or they'd probably have put me in a home for irregular verbs."

Timothy smiled.

"Tell me," the scribe asked with a twinkle in his eye, "do you think Our Savior knew the Latin tongue?"

"Well," Tim responded warily, "He might have

pleaded His case with Pontius Pilate in the Roman language. Certainly, Eusebius records a conversation between the Emperor Domitian and some of Jesus' relatives."

"So he does!" cried the old man with relish, "*Historia Ecclesiastica* 3:20. You have a good point there, Timothy," he exclaimed, adding cordially, "We must talk again."

"I look forward to it," Tim replied with equal warmth.

"In that case," said Ascarelli, "I'd like to leave you with a token of our little chat." He placed his wrinkled hands on the table and pulled himself wearily to his feet. "Take it," he said.

"What?" Tim reacted with astonishment. The scribe was pointing to the very bottle of tablets he had given him.

"They were all yours to keep," Tim protested.

"I know, I know," the old man said with a grin. "But if you take them back, I'll have an excuse to send for you so we can chat some more. Thank you. I feel much better. Pray for me."

Before a bewildered Timothy could respond with, "And you for me," the old priest had vanished.

———

As the months passed, Father Ascarelli's headaches seemed to increase, necessitating more and more of Timothy's visits to his apartment in the Governatorio, a large rambling building inside the Vatican.

Now and then, the old man would ask Tim to make a clean copy of whatever document he had just rendered. It was not long, however, before he casually added, "And if you see a rhetorical lapse here and there, don't hesitate to correct it. Remember," he said with a wink, "only popes are infallible."

By the spring of the year, the two had established a rapport that transcended not only aspirin but Latin as well. It was the closest thing to a father-son relationship that Tim had ever known. There was nothing he would not do for the papal scribe, and, perhaps more important, the feeling was mutual.

"I'm too old for this job, Timothy," he complained one afternoon, in his usual cranky tones. "But His Holiness trusts no one but me to latinize his words. It's too great a burden, so I had to offer my resignation."

"What?"

"Oh, it wasn't accepted, of course. I wouldn't have done it if I had thought there was the slightest chance. But I did receive a concession, namely permission—and stipend—to hire an assistant. Do you have any notion whom I should select?"

The two men smiled at each other.

"I have a thesis to finish," Tim answered shyly.

"Yes, but you are young and you can work on it at night, when fossils like myself are buried in their beds. Trust me, my boy. If you live up to the advance reputation I've given you, you'll fulfill your greatest earthly ambitions."

"And what do you think those might be?" Timothy asked warily.

Without directly answering his question, Ascarelli replied, "As I see it, the greatest pleasure on earth is dining at the pontiff's table." Mysteriously, he added, "They're not your usual vulgar Italian sort."

"What, Father?" Tim asked, genuinely puzzled.

"The wines, of course. They're French. Naturally, as an Italian I deplore the defection of Pope Clement the Fifth. But when the papacy finally returned from Avignon to its rightful home in 1377, it brought back barrels of the finest Burgundy. And pontiffs have continued to look north for God's most blessed grapes. *Experto crede,* they're worth working for. Good night, my son."

Despite his mentor's encouragement, on his way back to the Via dell'Umiltà, Tim lingered in the Piazza Navona, contemplating the extravaganza of song, women's laughter, and the clinking of glasses. He looked at the perennially festive Romans, and wondered if all he had sworn to forsake was worth the sacrifice.

47

Timothy

PONTIFICIA UNIVERSITAS
GREGORIANA ROMAE

AD DOCTORATUM CONSEQUENDUM
IN FACULTATE IURIS CANONICI

(Cum specializatione in Iurisprudentia)

R. P. TIMOTHY HOGAN

PUBLICE DEFENDET DISSERTATIONEM
DE IMPEDIMENTIS
MATRIMONII CLERICORUM

(Director R.D. Prof. Patrizio di Crescenza)

DIE VENERIS 26 MAIAS 1978, HORA 16 IN AULA MAGNA

In a matter of months—*de facto* if not *de jure*—Tim had become the papal Latin Scribe, and Father Ascarelli, the nominal holder of that office, served merely as his editor.

But when his manuscripts were handed back without even the slightest grammatical or critical notations, Tim began to wonder whether the scribe was reading them at all.

He finally worked up the courage to ask his mentor.

"Timotheus, my dear boy," Ascarelli replied, "why should I waste my failing eyesight studying a letter of appointment to a new bishop in Texas, when he won't understand anything but the fact that he's changing his ten-gallon hat—*petasus decem congiorum capax*—for a miter? I'd rather spend the time composing an article for *Latinitas* on my strategies for the game of American football—*pila pede pulsanda americana.*"

Sending various important papal communications to every part of the world had a twofold effect on Tim. First, it made him appreciate the longitude, latitude, and magnitude of the Catholic population. It also offered a taste of what it felt like to send commands to a place like, say, Sri Lanka, and know they would be obeyed without the slightest equivocation. The pope's pen could alter the destiny of millions with a single stroke.

Somewhere between encyclicals and letters of appointment, Tim managed to study for his exams, and to pass them all with distinction. When he and Ascarelli were topping off an evening of work— that is to say, *his* work—with a glass or two of *grappa,* Tim would be careful not to overindulge, for he would still have to bicycle back to the Via dell'Umiltà to study and write, while Ascarelli—and presumably the rest of the Vatican—slept.

Though the college building itself was a converted seventeenth-century convent, some evidence of modernity could be found in its small but well-equipped gymnasium. And since no amount of hard work rid Timothy of all his energies, he could sometimes be found at two or three in the morning at the rowing machine. To distract himself from other preoccupations, he had created a challenge: an imaginary trip from Italy to New York. Each evening he would log the number of miles he had rowed, hoping to reach two thousand by the end of his first year.

One night, as Tim was sweating his way toward the Azores, a voice from the not-too-distant past broke the spell of his athletic self-hypnosis.

"God, Hogan, what are you doing, trying to give yourself a heart attack?"

It was George Cavanagh, who had long ago on one hot afternoon in Perugia confided in Tim his fall from grace. Now he seemed transformed by the clerical collar he wore into a strangely imposing figure. Tim nonetheless groaned inwardly. He had been relieved not to see George for more than a year. Cavanagh was a painful reminder of his final afternoon with Deborah long ago.

"You should be asleep," Tim retorted with a gasp.

"How can I possibly sleep when my role model is still awake?" George smiled as he seated himself on one of the padded benches, picked up a dumbbell, and desultorily began to curl his arm in an approximation of exercise. "Really," he continued, "I'm not being sarcastic. I do admire you, Hogan. You're some kind of tactical genius. I mean, I've heard you praised as a champion of the left, the right, the conservatives, and the avant-garde. You're a real master of *romanità*."

Tim accelerated his stroke and began to breathe heavily, sucking in the air with a pulmonary wheeze.

"Don't tell me you don't know what *romanità* is, Hogan," Cavanagh continued. "It's the secret of success in Vatican society. The ability to sugar-coat enigma with charm. If Machiavelli were alive today, he'd probably write a book about you."

Tim glared at him.

"Come on," George said, his tone now one of candid admiration. "Word has it that Fortunato's invited you to teach a seminar in Canon Law."

Tim rowed on without comment as George continued to probe.

"Word also has it that you've turned him down. What exactly are you going to do?"

"Why don't you tell me, Father Cavanagh? You seem to know everything already."

"Well, all I've heard is that you've asked for a pastoral post back in the States. I know that 'work in the field' looks good on your C.V. But are you sure it's the right move to leave Rome just when your star is rising?"

"I'm a priest, not a politician," Tim said angrily.

George rose. "Sorry, Hogan," he said with undisguised exasperation, "I'm just lousy at *romanità,* otherwise known as artful groveling. *Pax tecum.*"

———

In late spring, Tim concluded his thesis. The Defense was set for the fourth week in May, under the aegis of Father Angelo Fortunato, the Dean of the Faculty himself.

"It's a great honor," Ascarelli assured Tim. "I, of course, will be in attendance. Which reminds me, I haven't received my invitation."

"To the Defense?" Tim inquired with surprise.

"Of course not. That is open to the public. I meant the reception in your honor."

"I'm afraid there isn't one," Tim replied.

"Are you mad, *figlio mio*?" Ascarelli scolded. "Or are you just trying to keep an old man from a decent meal?"

"Truly, Father, there's no party—"

"Aha," the scribe retorted, shaking an admonitory finger. "They just haven't told you yet. But I can assure you, when Dean Fortunato presides over a Defense, a lavish celebration always follows."

The scribe's words were prophetic. When Tim arrived back at the college a little after one in the morning, he found an envelope slipped under his door. The gold embossed Coat of Arms on the back bore the motto *Civitas Dei est patria mea*—The City of God is my true homeland.

Tim tore it open. In magnificent calligraphy, under a letterhead stamped *Cristina, Principessa di Santiori* and with an appropriately noble address near the Palatine Hill, he read:

My dear Father Hogan,

Forgive my boldness, but so many of your accomplishments have taken wing and flown over the Vatican walls, that I feel I already know you.

My good friend Dean Fortunato tells me that your "Defense" (which I am sure will be more of a eulogy than a questioning) will take place on the twenty-sixth of this month. As I understand it, no one from your family will be able to cross the Atlantic for this occasion, and so I take the liberty of proposing a reception and supper in your honor at my home.

If you find my proposal acceptable, please give me the names of any friends with whom you would like to share the celebration of your Doctorate.

Very truly yours,
Cristina di Santiori

Tim smiled with pleasure, then switched on his hotplate to boil water for coffee. There was much work still to be done before the sun peeked over the Esquiline hill.

It was only at six A.M. when he woke after a meager three hours' sleep to celebrate morning Mass that the significance of the letter began to sink in.

The Santioris were distinguished members of what was known in Rome as the *aristocrazìa nera*—"the Black Nobility." These were families of laymen who had for centuries been influential princes of the papal court, the so-called "Privy Chamberlains of Sword and Cape."

Some had hereditary duties at papal ceremonies. Dynasties like the Serlupi Crescenzi, who had served as Masters of the Horse for centuries. Or the Massimo clan, who held the hereditary office of Postmaster General.

But the Santioris claimed an even higher distinction. They had served as Grand Masters of the Sacred Hospice, the highest rank a layman could achieve in the papal court. Perhaps the most significant sign of their true nobility was the fact that their names never appeared in the press. When they gave a party it was not reported. Anyone worthy of knowing about it would have been invited, and that excluded the Fourth Estate.

As Tim was sitting in a corner of the refectory,

pensively spooning cornflakes, George Cavanagh appeared.

"May I join you, Father Hogan?"

Tim looked up, trying to disguise his annoyance, and replied desultorily, "Be my guest."

George, who had already seated himself, surprised Tim by his seemingly genuine cordiality. "Hey, listen, Hogan. I know it's open to everybody—but would it make you nervous if I showed up at your Defense? I mean, over the years I've needled you a lot. I was just wondering if my presence would put you off."

"No, that's okay," Tim answered. "Nothing could make me more nervous than I already am."

"Thanks. I look forward to not understanding a word."

Moved by this gesture of thoughtfulness, Tim immediately reciprocated. "George, there's going to be a little party afterward . . ."

"Santiori?" George smiled, his eyes widening eagerly.

"Yes."

"Thanks. I was hoping you'd ask."

———

Though its outcome was not in doubt, there was nonetheless an air of suspense at Tim's thesis defense. The *Aula Magna* was packed with students, faculty, and—at least somewhere in the crowd— the Princess of the Black Nobility with her entourage.

Tim had arrived fifteen minutes before the start of the ordeal, only to find Father Ascarelli already present. "My hearing's so antiquated I must always sit in the front row," the old Jesuit declared, then leaned forward to give his protégé some whispered advice—and a secret weapon.

"Remember. Despite the learning of those who will ask the questions—also be prepared for the idiotic ones. Just say '*non pertinet*' and move along. No one knows this topic better than you, since it is freshest in your mind. Dean Fortunato will of course pose a query, but it will be more like an oration to show how clever he is. Merely flatter him by agreeing wholeheartedly and proceed."

"Thank you, Father," Tim said with a wan smile.

"Now, take this," the old man urged, pressing something into his hand. It was in fact a Hershey bar.

"One of my former students sends me boxes from America," Ascarelli explained. "They're perfect for stimulating the mind."

Tim could not help laughing with joy at this eccentric gesture and willingly devoured the fuel as Ascarelli watched with satisfaction.

"One final word," Ascarelli called out affectionately as Tim was moving away. "These will be your last two hours as a student. *Enjoy* them."

In a way, it was like the final of a tennis match. Timothy skillfully volleyed back dozens of differing questions: powerful serves, carefully placed lobs, and some—as the old man had predicted—

completely out of bounds. There was even the cheering, although it was, of course, silent, except for the occasional murmur of appreciation from an elderly Jesuit in the first row: *"Bene . . . optime."*

When it was over, Tim's relief was tinged with a touch of sadness. Ascarelli was right. This had been his final moment to shine as a student.

———

The huge Palazzo Santiori sat in elegance atop the Via San Teodoro. Every one of its high-ceilinged rooms was graced by magnificent works of art, some dating back to the early Renaissance, when the artists had worked under the direct patronage of the family.

"This is unbelievable," said Tim, standing in awe before a depiction of the Annunciation by Raphael. He had steeled himself to meet modern power brokers, but was unprepared to confront Old Masters as well.

"The Santiori have always had an eye for talent." The princess was a short, buxom woman with gray hair, and eyes that outsparkled her many gems. "This version is earlier than the one in the Vatican. But really, when it comes to Raphael, there is no such thing as second best, don't you agree?"

"Oh, yes, of course," Tim answered quickly, wondering how it must feel to live in a house that held so many priceless treasures.

"Come, Father—may I call you Timoteo?—let me introduce you to some fascinating people. Drop over some other day and spend all the time you want looking at paintings."

Tim followed the principessa up the wide, sweeping marble steps. Her high heels clicked in near synchrony with the rapid beating of his heart.

After another flight of stairs, they came out onto a roof garden, lit by torches placed at intervals along the iron railing. The terrace commanded a breathtaking view of the Eternal City. From this vantage point one could see the entire Roman Forum illuminated by spotlights. Tim's eyes remained fixed on the noble remnants of Empire, partially because he did not feel worthy enough to face the living grandeur that was milling on the terrace.

The sound of a familiar voice brought his attention back to the present.

"*Nunc est bibendum*, 'now is the time to quaff,' as the poet says," he heard Father Ascarelli declare. "Horace was a truly Roman poet, was he not?"

Tim glanced at his mentor and was moved to quiet laughter. "You're certainly making good use of the occasion, Father," he remarked, looking at the flutes of champagne the scribe held in either hand.

"Well," Ascarelli joined the laughter at his own expense, "at my age I must make every effort to exploit the moment. I've already drunk your health, and will again. I'm grateful that you had the principessa put me on her list. Now I can die with an impeccable social pedigree."

"*Carpe noctem*," Tim said warmly.

"*Et tu, fili,*" Ascarelli responded and vanished in a sea of eminences.

At that very moment, Tim vowed to drink only mineral water so he would remember every face, sound, and syllable of this occasion . . . in his honor.

Nonetheless, he woke next morning with a headache. Not from anything he had drunk or eaten, but rather, he concluded, from yesterday's vast intellectual efforts—an afternoon of shining and a night of being shined upon.

He had returned to the college just in time for morning Mass, then climbed exhaustedly into bed, and slept through breakfast.

That evening, George sat down beside him in the refectory. "You almost could have been elected last night, Hogan."

"What?"

"By my count, there were sixteen Princes of the Church—and not all Italian either. When the Cardinal Archbishop of Paris comes to raise a glass to you, I'd say that you'd get all the French votes without much problem."

"Was he really there?" asked Tim ingenuously. For by now, he had learned to ignore his rival's caustic references to his ascent upon the ecclesiastic ladder.

"You mean you didn't see him? You probably were too busy staring at La Loren."

"What?"

"Come on, you'd have to be blind not to notice glorious Sophia and her attentive consort Carlo. We're allowed to look, you know. Who *did* you talk to, anyway?"

Tim spread one hand across his throbbing temples and said, "George, I'm trying to remember everyone I met, but it's impossible. And I'm not kidding. You can come up to my room and see the list I've written down—"

"Now that's an invitation I won't pass up," George reacted eagerly.

Later, as they leaned over Tim's wooden desk comparing scraps of paper, George remarked with undisguised awe, "This is a real honor roll. Are you still determined to go back to Brooklyn and hear adolescents and old ladies saying their confessions?"

"I'm going to St. Gregory's," Timothy answered firmly. "That's where I come from."

"Okay." George shrugged, "But for someone with your gifts I wouldn't think that was the best way to serve the Church."

"Well, what are your own plans?" Tim inquired.

"No doubt an unwise career move," George explained, "but I've requested a special assignment with the Jesuits in Argentina. I figure I'll probably have a better chance of getting to Heaven if I do good for others and not just well for myself."

"That's very commendable," Tim commented sincerely. "To be honest, I never thought of you as—"

"Altruistic?" George was not offended. "I know. I'm sometimes surprised myself by the growing strength of my Christian feelings."

———

The invitation came in the same near-parchment envelope with the Santiori seal.

My dear Timoteo,

The flowers you sent were both extravagant and unnecessary. For the real bloom at our little party was your extraordinary self. All my friends were captivated by your charm and wisdom.

I know that you must be terribly busy in these final days before your return to America, but I wonder if you could spare the time to come to the Villa for lunch this Sunday. I will be entertaining one of my relatives whom I am sure you will enjoy meeting.

It was signed simply *Cristina*.

———

This time there were only four of them, seated at great distances from one another at the long white-linened table in the sumptuous Santiori dining room. The princess, Timothy on her right, her sister Giulietta on her left—and, at the end, a handsome, gray-haired cleric in his midfifties.

He was introduced as the principessa's younger brother, Gianni, but Tim knew precisely how he was listed in the Pontifical *Annuario:* Monsignor Giovanni Orsino, Assistant Secretary of State for Latin America.

The brother was no less courtly and charming than the sister.

"If you do not mind," he said, with a puckish apology to Timothy, "I would appreciate if we could converse in English. That is to say, if you could speak English, and I would try to make myself understood on something better than the primitive level that I now possess."

"Of course," Timothy replied, politely adding, "But your English is very good."

"Please, *senza complimenti.* I would be more happy for you to correct me. I will take no offensive whatsoever."

"Of course, Monsignor," Timothy responded, ignoring the cleric's immediate malapropism. "But do you get to use much English in the Secretariat?"

"Not in my current situation," Monsignor Orsino replied. "The documents I deal with daily are of course in Spanish. And real Spanish, as they say, is merely Italian spoken with a lisp. But some day—"

At that moment, from far down the table, his older sister interrupted portentously, "Very soon, Gianni, very soon."

Orsino seemed to blush and pointing at Cristina said to Timothy, "Well then, as my optimistic sister says, 'very soon,' I may receive a new assignation."

"I believe Monsignor means 'assignment.' "
Timothy smiled politely.

The princess assumed the privilege of rank and completed her brother's thought. "Gianni is a very senior member of the Secretariat, and in eighteen months, when Bonaventura retires, the post of Apostolic Delegate to Washington falls open. And so . . ." With a delicacy uniquely Italian, the princess gracefully gestured the rest of her sentence, which seemed to indicate that she would see to it that her brother became Archbishop Bonaventura's successor. Hence the need to buff his English to a diplomatic shine.

"I wanted very much for you two to meet," she continued, "especially since all American episcopal appointments are made through Rome. And Rome depends heavily on the advice of its Washington Apostolic Delegate."

"Cristina," Tim protested, "I'm just going to be an assistant pastor. I don't even see myself as a bishop in my dreams."

"But *I* do," the principessa insisted.

———

As he walked slowly away from the Palatine Hill in the glow of the late afternoon sun, Tim thought that the title Princess, when applied to Cristina Santiori, was no empty designation.

Though her crown might not be visible, her power was.

48

Deborah

During the second half of Deborah's studies toward ordination, the focus changed from ancient law to modern life.

The aspiring rabbis were taught psychology—how to respond to the many cries of the heart they would receive from members of their congregations. Marital pressures, divorce, illness, death. The full cycle of grief.

"And here," Professor Albert Redmont emphasized, "the rabbi differs from the psychotherapist. For most doctors nowadays are too busy to give their patient much more than a pharmacological evasion to be swallowed three times daily. Rabbis have more potent medicine.

"Faith can lift the fallen. Even heal the sick, better than the scientist, whose powers are circumscribed by the frontiers of knowledge—which is where belief in God *begins*."

The future rabbis worked in hospitals, homes for the aged, and kindergartens. They learned first-hand how to confront an anguish that is even worse than death itself—the dying person's fears of the unknown.

"Hold my hand and repeat after me, 'Yea, though I walk through the valley of the shadow of death, I will fear no evil. For Thou art with me; Thy rod and Thy staff they comfort me. . . .' "

"Thank you, Rabbi Luria. Thank you for your kindness."

For Deborah, this human contact only magnified her love for the calling she had chosen.

———

For the High Holy Days in her senior year, Deborah was posted to a nonexistent congregation in New England.

That is to say, she would be temporary spiritual leader of a group of Jews who came together only on the so-called Days of Awe—the New Year and Yom Kippur—to expiate their sins and reinvigorate their faith.

The congregants in question were scattered throughout an area of some three hundred square miles near the Canadian border in New Hampshire and Vermont. Each year they would gather in the town hall or Unitarian church of a different village, bringing the one Torah Scroll—guarded all year round by an orthopedic surgeon—and absorb enough solidarity from their coreligionists to survive yet another twelve months in a region so remote that they were outnumbered by the black bears.

"Dean Ashkenazy," Deborah said politely after she had been given her assignment, "I don't want to seem as if I'm complaining, but most of my classmates have been sent to larger towns, even to colleges." She pointed to her distant bailiwick on the map. "Why me?"

"The truth?" the dean inquired.

She nodded. "Please."

"The college jobs are easy. Anyone can speak their language. Besides, if those kids feel strongly enough about a holiday to cut their classes and worship, then you've got an eager audience." He paused thoughtfully. "Deborah, the people you'll be preaching to are losing touch. They spend the year—especially at Christmas—wondering why they should work so hard at being different. They're a small group to begin with, but the rate of their attrition is alarming.

"So," he said, "I have to send the best we have." He looked at her and concluded, "And that, Rabbi Luria, is *you*."

49

Deborah

Laroche, Vermont, lay so far north that even in late September the leaves were already gold and crimson.

A sharp wind breathed a chilly greeting as Deborah stepped off the bus, her limbs stiff from the long journey, which had passed, it seemed, through all of Europe and the Middle East, as the Greyhound lumbered through such exotic towns as Bristol, Calais, West Lebanon, and Jericho.

Laroche was the last stop, and Deborah was by this time one of only two remaining passengers.

For a moment this caused some confusion, since a pair of middle-aged men bundled in parkas and scarves were waiting for "Rabbi Luria." Neither the eighty-year-old farmer nor the young woman in camel's-hair coat and briefcase seemed to fit their preconceived notion of a Jewish man of God.

448

The senior citizen was greeted by his family in the *joual* dialect of Quebec. By an uncomfortable process of elimination this left Deborah.

"Didn't they tell you I was a woman?" Deborah asked, as she noted the continuing uneasiness of Dr. Harris and Mr. Newman, the official welcoming party.

"Well, I'm sure they probably did," the doctor replied. "But I was so busy setting things up—not to mention setting broken bones—that I guess the whole notion didn't sink in. To be honest, HUC has usually sent us men."

"You mean so they could help you chop down trees and build the *sukkah* after Yom Kippur?"

"No, of course not," Mr. Newman said with an embarrassed smile. He opened the door to his station wagon for her. "I just wonder what the wives will think."

"I would have thought they'd be pleased to see a woman on the pulpit."

"Oh, of course," Newman mumbled. "It's just that you're so—"

"Young?" Deborah offered.

"Yes, there's that," he conceded, and almost involuntarily added, "And you're also pretty."

"Is that a plus or a minus?" Deborah asked.

Newman had painted himself into a conversational corner. The physician stepped in to rescue him. "Please, Miss Luria—I mean Rabbi—don't take offense. It's just that we're so isolated up here.

These gatherings are our only connection with what's happening in the Jewish world."

"Well," said Deborah lightheartedly, "I guess you might say *I'm* what's happening."

———

The Unitarian church was filled with people Deborah would never have thought of as Jews. It was as if their appearance had been altered by the strange clime and, compressing years of evolution, they had come to look indistinguishable from their gentile neighbors.

As the church organist struggled through the music Deborah had brought for him, and she rose to the podium in her white robes and square canonical hat, there were murmurs of wonderment from the worshipers and an uneasy tension Deborah could feel.

"*Shana tova.*" She smiled. "As you can see, you're getting something new for the New Year."

The laughter of relief that filled the church testified to the success of her tactic.

"We'll begin our service on page one thirty-one of your prayer books."

The organist struck a chord, and Deborah stunned her congregation with the beauty of her voice, as she sang in Hebrew, "How goodly are your tents, O Jacob," and then led them in the reading of the English translation. "Through the greatness of Your Love, I enter Your House. In awe I worship before the Ark of Your Holiness."

She continued. "In the twilight of the vanishing year, we turn to You as our parents have done before us in their generation. We come into Your Presence together with all other holy congregations of Your people . . ."

Her fervor united these scattered enclaves of people, who gathered twice a year to renew their identity and their faith. She, too, was swept up in the feeling of cohesion.

"May the sound of the ram's horn echo within us and awaken our longing for goodness and new lives in our souls."

By the time the service had reached the reading of the Torah from Dr. Harris's single precious scroll, Deborah had touched them all.

At the reception afterward, it seemed as if every congregant wanted to speak to her, not merely to shake her hand, but to take advantage of her presence for a kind of public pastoral consultation.

"You can't believe how much this means to us, Rabbi," said Nate Berliner, an orthodontist from a town near the Maine border. "My family drove a hundred miles to these services. And if next year you're a thousand miles from here, we'll drive there too."

"Why doesn't your seminary send people like you up here more often?" several worshipers asked. But most of the conversations were expressions of loneliness. How hard it was for them—as one man put it—"to keep our religious batteries charged. A jump-start twice a year just isn't enough."

"I'll speak to the dean," Deborah answered. "Maybe he can arrange for a rabbi to come up on a monthly basis."

"Then we could have a Sunday School for our kids," added another congregant.

"Just one thing," said Mrs. Harris, who had initially been outraged to see a woman on the pulpit. "They'd have to send somebody as wonderful as you."

———

When she told Danny about her experiences, he volunteered to return with her for the Day of Atonement.

It was not merely curiosity. Disenfranchised Jew though he was, Danny still trembled at the thought of God's Judgment. He wanted to observe this most solemn day in the company of the person he loved most in the world.

Deborah put him to good use, persuading him to chant the Torah portion to an admiring audience who could see he knew it practically by heart. At the very end of the long day of fasting and prayer in which the congregation stood in front of God's open gate, praying to be inscribed in the Book of Life for another year, Danny sounded the ram's horn.

He blew it with such vigor that Mr. Newman later remarked that he believed that it could be heard by God Himself.

During the long ride home Danny could barely contain his enthusiasm.

"Now I understand the phrase 'God Who watches over the remnants of Israel,' " he said. "Those people live in the opposite of a ghetto. It takes three hundred and sixty-five days to round them up. If you want a real challenge as a rabbi, Deb, why don't you apply to be stationed there when you graduate?"

"Sure, then Eli could go to a different school every day. Why don't *you* take the job?"

"May I remind you that I'm not a rabbi." He smiled evasively.

"That can easily be remedied, you know," Deborah countered. "I mean *I* don't have to tell *you* that it's not like becoming a priest. Any rabbi can say the words and ordain another Jew. So next year when I graduate—"

"I'll think about it," said Danny, trying to pretend she had not struck a chord. After a pause he asked, "When you said 'priest' just then—in fact, whenever you say that word—do you still think of Tim?"

Deborah answered quietly. "Yes. He's always somewhere in my thoughts. Especially on the Day of Atonement."

"It wasn't a sin," Danny asserted, gently putting his hand on hers.

She was silent for a moment and then said, "I keep wondering when the hell I'm going to tell Eli. I owe him the truth."

Danny nodded. "Speaking of full disclosure, have you thought how you're going to tell Papa you're going to be the next Rabbi Luria?"

"This was a good night to ask me," Deborah responded. "I made an oath during the closing prayers that I'd stop lying this year."

"When?"

"When I get the guts."

50

Deborah

As an elective course for her senior year, Deborah had chosen Modern Hebrew Poetry, telling herself she should make up for not completing Zev's course back in Israel.

By happy coincidence she found his name on the cover of the text they would be using: *The New Jerusalem Anthology of Modern Hebrew Verse,* translated and edited by Z. Morgenstern.

"What differentiates this new collection from all the others," Professor Weiss declared in his opening lecture, "is that Morgenstern not only knows the language, but he's a poet in his own right. . . ."

I never knew that, thought Deborah to herself. He never let it slip in class six years ago. Was it ego on his part—expecting all of us would know? Or maybe—as she thought more likely—he was simply shy. So shy, in fact, that he had waited one week too long to invite her for a cup of coffee.

Her attention refocused on the Professor's words just in time to hear, "Matter of fact, Morgenstern's reading some of his own verse at the Y next week. It's sold out already but if any of you care to go, I think I can arrange it—since he's staying at my house."

She wondered what to do. Not whether she would go or not, for that was far beyond the slightest doubt. Her only quandary was whether she should ask for a seat in the first row, if that were possible.

Would he be pleased to catch sight of her, smile, and therefore read with more emotion? Or would she embarrass him and throw him off balance?

Or, worst of all, would he not even remember her?

———

The night of the reading Deborah came home after her last class, had dinner with her son, and since Danny was out of town, left him under Mrs. Lamont's supervision before going out, explaining to Eli that she was going "to an important lecture."

The auditorium of the Ninety-second Street YMHA was filled to capacity as Professor Weiss walked to the podium to introduce the poet. The hall was so crowded she had to squeeze into a seat in the back row.

She scanned Zev's face from afar as he sat on a chair upstage. He looked the same—almost the same, she thought—although a little tired.

After Professor Weiss's flattering introduction, Zev stepped shyly to the podium. He reached into the pocket of a well-worn tweed jacket, and pulled out a pair of half-moon glasses.

Ah, thought Deborah, time doesn't stand still. He never needed those before.

She remembered with what passion he had read the Hebrew verses in their seminar. But there the room had been small, and there had been only twelve students. Now Zev's audience was in the hundreds, and his performance self-conscious bordering on the timid.

He began by reciting deft renderings of contemporary Hebrew poets and then a series of his own satirical vignettes of academic characters.

Only at the end did he read anything remotely personal, but it was the most courageous poem she had ever heard, a surgical exposure of his inner soul—an elegy to his son, newly *bar mitzvah,* who had died shortly thereafter.

Now it was clear why Zev had left these words for last. For, after reading them, he had no voice to go on.

The muted applause was not for lack of admiration, but a gesture of commiseration.

———

Professor Weiss had mentioned casually to Zev that one of the female rabbinical students had requested a ticket for tonight's reading.

"Deborah—what an incredibly nice surprise. How come you just disappeared?"

"It's a long story," she replied, elated to be shaking his hand.

"How's your little boy?"

"He's not so little anymore. He's in first grade at the Solomon Shechter School."

"That's terrific," he replied. "Say, the Weisses are having some people over. It's just a little buffet. I'm sure they won't mind if I bring along another guest. Are you—uh—here alone?"

"Yes, matter of fact," she answered. "And I'd love to come."

———

Though everybody at the party seemed to want a private session with the guest of honor, Zev managed to find a quiet spot to be with Deborah.

"That was very sad about your son," she said softly.

He simply nodded.

"I lost more than a child," he murmured. "My marriage fell apart. I guess we thought that if we split, the guilt would go away. I don't know about Sandra, but I still feel like a criminal for having normal blood cells and yet somehow causing his leukemia." He raised a hand to stop her before she could speak.

"Don't tell me it's irrational—I've spent too much time listening to a shrink tell me that. They don't seem to understand that nightmares haunt you even if you know they're not real."

"I understand," Deborah said quietly. Then quickly added, "So you were married when we met?"

"I plead guilty, Deborah. I wasn't the best of husbands. But I'm not that way anymore. Would you believe that in the eight months since our divorce, I haven't made a single pass at a woman?"

Deborah responded with a candor that astonished herself. "Would you believe that since . . . my husband died, I've never thought of a man . . . that way?"

Zev trapped her with his eyes. "Isn't it about time?" he asked gently.

She tried to avoid his gaze. "I suppose so," she answered, almost inaudibly.

"I wish I could be the one," he said softly. "But I don't think I can."

She was hurt. "Why not?"

"Because I'm not ready for an emotional involvement. And with you I couldn't be emotionally uninvolved."

"Would it be any different if the invitation came from me?" Deborah asked, surprised by her own words, "I mean, if I guaranteed you no emotional involvement, would you—?"

"Of course, Deborah," Zev replied affectionately. "But I don't think you're any more capable of casual lovemaking than I am."

As they discovered later in the evening, he was right.

———

Before this she had never cut a class. The day after she met Zev she cut all of them so she could be with him, in the hope of finding an answer to the urgent question: If they pooled their limited supply of love, would it be sufficient to sustain an enduring relationship?

After breakfast, they walked in the park and brought each other up to date on the various events that had occurred in their lives since she had been his pupil.

She was curious—and a trifle anxious to know his reaction to her imminent ordination.

"To be brutally frank, I have an instinctive antipathy to rabbis," Zev remarked. "But, of course, I've never kissed one before. Seriously, Deborah, I don't know if someone with your background can understand how much I hate the religious aspects of Judaism. To me the ultra-*frum* are rigid, doctrinaire, and arrogant. I'm sorry if this offends you."

"Offense has nothing to do with it. It's more like astonishment. Feeling the way you do, how on earth did you end up in Israel living on a starvation wage just to teach Hebrew literature?"

"Ah," he answered, raising his index finger demonstratively, "therein lies the difference. I may have misgivings about my religion, but I'm totally devoted to my cultural heritage. I love the Bible for the beauty of its poetry, its richness of sentiment. But I absolutely loathe the self-appointed interpreters who think they're all going to travel first-class on the chariot of fire when Elijah comes."

He tempered his outburst for a moment and asked, only half-joking, "Have I made you hate me yet?"

"You certainly seem to be trying," she said with a playful smile. "But I'll hear you out."

"I believe passionately that man's existence is territorial. And that goes for the Jew as well as his neighbor. *Every* people has to have a homeland."

"But what does this have to do with my becoming a rabbi?"

"I guess it was my way of saying it depends on what you stand for. I mean, if you're going to preach the dogma that we're 'God's chosen people,' then I can't honestly say I believe in what you're doing."

"What do *you* think I should be doing?"

He grew passionate again as he answered. "Reaching out to every complacent Jew, grabbing him by the collar, and telling him to love his neighbor—starting with his fellow Jew. I don't have to tell you Hillel said *that's* the basis of our whole religion, and the rest is commentary."

She smiled at him and said softly, "I think Hillel said it all."

Suddenly Zev turned and grabbed her shoulders. "Then I think you're gonna be one hell of a rabbi."

He took her into his arms. "And, Deborah, I want to be in the front row for all of your sermons."

As they walked through the park, Zev told her of the only palliative he had found from what was otherwise a life of constant anguish—work. He wrote and studied to exhaustion. Since his son had died, he had submerged his emotions like a swimmer under water and only surfaced for a breath of life when he was on the point of fainting.

"Sometimes I feel like a walking rain cloud," he said. "I seem to cast shadows over everyone I meet. I know I'm doing it to you right now. Don't you find my melancholia unbearable?"

She squeezed his hand. "No, I find it very familiar," she answered gently.

Zev stopped and looked at her intensely. "Then that gives us something in common—we each have half a heart. If we put the pieces together . . ."

She touched his lips gently to stop him.

"No, Zev, I didn't say that. I spent most of the night just watching you sleep, and even then I could see the sadness and loneliness on your face. I wanted to make it better."

"Well, you can," he insisted, "we can both—"

"No," she interrupted, "I also realized that I'm still part of a 'both.' I didn't give just half of myself to . . . Eli's father, I gave everything. I can feel how desperately you want to love and be loved. You deserve someone who can fill that need. I'm sorry, Zev. I only wish I could."

Zev's eyes grew sad again. "Deborah, are you telling me you intend to go through the rest of your life alone?"

"I'm not alone. I have my work."

"Yes, yes, I know," he retorted. "And you have your son. We've gone through all that. But what about a husband? Don't you feel the need for a man in your life?"

She lowered her head and said quietly, "I know what you're saying, Zev, but I also know I'll never be capable of loving anyone else."

"What about last night? Were you just using me as some kind of test case?"

She shrugged. She couldn't confess how painfully close to the truth he had come. "I'm sorry," she whispered. "I didn't even know myself."

Zev's yearning caught fire. "Dammit, Deborah, life is short enough. You're going to wake up some day to discover that you've waited until it's too late."

She looked at him mournfully and replied, "It's too late already, Zev. I'm sure of that."

He gripped her arms, fighting the urge to shake her. "Deborah, can't you understand—he's dead. Your husband's dead! When the hell will you come to terms with that?"

She looked at his contorted face and answered in a whisper.

"Never."

She turned and started to walk off. Even when she heard him calling she did not turn back.

"You're crazy, Deborah," he shouted. "You don't know what you're doing."

I do, she murmured to herself. I only hope some day you'll forgive me.

51

Daniel

A paradox: Why is it that even the happiest moments of life inevitably fade with time, but try as you may, you never forget the minutest detail of a catastrophe?

At precisely 5:16 A.M. on the last Wednesday in May, 1978, I had been blissfully sleeping in the Ritz Hotel Chicago when Deborah's phone call woke me. There was panic in her voice.

"Is something wrong with Eli?" I asked.

"No, no, Danny. It's Papa—"

"Is he sick?"

"Not yet, but I think this scandal may kill him," she replied. "He's been meeting with the elders all night."

"Hey, it's dawn," I protested, growing ever more afraid. "Has the synagogue been vandalized?"

"In a way. Papa's been betrayed by one of his

rabbis. And I'll give you one guess who the bastard is."

"Schiffman in Jerusalem?" I ventured.

"Let his name be erased forever!" Deborah spat out the supreme curse of our faith.

"What's he done? Calm down or I won't be able to understand."

"You'll understand, all right," she said bitterly.

And then she told me everything.

It seems the outwardly ascetic Rebbe Schiffman had been "borrowing" from our funds for years. That's a fancy way of saying he had embezzled money that pious people gave to help poor boys go to study in Jerusalem. Of course we have a genuine yeshiva promoting Torah studies, but some of the contributions were naively sent to what turned out to be Schiffman's own post office box.

Deborah told me of an incident that had occurred during her indentured servitude at the good rabbi's hovel.

There was a generous, kindhearted Philadelphia couple—Irv and Doris Greenbaum, self-made millionaires who had no children. Schiffman had somehow wangled five hundred thousand dollars out of them over lunch at the King David. Their contribution was intended to be for a much-needed dormitory. Somehow, the money found its way to an account in Zurich.

Recently, several months after Mr. Greenbaum's

untimely passing, his widow, accompanied by her niece Helene, had set out on a journey to visit all the places she and Irv had endowed with the fruits of their mutual labor.

First they visited a youth training center in the port city of Ashkelon, where she was heartened to learn about the many poor immigrants from the Arab countries who had benefited from the technical skills they had received there.

In Jerusalem the following morning they had taken a taxi to Mea Shearim and asked to be dropped at the *B'nai Simcha* yeshiva.

When they arrived, all they saw was a narrow two-story building which was obviously a dwelling that had been converted into classrooms. The school seemed to have no dormitory.

"There must be some mistake," Doris murmured to her niece, then asked their driver, "Are you sure this is the address the doorman gave you?"

"Of course, of course," the man responded, waving the paper in one hand and pointing to the sign above the building with the other. "Can't you see it says '*Yeshivat B'nai Simcha*'? "

"I'm sorry," said Helene, "but we can't read Hebrew. Maybe I can stop someone and ask."

"No, no," the driver quickly cautioned. "None of the men will speak to women, and most of the women won't speak to strangers. Let me try."

The two visitors waited in the taxi, which was

gradually becoming an oven, as the driver tried to find some passerby liberal enough to converse with a man who wore no skullcap.

He came storming back, poked his head into the open window, and said, "That man insists this is all there is. They don't have a dormitory. Their students live as boarders with different families."

Mrs. Greenbaum began to grow hysterical. "That's impossible," she cried. "Irv and I gave that money nearly ten years ago. We must contact Rabbi Schiffman immediately."

Once again their driver went to reconnoiter—even daring to penetrate the portals of the school. He emerged five minutes later and walked slowly back to his passengers.

"I'm afraid he's not here anymore," he reported.

"What do you mean?" demanded Mrs. Greenbaum.

"His assistant is now running the school. They say the Rebbe and his family left the country about a month ago."

"But I don't understand." Doris was growing increasingly distraught. "I wrote and told him precisely what days we would be here."

By now her niece had caught on to the situation. "That's probably exactly why he left."

Returning to the hotel, Helene called Mort, her lawyer husband in the States. It was he who had originally arranged for the transfer of the cash.

Though it was barely dawn in Philadelphia, Mort

promised he would get to the office and call them back.

A few hours later, he had the law firm's bank confirm that in early 1969 they had duly wired the money to the bank account named in the instructions given them.

Mort called the Jerusalem bank in question under the pretext that the Greenbaum Foundation once again wished to contribute to the *B'nai Simcha* and asked them to verify that their bank number had not changed.

His worst fears were confirmed. The account had been closed for nearly three years.

Not wasting any time, he shouted enough to get the branch manager on the phone and demanded to know the fate of the money his foundation had already donated.

The records showed that, within a day of its arrival, the five hundred thousand dollars had been transferred to an account in Zurich. This was all the banker's fiduciary ethics would permit him to disclose. The American lawyer would have to go through the normal protocol for any further information.

Two days later, the three Greenbaums were in Mort's Philadelphia office conversing on the speaker phone with the international leader of the *B'nai Simcha,* Rav Moses Luria.

In the interim Mort had investigated and discovered that over the years the good Rebbe Schiffman had appropriated nearly two million dollars for himself and was currently somewhere in Switzerland—obviously within visiting distance of the money.

The way Deborah told it, Papa had been almost berserk with shock and grief, especially when the lawyer informed him that a wire service reporter had already sniffed the story and could not be kept at bay forever.

Mort had promised to help as much as he could in trying to set things right before the scandal reached the press.

If he could be given a list of the contributors over the past ten years, Mort would then contact the parties concerned, swear them to silence, and explain that all the misdirected money would be repaid.

"But where am I going to get that kind of money?" Father had moaned.

"I'm sorry, Rav Luria," the attorney replied. "Miracles are your department, not mine."

I asked Deborah what emergency measures Papa was going to take, though I knew even a second mortgage on the school property would be pathetically inadequate.

Deborah, too, realized that there was no way our people could raise so vast a sum of money. But Father would not admit defeat, she said. In fact he had called a meeting of the entire community to take place at seven o'clock that evening in the *shul*.

"Danny," she pleaded, "do you think there's anything you could do?"

I was so thunderstruck that I could barely think. To be sure I was rich, but nobody keeps that kind of money on twenty-four-hour call. Though my heart sank, I nonetheless tried to reassure her.

"Hey, Deb, calm down and do everything you can to reassure Papa. I'll call you back in exactly three hours."

"Thank God, Danny," she responded. "You're our only hope."

I hung up, relieved that at least I had comforted her.

The only problem was that *I* didn't know what the hell to do.

52

Deborah

By 6:45, the synagogue was so packed that there were not enough seats for all the younger men, some of whom had returned from their university studies to be at this extraordinary gathering. In the balcony above, the younger women were seated even on the steps.

Promptly at seven P.M., Rav Luria rose, gray and trembling, went to the podium, and recited from Psalm Forty-six: "God is our refuge and strength, a very present help in trouble. Therefore will we not fear, though the earth do change, and though the mountains be moved into the heart of the seas. . . ."

He cast his sorrowful eyes on the sea of perplexed faces looking up at him.

"Friends—this is an hour of great danger. It is so grave that what we do tonight will determine whether we can remain together or will disintegrate into a thousand pieces, scattering into the void. I do not exaggerate. Nor do I fear that any of the words spoken here will go beyond these walls, since in our community brother does not betray brother."

He sighed deeply. "Perhaps I shouldn't have put it that way. Because one of our number has played Cain to the Abel of us all. The guilty party deserves no anonymity, so let me simply say that Rebbe Lazar Schiffman, the chief of our Jerusalem yeshiva, has absconded with money given over the years in good faith to foster the teaching of righteousness."

There were murmurs among the huge crowd, and the Rav let them crescendo. He was counting on their feelings of communal desperation to intensify their will to act.

"Now I could give this matter to the secular authorities and have them deal with it as the theft that it is. But that would rob us of our good name also, which the Torah teaches us is our most valued possession. Instead," he continued, "I have called you together this evening to make an extraordinary appeal. Our congregation is nearly one thousand in number. Some are teachers, shopkeepers, men of modest means. There are also businessmen whose wealth is considerable. We can clear ourselves of shame by raising the sum of . . ." He paused to take a breath and could barely pronounce a sum of such magnitude. Finally, he said, "Nearly two million dollars."

More murmurs. Fear was palpable in the air.

"We have already arranged second mortgages on this sanctuary and our school, but this will give us only slightly more than two hundred thousand dollars. The rest must somehow be found from among our brethren. Remember," the Rav went on, his voice quavering with emotion, "if we don't succeed, we will all be called criminals.

"This is not like a Yom Kippur appeal, where there's time to go home and discuss, to think, to weigh, to balance. You must give the ultimate of your resources—now."

As the rabbi spoke, Sexton Isaacs and some of the older boys from the school began to hand each member of the congregation a form mimeographed that afternoon. Upstairs, girls gave copies to the women.

"After filling these out," Rav Luria concluded, "I suggest that you rise and begin reciting the psalms. . . ."

The buzzing was loudest yet. The crinkle of paper and the creak of shoes on the old wooden floor added to the sound of chaos.

In a matter of minutes the congregants, having poured forth pledges from their coffers, rose one by one to pour out their souls in prayer.

Meanwhile, at the pulpit an extraordinary ritual was taking place. Sexton Isaacs was murmuring the contents of the pledge sheets to Dr. Cohen and two other elders of the congregation.

They had been feverishly engaged in this activity for forty-five minutes, when the Rav gave out so loud a sigh that it immediately silenced the worshipers.

"I regret to say we're nowhere near it. Our disgrace is inevitable. I will compose a short statement, trying to dissociate ourselves from Rebbe Schiffman's actions and pledging restitution though it take a hundred years."

Suddenly a voice came from the balcony.

"Just a minute, Papa."

All heads turned and looked up. Normally, the men would have berated a woman who dared to interrupt from behind the *mechitza,* but these were special circumstances. And this was the Rav's daughter.

"Yes, Deborah?" her father asked quietly. "Why are you interrupting?"

She moved to the very edge of the balcony and stretched out her arm. A pink rectangular paper fluttered in her grasp.

"Rabbi Luria," she said in a dignified voice. "With your permission, I'd like to make an announcement."

Sensing the anxiety of his congregants to hear what Deborah had to say, he responded with a toneless, "Go ahead."

"Ladies and gentlemen," she began. Behind her she could feel the women congregants bristle with uneasiness at the priority she had given them.

"What I hold in my hand," she continued, "is a banker's check made out to the *B'nai Simcha* in the sum of . . ." She paused. For she, too, had a sense of the dramatic. She then completed her sentence, ". . . one million seven hundred and fifty thousand dollars."

There were confused gasps. No one, not even Mrs. Herscher on the seat closest to her, could believe that they had heard correctly.

For all his wisdom, Rav Luria was genuinely baffled. "And is this person not present so we can thank him?"

"No," Deborah replied. "And he demands no thanks whatever. He has only one simple request."

Before the Rav could ask what it might be, his congregants had found their voices and were already shouting the same question.

"Our benefactor simply wants to be called to the Torah on Sabbath morning for the blessing that only Rav Luria can give him."

Thoughts like fluttering birds flew among the congregants: What a righteous man this must be. All eyes were focused intently on the Rav. They could tell from his expression that he had finally understood to whom he owed this enormous debt.

Yet they were thunderstruck by his response.

"You may tell your brother, Daniel, that however dire our circumstances, we will not compromise our principles. Redemption cannot be bought."

"Do you mean you refuse, Papa?" Deborah asked in hoarse astonishment.

"Yes, absolutely," said the Rav, pounding his fist on the lectern in an uncontrollable outburst. "I refuse, I refuse, I refuse!"

The entire congregation was on its feet. Voices shouted, "No, Rav Luria!" and "Bless him, bless him!"

Above all this din, the fiercest objection came from Deborah. "For the love of God, Papa, don't be so selfish—"

" 'Selfish'?" the Rav shouted furiously, his face reddening. "How dare you presume—"

Suddenly, he clutched his chest and staggered backward.

The congregation was shocked to silence even before the Rav's collapsing body touched the floor.

From the balcony Rachel Luria opened her mouth to scream, but no sound emerged.

Time seemed paralyzed as Dr. Cohen knelt down. Then from the farthest corner they could hear him whisper, "He's dead. Rav Luria is dead."

———

The moment the congregation heard the doctor's awesome pronouncement, they acted instinctively, saying almost in unison the prayer required upon hearing of a loved one's death: "Blessed is the Lord—a righteous judge."

The silence that followed was broken by the

chilling sound of all those present tearing a portion of their garments as a sign of mourning. It was as if the Heavens themselves were being rent asunder. A great leader had died in public, and they were all obliged to humble themselves.

Both Deuteronomy and *Talmud Sanhedrin* ordain that a body be buried on the day of death, if at all possible, even if it be at midnight. Thus for a man as great as Moses Luria no energy would be spared to make arrangements quickly.

As if by magic, several figures suddenly materialized, members of the *Chevra Kaddisha*—the Holy Brotherhood.

No one was sure who had called them. Yet, there they were, a special band of holy men prepared at all times to fulfill their solemn task of honoring the dead.

They transported Rav Luria's body back to his home. As his wife and daughters were left to wail and keen with the other women in a lower room, hurriedly the Brotherhood made preparations for a midnight burial.

Dr. Cohen and Uncle Saul, elders representing the congregation, stood as mute witnesses while the Holy Brotherhood went about their work by candlelight. Mystic tradition ordained that there be twenty-six tapers surrounding the body.

Their leader recited a prayer so ancient it was dated back to the first century. It implored the Holy

One to grant that the deceased may "walk with the righteous in the Garden of Eden."

Murmuring psalms and biblical phrases, the Holy Brotherhood placed a sheet on the legs and torso—for someone of the Rav's eminence should never have his nakedness exposed. They then washed his head and hair with various liquids, including raw egg, cleansed the rest of the body through the covering, and closed all its orifices with cotton.

At this point, two members of the society grasped Rav Luria's corpse and held him upright as others poured vessels of water over the dead man in a continuous stream, chanting, "He is pure. He is pure. He is pure."

They then began to wrap the body in a hand-sewn shroud, his prayer shawl, and a cowl for his head.

But there was a final ceremony to be performed before covering the dead man's face with a veil.

The leader of the Brotherhood addressed Dr. Cohen.

"This act should be done by his son."

"We've contacted Danny," the physician explained. "He's on his way from Manhattan. But who knows how long it will take? We're pressed for time. Besides, Rebbe Saul here is also a member of the family."

"No." The leader gestured imperiously. "It should be the son. We will wait a little longer." All stood motionless, some quietly reciting prayers, until at last Daniel Luria timidly entered the room, his face nearly as white as his dead father's.

"Danny," his uncle began in a voice which, even as he whispered, was an octave lower than everyone else's. "I'm glad you've come."

The new arrival was speechless. His eyes darted about the room, emanating fear.

53

Daniel

What I felt was actually beyond fear. It was kind of a mortal panic—expecting to be directly blamed for his death, and most of all, a dread of *looking at* my father's body.

But the greatest pain I felt was from the hopes that had been shattered by Deborah's phone call. What an irony. I had been waiting by the phone to hear the happy news that my father had agreed to bless and take me back into his favor. Instead, my sister's grief-numbed voice informed me that the man whose love I craved with every atom of my being had rejected me even in death.

During the endless taxi ride from Manhattan, I'd brooded on the event. I simply could not believe that anyone waiting in that room—where my father was lying—would countenance my presence.

And yet, though a prodigal, I was nonetheless

the only son, and as such had a special duty to perform.

The leader pointed at me. I hesitated. He was standing at the far side of the table, holding a gauze veil, but I did not think I could bear the sight of my father's uncovered face. I took several paces forward and still could not look down.

One of the assistants stretched out his fist, clearly wanting me to take what he was clutching.

"This is the sacred earth—earth from the Holy Land. You must put some on his eyes." He emptied the grains into my trembling hands.

At long last I found the courage to steal a look.

To my amazement, my father looked benign. In fact, he even seemed to smile, the way I still remembered him when I was young and had sat upon his knee. Now, paradoxically, I could not tear my glance away. I stared at Moses Luria, the man I had worshiped, loved—and feared—and was struck by a bizarre, irrational longing.

Can't I wake you up, Father? Can't you give me more time to make you understand? To try to tell you why I acted as I did? And most of all, to beg you to forgive me. Please don't go to sleep forever with hate for me entombed in your heart.

Uncle Saul touched me, dispelling my reverie of pain.

"Go ahead, Danny," he whispered gently. "It's getting late."

I took some earth and sprinkled it on his closed

eyes—and as I did so, accidentally brushed my fingers on his forehead.

It felt cold but not quite without life. Could he have heard my thoughts? The leader tapped my shoulder, motioning me to step aside. I forced myself to go and stand with Uncle Saul as they placed the cloth over my father's face and lifted his body into a plain pine coffin.

Half-hypnotized, I followed as they carried that box down the stairs. I saw Mama and Deborah trying to push closer, hoping to catch a final glimpse of their husband and father.

I squeezed through the crowd and embraced them. Deborah was mute with grief, but Mama managed to beg me softly, "Tell him I'll always love him, Danny."

It was only when I walked out of the house toward the hearse that the enormity of the moment hit me. The darkened streets were lined with people. Hundreds—perhaps thousands— of them. They jostled me to the head of the procession that was forming.

And these were not merely the *B'nai Simcha*. As we continued to follow the hearse, we passed through different neighborhoods where members of other sects stood reverently, paying their ultimate respect. My father's pious reputation far transcended the small confines of our territory.

At last, when we had reached the frontier of the outside world, we clambered into cars and began the drive to Sha'aray Tzedek Cemetery. I was now alone again with my thoughts—which turned back to Mama and Deborah. Since our women were forbidden from going to the cemetery, they were forced to stay at home, denied the honor and comfort of seeing Papa laid to rest.

I think I grieved for them almost as much as for him.

———

Suddenly, I saw the fires.

A second earlier, the window of our car had looked out on a blackness so profound it matched the inside of my soul. And now, flames were everywhere. Dozens of men had surrounded our car brandishing huge torches.

They removed my father's coffin from the hearse, and we began the stark convoy to his grave.

At one point in the seven stops for prayer, I dared to look quickly behind me. I saw Uncle Saul weeping as he recited one of the psalms in what sounded like a protracted moan. Behind him were my brothers-in-law, Dr. Cohen, the elders, and hundreds of people I did not know at all.

The frenzy of their mourning turned the event into a kind of ecstasy of grieving, which, illuminated by dancing flames, dizzied me. Now and then I could distinguish a word, a phrase from one of the psalms.

"Lord, make me to know mine end . . . how fleeting I am . . ."

I should have been praying too. I wanted to. But somehow I was too overwhelmed to make the words come.

At last we reached the newly hollowed grave. The pallbearers placed the coffin on the ground and waited for me to perform my filial duty—to say the words that every Jew can recite by heart, as if he had rehearsed for moments such as this throughout his life.

The huge throng hushed as, in a voice that barely escaped the prison of my throat, I started the burial *Kaddish:* "Extolled and hallowed be the name of the Lord in His world that is to be created anew, for He will revive the dead and raise them unto life eternal . . ."

The congregation joined me: "Praised be His glorious name forever and ever."

At this terrible moment I could not forget that this was the prayer my father had recited on my own symbolic death.

The pallbearers lowered the coffin into the grave as the leader recited: "O Lord and King who art full of compassion . . . in thy great loving kindness, receive the soul of Rav Moses, son of Rav Daniel Luria, who has been gathered unto his people. . . ."

I shuddered when I heard my father referred to as the son of the man whose name I bear. Except, of course, my grandfather had been *Rav* Daniel Luria.

At the end of the prayer, the cemetery was so silent that the flickering of torches sounded almost like gunfire. The leader of the society signaled to me. I knew my duty. I took up the waiting spade and shoveled earth upon the coffin.

Then, as others—countless, countless others—followed suit, I whispered Mama's message and walked off to drown myself in darkness.

54

Daniel

During the traditional seven days of mourning we all sat in our torn garments on boxes or low stools, enduring a million attempts at consolation.

It was a kind of limbo in our lives, punctuated only by the thrice-daily prayer sessions, during which we—the men—recited the *Kaddish*.

In accordance with an ancient custom, all mirrors in our house were either covered or turned to the wall. No one really knows the origin of this practice, but I personally think it is to keep the mourners from seeing their own reflections and dying of guilt for being alive.

The dignitaries who came from all over to pay their respects could say nothing to assuage my grief. The only thing that might have helped me was solitude. And that, ironically, became the only thing denied me.

By contrast, Mama seemed to take solace from the many women friends who flocked around her, sustaining a stream of sighs and syllables that—at least to her wounded soul—seemed to pass for conversation.

My heart went out to little Eli. Barely seven years old, he was not only traumatized by the event itself, but also upset by the sight of his grown-up relatives crying, and frightened by the crowds of black-coated strangers milling in the house and murmuring prayers at all hours.

Still worse, there was no one to pay adequate attention to his special needs. Too blinded by our own sorrow, Deborah and I simply failed him.

Yes, Eli understood death in the abstract. He had learned in school that Abraham was "gathered to his people" at the age of one hundred seventy-five, and though Methuselah's life extended an amazing nine hundred and sixty-nine years, even he ultimately left the earth. When it came to his grandfather, however, the phenomenon was too overwhelming to grasp. After all, his books were still set neatly on his shelves. There was even a faint smell of pipe smoke in his office. Eli was unable to believe that "Grampa" was not coming back.

I held him at my side during evening prayers, letting him know at least that the *Kaddish* was a special prayer for his grandfather.

Everyone remarked how well Eli was taking it all.

But of course, anyone with an ounce of understanding would realize that it was quite the opposite.

When my older sisters were not receiving visitors, they had their husbands to fill the void. But for most of the time Deborah had no one—except me when I could liberate myself from my well-intended comforters.

She was waiting desperately for the Sabbath. Not because our ritual of mourning would then be suspended. She had a more urgent reason: It would give her an opportunity to say *Kaddish* aloud—in the heathen precincts of Steve Goldman's Temple Beth El.

———

I was astonished to learn that my father's will had revived me from the dead. His final testament revealed what he had never said in life: that he had not totally despaired of my repentance.

The document expressed hope that I would be moved by the Father of the Universe to accept my destiny and follow in his footsteps. And if this should come to pass, he offered his fondest blessings.

But he was also pragmatic. In the event that the person he referred to as "my son Daniel" (the simple word "son" made my heart stir) was unable to serve, he decreed that his mantle be placed upon the shoulders of his beloved grandson, Elisha Ben-Ami, who, he believed, would become a great leader.

Furthermore, should he die before Eli was of age, Papa requested that Rebbe Saul Luria be appointed to guide Eli until he was old enough to take on the full responsibility.

Deborah was cast into an unbearable turmoil. Ironically, she who loved my father most had been the one most hurt by him. She had not gone through the trauma of her uncompromising rebellion to—in a symbolic sense at least—have her son taken from her. She had not bravely borne a son to sacrifice him to dogmas of the past.

She sat with clenched fists, twisting her tear-stained handkerchief, and poured out her thoughts to me.

She still could not suppress her consternation. Strangely, I found myself defending Papa.

"Deb, try to understand. He meant this as an *honor.*"

"No," she answered bitterly. "It was his own special way of punishing me. I can't believe that somewhere in his consciousness he didn't know what I was doing. He couldn't stop it when he was alive, but he . . . he's done it now."

"*No,*" I insisted, gripping her by her shoulders, "I refused and you can refuse on Eli's behalf."

And yet, she had pangs of ambivalence. "But then they'll have no leader. The *B'nai Simcha* will just dissolve. . . ."

"Look," I insisted, "if there's one thing our people have that sets them apart from all others, it is

490

their ability to survive. I promise you, Deb, they'll manage. In the meanwhile, thank God, Saul is strong and healthy and they respect him. Look how willing they were to take him as their leader until Eli is old enough to answer for himself."

"But they'll ask him then," Deborah protested.

"Right," I replied. "And then he can say no in his own voice."

The expression on her face suggested that she wanted to believe what I was telling her.

"Trust me, Deborah. Remember the words of Hillel: Be true to yourself and don't feel guilty."

At this point she looked at me, her face pale, her eyes reddened. "Don't you feel guilty too?" she asked.

I glanced for a moment over to the door that led to our living room where about a dozen visitors were chanting psalms.

Many of them had been in the group of elders led by Dr. Cohen who had cornered me the night before and tried to pressure me into succeeding my father. I had protested, telling them how I had strayed from the path of righteousness, that I was morally unworthy and spiritually dead.

They seemed not to listen, believing as they did that a full repentance would cleanse me in the eyes of God. They would have persisted forever had not Uncle Saul intervened, insisting, "Give him time to find himself."

Meanwhile, as our ritual mourning came to an

end, Saul—who had been a widower for nearly ten years—moved into our house. Though I knew his presence would be a comfort to my mother, it was still distressing to see him seated at Father's desk. Especially when he called me in to ask the most painful of existential questions.

"Tell me, Danny, what are you going to do with your life?"

I merely shrugged, unable to confess even to this profoundly good man that I now lived in a golden jungle, and I had hopelessly lost my way.

55

Deborah

"You're spitting on your father's grave!" Malka shouted.

The entire Luria family was up in arms. It was the first Sabbath evening after the official seven days of mourning had ended, and at Rachel's insistence ("I rule this house now.") Danny was allowed to attend.

Time had not stood still in the outside world, and the moment of Deborah's ordination was fast approaching. She had therefore chosen this night as the first remotely appropriate occasion for her announcement that she was going to become a rabbi. Her elder sister's reaction was predictable. Its vehemence was not.

Rav Moses' death revealed a well of strength in Rachel that none of them had ever seen. It became clear that, despite the difference in their ages, her husband had held her in high esteem and relied greatly on her opinion.

The succession to the Silczer throne might still have been in dispute, but there was no question about who now held the authority in the Luria family. That night Danny saw Rachel grow from Mama to matriarch. She stood up and addressed her children.

"Listen to me, all of you, and listen good. There will be no words of hatred expressed in this house."

Deborah leapt to her own defense. "Malka, I'll bet that you didn't know that we're all descended from a female rabbi—"

"There's no such thing!"

"Don't flaunt your ignorance in public. Her name was Miriam Spira and she's a glory to our heritage. All right, so maybe they didn't call her 'Rav Miriam.' But she did teach the Law and now, five hundred years later, the Lurias are still known everywhere as scholars."

"She's right," Danny interposed quietly but firmly. "She's absolutely right."

"*You*," Malka shouted, "you and your sister. You're both a disgrace to our family!"

At this point, still traumatized by his grandfather's death and frightened by this new outburst of emotion, young Eli burst into tears. Danny picked him up to comfort him. "I don't understand, Uncle Danny," the little boy sobbed.

"You will some day," Danny reassured his

nephew, secretly relieved that he did not have to explain why some people would regard his mother's wonderful accomplishment as a slap in the face to Almighty God.

———

The reaction of her sisters was so fierce that Deborah saw no point in informing them that she had all but accepted an out-of-town pulpit for the following year. The task she had taken on was especially challenging. The majority of her classmates did not feel they had the confidence to lead congregations on their own and were all seeking positions as copilots. They could thereby continue their education on the job—and learn from the senior rabbis' mistakes.

With her superb credentials, Deborah could set near-impossible criteria and fill them all. Having faced the daunting assignment of ministering to the New England Diaspora—not to mention having watched her father nearly all her life—she did not hesitate to present herself for the post of Senior Rabbi in a relatively young and growing community.

She wanted to stay within driving distance of New York so Eli could see his grandmother and visit the favorite sites of his childhood—the park, the zoo, the botanical gardens.

There was no shortage of possibilities to do this, and Deborah found a pulpit that offered the luxury of living in sylvan Connecticut and yet an easy journey to New York City.

Congregation Beth Shalom in Old Saybrook was relatively new. Moreover, because of its proximity to Yale, the percentage of intellectuals was high. There were no religious day schools like the one Eli had been attending in New York; but Fairchild Academy, with its reputation for high academic standards and liberal philosophy, was only a fifteen-minute drive from the gray saltbox house Deborah rented on the placid shores of Long Island Sound.

The night she officially accepted the appointment, Deborah was so excited that she took Eli to their neighbor Uncle Danny's to open a bottle of champagne. Somehow, her brother was far less enthusiastic than she had expected.

As soon as they were alone, Deborah confronted him.

"You're right, Deborah, I'm not crazy about the idea," he admitted. "I know there's a famous song, 'I Talk to the Trees,' but I never heard of anybody who got an answer. You won't like my saying this, but I think Old Saybrook is a picturesque cop-out."

"From what?"

"From eligible men. Did you ever think of that when you applied?"

"Yes," she answered candidly.

"So you want to be the first rabbi in history to take a vow of celibacy, huh?"

"Come on, Danny," she protested, knowing in her heart he was right. "I haven't done anything of the sort."

"But you have," said her brother shrewdly. "By choosing Old Saybrook you're *ipso facto* putting yourself out of circulation." He added in a wistful tone, "Besides, I'm gonna miss our heart-to-heart talks. You're not just my sister, you're my spiritual adviser."

"There's still the telephone."

"C'mon, Deb, you know that's not the same."

"Well, you can come up for weekends," she assured her brother affectionately. "And anyway, we've got two whole months of summer nights for you to unburden your heart."

Unfortunately, in the ensuing weeks Danny somehow could still not summon the courage to confide in his sister what was preying on his mind and gnawing at his conscience.

For when the grateful congregation had cashed the check that had been their salvation, they were accepting money that was not really his to give.

Since he'd had less than a day to come up with such a vast sum, he had been unable to convert his own assets in time. Hence, he had, with an act of desperate computerized legerdemain, temporarily "borrowed" the amount from the coffers of McIntyre & Alleyn. To be sure, he'd paid it back in less than a week—with interest. But there was no escaping the fact that by the letter of the law the noble end did not justify the dishonest means.

And some day—sooner or later—there would be no escaping the consequences.

PART V

56

Timothy

Father Joe Hanrahan was waiting by the gate at JFK Airport when Timothy's jumbo began to disgorge its passengers. They caught sight of each other at once. Taken by surprise, Tim stopped in his tracks. "How did you get past Customs?" he asked.

"It was easy, my boy." His old parish priest winked. "It only cost me a half-dozen blessings. The immigration fellas are God-fearing lads."

They embraced. "Tim, my lad," his first pastor said with deep affection. "It's good to see you again, especially with that collar. Actually that's the only change. You still look like the same schoolboy who threw a rock through the rabbi's window."

"You haven't changed either, Father Joe," said Tim with a flood of emotion, "although I hear that the diocese has."

"You could certainly say that," the older man

acknowledged as they walked toward Passport Control. "Your aunt and uncle weren't the only Irish family to move to Queens. All the old faces are gone now. And as you know, we've had a tidal wave of Hispanic immigrants."

"*Yo lo sé,*" Tim replied haltingly. "*Estoy estudiando como un loco.*"

Hanrahan smiled. "I should've expected you'd be prepared. Anyway, I've been limping along, and young Father Díaz has been a real help. He even celebrates one of the Sunday Masses in Spanish. Funny, our newest parishioners may be strangers to some things, but not to the Faith. They're a very pious lot."

"So I guess the parish school must still be flourishing," Tim offered.

"Uh, not exactly," Hanrahan replied, with a nervous cough. "We still have the kindergarten and first grade, but for the rest the young people have to take a bus to St. Vincent's. To put it bluntly, most of our faithful seem to have vanished. If it hadn't been for the Latinos, the church would be completely empty."

A shadow fell on Tim's heart at the prospect of seeing the windows of his old school darkened. "It's a pity," he remarked. "We shouldn't have charged tuition in the first place."

"You should've taken that up with your friends in Rome." The older priest sighed.

Tim did not know how to interpret this comment. Did his pastor know anything of the exalted circles he had lately come to move in? Very likely not. He was just venting his frustration at the prospect of leaving a parish less populous than he had received it.

"Naturally, there's a room waiting for you at the rectory," Hanrahan continued. "But if you'll forgive me, I've done a selfish thing."

"I don't understand."

"My mother died three years ago—"

"I'm sorry," Tim interrupted softly.

"Well, she was ninety-three and almost deaf, so probably it's better that she be where she can hear the angels sing. In any case, I'm still living in our old apartment, and I've taken the liberty of preparing one of our bedrooms for you. Frankly, lad, I'd be most grateful for the company."

"Of course, Father," Tim replied.

The skycap who lugged Tim's suitcases to Hanrahan's old Pinto refused a tip and merely asked the two clergymen to pray that his pregnant wife would produce a boy this time.

A few minutes later, as they entered the Brooklyn-Queens Expressway, the elderly priest commented, "Lord, I'm grateful that I'll have the pleasure of your company for a little while."

"You're not planning on dying?" Tim joked.

"No, no, not for a long while yet. It's just that,

from what I heard . . ." He paused, and then said wistfully, "They won't be keeping you here in Brooklyn very long."

———

"Bendígame, Padre. He pecado. Hace dos semanas que no he confesado."

As a pastor, Timothy found it difficult to sit on the other side of the curtain. Part of him still felt unworthy of discharging the duties of a priest, especially the role of confessor.

From beyond the lattice screen, a young husband was requesting absolution for his infidelity.

"I couldn't help it, Father," he protested. "This woman where I work was always teasing me."

The penitent took a deep breath. "I suppose I'm lying to myself. My body wanted her. I simply couldn't control myself." He began to sob softly, "Oh, my God, can I ever receive forgiveness for what I've done?"

Then came the moment when Tim had to admonish, uphold the law, chastise the sinner. He felt like a hypocrite. "My son, God sometimes puts temptation in our paths to test our true devotion to Him. And these are the times we must be strongest and prove the power of our faith."

———

With the aid of Ricardo Díaz, Tim learned to celebrate the Mass in Spanish and immersed himself completely in his pastoral duties. There were times when he did not leave the church until almost midnight. Yet who of his parishioners could have imagined that Father Timothy was afraid to walk the streets by day—for fear of seeing something that might make him think of Deborah Luria.

Finally, the tension became too great. He resolved to explore and hopefully to satisfy his gnawing curiosity.

He picked a rainy Sunday. It suited him because his black hat and black raincoat with its collar pulled up to protect him from the wind would make him less conspicuous when he ventured into the Lurias' neighborhood.

The downpour soaked him thoroughly. The heavy winds made others on the street pay more attention to their umbrellas than to passersby.

He walked first to the synagogue. It was still there, almost as it had been, though the gilded Hebrew letters on the sign above the door were slightly peeling, and the building seemed to sag with old age.

It was but several dozen yards to where, so many years ago—almost a lifetime in a way—he had on Friday evenings put out lights for pious Jewish families . . .

And met a pious Jewish girl . . .

He walked on, though with each step his legs seemed to grow heavier. At last he was in front of Rav Moses Luria's house, and stood there gazing at it. He looked up at the window he had broken—when was it, an eternity ago?

An elderly white-haired man noticed the unfamiliar figure standing motionless before the rabbi's home. His ingrained fear of outsiders made him suspicious.

"Excuse me, mister. Can I help you maybe?" he inquired.

To the old Jew's relief, the stranger replied in Yiddish. "I was just wondering if this was still the Silczer Rebbe's house?"

"Of course, how could it not be? What are you, from Mars or something?"

"And is the rabbi well?"

"And why should the rabbi not be well?" the man asked. "Rav Saul is in perfect health—may God shield him from the Evil Eye."

" 'Rav Saul'?" Tim asked, confused. "Is not Rav Moses the Silczer Rebbe?"

"*Oy Gotenyu*, you are out of touch, mister. Weren't you here when Rav Moses was taken off— may he rest in peace?"

"Rav Luria's dead?" Tim was rocked. "That's terrible."

The bearded man nodded. "Especially under such tragic circumstances."

"What circumstances?" Tim demanded. "And why isn't Daniel his successor?"

His elderly interlocutor grew uneasy.

"You know, mister, I think you ask too many questions. Maybe you don't know these things because they're none of your business."

"I—uh, I'm sorry," Tim stammered. "It's just that they were all friends of mine . . . a long time ago."

"Well, 'a long time ago' is a very long time," the elderly gentleman philosophized. "Anyhow, mister, I wish you a safe journey back to wherever you belong."

The man was glaring at him. Tim could remain no longer to contemplate the Luria residence, trying to read from silent brick the tragedy that had occurred. Thanking his wizened informant, he started off, wishing him *Shalom*.

He went to celebrate the evening Mass in Spanish.

———

Timothy gradually came to realize that his desire to return to St. Gregory's was, at least partially—perhaps completely—due to his yearning to be near where Deborah once had lived. To walk streets she might have walked. To let himself fantasize that he might see her coming around the corner, even if on someone else's arm.

Now, he regretted that he had not thought more clearly before making his decision to return. For this was a kind of purgatory he could scarcely bear. A self-inflicted punishment that drained his soul of passion for his sacerdotal work. It made him half a man and half a priest—as neither whole, as both a failure.

If this was the Almighty's way of testing him, he had surely failed and could now only sit anxiously awaiting God's retribution—and wondering what form it would take.

Then, to his eternal agony, he learned.

Tim was at his happiest when in the parish school. He visited often, teaching the youngsters prayers and religious songs, and trying to awaken the love of God in them.

He would go along on their outings, ostensibly to share the responsibility of shepherding them, but in truth because he felt most at ease in the outside world when he was in their company.

One sunny morning they were visiting the botanical gardens. The weather was exhilarating, and his heart grew light. Though other parts of the neighborhood had become almost unrecognizable, the beauty of the flowers had not changed.

He felt young again. And pure.

It was so warm that the children were able to sit on the grass to eat their sandwiches and milk. The Sisters asked Tim to say a few words.

Inspired by the miracles of nature around them, he quoted from Christ's Sermon on the Mount. Gesturing toward the gardens he pronounced, " 'Consider the lilies of the field, how they grow; they toil not, neither do they spin: And yet I say unto you, that even Solomon in all his glory . . .' "

He was struck dumb in midsentence. Scarcely fifty feet beyond where they were gathered, a dark-haired mother and her little boy were walking hand in hand, smiling and chatting with a petite, white-haired woman.

There was no doubt. It was Deborah and her mother. And her child.

Realizing that his own young audience had fixed their attention upon him, he rushed to conclude his words.

" 'Wherefore, if God so clothe the grass of the field . . . shall he not much more clothe you?' "

Striving to keep his emotions in check, he asked one of the girls, "Dorie, what do you think Jesus means by this?" As the little girl stood up and began her simple exegesis, Tim let his eyes focus once more beyond their group.

He could barely see her now in the distance. Yet even that sight was sufficient to tear at his heart. Deborah had come home. Married to another. To someone she had loved so much that she had borne a child to him.

That evening, he walked into the dining room and poured himself a large glass of whiskey. He then went to the living room, moved a chair close to the window, and opened it so the wind could soothe his face.

He took a swallow and began to berate himself.

Why are you surprised, for heaven's sake? Did you imagine she'd become some kind of Jewish nun and light a candle to you every night? You stupid Irish dolt. She's gone on with her life. She's forgotten. . . .

He raised his glass and toasted, "Good for you, Deborah Luria. You've wiped me from the slate of memory. You've given no more thought to . . . what we were."

He took another swig, and let the alcohol unlock his true emotions. At first he did not even realize it, but tears began to wet his cheeks.

And then he murmured half-aloud, "God damn you, Deborah. He can't love you half as much as I do."

57

Timothy

Tim did not dare to call from the parish phone, nor even from Father Hanrahan's house, since Sister Eleanor, who had been doing the priest's domestic chores for years, was apt to walk in any time.

Feeling guilty for his furtiveness, he bought a copy of *The Tablet,* handing the news vendor five dollars and requesting change in silver.

"Going to play pinball, Father?" the old man jested.

"Right you are, Mr. O'Reilly."

He even had to think about which phone booth to use, fearing he might be discovered by a chance parishioner.

As an act of desperation, he took the subway to Fulton Street, found an office building with a bank of telephones, and hid himself where he was certain he would not be seen or heard.

"Hello, Tim. Nice to hear from you."

"I'm grateful that Your Eminence had time to take my call."

"Don't be silly, I'm always glad to hear from you. Actually, this whole thing's providential, since I was planning to ring you. What's on your mind?"

"Eminence," Tim answered, "I—this is very hard to say . . ."

"Tim, your voice sounds despairing. I hope you've not lost your . . . commitment. Here in Boston, priests are leaving as if the whole cathedral was on fire."

"No, no," Tim rushed to say, "but I can't explain it on the telephone. Could I come up and speak to you privately?"

"Of course. I'll fit you in tomorrow morning if you can get up that soon."

"Thank you, Your Eminence." Tim sighed with relief.

————

Set on a hill in Brighton, the Cardinal's mansion was hardly grand by Roman standards, but in what was once a Puritan stronghold it was lavish enough.

Tim waited nervously on a bench at the end of a long marble corridor. Ten minutes later, a pair of tall mahogany doors opened, and the cardinal's secretary, a dark, broad-shouldered Cuban, began to motion the visitor to enter. He himself was suddenly blocked as Mulroney moved his portly presence to the doorway and called out, "Come in, my boy. Welcome to the land of the bean, the cod, and the Red Sox."

As he put his arm around Tim, and led him into a comfortable small parlor, he looked back at the Cuban priest. "Father Jimenez will bring us some tea, and we can start right in. I'd have invited you to lunch, but I've got to dine with a faculty committee at Boston College and try to hold my ground while they dun me for money. I thought I'd spare you that aggravation till you're a cardinal yourself."

His Eminence leaned back in a leather chair whose color almost matched his garb, and said, "All right, my lad, I've never seen those eyes of yours look dimmer. You're unhappy. Tell me what's the matter."

Tim had spent the night before wondering what pretext he could find, what story he could manufacture—and yes, if necessary, what lie he could pronounce—to induce the cardinal to have him transferred from Brooklyn.

"It's funny, Tim," Mulroney remarked, "I've known you since you were a fresh-faced seminarian, then a scholar-priest in Rome, and in all that time you never seemed to age a day. But now I see a shadow on your face. I can only conclude you're in the grip of a terrible crisis. And—notwithstanding what you told me on the phone—you're suddenly disappointed with the priesthood. Am I right?"

"No, Your Eminence," Tim quickly responded, "not at all. It's just—"

This was the sentence that he could not complete—until abruptly he decided that—despite the risk—the truth would serve him best.

"There's a woman—"

The prelate put his forehead in his hands and murmured, "Almighty Father, I knew it would be this!"

"Don't misunderstand," Tim interrupted quickly. "What I mean is—there *was*. She lived in my parish. . . ."

"Yes?"

"But this was long before I was ordained," he added frantically. "I was a seminarian—and, yes—I did sin with her." He hesitated for a moment and then added, "I loved her once with all my heart."

The cardinal fidgeted. "And now?"

"And now I'm back where I can see her. It's unbearable—"

"Is she married?" the prelate interrupted.

Tim nodded. "She has at least one child."

"Ah, good," the Cardinal could not keep from saying. "Have you two spoken?"

"No, I've only glimpsed her from afar. But it was—"

"The pain of memory?" the churchman inquired. Compassion colored his words.

"Yes, that's exactly it. I don't think I can survive much longer at St. Gregory's and not go mad."

Mercifully, Father Jimenez entered with a tray of tea and butter cookies. As he set it down on the Cardinal's table, Mulroney looked up at him and smiled. "That'll be fine, Roberto, you can leave it there." His secretary gave a reverent nod and quickly evanesced.

The Cardinal looked back at Timothy, whose blue eyes were broadcasting anxiety, and smiled. "Father Hogan, I was beginning to wonder if my faith was being tried. But, *Deo gratias*, you've restored it."

"I don't understand, Eminence."

"Tim, ever since I myself was honored with the Archdiocese of Boston, I've been searching for a pretext to get you transferred so I can watch your star rise without a telescope. Just a few days before you called, the perfect occasion presented itself."

He paused, then added with a mournful undertone, "I'm only sorry that the circumstances are somewhat unhappy. While you were at the Greg did you happen to come across a chap named Matt Ridgeway?"

"Once or twice. He was two years ahead of me, and I've always enjoyed his articles in *Latinitas*. He has such a sense of humor—not to mention a magnificent grasp of the language."

"You can't imagine what wonders he wrought for

the Latin studies in our schools," the Cardinal continued. "I appointed him a special director for Classical Languages, and he traveled the length and breadth of the Commonwealth spreading, so to speak, the gospel of the gospel." The prelate sighed. "He was such a gifted young man."

" 'Was,' Your Eminence? Is he ill?"

"To be frank," Mulroney answered somberly, "his departure is symptomatic of a kind of illness within the Church itself. He wants to marry. He says he can't bear the solitude. And, quite candidly, that's something even I can understand."

"Yes, Eminence," Tim replied, heartened by the sudden intimacy of their conversation.

"I'm doing my best to help Matt get his laicization from Rome, but that sort of thing is becoming much more difficult. I think the Curia, not to mention His Holiness, were a little startled by the number of defections when John XXIII 'opened the window.'

"Anyway, Tim, the point is that the Archdiocese of Boston is without a director of Classical Languages and without a strong-enough candidate to shoulder the burden. Surely this will make the authorities look with favor on your immediate transfer. How soon can you move up?"

"Could I discuss that with Father Hanrahan? I wouldn't want to cause him any undue hardship."

"Of course, Tim. But I'm sure that my old friend and successor, the Bishop of Brooklyn, can get him another A.P. in time for you to assume your duties on the Fourth of July. Then we could make it a double celebration."

The Cardinal glanced at his watch. "Oh my, if I don't arrive in time, I'll never be able to defend the Faith against those Deans at B.C."

———

Before boarding the return shuttle, Tim tried to phone Father Joe at the parish office to share the good news with him, but was told that Hanrahan had left for home.

Just then he heard the last call for his flight. He rushed to make the plane, already feeling lighter at having a burden lifted from his heart.

58

Timothy

Tim arrived back at the apartment a little after eight P.M. and knew instantly that something terrible had happened.

There was only a single plate set at the table, where gray-haired Sister Eleanor was sitting statuelike, her gaunt face a mask of worry.

"What's the matter, Nell? Where's Father Joe—has he been taken ill?"

"No, no," she replied. "But he's had to leave quite suddenly to give Last Rites—I know they call it something else now."

"Yes, 'Anointing of the Sick,' " Timothy replied impatiently. "Who's dying?"

The nun suddenly went pale. "I don't know. It's someone with pneumonia," she answered nervously. "I didn't catch the name."

Tim persisted, sensing that she was hiding something. "Tell me who it is," he demanded.

Browbeaten and frightened, the Sister blurted out, "Your mother, Father Tim. He's gone to see your mother. The hospital says she asked for him."

His mother?

If, as Tuck and Cassie had forced him to believe, his mother was incapable of rational discourse—or even recognizing her own son—how could she be lucid enough on her deathbed to remember Father Hanrahan and send for him?

Tim sprinted to the parish office and frantically searched the desk drawers for the key to their minibus while interrogating Father Díaz about the fastest route to Mount St. Mary's Nursing Home. He then dashed off into the street, climbed behind the wheel, fumbled for a moment trying to ignite the motor, and drove off with a jolt.

Tim pressed the pedal to the floor, driving recklessly. It was an almost suicidal act, as if he were afraid that what he would learn this night would so profoundly change his life that it might be just as well to lose it on the way.

Ninety minutes later as he stopped for gas, he suddenly noticed Hanrahan's old Pinto in the parking lot of the adjacent Howard Johnson's. While the attendant filled his tank, he dashed madly toward the diner, where he found the old priest sipping tea to calm his nerves.

For Tim this was no time to stand on ceremony.

"All right, Joe," he said abruptly, "don't lie to me anymore. Why did they never let me see my mother? I'll drive the rest of the way with you so you can tell me *everything*."

He had barely self-control enough to keep himself from grabbing the old priest and shaking him.

Five minutes later they were on the road again, Tim doing the driving—and Joe Hanrahan nervously trying to explain.

"You see, Tim, she was hallucinating. Saying things that could lacerate a person's heart."

"You mean you've heard her?"

"Yes," the priest admitted meekly. "It was my duty as a pastor."

"And what about my duty as a *son*?"

"It was to live your life, my boy."

"And all these years you've been lying to me," Tim raged.

Hanrahan was tight-lipped as they turned off the thruway and started to ascend a narrow winding road. In barely half a dozen minutes they would reach the hospital.

There, Tim would find the answers for himself.

———

Stone pillars and an iron gate. A painted sign on which two meager lines were traced: *Mount St. Mary's Nursing Home.*

Tim was too agitated to comment on the pallid euphemism for "asylum." All he could think of was that after so much pain he at last had reached the destination of his childhood longing.

A trio of nuns, one of them apparently Mother Superior, was waiting at the door.

"Father Joseph," they greeted him, anxiety and love commingled.

"Good evening, Sisters. Sorry this is such a sad occasion. Oh, this is my new Assistant Pastor, Father Timothy."

Two of them saw no special significance in Tim's presence. The third, a novice in her twenties, had not yet acquired the skill of looking at priests' faces without seeing them as men.

Flanking Hanrahan, the two other sisters escorted him along a darkened corridor.

Walking several paces behind, the young woman turned to Timothy and whispered, "Father, please don't be offended. But I'm struck by how your eyes resemble hers."

"Yes," he remarked softly, "I'm her son."

"I thought so," she whispered. "Margaret's talked about you often."

She has? he shouted inwardly.

"What did she say?" he asked aloud.

"Well," the young nurse replied, "she's delusional, as I'm sure you know. With due respect, it's clear you're not the Messiah."

"No," Timothy said, barely audibly. "What has she said that was rational?"

The Sister blushed. "That you were 'beautiful.' She spoke about your eyes."

Erich Segal

She only saw me for a week or so, and still she recalls my face, Tim thought. "Sister, what exactly is the diagnosis of her case?"

"Don't you know any of this?" the puzzled novice inquired. "Well, if you read her charts—and there's more than twenty-five years of them—the word that seems to recur is 'schizophrenia.' "

"What else do these reports say?" Tim asked her quickly, as he watched Father Joe and the other nurses disappear around a corner to the right.

"Well, lately her condition's been exacerbated by senile dementia. And of course this terrible pneumonia's raised her fever. I'm afraid you're going to find it quite upsetting to see her, Father."

"I'm prepared," Tim answered, staring into space. Not saying that he had been preparing for this moment all his life.

At the end of the long, silent corridor a ray of light shone on the dark linoleum. It was an open door. Father Hanrahan and the two older nuns had already entered.

Timothy was frightened to the marrow of his bones. The young Sister sensed it, and put her hand gently on his sleeve as they entered the room.

What Timothy saw was not a person. It was an emaciated wraith. Tufts of tangled white hair framed her wrinkled, hollow-cheeked face. The only thing that seemed remotely human were her eyes.

His eyes.

Despite the tubes in her arms, the woman was pulling at the bars that framed the bed. She was coughing horribly, her lungs full of fluid.

Then, their glances met.

Margaret Hogan merely stared. And mad and dying as she was, knew instantly who had walked into her life just at the end of it.

"You're . . . Timothy," she said hoarsely. "You're my son."

His heart was about to break.

Then once again a wave of madness washed across her consciousness. "No, you're the angel Gabriel, or Michael, or Elijah, come to take me off to Heaven. . . ."

Tim tried to catch Father Hanrahan's attention. To force him to acknowledge that even now, when she was all but covered by the shroud of death, Margaret Hogan still recognized her son.

How much more so would she have sixteen years earlier, when Tuck Delaney cruelly beat out of him all hope of seeing her?

They had all conspired to keep him from her.

"I'd like everyone to leave," Tim murmured with icy calm.

Not comprehending, the Mother Superior replied, "But Father Hanrahan's the—"

"I'm her *son*," Tim stated quietly.

The old man signaled the Sisters to depart. Suddenly, Timothy was alone with the woman who had given him life.

"Margaret," he said, fighting to keep control, "could we have a chat?"

She looked blankly at him.

"I've come to anoint you," he added.

"You mean Extreme Unction," she said.

"Yes." Timothy nodded.

Father Hanrahan had left his bag on the small table, and Tim withdrew the stole and placed it on his shoulders. He held the small bottle of oil in his hand as he sat beside his mother's bed, wondering how long she would remain lucid. Her racking cough increased his fears.

He tried to act the pastor. It was too late for him to act the son.

"Margaret Hogan, I'm prepared to hear your confession," he said softly.

His mother acted reflexively. She crossed herself and mumbled, "Bless me, Father, for I have sinned. It's been three hundred years since my last confession. . . ."

Oh, God, thought Tim.

She began to babble about angels, witches, demons. That she was the mother of a Saviour.

Tim shielded his eyes with his hand, pretending to listen as he tried not to cry.

Then, like bright sun piercing through a hurricane, she had an instant of clarity. "You're not a real priest. You're my little boy dressed up like one. You are my little Timmy, aren't you?"

Paradoxically, he was more shaken by her sanity

than her madness. He tried to answer calmly, "Yes, Mother, I'm Timothy. But I'm grown up now."

"And become a priest?" A look of confusion crossed her face. "No one told me that my baby was a man of God." She merely stared at him.

This was the moment. His only chance to ask.

"Mother, who was my father?"

"Your father?"

Tim nodded and urged, "Please try to concentrate. Tell me who he was."

She looked at him and smiled. "Why of course it was Jesus."

"Jesus?" His voice strained to prod her into thinking rationally. "It couldn't have been Jesus. He sits at God's right hand. Try to think. I know it was long ago."

"Oh, yes." She nodded. "Very long ago, and I've forgotten so much. Can't remember. No, no, I'm sure now it was Moses."

"Moses?"

"Of course," she answered with a manic look upon her face. "Yes, I remember now. Moses came to see me in the night. He told me I would have a son."

"A son?" Tim prompted her. "And am I that son?"

She looked at him again. "No, you're a priest. You've come to give me my Last Rites so I can be in Moses' arms again and see my baby Jesus."

Tim felt a knot in the pit of his stomach. Why can't I reach her? Why can't I make her tell me?

Then out of nowhere she blurted, "Oh, Father, bless me, I have sinned. I've sinned with—"

She could not complete her sentence. She had fallen back onto her pillow, and now lacked the breath of life.

In a daze, Tim acted to fulfill his priestly functions. He anointed her, and gave her absolution.

"In the name of the Father. And of the Son. And of the Holy Spirit."

Tim stood up and looked down at her. Then he leaned over, kissed her on the forehead, and at long last turned away.

59

Timothy

"Since almighty God has called our sister Margaret from this life to Himself, we commit her body to the earth from which it was made. . . ."

"Amen," said Timothy, echoed by the other mourners gathered at Margaret Hogan's grave.

They were not numerous. Merely her son, her sister, her sister's husband, and two of their three daughters. The third, Bridget, now married and living in Pittsburgh, saw no need to travel all that way to attend the funeral of someone she had never known.

After they each had sprinkled a handful of earth on Margaret's coffin, Father Hanrahan read, "Let not your hearts be troubled," from the Gospel of John. He concluded with Jesus' words to Thomas, "I am the way, the truth, and the life; no man cometh unto the Father, but by me."

The priest signaled the end of the service, and they all began to walk through the windy cemetery.

Tim remained at his mother's graveside, talking to her in death as he had addressed her in life, words to an invisible person.

As he rejoined the group, he could hear Tuck Delaney, bloated and balding, complaining to Father Hanrahan.

"Why was there no eulogy?" he inquired with a tinge of irritation.

"I'm sorry, Tuck. Her son requested that there be none."

His uncle glared at Tim, who answered solemnly, "I didn't want to hear a lot of phony words. Besides, there's already been so much falsehood I could choke."

"Now, Timmy," Officer Delaney chided, "is that how we're teaching our priests to speak nowadays?"

Father Hanrahan interceded. "Let him be."

They walked back in silence to the single dusty limousine that had brought them to the cemetery. Tim stood there as the others climbed inside.

"Come on," his uncle urged, "the radio predicted rain. Besides if we hurry we can miss the rush hour traffic."

"Fine," Tim replied sardonically. "I'd be mortified if I caused you to get caught in traffic. You all leave—I'll take the subway when I'm ready." He slammed the car door.

From inside, he heard his uncle tell the driver, "Let's get a move on. I can show you a good short-cut."

Tim walked back to his mother's grave. A few dozen feet from the freshly piled earth that lay on the remains of Margaret Hogan was the large marble tomb of one "Evan O'Connor, loving husband, father, and grandfather." O'Connor's foresighted family had provided a stone bench for people to sit down, to contemplate and pray for their relatives' immortal souls.

Tim stared at his mother's grave, thinking, You took the secret with you, Margaret Hogan. Now I'll never know.

He smiled bitterly to himself, and said, "For both our sakes, I hope it *was* the angel Gabriel, or even Jesus. Or Moses. . . ."

All of a sudden, he had a horrifying insight.

Moses, he thought to himself. Did she not know a Moses in her lifetime? *No,* it couldn't be. It's utter blasphemy even to think of it.

And yet . . .

And yet, he suddenly recalled a moment from adolescence. He saw himself at fourteen, sitting in that study, hearing a most holy man of God say, "When my wife died, Sexton Isaacs hired her to come in now and then. . . ."

And was not the man who had spoken these words named Moses Luria?

Tim frantically performed the calculations in his

head. If he was not mistaken—and dear God he wished he were—the year that Eamonn Hogan had been absent was the same year as Rav Moses' period of mourning. The pieces fit together with excruciating accuracy.

Moses Luria was young when his wife died. However much he was in pain, he was a man. And my poor mother in all her youthful beauty, and her innocence . . .

Probably she held the man in awe. Of course she did. He was a man of God, however different the God he worshiped. And with his eloquence, he might have—could have—wakened pity in her for his lonely state.

Darkness was enveloping the cemetery as Tim stormed toward the subway, trying not to think.

Trying to avoid the terrifying possibility that he, a priest devoted to the love of Jesus Christ, could be the son of Rabbi Moses Luria.

60

Timothy

By asking him to hear his confession, Tim wanted to make his worldly peace with Father Joe Hanrahan. For he knew he could no longer be a priest after what he was about to reveal.

"Bless me, Father, for I have sinned. It has been seven days since my last confession."

"Yes?" Father Joe inquired.

In agony, Tim whispered, "I have committed incest."

"What?"

"I've had relations with a woman whom I just discovered is my sister."

Father Joe was shaken. "Can you explain these fantasies of 'incest'?"

"They're all true," Tim raged. "I should have realized when the Jew himself said he had known my mother."

"The Jew?"

"Rav Luria—I hope he burns in Hell."

"You think the rabbi was your father?" the priest asked in amazement.

"I'm sure of it. Let him offer his own defense to his God. But what about me—do you understand *my* sin? What penance can you give *me* for all this? Nothing in this world could cleanse my soul."

There was silence in the room for several minutes. Then the old man, his voice quavering, asked, "Now will you hear *my* confession?"

Tim shook his head. "I can't, I'm not a priest. I'm really not a priest. Besides, you haven't given me my penance."

Father Hanrahan grasped Tim firmly by the shoulders and cried, "Hear my confession as your penance!"

Before Tim could protest, his boyhood parish priest sank to his knees and crossed himself.

"Bless me, Father, for I have sinned. It's been a week since my last confession.

"I have committed several mortal sins. Not merely in the space of time since I last spoke to you, but nearly all my adult life.

"I helped perpetuate a lie. My only excuse is that the truth I withheld was given to me under the seal of the confessional. No one—not even the Holy Father himself—could have released me from my vow of silence."

He paused, and then added, "But as a *penitent,* I can tell it to my confessor."

He looked at Tim, his eyes pleading for compassion, then began haltingly. "This was long ago—"

"How long?" Timothy demanded sternly. "Can you be more specific?"

He hesitated for a moment, stole a glance at Tim, and answered, "Before you were born . . ."

A shiver made his body tremble, but Tim responded simply, "Go on."

"A member of my parish confessed to me that he'd committed adultery and had made a woman pregnant. It was his wife's sister. He wanted her to have an abortion. Being a policeman, he knew the doctors. . . ." He took a deep breath. "But I dissuaded him. Then when the child was born, I lied on the baptismal papers. I put down the woman's husband so the child would be legitimate. I wanted to protect the poor sick woman. And the child . . . I wanted to protect the blameless little boy."

He lowered his head and began to sob.

Tim was electrified. *Tuck Delaney* is my father? That loudmouthed, craven animal? The very thought made him sick.

At this point the old priest looked up and met Tim's fierce glare. "That's my confession, Father Hogan," he mumbled. "Will you grant me absolution?"

Tim hesitated, then shot back, "I'm sure God in

His infinite compassion will bestow forgiveness on you." He paused, and then added icily, "I can never give you mine."

———

It was a muggy New York morning and, though clad only in shirtsleeves that exposed his beefy arms, Tuck Delaney was sweating as he mowed the front lawn of the white-shingled, green-shuttered Queens house to which he had moved his family several years before after making sergeant.

As he stopped, withdrew a handkerchief, and wiped his brow, Tuck saw his nephew striding toward him, wearing jeans and a faded satin baseball jacket.

"Hey, Tim," he scolded. "What kinda way is that for a man of God to dress?"

Tim ignored the reprimand.

"Shut up. You're no one to give me moral lessons."

His uncle bristled, and the back of his bull neck grew red with rage. "Hey, mister," he growled. "You watch what you're saying or, priest or no priest, I'll bust your chops."

In a way, Timothy was glad to see Tuck so belligerent. It made it easier to vent his anger when it was matched by equal animosity.

All during the subway ride to Queens he had wondered how he would broach this traumatic truth. Now the altercation had given him the perfect opening.

"You're a disgrace to the Force, Sergeant De-laney," Tim said bitingly. "I could have you up for child abuse."

The larger man's face seemed almost apoplectic with anger. "What the hell are you—"

Suddenly he realized that Tim knew. He froze, barely able to draw breath. "What're you trying to insinuate?" he asked with confused aggressive-ness. "You don't know what you're saying."

Tim looked at Tuck and felt a wave of shame that his progenitor could be such a callous brute. "I ought to kill you for keeping me from seeing her," he snarled through clenched teeth.

"Your own flesh and blood? I gave you life, boy." Tuck laughed nervously. "A holy man like you com-mitting patricide?"

"You killed my mother—you stole her life."

"Say it any way you want, you little bastard. 'Cause that's what you are, you know."

"There are words for what you are, Tuck. Far worse—"

Suddenly the policeman's face contorted into a cruel smile as he taunted, "Besides, I'm not even sure I'm the one. Your mother had real hot pants."

"Shut up!" Tim bellowed.

"Go on," Tuck sneered, cocking his fists. "Prove you're a son of mine. Try and belt me."

Tuck mistook his momentary inaction for cow-ardice and began to goad him with left jabs that lightly slapped his face.

Then Tim let loose the reins of self-control, pounding Tuck's ample belly. When the older man doubled over in pain, Tim delivered a punishing right to his jaw.

The moment he slumped to the ground, Cassie appeared at the porch.

"My God, Tim, what have you done?"

Tim held his aching right hand, gasped for breath, and murmured, "Why, Cassie, why?"

"For God's sake," she cried hysterically, running to her husband, who had risen to his elbows and was trying to gain the equilibrium to stand. "I took you in. Can you imagine what torture that was for me? What kind of priest are you?"

Tim looked down at both of them, his foster parents, and, eyes burning, replied from the depths of his bruised heart. "What kind of human beings are you?"

He turned and walked away.

61

Deborah

Officially, Deborah had been rabbi at Beth Shalom since the first of September and had already presided over two Sabbath services and a funeral. This had brought her into contact with some of the members of the congregation. But only on the eve of the New Year did she finally realize why the architect had designed the sanctuary to hold nine hundred worshipers.

With the completion of the circle of seasons, Jews all over the world would be gathering for their yearly expiation and atonement. The ritual catharsis available to Catholics at all times was theirs only on the High Holy Days. They shared a collective guilty conscience that drew enormous satisfaction from rising to confess in unison and of course to be further berated by their spiritual leader, garbed in white canonicals.

Traditionally on this occasion, the rabbi's sermon would be based on the biblical tale of Abraham being called upon to offer up his only son, Isaac, as a sacrifice to God.

But Rabbi Deborah Luria used this text merely as a point of departure. After a fleeting allusion to the piety of Abraham and the unquestioning obedience of Isaac, she continued, "Yet there are other sacrifices told of in the Bible that surpass the magnitude of Abraham's. For example," she went on, "in The Book of Judges, we find the story of Jephtha, a great hero who was obliged by a sacred oath to slay his only *daughter.*"

There was a stirring among the congregants. Few, if any of them, knew the story.

"Look at some of the significant contrasts," Deborah continued. "For one, Abraham never communicated his intent to Isaac—who we know from the commentators was no mere youngster, but actually thirty-seven years old at the time."

Her audience whispered to one another ("They never taught us that at Sunday school") as she went on. "In the story of Abraham and Isaac, there is no meaningful dialogue between parent and child. But Jephtha not only discusses his oath with his daughter, she actually encourages him to fulfill it.

"Unlike the case of Isaac, no angel appears at the last minute to say, 'Do not touch that child.' Jephtha must actually kill his own daughter." She could almost feel the shiver that ran through the silent sanctuary as she continued, "I believe that this is a truer story of religious devotion, one that makes us face the realities of life: That we must be ready to serve a God who sends us no angel, neither to rescue us, nor to tell us that what we are doing is right.

"And so, tomorrow when we read of Abraham's *willingness* to sacrifice Isaac, I will be thinking of Jephtha's daughter, whose name is not even deemed worthy of mention in the Bible. For throughout history, Jewish women have always been Jephtha's daughters."

———

It was indeed a good New Year for Congregation Beth Shalom and its new rabbi.

But it was not only the public Deborah they appreciated. It was also her devotion as a pastoral healer. Sometimes, in the tradition of her biblical namesake, she acted as a kind of judge in marital disputes. At others she counseled the distraught and comforted the bereaved.

Just a week after Yom Kippur, Lawrence Greene, a pediatrician from Essex, had a head-on collision when rushing to an emergency call late at night. Deborah spent nearly forty-eight hours at the hospital with Mrs. Greene until her husband was out of danger, leaving the woman's side only briefly to deliver and pick up Eli from school.

There was only one problem. And it did not take long for Deborah to realize it. Her personal life was a catastrophe.

Almost by definition, a rabbi's duties are performed at abnormal hours. This was doubly difficult for a young single mother like herself. Once they were ensconced in their new house and half-acre garden, Deborah was no longer able to provide her son with a Sabbath even remotely like those that had so formed her as a Jew. There had been much more to Rav Luria's Sabbath dinners than mere blessings and singing of songs. They were a weekly affirmation of the values of the family.

But she, Eli, and Mrs. Lamont made an odd Sabbath trio. After hurriedly dressing to be ready for Temple, she would gather her son and house-keeper to light the candles and help Eli with the blessings on the wine and bread.

They would quickly eat and sing a bit of the Grace After Meals before she had to rush off to Temple, put on her "uniform"—as Eli called it—and conduct Sabbath evening services.

Deborah did her best to compensate for her Friday absences by rehearsing her sermons with him on Thursday evenings and accepting his criticisms—some of which were quite helpful. "You wave your hands too much, Mom," he would say. "You look like you're flagging a cab."

Then there was Saturday morning. Once a month Beth Shalom had a children's service. She would leave him in the small chapel while she ascended to the sanctuary to lead the grown-ups. How could she have suspected that while she was uplifting their parents' souls, the children downstairs were teasing her son for being a rabbi's child?

When, as they drove home, she finally pried out of him the reason for his melancholy, Deborah could not keep from thinking of her brother's childhood agony as Rav Luria's son, and the strain it had imposed on him.

Her rabbinical studies had touched on "PKS" phenomenon, otherwise known as Preachers' Kids Syndrome—the unusual pressure put on clergymen's children. Now she had the dubious advantage of knowing about it without being able to deal with it.

On Saturdays when there was a *bar mitzvah,* Deborah could not depart until after the Grace After Meals. This meant that she would arrive home long after Eli had eaten lunch, and he would by then be glumly watching a ball game on television.

That evening she would have to rush out again on a round of sickbed visits that sometimes brought her home at two or three in the morning.

They would drive together to the Temple for Sunday School. They would separate at the doorstep—Eli heading desultorily for his classroom, hoping fervently that his mother, in her capacity as principal, would not pay them a visit this week.

———

Perhaps the biggest lie that Deborah had told herself was that she could make things right in a single afternoon. The time after Sunday School was to have been sacrosanct for mother and child to spend together. But of course she had not reckoned on certain inexorable facts of life.

For one, Sunday is the time favored by most couples for weddings. Also, because there can be no burials after Friday morning and all day Saturday, there would be a disproportionate number of funerals scheduled for Sunday. So much for the "sacrosanctity" of her parental time.

Deborah was conscientious and compassionate. She was dedicated. And yet while these qualities were also necessary for the exercise of motherhood, she seemed invariably to fulfill the rabbi's duties, not the parent's.

Her intuition told her that children like Eli know instinctively when they are being relegated to a back burner, responding with a direct protest to their elders. There would be only one problem. The communication would be in code. She would not receive a letter from her seven-year-old's attorney stating, "My client objects to your inadequate parenting and reserves the right to sue for any permanent damage that may occur as a result of your negligence."

Would that things were so simple. Instead, Eli's resentment might be expressed by various disruptive behavior patterns. And by the time his messages were decoded, perhaps it would be far too late.

62

Timothy

Timothy found the fury of the New England snowstorms empathetic with his own anger.

And he was grateful to have so much work to do—curricula to revise, schools to visit, lectures to prepare. Not that he hoped for any real relief. But at least he craved—and was sometimes blessed with—exhausted, dreamless sleep.

He told Cardinal Mulroney all he had learned about his bastardy and offered both to relinquish his position and his collar.

His Eminence, touched by Tim's candor, assured him that although a man born out of wedlock was technically ineligible for the priesthood, there was sufficient precedent in canon law to support his legitimacy as a cleric. "Yours is a classic case of '*ecclesia supplet*,'" he reminded him. "In other words, the Church stands behind you.

"And besides," he added with plain, unlatinate bluntness, "we couldn't afford to lose a man like you. We need a dozen more with their spiritual shoulders to the wall to keep it from falling down."

And so Tim attacked his new responsibilities with vigor.

Although Matt Ridgeway's departure was sorely lamented, his achievements were soon dwarfed by those of his charismatic successor. It seemed as if Father Timothy Hogan had been born to galvanize the young. Students hung on his every English word, and those who could not understand his dramatic allusions in Latin were inspired to learn the language, if only to appreciate them.

Nor were his superiors slow in rewarding him. Early in Tim's second semester Cardinal Mulroney called him into his office.

"I'm afraid I'm going to have to pull you off the road," His Eminence said sternly.

"I don't understand," Tim remarked, off balance.

"Then I've finally found a fault in you." The cardinal smiled. "You have no sense of your own worth. In any case, your many gifts have earned you the dubious honor of becoming my personal adviser."

"I beg your pardon?"

"You're young and wise. I need your help, if only to be good enough to justify Rome's faith in me. So I'm going to fix you up with an office and a secretary within shouting distance of mine. Is that all right with you, Tim?"

"Of course, Your Eminence," he replied, adding nostalgically, "but to be honest I'm going to miss those long drives between schools. The New England landscape can be very soothing to the harried soul."

"Don't worry about that." The Cardinal smiled. "In my chancery the staff is much too busy to be harried!"

He laughed heartily at his own joke.

———

It was not long before Mulroney began to employ Tim as an unofficial understudy at various fund-raising events. At first, Tim bridled at the task, knowing that his opening words, "His Eminence regrets . . . ," would elicit groans from the crowd who were expecting the man in the red hat. To his astonishment, there were no complaints. In fact, as time passed he was increasingly invited in his own right.

This at least gave him some "sins" to reveal at confession. For he had to acknowledge his own vanity—the palpable pleasure of being the object of admiration.

One spring afternoon at tea, the Cardinal inquired casually, "Tell me, Tim, what do you know about balance sheets, debits, credits, and the like?"

"Nothing at all, I'm afraid," he admitted.

"Good, I knew you were a kindred soul. I've been praying over this for a week now, and I've got the strong impression that our monetary dilemma needs an innocent—the lamb among the bulls, so to speak."

"I don't understand the reference, Your Eminence. Is it one of Aesop's fables?"

Mulroney's large pectoral cross fairly bounced from his chest as he shook with laughter. "Don't expect erudition from me, my lad," he replied. "It's just another of my idiotic mixed metaphors. The 'bull' is, I take it, good news on Wall Street, and the lamb—in this case two of them—you and I."

Thereupon, in unadorned language, Mulroney explained Boston's predicament—which was typical of every diocese in the country: Attendance was dwindling and donations were growing scarcer still.

"Naturally, we've got a large endowment," the Cardinal explained, "but that dates from the heyday of the Kennedys. Unfortunately, through the years our bankers have barely earned us enough to keep up with inflation. We'll be lunching with them tomorrow. We must be firebrands, lest our schoolchildren freeze for lack of winter fuel."

"I don't think I've ever given a thought to money in my entire life." Except to pay for a broken window, he added to himself.

"Good." The Cardinal smiled. "Then you'll be absolutely fresh!"

———

In a world of private banking dominated by the Protestant establishment, the Boston firm of McIntyre & Alleyn was a conspicuous exception. Indeed, their reputation—and their assets—had grown precisely because Catholic money wanted to be placed in Catholic hands. Their clients had weathered the crash of '29 because M & A knew how to do business only one way—conservatively. In the go-go '70s, however, this very virtue proved their most egregious drawback. And many accounts—some third-generation clients—abandoned their Stone Age strategies, preferring the tactics of such intrepid adventurers as Michael Milken of Drexel.

By the late 1970s they had closed their branches in Philadelphia and Baltimore, keeping their New York operation open in a cubbyhole—mostly for the sake of their letterhead. The firm's headquarters in Boston retained only the genteel mahogany-paneled suite in a venerable building downtown.

As the archbishop and his personal assistant stepped out of the elevator, they saw a workman kneeling before the glass doors of McIntyre & Alleyn, appending to the bank's title the gilt-painted words *and Lurie*.

"What kind of changes are you making?" the cardinal inquired, as he and Timothy sat in the boardroom with the two senior partners.

"New blood," said McIntyre Senior, "although

strictly speaking . . ." He paused for a moment and then said uneasily, "This Lurie fellow isn't really joining us. We're joining him. He's bought the majority stake."

The Cardinal of Boston grew restive. Tim expressed his superior's annoyance. "How could you do this without consulting His Eminence?"

"With respect," Mr. Alleyn countered gravely, "Mr. Lurie's activities have no relation whatsoever to the archdiocese's portfolio. His style is emphatically 'aggressive,' whereas we have standing orders from the chancery restricting us from being the slightest bit . . . adventurous."

"I beg your pardon, Mr. Alleyn," Tim interrupted. "I don't think you can glorify your investment strategy by calling it 'conservative.' As I see it you were so used to letting us live on annual contributions and interest that you never paid any attention to our capital. Now that they've both shrunk, administrators like myself are faced with the terrible prospect of having to close schools."

The cardinal leaned over and whispered to Tim, "Well done, lad. Would you like to take it from here?"

"Myself?" Tim gasped.

"If you like, I can leave you my hat," Mulroney joked, and then turned to the bankers. "Gentlemen, Father Hogan will handle matters from this point. You can assume that his opinions echo my own. I hope the Lord blesses you with the inspiration to get us out of this unholy mess."

In an instant the prelate had vanished, and Tim was left in the hot seat.

"What would you like us to do, Father Hogan?" McIntyre asked deferentially.

"I'd be grateful if you'd pull out the records and have someone translate them for me."

Mr. Alleyn realized this young priest needed to be placated. "We'll both stay. We can order in some sandwiches and work through lunch."

"Fine," Tim replied, "but while we're setting things up, why don't we ask the aggressive Mr. Lurie to join us?"

"Oh, I really don't think so," Mr. Alleyn said apologetically. "He works out of the New York office."

"Well," Tim commented, "perhaps he'd bestir himself to serve the Church."

"Uh, Lurie's not Catholic," said McIntyre. "I'm afraid he's a Jew."

"Mr. McIntyre, I find that remark unworthy of a Christian. Now why don't we get him on the phone?"

An intercom button was pressed, orders were given, and before Tim could finish the cup of coffee in front of him there was another buzz to say the new senior partner was on the speaker phone.

"Uh, hello there, Dan," Alleyn began politely.

"Sorry to disturb you, but as you know, one of the firm's oldest clients is the Archdiocese of Boston. I've got Cardinal Mulroney's assistant with me, and he'd like a few words with you."

"Fine. Put him on."

"Hello, Mr. Lurie. This is Father Hogan."

"Did you say 'Hogan?' It couldn't by any chance be *Timothy* Hogan?"

"Yes, as a matter of fact. Why did—"

At that moment each realized whom he was addressing, and the legate of the Cardinal of Boston—renowned for the brilliance of his Latin—began to speak to Mr. Lurie in New York—in Yiddish.

"Vos iz mit der nomen 'Lurie'?" Tim asked. Why are you calling yourself Lurie?

"Ikh hob shoyn gebracht genug shanda oif die mishpocheh," the voice replied. I've already caused my family enough embarrassment.

A moment later, the call concluded, and Timothy addressed those present. "Danny's agreed to take the next shuttle. Let's be sure we get him a sandwich. A cheese sandwich."

63

Daniel

After thriving in the perilous battlefield of commodities trading, I thought nothing could make me nervous anymore. Yet on the flight to Boston I was so unsettled I could barely read the newspaper.

It had been more than eight years since I had last seen my priestly "brother-in-law." So much had happened in the interim, especially to the most important person in our lives, who I knew would be the dominant presence in our confrontation, although hundreds of miles away.

The air would be charged with contrasting passions—my pious Catholic partners no doubt bowing and scraping to their archdiocesan officer, myself an alien religiously as well as financially. Underneath all the civil exteriors, there would be plenty of veiled hostility.

McIntyre & Alleyn would still be smarting from

my takeover of their cherished firm. They had conveniently forgotten that it was only young Pete McIntyre's extraordinary combination of arrogance and ineptitude that had brought them to the brink of bankruptcy the year before, and that I had appeared as a white knight to save the company with a deftly organized leveraged buyout.

Into this lion's den I would walk, a modern Daniel, where I would confront the man who had so wronged my sister and effectively destroyed her life, the man who, by denying him a father, had in a sense ruined Eli's life as well.

The first few seconds were of course the hardest. I entered the boardroom and saw Tim—perhaps five pounds heavier than when I last had seen him but otherwise unchanged. As we shook hands he mouthed some platitudes about my father's death. I acknowledged them politely and suggested we get down to the business at hand.

I took one look at their portfolio and realized that its mediocrity was not even the fault of some cretin like Pete McIntyre. It was a case of plain and simple neglect.

While in the outside world the prime rate was hovering around twenty percent, they were still holding government bonds harking back to World War II, which were earning a mere three or four percent. By the time we broke for lunch I had set out a preliminary restructuring plan, and Tim was effusively grateful.

Fortunately, McIntyre & Alleyn obviously felt some kind of *noblesse oblige* to keep Tim company. So we were not alone when we munched our sandwiches, and Father Hogan could only make the obvious small talk, like asking how I, who had once embarked upon a career dedicated to upholding the values of the past, ended up seeking value in futures.

I gave him a short course in options buying, beginning with my Russian wheat ploy in the summer of '72. I then described the exploit that won me the directorship of a commodities fund that M & A had launched—the reward for my astute prediction of the rise in soybean futures during June 1973.

"It was all because the anchovy crop in Peru failed," I explained.

Tim was incredulous. "Come on, Dan. Now I know you're pulling my leg."

"No, honestly, Tim. Breeders all over the world use ground anchovies for livestock fodder in exactly the same way they use soybeans. The Peruvian fishermen's misfortune was the Iowa farmers' windfall. Soybeans rocketed to twelve bucks a bushel. It was phenomenal."

"No, Father Hogan," Mr. Alleyn interposed with a grudging compliment, "the real phenomenon was that Danny had us perfectly positioned to reap this windfall."

I tactfully neglected to mention that shortly after this, against my advice, Pete had put himself on the wrong side of every yo-yo fluctuation in the price of gold and been forced to sell me his birthright, so to speak.

After we had worked for another two hours or so, I excused myself in hopes of catching the five o'clock shuttle. Tim insisted on taking me to the airport in the car the archdiocese had put at his disposal. It was not really an unalloyed gesture of friendship, since I knew full well that I would be interrogated along the way.

Since it was a short journey, he did not waste any time. Abruptly, he ceased to be the confident churchman and hesitatingly inquired, "How's Deborah, by the way?"

"Fine," I replied without elaborating.

"I, uh, assume she's made you an uncle many times over," he said, still probing.

At this point, I figured the best way to extricate myself would be the hypocritical but effective tale of Deborah's "tragedy."

"She's got one boy," I said tonelessly. "Her husband died."

"Oh, I'm sorry," he replied in a shocked voice.

I could tell he was about to plead for more details when, happily, the Eastern Airlines terminal came into view. He had just enough time to murmur something about giving her condolences when our car glided to a halt, and I hopped out.

I wanted to run straight through those glass doors, but something made me glance back at Tim.

He seemed so forlorn and—I guess "helpless" is the word—that I felt a need to comfort him.

"Hey," I murmured. "Deborah's a strong woman. She'll get over it."

With this I walked away, trying not to think of the ineffably sad look on Timothy's face.

64

Timothy

Danny's words had torn open the scar of memory.

The discovery that Deborah had borne a child to another man had been a kind of final, albeit implicit, rejection of his own enduring affection.

In the preceding years, Tim had often conjured up her image, joining her in a world without boundaries—a garden (for that was the literal meaning of "paradise") where they could walk hand in hand, freely sharing each dimension of their love.

This had been painful enough. But at least there had been the paradoxical comfort of her unattainability. Now his dream of holding her was once again a possibility—a theoretical one, to be sure, but nonetheless a possibility.

And there was more: He still loved her so much that he even wanted to comfort her for the grief of her lost husband.

———

"Hello, Father Hogan?"

He recognized the voice and could even put a face to it. It was Moira Sullivan, a lay teacher whose Latin class he had visited when he was touring the Sacred Heart Academy in Malden. He had noticed how much the youngsters loved her. There was a gentleness in her manner and a lilt in her voice. She had blond hair.

And yes, he had admitted to himself, she would no doubt have been attractive to any man who had not taken holy vows. If further proof were needed, she wore a wedding ring.

During a luncheon-conference in the Staff Room, she had addressed several questions to him and at other times flatteringly referred to some of his earlier remarks ("As Father Hogan mentioned . . .").

Now, some ten days later, she was telephoning him.

"It's nice to hear from you, Mrs. Sullivan."

"I just wanted to thank you for the lovely letter you wrote Sister Irene."

"I meant every word," Tim assured her. "You're a wonderful teacher—*ornamentum linguae Latinae.*"

"Oh. . . ." There was shyness in her voice now.

"Um, anyway, I took the liberty of calling to ask whether you'd been able to get a copy of the new textbook I mentioned—"

"Yes—the Cambridge Latin Course. On your recommendation, I ordered it that very afternoon."

"Oh." The disappointment was undisguised. She hesitated. "Did it live up to my rave review?"

"I'm sure it will, but I had to special-order it from Blackwells, so I haven't actually gotten my hands on it."

There was a momentary pause before the teacher spoke again.

"In that case I wonder . . . perhaps you'd like to see my copy. I mean . . ." Her voice suddenly accelerated. "Could I take the liberty of inviting you to dinner . . . at my home? I know how busy you are, so if you can't come, I'll understand."

"Not at all," Tim replied. "I'd very much like to meet your family as well. If I recall correctly you mentioned two daughters. . . ."

"Yes, they'd be absolutely thrilled if a priest from the chancery came to dinner." An uneasy silence. And then, "You see, my husband . . ."

"Does he teach as well?" Timothy inquired cordially.

Another pause. Moira Sullivan's answer was quiet. "He's dead, Father. He was killed in Vietnam eight years ago."

Consciously at least, Tim saw nothing out of the ordinary. A dinner with this widowed mother would be altogether within the scope of his pastoral duties.

———

Paperbacks filled the white laminated shelves lining the walls of her Somerville apartment. Tim could not keep from thinking that Moira's husband had built them himself. Indeed, though she and her two daughters, ten and eleven, were lively and hospitable, the atmosphere was charged with innumerable reminders of her husband's absence.

Moira talked nervously about schoolwork, her family, and other trivialities of everyday life, which were nonetheless foreign to Tim. Only once or twice did she mention Chuck, and even then referred to him almost in the abstract as "my husband."

The little girls, though, had not yet mastered the art of social masquerade. Even when they smiled, sadness never left their eyes.

Tim could see they were comforted (for that of course was the purpose of his visit) by the mere fact that he paid attention to the details of their studies, to Ellen's tales of hockey practice and Susie's pride at having been chosen for the choir.

They were a close-knit family, united by their loneliness. Tim's heart went out to them. They were such innocent girls, defenseless in a world that still viewed the offspring of a single parent as somehow defective.

Worse, by some bitter psychological irony the

children of divorce were somehow socially more welcome than orphans. It was as if the girls bore some blame for their father's death—their schoolmates shied away from "catching" their bad luck.

Moira herself, vivacious and pretty, did not deserve the fate dealt her. Yet how many husbandless victims of the Vietnam war had cried in his confessional? And, sadly, the more children, the more tears.

"You must be sick to death of being asked to dinner, Father," Moira remarked as they were sitting at the table.

"Only when I have to give an after-dinner speech." Tim smiled. "It's a pleasure to be off-duty—and in such charming company."

He winked at the girls, who blushed with delight.

Moira was perceptibly nervous. But she knew both from experience and instinct how to behave as "a wife." For although Tim was a priest, he was nonetheless the man whose presence transformed their group into a family.

Tim sensed this and was secretly embarrassed and unsettled by the pleasure it gave him.

At nine o'clock Moira disappeared for a few minutes when the girls went to bed and left him with her copy of the Cambridge Latin Course, which he duly perused. He had moved on to browse through her library when she reappeared with coffee.

"You've got some fascinating books. I could

spend weeks on your theology collection alone," he said. "I envy you—where do you find the time?"

"Well." She smiled self-consciously. "As you see it's still early and the girls are asleep. If you weren't here I'd probably read for three or four hours."

Part of Tim sensed the subtext of her words, yet instead of changing the subject heard himself say, "Not every night, I'm sure. I mean, you must have a busy social life."

Moira answered candidly, without self-pity. "No."

She paused and then added, "Maybe that's part of what draws me to the Church. In what you flatteringly called my theology section, I've got William James's *The Varieties of Religious Experience.* His primary definition of religion is man's way of dealing with solitude."

"Yes," Tim acknowledged. "That certainly could apply to the priestly calling."

He immediately regretted having said something that might misguidedly lead her on. Learned allusions notwithstanding, he sensed the direction of her thoughts, which he tried to deflect.

"You must miss your husband."

She replied with bewildering certainty, "No." Then she explained. "Chuck and I were both kids. Neither of us knew what marriage was. By the time he learned he didn't like it, we already had the girls, so the only viable option for a nice but immature guy like Chuck was enlisting in the Marines. I hope this doesn't sound too cynical, Father—"

"Tim. Please call me Tim. And, no, I understand what you're saying. Sometimes I think we don't have enough instruction before marriage. After all, it is a kind of frightening leap of faith."

She looked at him and answered, "Yes. And I imagine you know more about it than the average husband."

Distracted by a guilty conscience, Tim was caught off guard. Perhaps she sensed his embarrassment and diffused any potential misunderstanding by adding, "I mean, you must counsel dozens of couples every month. You certainly know what a good marriage *isn't.*"

Tim nodded and smiled at her warmly. It was simply a chaste gesture of affection, but Moira was herself too starved to notice the distinction.

Her tone of voice changed, and he knew instantly that she was speaking to him as a man.

"Ever since I can remember one or another of my friends has had a crush on her priest. I suppose your female parishioners must be in desperate straits."

Timothy laughed, hoping to reinforce the slender pretext that they were discussing other people.

"Yes, I'm afraid now and then I do encounter an overenthusiastic teenager. . . ." His voice trailed off.

She looked at him and whispered, "How about thirty-four-year-old widows?"

Despite himself, he saw the curve of Moira's breasts beneath her white blouse and was frightened of his own thoughts.

He sensed how much she needed physical comfort. And was disquieted to think that *he* might, too. It took all his inner strength to prevent them both from losing control. "I'm sure you understand the commitment of a priestly vow."

"Oh," she said, blushing. "Have I really come across a man beyond all earthly temptation?"

"Yes," Tim replied, feeling a qualm of guilt even as he said it.

"God, I feel so embarrassed. Have I offended you? Will you hate me forever for this?"

She had now drawn closer, her face so near that it was a supreme effort for Tim to dull his sensibilities to her beauty. He spoke gently.

"No, Moira. I'm not offended. If it can be of any consolation, I understand in ways I simply can't explain. I hope we can still be friends."

She stared at him with admiration.

"Oh, yes. I hope at least for that."

It had not been easy for Tim, for as a man he could not deny that she was attractive. And yet the priest in him had prevailed. So much so that he felt secure enough to kiss her on the forehead and whisper, "Good night. God bless you, Moira."

Outside, unable even to turn the ignition, Tim slumped against the steering wheel. Something in him shared the hurt that he had inflicted upon her.

And he despised himself for the lie he had told—
that as a priest he was above all earthly desire.

For what had saved him from temptation was not
merely religious scruples, but rather his unabated
yearning for Deborah.

65

Daniel

"Well, Mr. Lurie, indulging in a bit of peculation, are we?"

"You could have knocked, McIntyre," Danny replied with annoyance, as the young partner unceremoniously entered his office.

"Oh, I beg your pardon. I didn't realize you were such a stickler for protocol."

Peter McIntyre III was being unusually arrogant to the majority stockholder in his family's firm. He further outraged Danny by sitting down and propping his expensive Gucci loafers on the edge of the desk, remarking, "I bet you didn't even think I knew that big a word, huh?"

"Frankly, no," Danny answered with irritated impatience.

"Actually it's related to the Latin *pecunia*, meaning money, which is itself derived—you won't believe this, Danny—from *pecus,* meaning cattle."

"Hey, will you get the hell out of here—"

Peter ignored him and continued with a grin. "Wonderful thing, Latin. Who would have thought that 'peculation' came from the word for cows? But then I guess they didn't teach Latin in the schools you went to, eh, Dan?"

He leered at Danny for a moment and then drove home his point. "But anyway it's a crime, and you've committed it."

Enraged, Danny stood up, leaned over, and shoved McIntyre's feet off his desk.

"Now what the hell's on your mind, Pete?"

"Well," McIntyre began, "my family's name for one. Mr. Alleyn's for another." He paused, aimed, and then fired: "And your head."

Peter McIntyre III was determined to play out this moment for all it was worth.

"There must be a Jewish word for what you did, Mr. Lurie, something like 'misappropriation of funds,' 'embezzlement,' or 'fraud'—check where appropriate."

Danny shivered inwardly.

"You know something," Pete went on quietly, "when I first met you, I thought you were the smartest guy who ever lived. In fact, I tried to copy you down to the slightest detail just to see if I could latch on to the secret.

"I bet you didn't even notice that when you

started going to Francesco for your suits, I had him cut mine too. I tried to keep up with all the reading you did. I even took a course in computing—which was one of your great gifts to our firm."

Disquieted by this sudden flattery, Danny still did not say a word.

"I'll even make a confession," McIntyre continued. "I'd sometimes come back at one or two in the morning, when I knew you were working at home, and study all the documents on your desk, the words you'd circled, the notes you'd made—"

"In other words," Danny murmured angrily, "you were a sneak thief."

"Call it what you wish," Peter conceded. "But it's small potatoes compared to what you've done. I mean, your Walston Industries caper was a dazzling bit of legerdemain, which in other quarters might even be called grand larceny."

Danny caught his breath. Since his urgent but short-lived "borrowing" of one and three-quarter million dollars from the company coffers was nearly two years behind him, he had been lulled into a false sense of security. Still, he replied in what he hoped were confident tones.

"The fund I run for this firm is audited every six months, Peter. There's never been the slightest question—"

"Oh, I know," McIntyre answered. "There's no one better at the old financial soft-shoe than Dan the Man. By the time you came up for scrutiny you had everything perfectly back in place. You'd already 'bought' Walston Industries and unloaded it—"

"For a *profit*," Danny interrupted.

"Nominal, my friend, nominal," his antagonist rebutted. "By curious coincidence a sum precisely equivalent to interest at the prime rate for the six days you held it. Now, dumb gentile that I am, I can't understand why a guy with your smarts didn't turn a better profit than that."

"What's your point?" Danny demanded.

"What I really want to know is what was *yours*. You must have done something incredibly . . . borderline with that dough. And my insatiable curiosity impels me to find out what."

"Suppose I needed liquidity really fast to cover a temporary shortfall? Anyway, there's no proof I ever did."

McIntyre took his time, wanting to savor this moment like the last drop of a vintage port.

"I guess real computer literacy hasn't hit Wall Street yet, Dan. Those poor backward supervisors only audit your printouts. They don't inspect what might still be lurking deep down in your database."

"Were you actually devious enough to check the contents of my private computer?" Danny was livid.

McIntyre nodded unrepentantly. "Lucky for the firm I did," he said. "I don't have to tell you what would happen if the S.E.C. got wind of this. Not only to you but to the entire partnership—a respected institution founded before your relatives were even puked up on Ellis Island."

He paused for a moment. "That's why I'd like to see this thing worked out privately," he said. "By the way, only my father and grandfather know about this. They've authorized me to speak on their behalf."

"About what?" Danny asked.

"About something you probably won't understand—preserving our good name. So here's our proposal, which we regard as fair, equitable— and completely nonnegotiable."

Danny held his breath as Peter strode up and down the large office, like a player warming up before a championship game.

He stopped at the farthest corner of the room and said softly, "You'll sell us back your majority holding in McIntyre & Alleyn, for fifty cents on the dollar."

"That's outrageous."

"Oh, I agree," Pete replied with mock commiseration. "Believe me, Dan, I fought like hell for you. My father really didn't want to go above twenty-five."

Danny was speechless.

McIntyre continued, "Would you like a little time to think it over—say five or ten minutes?"

"What if I refuse?"

"Oh, that's the beauty of it—you don't have a

choice. At the worst, the McIntyres and the Alleyns only risk embarrassment. You, my good man, risk going to the clink. Know what I mean?"

Danny flopped into his large leather chair. He closed his eyes for a moment, then sighed.

"Okay, draw up the papers and I'll sign them. Just get the hell out of my office."

"Sure, Danny, sure. The documents'll be ready by eleven tomorrow, and we'd be very grateful if you were out of *our* office by twelve. Naturally, we'll forward your mail."

Again Pete smiled and held out his hand in valediction.

"Hey, I feel terrible leaving you here all alone. Could I buy you a drink or something? I mean, if you did something crazy like jump out the window, that would kind of spoil the whole negotiation."

Danny picked up the small gold clock on his desk—a Christmas present from the entire staff of the Fund—and hurled it at Peter McIntyre with all his might. It missed and shattered painfully against the wall.

"Don't worry about it, Dan." McIntyre smiled casually. "We can have the wall fixed. Good night, old buddy."

66

Daniel

I suppose anyone else in my position would have jumped off a bridge. But far from being desperate, I was curiously relieved. God had punished me for what had clearly been a sin. Though my motive had been only to save the *B' nai Simcha* from Schiffman's larceny, and though the reason I had not paid that money back immediately was that the seven days of mourning for my father intervened, had I misappropriated the money for no more than thirty seconds, I would have been no less guilty.

Therefore, instead of drowning myself, or my sorrows, I went up to the little *shtibel* in the Bronx where I was now a regular. I knew that even late at night there would be one or two people studying the Bible and I could join them. Still, one of the scholars, Reb Schlomo, could sense that something was on my mind.

"You got troubles, Danileh?" I merely shrugged, but he took the response as being affirmative. "Trouble with your wife?" I shook my head. "Your health?"

"No."

"Money troubles?" he pressed on.

Rather than be impolite, I answered, "Sort of."

"Listen, Danileh," the old man said compassionately. "I'm not exactly Rothschild, but if you need a few dollars, I could maybe tide you over."

"That's very kind, Reb Schlomo," I replied. "But all I need is your companionship. Why don't we read some Isaiah?"

"Fine, then, Isaiah it is."

Three or four of us stayed up through the night, pausing only for glasses of tea. After morning prayers I finally found the courage to go home and face the rest of my life.

The lamp on my Ansafone was blinking. There was one message: "Will you please call Dean Ashkenazy at HUC."

Five minutes later I was on the line with the head of Deborah's old seminary. "Danny, I hope you don't mind but I got your number from your sister," he said. "I wouldn't bother you if it wasn't really serious, but I need your help."

"How can I possibly help?"

"You know that 'nonexistent' synagogue up north where Deborah cut her teeth?"

"Sure, how could I forget those people?"

"Well, you'll be happy to hear they haven't forgotten you, either. Which is especially fortuitous since the man I was sending up this year has decided to play semipro football instead of becoming a rabbi. So I'm stuck. Will you do it, Danny?"

"By myself?"

"You mean you've forgotten how to read Hebrew?" the dean quipped.

I did not laugh. "With due respect, sir," I protested, "I'm not . . . legitimate."

"Come on, Danny," he chided, "You know perfectly well that any Jew can run a service. Those people up north are counting on you to lead prayers—and especially to blow the *shofar.*"

"Will I have to give a sermon, too?" I asked nervously.

"Absolutely," Ashkenazy replied. "And I know you'll really enjoy going back to the books and preparing some good ones."

———

I don't have to tell you he was right.

I began to haunt the library at HUC and grew increasingly stimulated by the sort of avant-garde theology that was emanating from a whole new generation of scholars. In fact I loved so many of the books that I threw caution to the winds and actually went out and bought most of them.

I had not been so intellectually ignited since I had taken Beller's course. When I revealed my new enthusiasm, Aaron even joked that I was "defecting to God," but curiously I sensed that something in him was pleased.

I found myself studying till three or four A.M., unable to tear myself away from the excitement of putting new perceptions onto paper.

Finally, two days before the New Year I set out, my rented station wagon loaded with books, my head filled with ideas.

I was no Deborah, but I think what I had come to call the "freeze-dried" congregation (add water once a year, and it fills the hall) responded to my enthusiasm.

Paradoxically, it was an initiation for me. Though I had read from the pulpit hundreds of times in my life, I had never given a sermon. Even my *bar mitzvah* speech, as is customary among the Orthodox, was merely an interpretation of the text to show my learning. This time I was expressing my own ideas and personal feelings, which I wanted to share with the congregation.

About our traditions. Our heritage. About what it meant to be a Jew in the year 1980. This was especially meaningful for them, since for the remainder of the year they were awash in a sea of Christians who, however tolerant, were unaware that we were their spiritual ancestors.

I tried to make everything relevant. During the Prayer For Our Country's Leader, I referred to President Carter's achievement in effecting the peace treaty between Israel and Egypt, and expressed our hope that it would ultimately bring harmony to that entire troubled region.

At first, I was embarrassed by the fact that they hung on my every word. But gradually my super-ego permitted me to take some pleasure, and by the closing prayer on Yom Kippur, I actually felt pride.

Dr. Harris insisted that I remain after the final blast of the *shofar* so I could have dinner and a chat with him and several of the officers.

I thought at first they were trying to fix me up.

"Are you married, Rabbi Luria?"

"No," I replied, "I don't seem to have gotten around to it. And by the way, I'm not an official rabbi."

"It doesn't matter," Mr. Newman interposed, with a kind of quiet passion. "You are to *us*. And our reason for asking is simply to find out if you have any ties in New York."

"Only striped ones," I jested. By now I sensed where this was leading.

They went on to tell me that during the previous year they had regularly talked about getting a permanent wandering rabbi for their scattered community.

"I think of us as a lot of loose beads," Dr. Harris put it metaphorically, "and we need someone to make us into a necklace. We were hoping you'd be interested."

"So you'd like me to be your piece of string." Although I said it lightly, I was genuinely touched.

"Look at it any way you want," said Mr. New-man. "We've canvassed the members. If you could visit each of five towns on a different day of the week you'd just about cover all of us. We think we could afford to offer you twenty-five thousand a year—we might be able to stretch a little more, but not much. Of course we'd take care of your travel expenses." He added diffidently, "Do you think you could manage on that?"

Little did he realize how momentous his words were to me. If they were asking me whether a modest salary would be adequate, then they knew nothing of my other life . . . my peculation. To them I was still pure. And the thought of leaving my sins behind me made his offer seem like a gift from Heaven.

"Dr. Harris," I said softly, "I feel honored."

There was a universal sigh of joyful relief. "Danny," Mr. Newman said with emotion, "we're all grateful. You can't imagine what you're doing."

And I, for my part, was unable to say that *they* could not imagine what I was doing, either. They could never know that I had just discovered what I wanted to do with the rest of my life.

Not be a big rabbinical heavyweight, being bowed and scraped to. Or sit in judgment over other people's behavior before I arrogated to myself the right to render a judicial verdict.

Nor bow before the golden calf, either.

The New Testament may not be my Bible, but I

found it to contain some important thoughts. For example, "the love of money is the root of all evil." This had all the more effect upon me since it comes from the First Epistle of Paul to Timothy, and the whole phrase concludes that while some have coveted it, "they have erred from the faith and pierced themselves through with many sorrows."

As far as I was concerned, I had erred right back to the faith. For the simple reason that I felt needed.

67

Deborah

It was early spring in the third year of Deborah's ministry. She was conducting a seminar on the upcoming Passover festival when her secretary politely interrupted to say that Stanford Larkin, Eli's headmaster, was on the telephone. At first she feared that her son had been hurt. She was right, but did not realize the nature of the injury. Mr. Larkin wanted to set up an appointment. She implored him to see her right away, and he agreed.

"He's a really lively boy," the headmaster began.

Herself a counselor, Deborah knew full well this was a euphemism for rowdy.

"He's also extremely energetic."

She knew this meant belligerent. She only wondered how far Eli had gone.

"In one sense, I have to admire his courage," Larkin continued. "I mean, he's not afraid to take on boys twice his size. The only problem, Rabbi, is that he's always the one who starts the fights."

The headmaster continued. "It's been my experience that when children act like this they are calling to us, signaling for our attention."

Consumed with guilt, Deborah nodded. "What do you suggest we do, Mr. Larkin?"

"Well, I'd strongly urge that Eli be evaluated by a child psychologist."

Her heart fell, but Deborah managed to respond, "Yes, yes, you're quite right. If there's someone you can recommend . . ."

Larkin took a piece of paper from his desk and handed it to her. Written on it was the name Marco Wilding, Ph.D. Lest Deborah think the conversation could have ended otherwise, included at the bottom was the exact date and time Dr. Wilding had agreed to see her son.

After three one-hour sessions with Eli, the psychologist arranged a fourth with Deborah herself.

As Dr. Wilding leaned his forearms on his desk, emphasizing the muscular shoulders of the football lineman he had been in college, he pronounced a clinical, incisive diagnosis to a woman he was clearly at the same time sizing up. This did not make it any easier for Deborah to accept his opinion.

"You've got to get on his wavelength," he began. "You still think of him as a kid, but even boys of nine are becoming aware of their gender. And psychologically at least, he's on the horizon of manhood. Does that make sense, Deborah?"

"I think so, Doctor," she replied in a tone intended as a subtle reprimand for his cavalier use of her first name.

"I mean, tell me," the psychologist continued, "are there any men in his life?"

"He's got my brother, Danny."

"And how often does he see him?"

"Every few months. On vacations mostly."

"Well that scarcely counts, wouldn't you say? When Eli gets up in the morning there's no one shaving in the bathroom. No one tossing a football with him on the weekends. No one showing him how to box—"

"He fights enough during the week, thank you," Deborah interrupted coolly.

"Ah," said Wilding, with a knowing smile. "That's precisely it, Deborah. He fights because nobody teaches him to box. Does that seem paradoxical?"

"No, Doctor," Deborah confessed.

"How about you?" he inquired. "Are there no men in your life? I assume as a rabbi you would come into contact with many."

"Yes. But precisely because I am a rabbi, the relationship has to be strictly pastoral. Do you get my point, Doctor?"

"Loud and clear," he answered. "But don't you think your problem's quite germane?"

"My problem?"

"Deborah, you're young, attractive—and unattached. I assure you—and I'm speaking now with total objectivity—that if you had a stable relationship, it would do wonders for your son. Now, when do you think you'll be ready to remarry?"

Deborah was offended but inwardly she had to concede that the question was legitimate. She replied with quiet candor, "Never. I don't intend to."

"What makes you so adamant?"

"*That* is none of your business. Now, if you'll stop grinning at me like a toothpaste commercial and tell me what I can do to help my son, I'll leave and let you upset your other parents. By the way, are you as blunt as this with the fathers?"

"Absolutely." Wilding smiled. "And you'd be amazed how passively they take it. You've got a lot of spunk, Deborah. If you're as brave as you're coming on now, you'll do what's right for the kid."

"And what in your opinion is 'right'?"

Wilding looked her in the eye and said two words: "Military school."

"What?"

"All right, call me a fascist reactionary. But Eli needs discipline. And yes, call me a sexist—but he needs some paradigms of masculinity to emulate."

"Oh, come on, Doctor. Can you actually see my son marching around in a uniform saluting people all day long?"

"Yes," the psychologist answered, pounding his

desk for emphasis. "And I can see it doing him a world of good. Of course, if you object to that much regimentation, there are always the traditional boarding schools—"

Deborah could tolerate no more.

"You're bent on taking him away from me, aren't you?"

"I'm just trying to help him, Deborah," Wilding replied with the first hint of compassion he had displayed that afternoon. "And I'm telling you what I believe he needs."

"Then perhaps you can give me one alternative that doesn't get me out of the picture."

Marco Wilding rested his square jaw in his hand, reflected for a moment, and then spoke. "Okay, I should've thought of this before. . . ."

"Yes?" Deborah asked impatiently.

"Your kibbutz—he loves it there. He lives for the summers and dies at the thought of having to leave. Have you ever thought of going back with him permanently?"

"You mean just give up everything—my job, all my responsibilities?"

Suddenly Dr. Wilding's face grew somber. He looked the mother of his patient squarely in the eye.

"I would think your first responsibility would be your son. And that, Ms. Luria, is all I have to say."

———

For once her brother refused to discuss it with her.

"But, Danny, you're the only friend I have. Just

put yourself in my place for a minute. What would you do?"

"I'd go right out and marry the first remotely eligible girl I could find."

"You're not serious. You mean 'love' wouldn't come into it?"

"Listen," he retorted. "I'd do it out of love for my *kid*. In fact, I'd do it if you wanted Eli to live with me. You know, so much of my unofficial rabbinical counseling involves screwed-up parents with screwed-up kids. I'm convinced that a spouse can survive almost anything—but a child can't."

Just then the doorbell rang. They made a date for another chat at ten that evening, and Deborah rushed to the door.

There were two people there. But at first Deborah did not even notice Jerry Phillips, Eli's Phys. Ed. teacher. All she could see was the blood smeared over her son's small face.

"Oh, my God!" she gasped. "Eli, what's happened to you?"

The boy lowered his head. The explanation was left up to Jerry.

"He's okay, Rabbi. Just a bloody nose that'll clear up with a good wash. Unfortunately it's the other fellow, Victor Davis. . . ."

Oh, God, Deborah thought to herself, and a congregant, too.

"He started it!" Eli interrupted in angry self-defense.

Ignoring him, Deborah asked the teacher, "What exactly happened?"

"Before I could separate them, Eli decked the Davis boy, and Vic kind of hit his head on the wooden floor."

"Is he okay?"

"Let's hope so," Phillips answered uneasily. "He's at Middlesex Hospital being X-rayed right now. Which reminds me, I promised to meet the parents there." He looked awkward and embarrassed. "I . . . I'm really sorry about this, Rabbi," he mumbled.

"Please, Mr. Phillips," she replied uncomfortably. "Thank you for understanding," she said, adding, "And thank you for driving him home."

Deborah closed the door, looked at Eli, and shouted, "You should be ashamed of yourself!"

But the boy persisted in his self-defense. "Mom, I swear he started it. He kept elbowing me in the neck."

For an instant, Deborah tried to visualize the scene and realized that Eli's antagonist must have been considerably taller. Still, bravery was no excuse for pugnacity.

"All right, let's get in the bathroom and clean you up."

As she rubbed her son's cheeks with a cold cloth she could feel him wince. Whatever the outcome, he had obviously taken several hard blows and was manfully trying to disguise his pain. It was all she could do to keep from hugging him.

Ten minutes after she had sent Eli to his room to finish his homework, the phone rang. It was Mr. Davis.

To Deborah's anxious query regarding his son's condition, he growled only that there was no concussion but "it could have been a heck of a lot worse."

"I can't tell you how sorry I am," Deborah offered.

"*Sorry?*" Mr. Davis answered. "I would think you'd feel ashamed. That's no way for a rabbi's son to behave."

She wanted to interject that most nine-year-old boys are prone to aggressiveness—regardless of their parent's occupation. "The horizon of manhood," as the good Dr. Wilding put it.

"I mean, really, Rabbi," he continued his harangue, "you should be setting an example in this community. It's disgraceful that my so-called spiritual leader's kid acts like a hooligan. I'm warning you, if I ever see your boy at basketball again, I'm resigning from the Temple."

Seething, Deborah could manage just one final burst of civility.

"I'm grateful to know your position, Mr. Davis," she answered coolly. "Good night."

She put the phone down, buried her face in her

hands, and tried to think clearly. If young Davis was anything like his father, it was no wonder Eli had belted him.

She went up to his room. Light still shone under his door.

She knocked softly. There was no reply. She slowly opened the door and saw her son curled up under the blankets, fast asleep. His reading light was still on.

Some instinct made her glance at his bookshelves, and she instantly realized that something was different.

Everywhere they went Eli carried with him, as a kind of holy icon, a framed photograph of his "father" standing proudly by a Phantom jet, the Star of David clearly visible on its side. He always placed it near his bed so he could see it before going to sleep. This was perhaps the most painful of all the lies she had been a party to. Every night when he said his prayers Eli would always conclude with, "Good night, Mama," and then add in Hebrew, "Good night, *Abba.*"

Suddenly, it struck her what was wrong: The frame was empty. What had he done with the picture? Some irrational fantasy made her first think he had somehow discovered the truth and torn the photograph into a million pieces.

Yet a closer look at her sleeping son revealed where the photo now was—in Eli's embrace.

She had all she could do to restrain her tears as she

leaned down, gently brushed aside a lock of blond hair, and kissed his forehead. Then, turning out the light and closing his door, she went downstairs to make the most important phone call of her life.

———

At breakfast she tried to restrain her emotions so the subject would come up naturally. Though she avoided all mention of the previous day's brawl, Eli was nonetheless sullen and withdrawn. She sat down across from him, took a sip of coffee, and opened the conversation.

"Eli, do you like it here?"

"What do you mean by 'here'?"

"I don't know, Connecticut, your school—just 'here' in general."

"Yeah, sure," he replied blandly. "I mean, it's okay." He studied his mother's face to decipher her intentions. "How about you, Mom, do you like it?"

Ah, that was a tough one. She had prepared no text for this.

"To be honest, Eli, I'd be happy except that something tells me you're not."

"Hey, I don't know what you're talking about," he replied defensively. "Why don't you say what you want to say?"

"Well." Deborah hesitated, trying not to betray emotion. "Sometimes I miss the kibbutz, don't you?"

"We go there in the summer, so how could I miss it?"

"You could miss it in the winter," his mother suggested. And then asked, "Do you?"

The little boy paused. "Sometimes . . . ," he confessed in a whisper.

"Well then, how would you feel if we went back for good?"

"What about your job?" he protested—a little too quickly.

"Well, basically I'm a teacher. A rabbi doesn't necessarily have to put on a robe and give sermons. Bible Studies are part of the general curriculum, and I could teach them in the Regional Kibbutz High School."

The boy was silent for a moment, and then asked quietly, "Who says they'd give you a job?"

She smiled. "Grandpa Boaz says. I spoke to him on the phone last night."

For a moment there was total silence. Deborah was moved as she watched her son try to suppress his growing elation.

"Really?" he asked.

"Really," she answered.

Eli looked at his mother wide-eyed and then suddenly, as if propelled by an engine, ran into her arms.

68

Timothy

Few realized that despite his vast popularity, Timothy was not yet an official member of the Boston archdiocese. A priest moving from one bishopric to another is required to spend two or three years of "incardination."

When Tim's pro forma trial period was concluded, Cardinal Mulroney held a small dinner in his honor at which he bestowed upon him the title "Monsignor."

This only swelled the number and variety of invitations he received, ranging from orphanages to formal fund-raising dinners.

Understandably, Tim felt more at home at school picnics and Knights of Columbus barbecues than at black-tie banquets at the Ritz Carlton, where sedately elegant Catholic matrons felt secure enough to ask him to dance without fear of arousing their husbands' jealousy.

After endless months of "socializing for God"— as Mulroney lightheartedly referred to it—Tim had started to put on weight, and he forced himself to jog around the Boston College reservoir instead of eating lunch.

One blustery afternoon, he was astonished to see his secretary, the normally phlegmatic Sister Marguerita, scurrying toward him without a coat, waving an envelope as if to flag him down.

"Monsignor," she called out with a thrill in her voice, "you've got an invitation from Washington!"

"That's still no excuse for you to go out without a coat, Meg," Tim joked as he reached her, struggling to regain his breath in the cold air. "President Reagan?"

"Almost as lofty," she puffed. "It's from the Vatican Embassy."

Though he affected surprise for her sake, Tim strongly suspected what the letter contained.

Less than a year earlier, in January 1984, Ronald Reagan had reestablished the formal diplomatic ties with the Vatican which had been suspended for more than one hundred years. From now on, the apostolic delegate from Rome would be addressed in Washington as "His Excellency the Ambassador."

The invitation in Tim's hand requested the pleasure of his company at a Gala Reception to welcome the new Vatican Envoy to America, none other than the principessa's beloved brother, Archbishop Giovanni Orsino.

"Isn't that splendid, Monsignor?" Sister Marguerita gushed.

Affecting a stern gaze, Tim cautioned her, "Meg, this is confidential—I don't want to hear any of it buzzing about the third floor of the Residence." His secretary nodded, blushing slightly. No doubt they already know, Tim mused to himself.

———

The lights of the Vatican Embassy on Massachusetts Avenue shone bright enough to be seen by air traffic in the sky as an endless cavalcade of limousines drove up and disgorged the aristocracy of Washington.

Tim was already inside when he heard the trumpets blaring "Hail to the Chief." He watched with awe as President and Mrs. Reagan appeared at the head of the staircase, both smiling broadly and waving. They went straight to their host, Archbishop Orsino, who greeted them warmly and introduced them to various members of the American Catholic elite.

Cardinal though he was, Mulroney nonetheless felt awkward in the company of high-ranking diplomats and government officials. As a result, he spent most of his time talking shop with his fellow Eminences from New York, Chicago, Los Angeles, Detroit, and Philadelphia.

Tim could enjoy no such fraternity and hence drifted shyly to the periphery, gazing at the glittering armada of guests, which included, among the many luminaries from Capitol Hill, Senator O'Dwyer from Massachusetts, who had visited him so long ago at St. Athanasius'. He stood immobile for several moments until suddenly hailed by a familiar voice.

"Hey, Hogan," came an incongruously raucous salutation. Tim turned to see George Cavanagh, dangling a half-filled glass of champagne in his hand.

"I thought you were still in the wilds of South America," Tim remarked as the fellow seminarians shook hands. "I never expected to see you at an affair like this."

"Well, this is just another kind of jungle, isn't it?" George responded with undisguised irony.

"How've you been?" Tim asked, while trying to assess the genuineness of his old acquaintance's cordiality.

"Tired, Father—I should say *Monsignor*— Hogan. I can't tell you what it's like to try to shepherd the flocks south of the border. I only survived because *their* faith sustained me." He took a swig of champagne and sighed. "But I'm all played out, Tim. I can't take any more of this guerrilla warfare."

"You're not leaving the Church, are you, George?"

A light immediately rekindled in Cavanagh's weary eyes.

"No, I'm not giving up *that* fight. But I've become a 'company man.' Next month I'm being consecrated Auxiliary Bishop of Chicago. You'll get your invitation."

"Oh," Tim responded, surprised at first. Then, with genuine warmth he added, "Congratulations are in order, Your Excellency."

"Not really," George replied disconsolately. "It was a simple *quid pro quo*."

"I don't understand."

"My newspaper, Monsignor. That's all I had to give up. *La Voz del Pueblo* is now silenced."

Before Tim could respond, George quickly added, "Of course, that doesn't mean I'm totally compromising my principles. But at least I'll have a chance to express them from a pulpit instead of a tree stump in a tropical forest.

"To be honest, I'm looking forward to it. Not just having running water and a good bed. But to be nearer a source of spiritual comfort for those awful nights—you know, when your soul can't sleep."

Tim nodded. "I have had my share of those."

George downed the rest of his drink and continued. "Just between the two of us, Timmo, sometimes I wish our prayers could be sent by registered mail—just so's we'd be certain *once* that they'd reached their destination." Weaving slightly on his feet, he slurred, "Hey, I'm getting a bit seditious, aren't I?"

"No," Tim answered quickly. "Just a little drunk. I think you ought to go home and go to bed."

"Home?" George countered. "Where is 'home' to a Catholic priest? At the moment there are four of us in a suite at the Watergate. Can you imagine, Timmo? The *campesinos* are starving in Nicaragua, and we're enjoying twenty-four-hour room service."

Tim began to nudge his friend toward the door. Once outside, he helped him find his driver, and when George was seated in the car said reassuringly, "Hey, Cavanagh, if it means anything, I admire you. I really do."

George looked up and asked woozily, "Are you serious, Hogan?"

"I wish I had your heart," Tim said affectionately.

"I don't believe you. But I wish I had your *head*. Good night, Monsignor."

With that Cavanagh pressed the electric window closed and waved to the chauffeur to drive off.

When Timothy returned to the festivities, the host himself came up to him.

"*Caro Timoteo,*" said Ambassador Orsino, "I've been looking everywhere for you."

"I'm happy to see you again. How is your sister?"

"Blossoming as ever. She sends her most fond

regards," Orsino replied. "But I want to talk to you more privately. Are you free for breakfast tomorrow?"

"Yes, any time you'd like."

"Good. My car will pick you up at 7:45. *Buona notte.*"

———

The Washington morning was unseasonably bright and warm. An elegant table was set on the terrace of the Ambassador's residence, and a white-gloved butler was standing at a respectful distance. Apart from him, there were just the two of them—Tim and the principessa's brother.

"Please, Tim, call me Gianni," the diplomat insisted. "I have been hearing some wonderful things about your various accomplishments in Boston. Apparently you are skilled alike in Latin books and ledger books."

Tim could not suppress a smile. "Actually, it has been very rewarding. The response from the people—"

"And the rank? Do you not also enjoy being called 'Monsignor'?" When Tim hesitated, Orsino urged him to go on. "A touch of vanity is not so sinful. I freely confess to you that for all the titles I already own, I am always delighted when I receive a new one."

Tim smiled at this childlike candor.

"And you have more than earned your honors, I

can assure you. In fact, sitting on my desk I have Cardinal Mulroney's request to elevate you to . . ." His voice trailed off, then continued in a theatrically dismissive tone. "But no. You are too valuable to languish in Boston even as an Auxiliary Bishop, my boy. You are needed in Rome."

The mere mention of his beloved city stirred Tim's longings.

"What exactly would I be doing?" he asked, trying to hide his excitement.

"Well," said the Ambassador, "I'm afraid it won't be as easy as translating Latin epistles. I have persuaded the Holy Father that you have asbestos enough in you to commute between the frying pan and the fire." He grinned. "That was very elegant English, no?"

"Yes, uh—Gianni," Tim said, all the while dazed by the notion that his name had been pronounced, in any context, by the Pope himself.

Orsino took a sip of coffee, wiped his mouth, then leaned on the table looking at Tim.

"The frying pan is South America, Timoteo," he uttered in confidential tones. "No one can testify better than I how badly we need help there. The 'fire,' I'm afraid, is Franz Cardinal von Jakob, formally Archbishop of Hamburg. You of course know the post he holds now?"

"Yes," Tim responded. "He's Prefect of the Congregation for the Doctrine of the Faith."

"Have you ever met him?" asked Orsino.

"I'm afraid I don't move in such exalted circles," Tim replied.

"Actually, you do." The Ambassador smiled. "I saw him at your thesis defense, although true to character he didn't attend my sister's party. Between the two of us, he's an impossible man. But then he has an impossible task. Only a Prussian, I think, would undertake to reeducate the dioceses in Africa where the Mass is chanted to jungle drums and the only concession to celibacy is that local priests do not lodge with their wives and children.

"I don't have to tell you," Orsino added, "von Jakob rules with an iron fist."

"It stands to reason," Tim remarked wryly. "The 'Sacred Congregation' has a long history. Especially under its former name—the Inquisition."

"But believe me, Timoteo, Africa compared to South America is child's play. And *I* can testify to that. The Jesuits are putting unacceptable ideas into the heads of our faithful. This business about 'inculturation' is madness. The next thing we know they'll be singing hymns to tango music. Unless we can get these revolutionaries under control, the Holy Father will have to abolish the Society of Jesus, as Clement XIV did. It's war, my boy."

"But I don't see where I fit in." Tim was genuinely puzzled.

"Ah," said Orsino, rising to his feet so he could pace the terrace and gesticulate more widely.

"That's precisely the point. You're a learned churchman. A charismatic speaker. And most of all a man with unshakable faith in Rome.

"Upon my strong recommendation, it has become the wish of both Cardinal von Jakob and the Holy Father himself that you take the post of Special Envoy from the Curia to the Dioceses of Latin America."

"All of them?"

"Only the ones where the Jesuits are making trouble," Orsino replied, and then grinned. "So I guess that does mean all of them. There must be no more incidents like the Sandinistas' humiliation of His Holiness during his tour of Nicaragua. Our South American priests must be convinced to ignore the inflammatory Jesuitical press—"

"Like *La Voz del Pueblo*?"

"Precisely," the diplomat agreed. And then deftly changing the subject, he asked, "Now can you be in Rome by the end of the month?"

"I think so. Of course I owe Cardinal Mulroney the courtesy of—"

"Oh, there is no problem with that," Orsino commented, a twinkle in his eye. "He is very proud of you, indeed. And since time is of the essence, I'm sure you don't mind if we have the ceremony in Rome."

"What ceremony?" Tim inquired.

"I thought you would take it for granted." The Ambassador smiled ingenuously. "We would not entrust such great responsibilities to a nuncio below the rank of archbishop. Congratulations, Your Grace."

———

As his air-conditioned limousine floated through the hot and humid streets of Washington, Tim was torn with ambivalence.

There is no priest in the world who would not be euphoric at being granted the royal robes of the episcopate.

And yet not everyone would pay for it by serving the . . . Inquisition.

69

Daniel

Within a month of accepting Dr. Harris's offer, I sold my New York apartment and bought an A-frame chalet in Lisbon, New Hampshire, putting the remainder of the money into Treasury bonds. I had lost all desire to deal with Wall Street, and in truth, I had always known that making money did not make me happy.

I chose Lisbon not just for its exotic name, but because it was central to the five-village cluster in which I was now serving as unofficial spiritual adviser. Also it was a snowball's throw from the Vermont skiing areas of Stowe and Sugarbush. I had intended to take up the sport, not out of any athletic urge but because I had always heard it was a great place to meet single girls from New York. It was probably true—but who had time to find out?

In due time I had expanded my operation—most

importantly by taking one or two young congregants over to Israel each summer. While I visited Deborah and Eli, members of my scattered flock could take courses in Hebrew and generally drink in their heritage. This produced instant Sunday School teachers. Gradually I built up a strong team.

I had so completely thrown myself into my work, driving from town to town, leaping from festival to festival, I could scarcely believe that nearly four years had passed since I had become what I chose to call "a rabbi without portfolio."

Only once did I actually realize how quickly sand was passing through the hourglass: in Israel in May for Eli's thirteenth birthday—and that most important landmark in his spiritual life—his *bar mitzvah*.

The kibbutz had no chapel, so Deborah made arrangements with the rabbi of *Or Chadash* in Haifa—one of the first Reform synagogues in Israel—an attractive little building halfway up Mount Carmel.

The rabbi even invited Deborah to share the pulpit with him for that occasion—and especially to sing all the Torah portions preceding Eli's.

Yet an unexpected shadow of melancholy fell on what should have been a completely joyous occasion. For in addition to the kibbutzniks who came in a stately convoy of asthmatic buses, there were six men in their early forties who had made the journey from various parts of the country. They turned out to have been pilots from the same squadron as the "father" of the *bar mitzvah* boy.

Boaz and Zipporah were deeply touched—and Eli was almost speechless with emotion when he heard who these men were. Deborah quickly arranged to have Colonel Sassoon, Avi's wing commander, called to the Torah, just preceding me, Boaz, and herself.

Eli's eyes were riveted on these men, as if he were trying to pierce their memories in hopes of getting a glimpse of his father.

And I couldn't keep from noticing, both during the service and at the party back at the kibbutz, that Avi's comrades kept staring at Eli, no doubt wondering how the hell olive-skinned Deborah and even darker-skinned Avi could have produced such a *blondini*.

The only trouble was, Eli noticed, too.

That night, while the adults celebrated in the refectory, Eli had a party for his classmates from the Regional High School—male and female—at the sports hall. They were having a good time, judging from the giggles I overheard when passing by on the way to my guest room to pick up a sweater.

Suddenly, I heard Eli's voice.

"Hi, Uncle Danny."

"Hi, you were great today, kiddo," I hailed him.

"Thanks, Danny," he answered, with something

less than euphoria. "But would you tell me the truth?"

"Sure," I answered, my preoccupations making me a little anxious about just what he wanted told with candor.

"Did my voice break during the *Haftorah*?"

"Not at all," I assured him avuncularly. "It was all in splendid baritone."

"Gila says my voice broke."

"Who's Gila?" I asked ingenuously.

"Oh, nobody," he replied. This time, his voice did break.

"Aha, so she's the woman in your life I've heard Boaz talk about."

"Don't be stupid, Uncle Danny, I'm too young for girls," he protested too much.

My years as a woodsman-rabbi had indeed given me acumen in the judging of human relationships, even among adolescents.

"She's a real winner," I commented.

"Gila and I are both going to serve in the Air Force," he said proudly.

"Hey, that's five years down the road. You shouldn't be thinking of that stuff on the night of your *bar mitzvah*."

His voice suddenly became somber. "Uncle Danny, in Israel, the minute your *bar mitzvah*'s over that's *all* you think about."

At that moment, despite the party wine I'd

imbibed and the balmy air, I felt cold sober. How could any kid ever have a normal childhood given this ineluctable fact of life?

Still, my childhood hadn't been that wonderful. Maybe I'd have been better off knowing exactly where I was going at eighteen—with no option for dropping out.

I tried to put my arms around my handsome nephew. But even at thirteen he had grown too tall for me to do anything but give him a slap on the back.

It was only when I realized that he had no reason to walk all the way to the guest cottages that I knew our encounter had not been a chance one. And that what Eli most wanted from me on this night celebrating his induction into manhood were some plain home truths.

"Uncle Danny," he began. He was trying to sound calm. "Could we talk, you know, man to man? It's something really important. You're the only guy in our whole family that I completely trust."

Oh, God, I felt as if the sky were going to fall on my head.

"If you're going to ask me the facts of life," I said jocularly, "I'll tell you as soon as I learn them myself."

"No, Danny. This isn't funny," he persisted.

"Okay then," I capitulated. "Tell me what's on your mind."

By this time we had reached my bungalow and we both sat down on the steps.

At first he merely stared in the direction of the lake. Finally he began.

"Uncle Danny, all this week Boaz and Zipporah's relatives have been coming in from Tel Aviv and even Chicago. They spent hours and hours talking about old times and looking at photographs."

I had no illusions about where this was leading.

"It's crazy," he continued wistfully, "they've got millions of pictures. Even some old fading brown ones from Budapest. And there must be a million pictures of Avi as a little boy."

He lowered his head and murmured painfully, "But there are *no* pictures of Mom and Avi. Not a single one. Not even at their wedding." He paused and then confronted me. "What do you think that means?"

My mind raced to find a quip, a diversionary joke—something to get me the hell out of this corner. But I knew my nephew was too smart—and the power of truth stronger than both our wills.

"I never met Avi," I finally answered, making the only honest claim I could.

"That wasn't the question," Eli said somberly.

"Oh?" I responded. "Then what was the question?"

Eli looked at me and said quietly, "Are you sure he was my father?"

Despite the fact that I'd had at least a quarter of an

hour to arm myself with evasionary weapons, I was powerless. I just froze. Finally, he put me off the hook.

"That's okay, Danny," he said softly. "You don't have to give me an answer. The look on your face said everything."

70

Daniel

Two days later I drove Eli to Jerusalem for his "second *bar mitzvah*." As the Silczer Rav, Uncle Saul could not for diplomatic reasons attend Saturday's ceremony. But I agreed with him that we should honor my father's memory by having Eli called to read the Torah during a Monday morning service at the Wailing Wall.

Deborah could not bring herself to come. There was the legitimate objection that she would be separated from her son and pushed into the crowded women's section. Then there was the memory of the riot, from which she still felt psychological scars.

And I suppose there were other memories too.

Needless to say, the entire Jerusalem *B'nai Simcha* community was present, including the yeshiva boys, who were doubly grateful for the half-day

holiday. Like myself, Eli could work both sides of
the street. He was as much at home among the
merrily dancing *frummers* as he had been among
the discoing kibbutzniks.

Afterward, during the wine-and-cake reception
back at the school, Saul called me aside to discuss
some Silczer business.

In the years since my father's death, he and the
Jerusalem Elders still had not agreed on a site for
the yeshiva dormitory.

He had kept me up to date, not because I was one
of the clan, but because, despite Doris Greenbaum's generosity in declining repayment of her
gift, Saul regarded the money as my personal contribution, though of course he had no idea of the
price I had paid.

This time, he was intent on resolving the question of the dormitory once and for all. A week
earlier he had taken me on a tour of the available
buildings in Mea Shearim—and even beyond its
periphery in the contiguous neighborhoods. The
places were cramped and the prices astronomical.

In my opinion, the best we had seen was a three-
story building of Jerusalem stone that had nearly
turned gray with age. We could probably have converted it to a dorm for about sixty yeshiva boys,
who would then have an easy walk to class. But
today Rebbe Bernstein, the chipper and scru-
pulously honest successor to the abominable Schiff-

man, had a new proposal to put before my uncle, who wanted me to hear it too.

As Eli happily wandered off on his own, his destination Richie's Pizza on King George Street (for a kibbutz kid he certainly knew where to meet girls in the big city), we sat in the principal's office drinking glasses of tea as Rebbe Bernstein introduced us to a slender black-coated gentleman named Gordon. After pinning a large map onto the bulletin board he launched into his presentation.

"This, honored rabbis, is the magnificent new township of Armon David—designed with wide streets, the finest materials, and magnificent amenities. And believe me, your neighbors will be strictly the *frummest* of the *frum*."

He paused to let us assimilate these attractions and then continued. "What's more, on the new road promised by the Ministry of Housing, it will be a mere twenty minutes' bus ride—thirty at the most—from where we are now sitting."

Naive visitor that I was, especially feeling that unique elation at being in the Holy City, I was at first captivated by the thought of a place nearby with not only large airy rooms, but even a patch of greenery. The way they worked those kids, it would certainly do them good to have some fresh air that was really fresh.

Then all of a sudden it occurred to me. Even

allowing for the developer's hyperbole, his township was a good deal farther from Jerusalem than would be appropriate. In fact, it looked suspiciously close to the Arab villages of Dar Moussa and Zeytounia.

This prompted me to ask, "It all looks very impressive, but can you tell me on which side of the Green Line it is?"

Gordon was highly offended.

"Surely the son of the great Rav Moses Luria—may his righteous memory be for a blessing—does not believe in absurd territorial quibbles. All of this land was given to our people by Almighty God."

I had to keep myself from asking, If the Holy One had given us this territory, how come this guy was selling it again? But I had more important things to say. I turned to Saul but intended my remarks for all those present.

"I have every respect for Mr. Gordon's talents as a town planner, but I'm afraid the *B'nai Simcha* have certain responsibilities, don't you agree, Uncle Saul? I mean, if we should move to Armon David—"

"You would have space for a hundred students." Gordon interrupted so quickly, a touch of panic showed.

"That's not the point," I retorted, still addressing myself only to Saul. "If we were to build our dormitory beyond the Green Line, that would be construed as a political statement. It would suggest that our community approved of confiscating Arab territory."

Gordon misunderstood my criticism, or chose to. "In other words," he trumpeted, "you would not just be gaining a magnificent living complex, you would be striking a blow in favor of Greater Israel."

All eyes were on Uncle Saul, who stroked his beard and answered quietly, "I don't believe in striking blows, metaphorical or physical. Danny is right."

Gordon was sizzling. Studiously avoiding me, he addressed his remarks to what he sensed might be the weak link in our chain, the diminutive Rebbe Bernstein. "Think of the *skandal* if people should hear that the current Silczer Rebbe renounces our nation's claim to even a millimeter of sacred land."

"Excuse me, Mr. Gordon," Saul said quietly but firmly. "I don't recall using the word 'renounce.' But while we're making accusations, let me tell you that the primary rule by which a Jew must live is *Pikuach Nefesh*—the respect for human life."

Good for Uncle Saul! I followed him into the fray.

"Surely, Mr. Gordon, you remember Leviticus 19:16. 'Neither shalt thou stand idly by the blood of thy neighbor.' On those grounds alone your proposal is out of the question."

It may seem hard to believe, but all the developer said in the time it took him to fold up his map and make an infuriated exit was a single, "Hmph!"

Which I took to mean that the *B'nai Simcha* are

spiritually bankrupt, they're not real Jews, let them go back to Brooklyn, the whole bunch of them. All spiced with choice epithets.

We all sat quietly in the room for a moment. A smile of relief crossed Rebbe Bernstein's face as he looked at my uncle.

"Thank you, Rav Luria," he murmured.

My uncle beamed at me. "I was very proud of the way you acted, Rebbe Daniel," he said affectionately.

With some embarrassment, I reminded him that I was not really a rabbi.

But he responded, "You are, Danileh. You are."

———

As Eli and I were driving back to the kibbutz, he seemed curiously carefree for someone who had experienced such a serious identity crisis only forty-eight hours earlier. He was even humming the latest tunes from the Israeli hit parade.

I didn't have the guts to ask him how he had come to weather his existential crisis with such aplomb—not to mention speed. Happily, as darkness began to fall, he took the initiative.

"Remember that talk we had the other night, Uncle Danny?"

"Yeah," I answered laconically. How the hell could I forget it?

"Well, I confronted Mama and she told me the truth."

She did?

"I suppose you knew about it all the time," he generously allowed.

To which I replied with a noncommittal, "Mmm."

"So what?" he said.

"So what, what?" I asked.

"So my father and mother weren't married. What difference does it make?"

"You're right," I assented. "By Jewish law you're kosher enough to marry the Chief Rabbi's daughter."

We drove for about a kilometer and then he asked me with a mischievous smile, "Is she cute?"

"Who?" I asked, a bit confused.

"The Chief Rabbi's daughter," he replied. "I might be interested."

So Deborah had postponed the inevitable. But sooner or later, somebody would have to come up with the guts to tell Eli the truth. Meanwhile, as the saying goes, "We should thank God and take each day as it comes."

We arrived at Kfar Ha-Sharon just after dinner. Eli with his youthful vigor was willing to forgo a meal in exchange for permission to hitchhike to Gila's kibbutz, so I had a quick bite with Deborah in her *srif*.

She was pleased to hear about all the events in Jerusalem that day, and even went as far as to comment, "That was a very gutsy stand for Saul to take."

"What about me?" I protested, wanting my share of kudos. "I started the whole argument about the Green Line."

"Granted, that took courage," Deborah commented. "But the difference is you're going to go back to the woods, and Saul's going back to Brooklyn where he'll have to face the wrath of God knows how many *frummers*."

71

Timothy

Fifty days after the Resurrection, the eleven apostles had gathered in a room in Jerusalem during the Jewish Festival of Weeks. Suddenly, they heard the rushing of a mighty wind from Heaven and the Holy Spirit appeared before them as tongues of fire.

This blazing epiphany is commemorated by the Feast of Pentecost, a favorite occasion for the ordination of bishops. The ceremonies are a dizzying explosion of red, a reminder both of the flame and the blood of the apostles, all but one of whom was martyred.

On Sunday, May 26, 1985, in St. Peter's Basilica in Rome, Timothy Hogan stood face to face with His Holiness the Pope, the Holy Father all in scarlet, except for the white of his skullcap, and flanked by two cardinals, one of whom was the Archbishop of New York. Like the others about to be ordained, Tim wore a pectoral cross—the only addition to his simple priestly garb, which he was wearing for the final time.

Looking at Tim with his piercing eyes, the Pope as Principal Consecrator questioned his readiness to assume the duties of a bishop. "Are you resolved to be faithful in your obedience to the successor of the apostle Peter?"

Tim managed to whisper, "I am."

He knelt. The warm hands of the Holy Father touched his head. I am as close to God as I ever will be in this life, he told himself.

After the two cardinals also placed their hands on Tim's head, the Pope anointed him with oil, tracing the sign of the cross with thumb and forefinger.

Such was the silence in the massive basilica that His Holiness could be heard to whisper, "*L'anello*." He then said quietly in Italian, "Your hand." Tim complied and stretched forth his wedding finger as the Holy Father pronounced in solemn tones, "Take this ring, the seal of your fidelity. With faith and love protect the bride of God, His holy Church."

Tim was engulfed by a wave of sadness. This is my wedding, he thought to himself. The only wedding I will ever know in my entire earthly life.

As Archbishop Timothy Hogan bowed to receive the pontiff's blessing, he glanced swiftly into the crowd of spectators and saw his beaming mentor,

Father Ascarelli. His presence only emphasized Tim's feeling of unworthiness. For someone of Ascarelli's gifts, the cardinal's hat would have been an easy prize. Yet, a true Jesuit, he scorned high office.

When Tim had asked years earlier whether scarlet robes attracted him, the old man had shaken his head and murmured, "*Sacerdos sum, non hortus.*" I'm a priest, not a flower garden.

The pontiff placed the white-and-gold miter on the new archbishop's head and then handed him as the final symbol of pastoral obligation, the shepherd's crook.

At the end of the Mass, as the choir was still singing exultant hallelujahs, Tim returned to the sacristy, changed from his regal trappings, and walked out into St. Peter's Square. The Swiss Guards in their orange-and-black striped uniforms and medieval armor maintained a path through the sea of people.

He was now officially archbishop of the church of Santa Maria delle Lacrime. This was a mere formality since bishops appointed without a specific diocese nonetheless are given a nominal affiliation with a church in Rome.

Santa Maria had been "offered" to Timothy by the principessa as a gesture of affection. In a way, this ethereal association added to the unreality of it all. Could he, Timothy Hogan, onetime incorrigible street-fighter from Brooklyn, actually be endowed with the purple of the episcopate?

Lost in thought, he was about to cross over to the Via della Conciliazione when he heard a nasal cry behind him, "*Vostra Grazia, Vostra Grazia.*"

He turned as a small middle-aged man in a frayed black corduroy jacket and beret scurried up to him still calling, "Your Grace, Your Grace."

Timothy stopped and inquired, "Yes?"

"At your service, Your Grace," the man puffed deferentially. "Here is my card."

LUCA DONATELLI
VIDEO PHOTOGRAPHER
FOR ALL OCCASIONS

"Please accept my humble congratulations and feel free to call upon me for an indelible memento of this great occasion. Naturally, I can do either VHS or Beta."

———

The celebration was at the principessa's villa.

Nothing seemed to have changed at the Santiori residence—including the hostess herself, who had miraculously retained her youth and vigor by a strict regime of diet, excrcise, prayer—and yearly trips to Dr. Niehans's exclusive clinic in Montreux.

As he entered the villa, Tim impulsively embraced the principessa, almost lifting the petite woman off the ground. "*Grazie*, Cristina," he murmured. "*Grazie per tutto.*"

"Don't be silly, Your Grace," she smiled broadly.

"You have risen by your own merits. I only pride myself in having been among the first to find them."

"With due respect, *Vostra Altezza*," Father Ascarelli interrupted. "I found him before you did." He embraced his protégé, murmuring. "Purple suits you, my boy. Continue to serve God as you have."

There were nineteen guests at the long table, since Archbishop Orsino had telegraphed his regrets at the last minute. The crystal shone, and the wine, from the Santiori vineyards in Tuscany, matched the color of the diners' vestments—except those of Father Ascarelli.

Tim was introduced to a number of foreign bishops making their *ad limina* visits to Rome as well as to several prefects of the Vatican Sacred Congregations. When the Cardinal of New York City shook Tim's hand, he remarked with theatrical emphasis, "Archbishop Hogan, I am charged with the sacred duty of conveying an important message to you." He paused for effect and then continued, "My colleague, the Cardinal of Boston, has entrusted me with the expression of heartfelt affection and congratulations from a list so long that I have no doubt it includes the entire Boston Red Sox!"

Tim was about to reciprocate with a message of gratitude when the principessa appeared. Taking him by the arm, she smiled at his red-clad interlocutor.

"Your Eminence will excuse me," she bubbled, "I must steal the archbishop away for a moment, since one of my guests unfortunately has to rush off to a plane."

As he was whisked away, Tim could not help but think, What authority this little woman must have, to be able to preempt the most powerful prelate in the United States.

The other guests were long gone when Ascarelli insisted that Tim sit with him overlooking the empty forum.

"I know what you're thinking," the old man murmured.

"Do you?" Tim asked, his mind slightly blurred by the length and excitement of the day.

"You're wondering whether it's your own merits or the principessa's *romanità* that won you your appointment."

Tim's silence was assent.

"Believe me, you know I'm parsimonious with flattery. You well deserve your rank. The only influence she used was to get you affiliated with her own church. There were a great many fighting for that honor. These *aristocratici* own some of the most famous churches in Rome. Even that jewel in the Piazza Navona is private real estate."

"Do they charge rent?" Tim joked.

"Each in his own way," replied Ascarelli. "I'm told the principessa is satisfied to accept as recompense one dinner a year with His Holiness. But you'll learn all about this when your time comes."

"My time for what?" Tim asked.

"Come on, my boy, you don't have to use *romanità* with me! You know that of all your classmates you're by far the most *papabile*."

"Pope? Don't be silly," Tim answered dismissively. And fell silent.

In such proximity to the Roman Forum, Ascarelli's rhetoric was unstoppable.

"Amazing, isn't it, that the papacy is the last modern institution with the qualities of a Renaissance court—offering advancement based on talent. My good friend Roncalli—John XXIII—was the son of a poor Bergamese farmer. And Luciani—John Paul I—was the son of a migrant worker. Indeed, my father employed him in our vineyards on several occasions. And what's more," the scribe added with a chuckle, "our Church has chosen three Jewish pontiffs."

"What?" Tim assumed this was another of the old man's practical jokes.

"The Pierleoni family," the scribe explained. "Once upon a time they were solid citizens of the Roman ghetto. Then, after a little holy water was splashed in the right places, they went on to produce Popes Gregory VI and VII and Anacletus II. So it would hardly be earth-shattering if an Irish boy from Brooklyn—"

"Father Ascarelli," Tim demanded plaintively, "what makes you think I harbor such lofty ambitions?"

The scribe looked at him for a moment. "Your eyes, Timoteo. I look in them and see what can only be described as . . . longing. I can't imagine why else you would be so unhappy."

72

Timothy

By the time Tim had returned to his new quarters in one of the elegant prelatial suites at the North American College on the Gianicolo, slender threads of dawn were streaking the sky. Under his door he found a linen envelope containing a card with the papal seal and a small handwritten note:

His Holiness requests your company
for the celebration of Mass at 6:00 A.M.
Monday 27 May.

Tim glanced at his watch. There was barely enough time to shave and change.

Yet by a quarter to six he was waiting in the incongruously modernistic papal chapel, fresh and awake thanks to the unfailing combination of caffeine and adrenaline.

A cluster of papal household nuns, all in black except for a single red heart embroidered on the breast of their habits, were already kneeling in prayer.

At precisely five minutes to six, the pontiff strode in, followed by three or four other clerics in various garb. Spying his new archbishop, he smiled and offered his right hand. *"Benvenuto, Timoteo."*

Tim was about to kiss the papal ring when His Holiness demurred, "Please, we are about to pray. Before God we are all equals."

After intoning the Mass, the pontiff beckoned Tim to join him in his velvet-lined elevator. The only other passenger was a priest whom Tim recognized as the papal secretary, Monsignor Kevin Murphy. This freckle-faced, red-haired Dublin boy was known to jog ten miles along the Tiber before anyone else in the Apostolic Palace had put on slippers.

As His Holiness introduced the two young men, he joked, "As you know, Timoteo, I'm here to serve God. But it is Kevin who fixes the agenda. Bear that in mind."

Tim and the Irishman exchanged smiles as the elevator came to a stop. Its passengers disembarked into an elegant *sala* whose vaulted, gilt-stuccoed ceilings and artwork made the illuminated panels in the papal chapel seem like Hong Kong plastic. Other high Vatican officials were waiting to join the Holy Father for a working breakfast at the large oval table.

It was easy to distinguish Franz Cardinal von

Jakob, for the strapping German stood nearly a foot taller than the other prelates, his height accentuated by the straightness of his posture. Tim took the initiative and introduced himself.

The austere von Jakob responded with the semblance of a smile and a laconic, "Welcome, Your Grace."

It was not surprising that von Jakob was seated at the Pope's right hand. Tim was somewhat overwhelmed, however, to discover that he had been placed directly opposite. It was—it seemed to him—as if the pontiff wanted to assess him at close range.

The German wasted no time and immediately began his catechism to determine how acquainted Tim was with the Church's problems in Brazil.

"Well, I know it's the biggest Catholic country in the world—and the poorest," Tim replied nervously. "Some say we should be doing more to help them—including a lot of their own priests."

"They rant about 'the triumph of the proletariat,' " the Cardinal stated with irritation. "It sounds like something from *Das Kapital*."

The pontiff then declared in quiet, measured tones, "I am convinced that the true Armageddon will be between the soldiers of Christ and the dark forces of Marx."

"The Brazilians are on the verge of rebellion," von Jakob continued. "The priests stirring up the peasants are encouraged by some of our most charismatic theologians, especially the over-esteemed Professor Ernesto Hardt."

Tim nodded. "I've read a few of his articles. He's certainly a persuasive advocate for reform."

" 'Reform' is the key word," the German pronounced. "The man thinks he's another Martin Luther. We're most disturbed by the rumor of a book he's preparing. They say it could be the rallying cry the Brazilians are waiting for."

A voice at the other end of the table inquired, "I still don't understand, Franz. Why can't your office simply order him into penitential silence? This certainly proved successful with his countryman, Leonardo Boff. . . ."

"No, Hardt's too dangerous," von Jakob responded. "Unless we handle him carefully, he'd leave the Church—and God knows how many thousands he'd take with him." He turned to Tim and asked, "Do you have any idea of the inroads the Protestants are making?"

"It seems more like a tidal wave," the new archbishop acknowledged. "I've read a report estimating that every hour of the day, four hundred Latin American Catholics leave the Faith."

There were murmurs of distress from all around the table.

Von Jakob continued to address Tim. "It is for this reason that you must persuade Hardt not to publish his book. I needn't tell you how important this assignment is."

Timothy had led a sheltered life. Even as far as Church politics were concerned, he was an innocent. But this did not mean that he was without scruples, and the idea of suppressing a book—any book—struck him as morally repugnant.

He wondered if George Cavanagh would have accepted this assignment. And he wondered something else.

"With respect," he asked, trying to hide his discomfort, "how did you come to choose me?"

"For a diabolical genius like Hardt, we needed a very special envoy. When I called Archbishop Orsino in Washington, he unhesitatingly suggested you."

"But are you aware that I don't speak a word of Portuguese?" he asked.

"You are fluent in Latin, Italian, and Spanish," said the Cardinal, holding up a document that was obviously part of Tim's dossier.

His Holiness added affably, "I've had occasion to learn a few words for my South American journeys. And with no disrespect to our Lusitanian brothers, I found that to speak Portuguese, you merely have to talk Spanish with pebbles in your mouth."

There was a ripple of appreciative laughter.

"In any case," von Jakob continued, "my Congregation has expert language tutors whose total immersion technique would be the envy of Berlitz. I have no doubt that in three months you will be speaking Brazilian Portuguese like a native."

"There is only one problem," His Holiness added good-humoredly. "You then have to discover *what* to say."

On this note, the breakfast was adjourned.

As the princes of the Church dispersed to their several domains, Tim followed Monsignor Murphy to his office, which served as a sentry post for the pontiff's inner court.

The papal secretary explained that Tim's linguistic inculcation would consist of three daily four-hour sessions, each with a native Brazilian priest. They would even remain with him during meals, making sure only Portuguese was spoken.

"After that," Monsignor Murphy joked, "you can relax with some light reading—like the history of Brazil."

"Thank you, Monsignor," Tim responded. "But something tells me these language lessons will be less of an ordeal than what comes after."

The papal secretary hesitated, and then lowering his voice, said, "Your Grace, may I tell you something in confidence—as one Irishman to another?"

"Of course."

"I think you should know that you're not the first legate to be sent to Ernesto Hardt."

"Oh," Tim replied, "and what happened to my predecessor?"

Murphy's answer was laconic.

"He never came back."

73

Deborah

Dear Deb,

I enclose an item from the *Boston Globe*—which I'm pretty sure escaped the attention of the Israeli press.

To be honest, I hesitated before finally deciding to send it. I mean I know Tim's always somewhere in your thoughts—how could it be otherwise when you see his face every time you look at Eli?

But I still wondered how you might feel on the far-off shores of the Galilee to learn about your "old friend" becoming an archbishop.

Would it make Rabbi D. Luria happy—proud, even?

And then the 64-shekel question: How would it make Eli feel?

Don't you think he deserves to know his father is a Christian? And more important, the bitter truth that even if his father were the pope—and in Tim's case that is even a possibility—he would still be despised by the anti-Semites of the world for having Jewish blood.

Far from injuring him, it would actually give more meaning to the life that he will soon be risking for us all. . . .

If that is a sermon, so be it. If you won't say amen, then I'll . . .

Two days later

I still can't finish the preceding sentence. Maybe you will.

All my love,
Danny

———

Though she was determined to keep the enclosed picture, Deborah knew she should have burned her precious letter. Was not the photograph enough? Could not she feed her soul merely by looking at his picture and letting her heart provide the text?

Yet some inward force compelled her to hold on to everything that Danny had sent. And even afterward it was not hard for her to comprehend why she had merely placed these documents in the top drawer of her desk.

She had spent the fourteen years since Eli's birth desperately searching her heart to find the proper words. Now, she had them. But like a coward—or so she later thought—instead of facing him to let him know the truth, she simply left the letter where he was certain to find it.

Nor did it take long.

The following evening, Eli did not appear in the refectory for dinner.

At first, Deborah merely thought he had—yet again—stayed late with Gila at her kibbutz. But when she got home and discovered Danny's letter crumpled into a ball in the center of the floor, she called her son's girlfriend, who only compounded her dismay by saying that Eli had not even been in school that day.

Deborah hung up and ran to share her anxiety with Boaz and Zipporah.

To her surprise and relief she found that Eli was at their *srif*. And judging by the thickness of the cigarette smoke, the conversation must have been going on for several hours. Her son stared at her, his angry eyes burning with betrayal.

"Eli—"

He turned his back to her.

"You have every right to hate me," she said helplessly. "I should have told you long ago."

"No," Boaz interceded. "We're all to blame. As I've been trying to convince him since he got here. *We* were the ones who put you up to it."

Zipporah nodded wordlessly.

Eli began to vent his rage, starting with his "grandfather."

"How could you do this? How could you desecrate your own son's memory?"

This at least was something to which Boaz could respond.

"I—we did it as an act of love."

"Love," the young boy sneered. "Who for? Some Christian that my so-called rabbi mother went to bed with?"

"Eli!" Deborah snapped. "You have no right to talk that way."

"Oh, no? You should be ashamed. . . ." His rage continued though he had exhausted speech.

It was Deborah's turn to try to make him understand.

"Eli, I am ashamed. But only for lacking the courage to tell you. There's one thing I insist you understand because it's why you came into this world." She paused and then continued softly, "I loved your father. He was kind and good—and pure of heart—and I swear to you our love was mutual."

Eli turned to look at Boaz and Zipporah. Contrary to his expectations, they both nodded.

"Your father was a *mensch*," Boaz asserted.

"Which 'father' do you mean? Your son or . . . my mother's 'priest'?"

Again, Eli's piercing stare took in all of them.

Deborah was paralyzed, but Boaz answered passionately.

"I don't have to tell you what a man our son was. You've been hearing that for fourteen years. The only lie we ever told you was that he'd been your father. And I tell you frankly, Eli, even if you cut me dead from this day on, I'll always be grateful for the time you let our boy live on in you. And now," he said, "I want you to apologize to Deborah. She barely knew him—and for that part of the lie your anger rightfully should fall on me."

Eli was confused. "But, Boaz," he stammered, "I . . . I'm not angry at you."

"Why?" the old man countered. "You mean you hate Deborah because your father was a Christian? Dividing the world into 'them' and 'us' is the kind of twisted thinking that created the Holocaust. I have the right to say this because that arbitrary hatred lost me my parents *and* my son. The most important thing is not to be a Jew or a Christian, but to be good. Your father—whom I knew—was good."

At last Deborah found her voice.

"He still *is*," she said with quiet strength. "Tim is still alive. And now I owe it both to Eli and to Tim to have them meet each other."

"Never!" the boy shouted. "I never want to meet that man."

"Why?" Deborah demanded angrily. "You've

been castigating all of us for sheltering you from the truth. What are you afraid of now—that you might like him?"

"How could I after what he did?"

"No," Deborah exploded. "You're wrong if you imagine he abandoned me. He offered to . . . leave the priesthood . . . live in Jerusalem. And afterwards I never told him about you. He still has no idea."

A look of consternation crossed the boy's face as Deborah continued.

"God knows I love you, Eli, and I've tried to be as good a parent as I could. But I realize now that I was wrong. I'll never forgive myself for letting you grow up without a father."

The boy's eyes filled with tears.

Until this moment, Zipporah had only been a witness. Now she spoke in judgment.

"How much longer must I listen to this? How much more can we apologize and flagellate our guilty consciences? We're all alive. And until yesterday we loved each other like no other family on earth. How could we"—she focused her gaze on Eli—"let a simple piece of paper alter that? Now, I suggest we have a glass of schnapps." Looking again at Eli she cautioned, "Just a drop for you, *boychik*. And then we'll sit down and talk until we can remember who we are and what we mean to one another."

They kept talking through the night. Eventually,

when nothing was a certainty except that they all had experienced some sort of catharsis, Rabbi Deborah Luria said to her son, "All right, Eli, when do you want to go with me to Rome?"

The boy replied from the embers of his anger, "Never."

PART VI

74

Timothy

Tim's mind was playing tricks on him. After ten hours' flight, the drone of the Varig Airlines DC-10's engines began to sound as if they were tiring. He asked one of the ever-attentive stewardesses for another cup of black coffee and jokingly suggested that she make sure the pilot had some, too. The young woman smiled at His Grace's sense of humor and hurried off.

While all the other passengers in the first-class compartment slept, Tim was hard at work preparing for his first mission as papal nuncio. Every time he had been paroled from his linguistic imprisonment, he had gone immediately to von Jakob's office to study the massive dossier on Hardt, creating his own abridged version for the trip itself.

Born in Manaus on the Rio Negro in 1918, the son of a Swiss immigrant and a *mameluca*, a woman of mixed Indian and Portuguese stock, Ernesto Hardt had been educated by the Franciscans and upon graduation joined their number. After studying in Rome, where he received his doctorate from the Gregorian, he taught in Lisbon until 1962 when he returned to assume the first Chair of Catholic Theology at the newly founded University of Brasília.

These bare facts filled less than a page. The rest of the file consisted of Hardt's vast bibliography and annotated critiques by various conservative Vatican scholars. Von Jakob's initialed marginalia were conspicuous by their frequency and acerbity.

A subsequent section devoted exclusively to correspondence between Rome and Brasília consisted mostly of reprimands for Hardt's dissident behavior with polite but evasive replies like, "It is difficult to preach the word of God in a land which He seems to have forgotten."

Tim continued to leaf through Hardt's publications—in Spanish, for they had achieved a wide circulation across Latin America. There was no question that they voiced a plea for the downtrodden, but their phraseology, though polemic, was soundly based on Scripture—indeed, on the Old Testament.

There were many labels one could pin on Hardt, but "Marxist" was no more appropriate than "fundamentalist Christian," although he advocated a literal reading of the Bible. For example, he made much of the incident recounted in three of the four gospels, when a pious young man asks Jesus what more he can do to be sure of life eternal. Christ answers: "If thou wilt be perfect, go and sell that thou hast, and give to the poor, and thou shalt have treasure in heaven."

Could any fair-minded Christian denigrate the Saviour's injunction as mere socialism?

With every turn of the page, Tim expected to see more heretical and inflammatory utterances, but thus far he could find no reason to believe that Ernesto Hardt was dedicated to anything but the word of God.

———

The city of Brasília was designed to look like an airplane from above. But to those who know it, it seems more like a wilting crucifix.

Until the 1940s, Brazil's huge Mato Grosso was the last great unexplored area on earth. But for nearly two centuries Brazilian governments had dreamed of building an inland capital city, a beam of light in the very heart of darkness.

Nearly every history of modern architecture contains photographs of architect Oscar Niemeyer's stunning skyline, especially the dramatically tapered conical cathedral.

The futuristic, magnificently planned city was opened to receive its inhabitants in 1960, having leapt from drawing board to reality in little more than three years.

As the plane from Rio taxied to a stop, Tim picked up his briefcase and black raincoat (for the long wet season lay ahead of him, should his mission prove difficult), and walked through the hatchway into the sleek marble terminal.

The Vatican ambassador, Monsignor Fabrizio Lindor, his rotund figure dressed impeccably in a lightweight suit, looked remarkably fresh despite the lateness of the hour. He walked toward Tim, proffering his hand.

"Benvenuto, Vostra Grazia. I know how exhausted you must be, so give Father Rafael your baggage tags and come out to rest in the car."

Tim had barely enough energy to nod as he followed the diplomat through the tall glass doors to a black Mercedes limousine waiting conspicuously in the No Parking zone.

"We were instructed by Cardinal von Jakob to book you a hotel suite. I've reserved the best at the Nacional, but I wonder if you wouldn't feel safer— er, more comfortable, that is—staying in one of the embassy guest rooms."

"Safe from what?" Tim inquired, slightly aroused from his torpor.

The Ambassador shrugged. "We're very far from the Vatican, Your Grace, and very near the dense jungle."

During the nearly two hours of his connecting flight from Rio Tim had prepared himself to confront the Vatican ambassador with an urgent demand for information.

"Monsignor Lindor, did you know my . . . predecessor?"

"Are you referring to Archbishop Rojas?"

"Yes. Did you know him?"

The diplomat hesitated before responding. "Briefly, yes. He was not with us very long."

"Oh?" Tim remarked casually. "Did he fall under Hardt's fabled spell?"

"Well, yes," the envoy answered uneasily. "You might say that. He did embrace Liberation Theology and at Hardt's suggestion went to work for Bishop Casaldáliga in the Amazon."

"Is there any way I could get to speak to him?" Tim asked.

"I'm afraid not," the Ambassador replied. "Rojas is dead. He was shot, actually."

"Does anybody know by whom?"

"From what I hear it was a mistake," said the Ambassador. "During a protest march, he'd linked arms with Casaldáliga. There was an assassination attempt. The gunman hit Rojas instead." Tim thought he heard him add under his breath, "Worse luck."

As they drove through the empty nocturnal streets of the city, its stark buildings like huge illuminated stalagmites against a blue-black sky, Ambassador Lindor rhapsodized at length about his nostalgia for Rome. Tim took this to be an unconscious revelation that the Vatican's representative was ill at ease in this sinister Disneyland.

As they neared the hotel, Lindor remarked cordially, "I expect you'll want to rest tomorrow, but if you wish I can come by in the late afternoon and give you a tour of the city."

"That's very kind, Monsignor," Tim answered. "But I don't think I'll get much sleep tonight, and I'm anxious to get started. Does Father Hardt know I'm coming?"

"Well," the Ambassador temporized, "we haven't sent him an engraved announcement nor—as you instructed—have we set up an appointment. But somehow he still receives messages on the Franciscan grapevine. So I think it's fair to say you won't be surprising him."

"I had no such illusions," Timothy assured him, continuing, "But my notes say he lectures only once a week and spends the rest of the time, as they euphemistically put it, 'in the field.' I believe tomorrow is that weekly occasion, and I wouldn't want to miss it."

"I have all his classes tape-recorded," the Ambassador offered. "You could listen to him in the comfort of my office."

"That's all right," Tim replied. "I've also read the transcripts. But there's nothing like seeing the man himself in action. Don't worry, Monsignor, I won't defect." He looked hard at the corpulent diplomat, who appeared to squirm uneasily.

"To be honest, Your Grace, he's a second Savonarola."

"Are you suggesting that Hardt be burnt at the stake?" Tim asked facetiously.

"Of course not," the Ambassador responded. "That would be too good for him."

———

The management had welcomed Tim to his suite with a basket of fruit and bottle of wine, but instead he took a can of Antártica, a local beer, from the minibar and sat down on his bed. Without the benefit of a glass, he took a cool mouthful and caught sight of himself in a mirror above the writing table.

"You still look fighting fit, Hogan," he told himself. Indeed, the only uncomfortable moments for his vanity nowadays came when he brushed his hair and found an increasing number of blond strands in the bristles. He could not suppress a shudder at the prospect of growing bald. Not because of vanity on his part, but if the inevitable process continued, he would look less like Timothy Hogan and more like the despicable Tuck Delaney.

He drained the beer, leaned back, and fell asleep on top of the bed.

The following morning he was enjoying a breakfast of fresh fruit and strong coffee when the Ambassador phoned.

"You were right," he reported. "Hardt lectures this afternoon from four till six. I'll send an Embassy car to take you."

Tim could not help noticing that the diplomat did not offer to go along.

"No, that's all right, Monsignor," he replied. "I think I might enjoy taking the bus."

The University of Brasília—another Niemeyer gem—was situated on the northeast periphery of the city. Tim stepped off at the university bus stop on the Eixo Rodoviário. As he crossed the campus he was struck by the varied hues of the students— in attire no less than complexion. He himself was dressed in "civilian" clothing—not even wearing his pectoral cross.

Ordinarily, lectures on religion took place in the Instituto de Teologia, but Hardt's classes were so popular that they were held in the highly banked amphitheater in the science building.

Ironically, the words of God would be discussed in the domain where science was king. Hardt's podium was flanked by gas spigots and other trappings of the modern laboratory.

At precisely 4:15, Ernesto Hardt—a tall, stoop-shouldered man with leathery skin and a flowing white mane crowning his high forehead—marched toward the podium. He wore corduroy pants and a short-sleeved khaki shirt opened sufficiently at the neck to reveal a small gold cross.

Tim was seated discreetly in the back. When the

rest of the spectators rose in a gesture of respect he had to scramble to his feet to avoid attracting attention to himself.

Hardt carried no briefcase, book bag, or notes. All he brought to the podium was a tattered leather Bible, which he scarcely consulted during the entire hour and a half of his lecture.

His subject for the day was Jesus' Sermon on the Mount.

But when he quoted "Blessed are the poor in spirit," he interpreted it as praise for the materially impoverished.

"Now what exactly does our Lord mean when he says, 'Blessed are those who hunger and thirst after *righteousness*'? Could Jesus have been referring simply to some abstract concept of justice? Of course not. The key words are 'hunger' and 'thirst.' In our religion, 'righteousness' has to mean an equitable distribution of food among the peoples of the earth.

"We find the same thought processes in the Dead Sea Scrolls, notably the so-called *Thanksgiving* and *War* documents, which date from the same age as Jesus. So we can have no doubt as to what Our Lord intended."

His penetrating gray eyes scanned every face in the auditorium before his swelling voice proclaimed, "There can be no justice in the world until there are no hungry people!"

Tim could only wonder whether the crowd

surrounding Jesus would have reacted to these words with as much enthusiasm as Hardt's audience, who cheered vociferously.

Withdrawing a crumpled handkerchief Hardt wiped the sweat from his cheeks and brow.

"The first action in the service of God is not prayer but commitment. Not sacrifice but giving. Only then can we begin to talk about other kinds of righteousness."

His dark brown face now glowed red. He had made his point, for without even mentioning his adversary, he had damned the Catholic Church. He had taken Christ from Rome and brought him, living, breathing, and preaching, to the heart of the Brazilian jungle.

Leaning against the wall under a banner broadcasting *E Proibido Fumar*, Hardt reached into his breast pocket, pulled out a package of Marlboros, and lit one. After inhaling deeply he once again approached the lectern.

"The class is officially over," he began in colloquial Brazilian dialect. "But for any who are interested, I have a few words to say about freedom."

No one moved. Hardt continued, "Any schoolboy knows the unspeakable practice of slavery was officially abolished in our country by Joachim Nabuco in 1888. But some people still haven't heard the news. So instead of going to church on Sunday we're traveling to São Jodo to demonstrate at the Da Silva ranch. Those interested in painting placards should see either Jorge or Vittoria afterward."

He pointed to a pair of young assistants dressed much like himself and holding clipboards ready to enroll foot soldiers in the army of justice.

"Our lecture next week will be on Old Testament echoes in the Gospels, so be sure you have the proper texts with you. *Vai com Deus.*"

A bustle ensued as the students went their various ways. Not a few stopped to sign up with Jorge and Vittoria. The exodus occurred so swiftly that Timothy found himself rooted to his chair, face to face—albeit at a distance—with his heretical quarry.

The Brazilian spoke first.

"Good afternoon, Your Grace. I hope my lecture wasn't too elementary for you."

"On the contrary, Dom Ernesto," Tim replied. "It was very enlightening. May I invite you for a cup of coffee?"

The professor smiled. There was a quality in Hardt's demeanor that Tim had never seen before in a man of God. Somehow his eyes were clearer and he radiated peace of mind.

"Not in a country where coffee is the only nonluxury. But since I presume the Vatican's paying, why not revise your offer to a good bottle of *vinho verde*?"

"Very well," Tim answered affably. "*Vinho verde* it is. Can you suggest a place?"

"If you don't mind simple food I'd like to invite you to my home for dinner. How does that sound?"

"That's very gracious," Tim replied. "If you'll give me directions . . ."

"It's a little complicated. I think it would be better if I picked you up myself. Is seven-thirty all right?"

"I look forward to it."

"As I," Hardt replied, adding mischievously, "It would be especially festive if your budget allows you to bring several bottles. *Cenabis bene apud me*—if you know your Catullus."

"*Constat*," Tim responded.

With that Hardt smiled, added "*Pax tecum*," turned, and started toward the rear exit where Jorge and Vittoria were waiting.

75

Timothy

At 7:15 Tim was standing in his best lightweight black suit in front of the Hotel Nacional with two green bottles under his arm, wondering what sort of a vehicle Hardt would arrive in.

He concluded that it would most likely be something conspicuously proletarian—a dump truck or a donkey.

He was both right and wrong, for at precisely seven-twenty-nine (was it the punctilious Swiss in him?) Hardt drove up in a Land Rover of so old a vintage that had it been a wine it would have been a *gran reserva*.

"Step in, step in," the older man called in a friendly voice. As Tim mounted the vehicle, the theologian eyed the bottles. "Ah, you're a man of your word. That vintage must have set the Vatican back a pretty penny!" He floored the accelerator, and with a jolt and a heave, the car ground into a forward motion.

As the two men rode they engaged in casual dialogue about the astronomically high prices in Brasília. In no time they had driven through the Eixo Rodoviário Norte and out onto the highway.

After ten minutes Tim commented, "Have you always lived this far out of the city?"

"No," Hardt replied. "When I was still enjoying the favor of the Church I had digs near the cathedral. But now I'm in one of the 'anti-Brasílias.' It's not as convenient, but it keeps me closer to the people."

" 'Anti-Brasílias'?" asked Tim.

"Otherwise known as *favelas*—which is another way of saying 'shantytowns.' I don't have to tell you this is the most thoroughly planned city in history. The designers only forgot one thing—living quarters for the *candangos*, the pioneers who actually did the construction work. Nowadays," he went on, "the poor people are stuck in *favelas* which ring the city like beads on a necklace—only not so pretty. Some are as much as thirty kilometers out of town."

"That's a pity," Tim commented.

"Indeed, Your Grace." Hardt grinned cynically. "The city planners thought of everything except the people." With a glance at Tim he added, "Sounds a little like the Vatican, doesn't it?"

It was more than half an hour before they turned off the highway down an unpaved road into a sprawling agglomeration of hovels. Some of the structures were of corrugated steel, others of cinder blocks, no doubt borrowed from various city building sites. From the roof of each dwelling, tall TV aerials reached desperately into the evening sky.

The street—if one could call it that—was even narrower and bumpier than the road. Hardt was perpetually sounding his horn to chase chickens and children out of his path.

Hardt's home was somewhat grander than the others. Even from the outside Tim could hear the electricity generator sputtering and could smell its pungent black exhaust. Though he was nearly twice Tim's age, Hardt bounded easily from the Land Rover onto the ground and rushed around to help his guest dismount.

"That's all right," Tim said good-humoredly, "I can manage without breaking a leg."

"I know, Dom Timóteo. But I was concerned about the *vinho*!"

At this moment a dark, barefoot boy of about ten, in shorts and sleeveless undershirt, came rushing up to them shouting, "Papa, Papa!"

Hardt reached down and picked the lad up into his arms, showing him proudly to Timothy.

"This is my son, Alberto."

Somehow in the dusky light of the squalid *favela*

653

Hardt's flagrant violation of priestly celibacy did not seem relevant.

Tim glanced around, wondering how human beings could tolerate such conditions, but all he could say was, "This is quite a place."

"Yes. I think after this, Hell must look like Miami Beach. Do you realize there are . . ."

Suddenly, they heard a woman's voice call out.

"Stop your sermons, Ernesto. He's our guest."

Tim turned to find a young woman in her early thirties whose smile was accentuated by gleaming black hair and dark skin.

"Also, please forgive his lack of social graces," she implored her visitor lightheartedly. "I'm afraid a Franciscan education doesn't include how to introduce your woman." She held out her hand and said, "I'm Isabella. I hope you're not too jet-lagged to enjoy the evening."

"Thank you," Tim replied cordially, totally enchanted by this woman who was surely young enough to be Hardt's daughter.

Indeed, the old man seemed to be able to read his mind.

"I suppose you're thinking how a decrepit *velho* like me came to win such a young gazelle."

Isabella smiled at Tim. "Don't indulge him. That's just a sneaky way of boasting about his machismo. We met as good Brazilian Catholics should—on a picket line. I was reading Law at the university."

Hardt blithely concluded the anecdote. "And Isabella took pity on a poor bachelor who didn't know the truth of Proverbs 31, that a good woman is more precious than rubies."

Tim knew the verse and immediately quoted St. Jerome's Latin:

"*Mulierem fortem quis inveniet.*"

This pleased Hardt immensely.

"What a pleasure to hear a Catholic quoting Scripture," he said mischievously. "They usually confine themselves to quoting other Catholics."

He looked squarely at Tim with his clear gray eyes, hoping to elicit a smile. At last, he did.

"So," he said, ushering his guest into the house, "at least they haven't sent me a dour one this time. Excuse me, Dom Timóteo, may I offer you a drink? Sherry, perhaps?"

"With pleasure," Tim replied as Hardt placed a hand on his shoulder, leading him toward the study.

Although lit only by a single flickering lamp, the brick and lumber bookshelves held not only books but the latest journals of theology and biblical criticism.

"Were you at the Greg?" Hardt inquired.

Tim nodded.

"Biblical Institute?"

"No, Canon Law."

"Ah!" said Hardt, disappointed. "A total waste of time! Will you drink to that?"

"Only if I have the right to appeal," Tim joked.

"Tonight all you can appeal for is another drink," Hardt replied, pouring two large glasses of amber liquid from a bottle with no label.

After motioning Tim to sit on a well-worn sofa, Hardt sat behind his desk and listened as the young archbishop posed his first serious question.

"Dom Ernesto, you knew I was coming. You recognized me immediately. I'm surprised you didn't know my whole *curriculum vitae*."

"Ah, Timóteo, I hope you won't be offended, but there's no dossier on you yet. In fact, I think that's one of the reasons they chose you. Tell me," he continued, "why do you think the Vatican has wasted so much effort trying to gag pastors in the middle of the Brazilian jungle, eh?"

" 'Gag' is a bit brutal, Dom Ernesto."

Hardt leaned over his desk and said with unconcealed anger, "So is 'penitential silence.' And that's how your von Jakob muzzled my dear friend and brother, Leonardo Boff. When you next see His Eminence Cardinal von Jakob, tell him that he's forgotten the Gospel of John, chapter eight, verse thirty-two."

Tim immediately quoted, " 'And ye shall know the truth, and the truth shall make you free.' "

"Bravo, Dom Timóteo. And do you believe it as well as remember it?"

"Of course," Tim responded.

"Then why don't you spend your energies on something worthwhile?"

"Like what?" Tim inquired.

Hardt leaned across the desk and with an expression almost devoid of a smile said sternly, "Like getting my book published in English."

Before Tim could respond, Isabella poked her head in and said, "It's ready and it's hot. You can continue your dialectic at the table."

The dining room was actually a long, narrow wooden table in the corner of the kitchen, warmed by the same wood-burning stove that was used for cooking. Two children were already seated—the boy Tim had seen and a younger girl who was introduced as Anita.

"I hope you don't mind eating with the family," Isabella remarked. "But Ernesto is on the road so much that he rarely gets to see them."

"Not at all," Tim assured her. "I enjoy talking to children."

"Yes," Hardt agreed. "The younger the better. Before they learn how to lie."

The host took a massive stewpot from the stove and placed it on a corrugated tin tray at the center of the table. He then sat down, and the rest of the family followed his lead in bowing their heads as he said grace in their dialect. Hardt looked at the "Pope's Man."

"Dom Timóteo. You're our honored guest. Would His Grace like to say his grace?"

The children giggled, suggesting that they knew more English than Tim had supposed.

Tim felt it was time to assert his orthodoxy and took the opportunity to pronounce, "*Benedicat dominus et panem et pietatem nostram, amen.*"

With a big ladle, Hardt placed some stew on Tim's dish, explaining it was called *xinxim de galinha*. As Tim tasted what, despite its exotic name, was more like watered soup, Hardt produced the two green bottles and opened them with gusto.

During the meal, Tim talked to Isabella, whom he found to be well informed on matters both ecclesiastical and secular. She explained that she used her law degree to work three days a week for an agency providing legal aid for the Indians.

The company of these lively children—although he did not speak a word of their dialect—pierced Tim's heart.

Still, he was wary, knowing he was the focus of a brainwashing exercise, which he was determined to resist.

After dinner the two men retired to the study. Hardt opened the bottom drawer of his desk cabinet and withdrew a treasure—*ginjinha,* a potent liqueur derived from morello cherries. He poured each of them a glass and then sat down.

"Timothy," Hardt began a new chapter of their dialogue. "Why does von Jakob think that even if I burn my manuscript my ideas will die? You saw that lecture room. There were at least four hundred people taking notes. I even saw a few with tape recorders. Did Jesus give out pamphlets?" he asked, fixing Tim with his piercing gray eyes. "And I don't mean that disrespectfully. He preached the Word. He preached Mosaic law cast in a new dimension, crowned with love. Hasn't von Jakob learned from history that you can burn old books— even suppress new ones—but you can't kill the Word?"

Tim thought for a moment, then asked softly, "Just precisely what do you have against the Catholic Church?"

"I can only tell you what's wrong in Brasília, Tim. Have you seen our cathedral? It's one of the most beautiful churches ever built. It looks like a supplication cast in stone." He slammed his desk. "But it's *empty,* Timothy! It's all ceremony and no substance!

"How could I as a priest celebrate the Eucharist and put a wafer in the mouth of a man who doesn't have a piece of bread? I ask you, Tim. Do those starving people have to wait for the Messiah to return before they have enough to eat?"

The priest stretched his legs out before him and leaned back in his creaking chair.

"Do you know, Timóteo, half the land in Brazil is owned by only five thousand individuals. Imagine, Tim. Imagine if all the territory between New York and Chicago belonged to fewer people than fill one section of Yankee Stadium. Meanwhile, seventy million of our people suffer from malnutrition, and in Africa—the Ivory Coast, where the people are just as hungry—they're building a cathedral *twice* the size of St. Peter's. It's monstrous!"

Timothy was appalled. "Is that what's in your book?" he whispered.

"Be serious, this information is in every World Almanac."

"Then what can you possibly say that would be more outrageous?"

"Nothing, really," Hardt said quietly. "It's just that instead of merely printing statistics like an almanac, I pin the blame squarely on the Church."

Suddenly, Hardt glanced at his watch.

"My God, it's nearly one. You must be absolutely exhausted from your journey and my tirades."

"No, not at all," Tim protested. "But I do think I should be getting back to the hotel."

"Fine," said Hardt. "I'd be glad to drive you."

"No, no. There's no need. I can—"

"—Call a cab?" His host laughed. "We don't have a phone. And the next bus leaves at five A.M. loaded with laborers. Your only choice is myself as your chauffeur or the couch you're sitting on, which doubles as a bed. Considering the amount of alcohol I've consumed, I suggest you accept the latter."

"I'll settle for the couch," said Tim good-humoredly.

"Fine. Let me get you something to sleep in." Hardt left the room and quickly reappeared with a track suit in the colors of Brazil's international soccer team.

"This was the only contribution to our cause by the right wing—Jose Madeiros, the team captain, to be specific," he explained, adding, "I'm going to auction it, so try and make it look as if nobody slept in it. Can I get you anything else?"

"No," Timothy said, his lids growing heavy. "I'm fine."

"Oh, yes," Hardt said in parting. "What you Americans call the little boys' room is at the end of the back garden. Or if you feel in a populist mood, the communal latrine is down the road to the right. There's a flashlight on my desk—you won't need to ask directions!"

At last Tim was alone. He undressed and carefully folded his clothing on the chair behind the desk. It was now cold, and he was glad that Brazil provided its athletes with the finest Adidas garments.

He looked around the room and suddenly thought to himself, I could find that manuscript in no time. Even if it's hidden behind the books I could just take that flashlight he so generously offered me and . . .

He stopped himself. He was a priest, not an undercover agent. Besides, he already knew that he wanted to see the book for selfish reasons. To read it and learn Hardt's secret thoughts.

76

Timothy

The first kettle of boiling water next morning was for coffee, the second to enable the men to shave.

"Do you have anything planned for today, Dom Timóteo?" Hardt asked as the two of them shared a single metal mirror.

"Not really. The ambassador gave me an open invitation for dinner but I can skip that. I'm due to celebrate eleven o'clock Mass on Sunday."

"Well, you can make up your mind about that after this morning," Hardt commented in a cautionary tone. "What I show you today may make you lose a little fervor."

No, Tim thought to himself, this glib heretic will not dissuade me from celebrating the Eucharist.

The entire Hardt family once again gathered

around the table for a breakfast of fried bananas, and, of course, more coffee.

Young Alberto pointed at Tim's sweat suit and giggled.

"*Futebol, futebol.*"

"*Sim,*" Tim replied with a grin. "*Te gosta de futebol?*"

"*Sim, senhor.* Are you coming to the game today?"

"I don't know what your father has planned for me today." Tim turned to his host. "Ernesto?"

"Don't worry," the priest said affably. "That's going to be part of your grand tour of the slums."

After the two men had helped clear the table, Isabella began to give a squealing Anita a thorough hair-wash in the sink, and they returned to the table for their third cup of coffee—and Hardt's third cigarette of the day.

"You ought to give up smoking, Dom Ernesto," Tim suggested. "It can kill you."

"And you ought to give up celibacy," the priest retorted. "It'll kill you even faster."

"Why do you say that?" Tim asked uncomfortably.

"I saw your face when you were talking to Alberto." Suddenly, he shifted gears, "And by the way, he'll be angry as hell with me if I'm late to watch him play. Let's go."

Tim rose and followed Hardt out into the muddy

streets, sinking into the puddles of dirty water in his highly polished black leather shoes.

As they began their tour of the *favela*, Tim realized how much of the utter squalor of the place had previously been shrouded in darkness. It was noisy, dilapidated, foul-smelling, and unsanitary.

Perhaps half a dozen other houses had a generator like Hardt's. The only water supply for the whole village came from two communal pumps. As Tim stared Hardt read his mind.

"Yes, Dom Timóteo. It is polluted. And yes again, everything we served you was thoroughly boiled first. This is actually where my brothers and I have made some progress. We've taught some elementary hygiene here and dramatically reduced the dysentery rate."

Beyond the suffocating cluster of houses they reached a sodden field where Alberto and two dozen or so others like him were engaged in a spirited soccer match, the goals on either side marked by two empty oil drums.

Even as they played, members of both teams managed a friendly wave to their resident priest.

"*Oi*, Dom Ernesto. *Como vai?*"

"*Bem, bem,*" Hardt answered as he waved back.

"They look like they're having fun," Tim remarked. "What other activities do they have?"

"None," his Brazilian host replied. "Besides, we're too busy to pay much attention to the healthy ones. Let's go."

As he led Tim back through the narrow streets of the town, Hardt continued his commentary. "As you might imagine, here in what you North Americans call the Third World we have a very high birthrate."

"Yes," said Tim quietly. "I imagine you do."

"But what keeps our burgeoning population in check," Hardt went on ironically, "is one of the highest infant-mortality rates in the world. A baby born here is ten times more likely to die in its first months of life than one in, say, Ohio.

"At the other end of life—if we're willing to stretch that definition to describe a person inhabiting a *favela*—the average Brazilian will die ten years sooner than his gringo cousin in the States."

They walked several muddy paces in silence until something occurred to Tim. "I hope I don't sound paranoid, Dom Ernesto. But every so often we pass a group of rather muscular residents who seem to be—I don't know—sizing me up."

"Don't worry," Hardt answered. "They won't bother you."

"But who are they—some sort of gang?"

"That's such a pejorative term, Your Grace. They're not only outstanding citizens of this *favela*, but they're members of the *associacão dos moradores*. You might say they're our 'residents' association.' In short, they look after things and do for us what the government doesn't."

At that moment, the two men reached a large

building that seemed out of place in these surroundings. It was a long, white, barnlike structure with what appeared to be two floors.

"This skyscraper is our hospital," Dom Ernesto explained.

"And are those men sitting in front *moradores* or doctors?"

"Neither," he replied tonelessly. "They're undertakers."

Hardt looked soberly at Tim. "You don't have to go in. Some of the diseases are quite contagious."

"That's all right," Tim said, shoring up his courage.

———

He could never have been prepared for what he saw. Though he had visited the sick and dying in many hospitals, he had never attended terminally ill people who were not receiving any medical care.

The huge dormitory echoed with the wails of the young and groans of the old. Suddenly, Tim felt Hardt's hand affectionately on his shoulder. Ernesto spoke gently.

"I understand, brother. I've come here every day for the past ten years, and I still can't get used to it."

"Aren't there any doctors?" Tim asked, his stomach in knots.

"Of course," Hardt replied. "They come, they make rounds, they go. Sometimes if a big drug company has been munificent, they leave painkillers or some very avant-garde medicines."

"Well, at least that's a consolation," Tim remarked.

"Ah," Hardt said. "You must understand that for all the generosity of the world's pharmaceutical companies, they prefer to sell rather than donate. This means we get drugs that for one reason or another have been declared unsuitable for 'civilized' consumption." He added, "I don't have to tell you how much Thalidomide we got free.

"We do have nurses. One or two of them are fully qualified. Most are *moradoras* who just give injections, carry off the dead, and change the bedclothes." He sighed heavily. "This is the one time I wish I were a doctor. All a priest can do is give last rites and try to offer some explanation for why God is taking them so young."

Tim looked around him at the patients on their low beds, some writhing, some spasmodic, most of them inert. Surely, he said to himself, this must be what Dante's inferno looked like. Gradually a sound reached his consciousness, rising above the moans of the dying.

"I can hear children."

"Yes." Hardt locked him with his gaze, this time his gray eyes emanating sympathy for Tim. "They're on the second floor. If I told you it was ten times worse than what you're seeing now, I wouldn't be exaggerating. Are you sure you can take it?"

The fervor in Tim's own eyes answered Hardt even before his words.

"Didn't our Lord say, 'Suffer the little children to come unto me, and forbid them not; for of such is the kingdom of God'?"

"Good, my brother," Hardt remarked, gripping his upper arm affectionately. "You have all my admiration."

Hardt led the way up a creaking, makeshift wooden staircase to the second story.

Tim was sickened by the sight and smell of what was before him. Wretched little children, pale and scrawny, some with distended bellies, lay passively whimpering on mattresses, the smaller ones cradled in their mothers' arms . . . dying.

"Tell me," Tim asked hoarsely. "How many of these kids will ever leave here alive?"

For all Hardt's penchant for polemics, this time he was unwilling even to talk.

"How many, Dom Ernesto?" Tim persisted.

"Sometimes," Hardt began, "sometimes, God sends a miracle." He paused again and in a lowered voice added, "But not very often."

Tim felt helpless and angry.

"What are they suffering from?"

"The usual infant scourges—dysentery, typhus, malaria, and of course, since disease is the only area in which we're up to date, we're starting to see cases of AIDS."

"This is inhuman!" Tim exploded. "There are supposed to be six major hospitals in Brasília."

Hardt nodded. "There are—but we're somewhat out of their district."

Struck by a sudden notion, Tim turned and appealed to Hardt.

"Can you take me to my hotel and back?"

"Certainly," his host replied, sounding confused. "But why?"

"Don't ask. Let's just say I want to do something special for these children."

"In that case," Hardt responded, "you'd be better off helping some of the guys downstairs hammer little coffins."

Tim lost his temper. "For once, Dom Ernesto, I'm talking to you as an archbishop. Now do what I say!"

Surprised, Hardt merely shrugged his shoulders and started downstairs ahead of Tim.

———

At the sight of Hardt's mud-caked Land Rover, the doorman at the Nacional made haste to direct it as quickly as possible toward the parking lot until he saw the driver.

"*Bom dia, padre*. May I take your car?"

"Thanks, but we'll only be a second."

"In that case, leave your vehicle right here. I'll guard it like a lion."

Hardt winked at Tim as if to say, You see who's boss around here.

Minutes later Tim was back in the car, this time carrying his black valise.

"May I ask what you've got there?" said Hardt as he gunned away from the curb.

"No, brother," Tim replied. "It's official church business."

For the rest of the journey they listened to a feverish soccer game on the radio.

When they reached the village, Timothy excused himself and went into Hardt's office. As he quickly changed his clothes he could hear Isabella and Ernesto expressing their curiosity in rapid dialect.

When he emerged moments later, the sight of him took their breath away. He was wearing the full purple regalia of a Roman Catholic bishop.

"What on earth do you think you're doing?" Hardt remarked sarcastically. "It's at least two months until carnival."

Tim was not amused. "I'm going to the hospital again. You don't have to take me. I know the way."

Without waiting, he strode swiftly out of the house. Bemused, Ernesto and Isabella followed him through the mire.

Twenty minutes later they discovered that not all of Heaven and Earth was dreamt of in Liberation Theology. As Tim knelt by the side of the children one by one, chatting with them, each in a language the other could not understand, and, most of all, *touching* them, the Hardts could see from afar how Tim made the children laugh and the mothers cry. Each time he formed the sign of the cross and moved on to the next patient, the tearful mothers would bless him and instinctively grasp his hand to kiss it.

When he reached the far end of the dormitory, Tim looked back across the sea of children and saw Ernesto and Isabella smiling. He had just performed his most meaningful service since he had entered the priesthood.

When they were back in Dom Ernesto's house, Isabella poured the coffee as Hardt commented.

"Was that supposed to be a lesson to me in pastoral healing?"

"Dom Ernesto," Tim replied, "if you found something that enlightened you, please take it with my compliments. As far as I was concerned, I wanted to prove for myself and to you that there is something good in the power of Holy Mother Church."

But Hardt was not convinced.

"Tim," he began, "with your purity of spirit, you would have moved those poor children if you'd been dressed as Santa Claus."

"I don't agree," said Isabella. "These people know that all bishops wear purple. They've just never seen one." Turning to their guest, she reiterated, "You're right, Dom Timóteo."

"Thank you," Tim replied. "And if it will mean anything, I'd like to celebrate Mass there tomorrow. Once on each floor."

Hardt made a surprising request. "Would you allow me to assist you, Dom Timóteo?"

As the weeks of Tim's "visit" grew into months, the two men's conversations grew more intimate. Tim came to prefer the warmth of the Brazilian's household to the luxury of his hotel. They often spent entire nights discussing Scripture . . . and their innermost feelings.

One evening Hardt, as ever puffing on a cigarette, asked his guest, "Tell me, my young friend. Have you never loved a woman?"

Tim hesitated for a moment, not knowing how to react. Even in this remote and alien place, visions of Deborah had continued to surface in his subconscious. Still, he had never talked about her to anyone except his confessor, and even then he had not pronounced Deborah's name nor described what it felt like to love her. He had spoken only of sin but never joy. Now he wanted to open his heart to this man he so admired.

The Brazilian priest listened intently and did not interrupt Tim even when his narrative became elliptical and some details were jumbled.

When Tim had concluded, Hardt said gently, "I think you should have married her." He inhaled deeply, then asked, "Don't you?"

"I had made a commitment. I was marrying the Church, Dom Ernesto."

"And in so doing you were perpetuating a false dogma. Of all the scriptural passages I could adduce, there is nothing more ironic—nor appropriate—than chapter three of the First Epistle to Timothy. You of course recall that here St. Paul himself sets out the requirements for a good bishop, insisting that he must be 'blameless, vigilant, sober—' "

The reflexive scholar in Timothy filled in the missing part of the quotation. ". . . And 'the husband of one wife.' "

"Can you tell me truthfully, do you still think of her?"

Tim let his eyes blur so that he would not have to see the older man's reaction.

"Yes, Ernesto. Every now and then I see her face."

"I feel sorry for you," Hardt said with compassion. "For you'll never know the very special love I share with my Alberto and Anita."

Tim shrugged.

"Would you know how to find her?" his Brazilian friend inquired.

Tim hesitated, then at last allowed, "It wouldn't be impossible."

They sat silently for a moment. At last Hardt spoke.

"I'll pray for you, my brother."

"For what, exactly?"

"For you to find the courage," he replied affectionately.

77

Daniel

It was like entering a time warp. One minute I was walking the sophisticated streets of Gallic Montreal; a few blocks later I found myself in a neighborhood that could have been New York's Lower East Side a hundred years ago.

The streets were elegant enough—St. Urbain, Boulevard St. Laurent. But that was the extent of the area's Canadian character. All along the Boulevard, which the locals refer to as "the Main," the shop names were in Yiddish—the language I heard everywhere in the loud negotiations between the pushcart vendors and their black-coated, bearded clients.

After working in rural New England for nearly six years, I missed these sights and sounds of my childhood.

I confess that "the Main" made me nostalgic. Except for one thing. *I* was no longer wearing the team uniform. My garb was in no way Jewish enough for the denizens of this area. They stared at me as if I had two heads—neither of which wore a skullcap.

Nonetheless, the only way I could recharge my ethnic batteries was by going to St. Urbain Street, and I did so as frequently as possible.

Whenever I needed a new Jewish book—or a rare old one—the closest city to which I could go to browse was Montreal. So every few months I would make a bibliophile's journey for the sheer pleasure of holding new books and leafing through them.

On this fateful Sunday, I fortified myself with two really good hot pastrami sandwiches—a kind of ambrosia impossible to find in northern New England. Then, I headed for my destination, the Eternal Light Bookshop on Park Avenue.

I always called ahead to say I was coming so that Reb Vidal, the learned proprietor, would be sure to be there. I had come to rely on him to keep me up to date with what was new in the Old Testament, but on this particular day when I entered the shop he was nowhere in sight, and an ancient, stoop-shouldered clerk was off in a corner chatting in Yiddish with some customers.

I proceeded to check out the "Just Arrived" table.

I can't describe the feeling. In Brooklyn I took it

for granted. Yet here, as a fugitive from a hermetic sylvan province, I first began to appreciate the true joy of touching a book in the holy language.

I whiled away twenty minutes or so. Then I began to grow restive, so I went to get some further elucidation at the counter where the old-fashioned cash register stood. Perhaps there might be a message for me.

It was at that moment that my life changed.

Seated there was a fresh-faced girl in her late teens, with the deepest brown eyes I had ever seen. Even from afar I could sense the emanation of what the mystics called *shekinah*, the quintessence of divine radiance.

I approached respectfully and said, "Excuse me. I'm looking for Reb Vidal. He was supposed to—"

She immediately turned her back to me.

God, what a heathen I had become! No well-brought-up Orthodox girl would ever speak to a male stranger. Clearly she was present in that shop only to serve the female clientele.

Awkward fool that I was, I tried to apologize—which only exacerbated matters.

"Please forgive me," I babbled, "I meant no offense. I mean . . ."

She turned her head again and addressed the old man in the corner in Yiddish. "Uncle Abe, would you kindly help this gentleman customer?"

"Just a minute, Miriam," he replied. Then

added, "He looks like a *shaygetz* to me, so go in back."

I bristled. He had described me with the ultimate Orthodox disparagement for another Jew—calling me a gentile.

I would have been furious except that, at least by my outward appearance, her uncle was absolutely right. After all, with my crew-neck sweater and open collar, not to mention my uncovered head and the outrageous shortness of my sideburns, I was clearly an alien.

Uncle Abe was glaring at me from across the store, and I could even hear him mutter, "What *chutzpah*." Thereafter he deliberately took his time with the other customers, probably hoping I would go away.

Finally he rang up their sale, and the store was completely empty. As I walked up to him, he inquired, "*Oui, monsieur?*"

Who the hell did he think I was, Yves Montand? In any case, to his great relief, I answered in Yiddish, hoping that would convince him that I was at least within the pale of acceptability.

"May I help you?" he asked with a touch of irritation.

"I'm looking for Reb Vidal," I replied. "I called ahead to say I'd be here today."

His eyes lit up in recognition. "Oh, you must be the cowboy."

"The what?"

"That's what my brother calls you," he said. "He had to take his wife to the hospital, and he sends you his excuses."

"Is it serious?" I asked.

"Well,"—he shrugged—"when you've spent your childhood in Bergen-Belsen instead of kindergarten, everything is serious. But—God willing—it's just another of her blood pressure attacks. Now may I help you?"

"Please give my best wishes to Reb Vidal for his wife's recovery," I said. "Meanwhile, I'd like to take a look at Alfred J. Kolatch, *The Jewish Book of Why*."

"Why?"

"That's the title," I answered.

"I know the title, young man," he replied. "I just wanted to know why you should be interested in such a work. Are you Jewish?"

"Are you kidding? Can't you tell?"

"Not by the way you're dressed. But I'll take your word for it. Just explain to me why you need a book which tells you what any yeshiva *bocher* of six already knows."

"This may come as a surprise to you," I retorted. "But not everybody in the world has had the benefit of yeshiva training. I have a lot of students desperate to learn about their heritage who can't read Hebrew. Now could I impose upon you to show me that book?"

Uncle Abe shrugged, reached beneath the counter, and withdrew a blue-and-red volume. Glancing at it I was immediately convinced that it was a delightful way of explaining Jewish customs.

"This is terrific," I said, looking up at him. "Can you order me two dozen?"

"It's not impossible," he responded vaguely, obviously intent on sparing me the pleasure of a simple yes.

Just then his glorious niece reappeared. "Uncle Abe, Papa's on the phone."

"Oh," said the old man in a worried tone, and as he turned away mumbled to me, "You wait quietly." Then, as he passed the counter, he said to the young girl, "Don't speak to the cowboy, Miriam."

She nodded obediently, and her eyes followed her uncle as he disappeared to the back of the shop.

I know, chapter and verse, that what I did next was wrong. But I did it anyway. And the reason couldn't be found in any Jewish Book of Why. I addressed the girl.

"Miriam, are you still in school?" I asked timidly.

She hesitated for a moment and then, glancing furtively behind her, turned to me. "It's not proper that we speak like this," she said uneasily.

But she didn't walk away.

"I know we shouldn't," I replied. "The prohibitions can be found in the Code of Jewish Law 152:1, and *Shulchan Aruch Even Ha Ezer* 22:1 and 2."

"You know the *Shulchan Aruch*?" she said with surprise.

"Well, I've studied a bit and I know the *unabridged* version pretty well."

"Oh," she said, "that must be why Papa likes you so much."

I was astonished. "You mean Reb Vidal has actually spoken of me?"

She blushed and again glanced over her shoulder. "My uncle will be back in just a moment. I'd better—"

"No," I stopped her. "Just one little second. What exactly did your father say?"

She answered shyly and quickly, "That you were . . . very learned. That it was a pity—"

"A pity that what—?" I interrupted urgently.

"That you were—"

At that frustrating moment, Uncle Abe reappeared and glared at Miriam. "Have you been talking to this stranger?" he asked sternly.

She was tongue-tied, so I interceded. "It's my fault, sir," I insisted. "I was just asking her what time it was."

"You don't have a watch?" the old man inquired suspiciously.

"Uh," I answered, groping for a pretext, "Uh— it's stopped." That was even half-true. For in a cosmic sense, time had stood still from the moment I set eyes on Miriam Vidal.

He ordered his niece to go out while he would

"take care of this tourist." But I was heartened to see that Miriam disobeyed him. She remained rooted to her post behind the counter, drinking in every word of our conversation.

"All right then, mister," he said curtly. "Have we done all our business for today?"

"No," I answered, "I haven't driven two hundred miles just to order one book. I was looking forward to discussing publications on mysticism with Reb Vidal."

"Well, you'll have to do that next time. Have a nice journey home."

Before he could turn his back on me, I stopped him with the next question, "Scholem?"

He sneered at what he chose to regard as a mispronunciation. "*Shalom* to you as well."

"No, no," I persisted, "I mean Gershom Scholem. He writes on the *kabbalah*."

He took this remark as the ploy it was and answered dubiously, "What particular title were you interested in?"

"Well, I'd like to see what you have."

"Certainly," he replied and pointed to the opposite wall. "Mysticism's over there on the top three shelves. If you need any advice just ring the bell on the counter and I'll come out. Now, if you'll excuse me."

He turned and saw his niece still standing there.

"Miriam," he said with a frown, "I thought I told you to go."

"I'm not talking to him or anything."

"But you're *looking*," her uncle snapped. "And you know what the Code says about that."

This was my moment. I intervened with as much hostility as I could put into a single sentence. "And in precisely what tractate does such an interdiction appear?"

Uncle Abe was stumped. "Uh—it doesn't matter, I just know that it's forbidden."

"I beg your pardon," I replied, warming to the fray. "According to Chapter 152:1 of the Code, *I'm* forbidden to look at Miriam—which, as you can see, I'm not doing. It's forbidden for me to look at her and say that her hair is the loveliest I've ever seen, her voice the loveliest I've ever heard. But of course I'd never do such a thing."

I stole a look at her out of the corner of my eye. She was smiling.

"In any case, I've already got all the Scholems you have in stock, so I'd better leave it for another visit. But could I prevail upon you to leave a message with Reb Vidal?"

"Perhaps," the curmudgeon replied. "What is it?"

"Naturally I'll write him a formal letter, but I'd like the honor of being formally introduced to his daughter—in the presence of a chaperone, of course."

"That's out of the question," he retorted. "She's a pious girl—"

"Don't worry," I persisted, "I'll wear a skullcap—I'll even wear black clothing and a fur hat if I have to."

"Are you mocking us?" asked the old man.

"No, I'm just trying to convince you that I'm worthy of an audience with your niece. Anyway, at least let her father decide."

"No, he won't approve, I'm absolutely certain," the man said adamantly. "You come from somewhere in the woods. We don't know your family or anything."

I think I can point to this as the moment I took pride in my upbringing for the first time. All I needed now was to be precisely who I was.

"Do you happen to have a copy of *The Great Book of Hasidic Tunes*?" I asked ingenuously.

"Certainly, both volumes. Are you interested in buying it?"

I answered his question with one of my own. "Do you happen to be acquainted with the tunes therein?"

"Some of them," he answered. His averted eyes told me he was feeling slightly intimidated. "The famous ones, of course."

Again I sneaked a furtive glance at Miriam, who was watching wide-eyed.

I began to hum, "*Biri biri biri biri bum.*"

The old man stared at me as if I were a lunatic.

Encouraged by his consternation, I began to snap my fingers and sing at the top of my voice.

"Do you recognize this one, Reb Abe?"

"Of course. It's by Moses Luria, the late Silczer Rav, may he rest in peace. Everybody knows it."

"Well, I'm his son—*biri bum*."

I heard a little gasp, and turned in time to see Miriam covering her mouth. But she did not cover her eyes, which were sparkling. The old man stood there gaping, at a loss for words.

Just then a voice boomed, "Abe, what are you doing?"

The old man whirled to see his portly brother, Reb Vidal, stride in.

Now poor Abe was all aflutter. "This *meshuggener*, he's singing. He says he's—"

"I know, I know. I just want to know why . . ."

"Why what?" the befuddled uncle asked.

"Why *you're* not singing too?" And then the good Reb Vidal let loose a cannonade of laughter.

———

Needless to say, I got my audience. More than that, I was invited to spend an entire Sabbath weekend with the Vidals. I was billeted in Uncle Abe's basement apartment on Clark Street.

For the rest of the week I desperately tried to grow my sideburns, and thanks to my dark hair, had pretty much achieved the statutory minimum length by Friday afternoon.

As I unpacked my suitcase in the guest room— an elaborate word for the large closet I would be occupying—I recalled my frenzied activity in the past few days. I was desperate to obtain the trappings of orthodoxy, and must have gone into every store I could find to obtain the appropriate—and best-cut—Orthodox attire. I examined myself in the mirror and heard a voice ask, "Hey, Danny, where've you been?"

Miriam's mother had gone to great effort and expense to prepare that meal. They had even invited a brace of elderly cousins named Mendele and Sophie. My own contribution was a bottle of Château Baron de Rothschild, a strictly kosher red Bordeaux from France.

My only worry was that I might spill some of it on their precious white tablecloth, since from the moment I walked in I could not keep my eyes off Miriam. She looked lovelier than ever in a blue-and-white dress with a high lace collar and cuffs, her face angelic in the flickering candlelight.

I felt a curious conflict of sensations. On the one hand, I was happy, even flattered, that Reb Vidal had obviously gone through every songbook in his shop to make sure he sang as many Lurianic melodies as possible. On the other, I began to wonder if I could endure being accepted merely as my father's son. But then I persuaded myself that if our biblical ancestor Jacob could work fourteen years in Laban's fields to win his beloved Rachel, I would be able to survive my family's eminence and still win Miriam on my own.

"By the way," Reb Vidal mentioned during the

fish course, "I see from *La Tribune* that your uncle is causing quite a stir."

"How so?" I asked in genuine ignorance. Though I called home weekly, most of the conversation consisted of a bombardment of questions from my mother, all of which seemed to boil down to unending variations on the theme: Was I dressing warm?

My host explained. "It seems he's signed a petition in *The New York Times*, along with some Conservative—and even Reform—rabbis, urging the state of Israel to give up land on the West Bank in exchange for peace. That's unprecedented for a man in his position."

I could not help beaming with pride. Not only had Saul acted as a leader should—to think of his people's welfare with *vision*—but he had bravely done it in the most public of forums.

"Apparently, he's been criticized by many Orthodox rabbinical leaders. And I'm sure it didn't win him many friends in Brooklyn," Reb Vidal added. "Do you think he did the right thing?"

"Absolutely," I remarked. "A leader's first obligation is to safeguard the survival of his people. Saul had legitimate doctrinal reasons. Besides, the Bible itself gives contradictory boundaries for the Jewish State. There's Genesis 15:18, which rather ambitiously claims for us all the land 'from the Nile to the Euphrates,' while Judges 20:1 mentions only 'Dan to Beersheba,' which wouldn't even give us Haifa and the Negev."

"I agree. It's a very difficult question," Reb Vidal said. "I'm afraid there are no easy answers."

We sang and we ate. And then we sang again. I loudly, to be sure that Miriam could hear, and she so shyly and softly that at times I thought she was merely mouthing the words. All through the meal I could not help but notice the relatives—even Uncle Abe—looking at one another and nodding.

A little after ten, I took reluctant leave of the Vidals and walked slowly back with Abe. It would be noon till I would see my Miriam—Oh, God, please make her *mine*—unless I dared to sneak a look up at the ladies' gallery tomorrow morning, something I knew I would not risk under the circumstances.

Having been a widower for many years, Abe was grateful for my company. We sat in the shadows of his front room and exchanged family histories—though naturally he knew most of mine. He went to great pains to emphasize that their family were direct descendants of Chaim Vital, who had studied in the Holy Land with Isaac Luria in the late sixteenth century.

Their particular branch had settled in southern France, where the medieval popes permitted Jews to live in certain areas, among them Avignon and Aix-en-Provence. The Vidals had been French for more than five hundred years, till the Nazis came and decided they were just another kind of oven fuel. Those who survived the war, knowing no

English, chose to emigrate to Quebec. And so here they were.

I hazarded a delicate investigation. "How old is Miriam?" I asked.

"Eighteen, God bless her," Abe replied.

"How come she's not married already?" I asked, quickly adding, "Not that I'm complaining."

"Ah," said Abe with a smile, "my brother says it's because he can't find anyone suitable. But frankly, when your youngest child is your only daughter, and that daughter is a pearl like Miriam, you hesitate to let her go.

"Actually, for the past year or so, he's been resigning himself to compromise and has been talking with some families. I think he even liked the Dessler boy, but then Miriam objected—"

"On what grounds?" I asked anxiously, hoping it was not because Dessler was an old man like me.

"She said he wasn't *frum* enough."

My heart sank, and I began to ache at the irony of it. Had I followed in the footsteps of my father there would have been no question of my orthodoxy. But now—at least in Reb Vidal's eyes—I was a "cowboy," almost a creature from another planet.

I spent a sleepless night tossing and turning, wondering whether there was time enough for me to repent. Even a loving, overly possessive father like Miriam's would not permit himself to let her stay unmarried to the age of *nineteen*. My time was short.

In *shul* the next morning I was given the singular honor of being called to read the portion from the [...] I lacked Deborah's vocal talents, I [...] a good pair of lungs, and I knew that in our tradition loudness can sometimes compensate for being off key. I chanted both the prayers—and the [...] myself at the top of my voice.

As I mounted the podium, I was more nervous than at my own *bar mitzvah*. My heart beat faster, [...] my palms were even clammier. For on that [...] day I was only becoming a man. Had I faltered or forgotten blessings, I would have had another chance. This time, my goal was to become [...] husband, and I had no doubt that the pious Miriam, up in the balcony, would be following every [...]

When my performance ended, I could hear animated buzzing from every corner of the men's section. Here and there I even got a snatch of dialogue: "Rav Luria's son . . ." "I think Vidal's made a match." "If Miriam says her usual 'no,' I want him for my daughter."

A wonderful thing happened during the lunch that followed. As our host was discussing that week's scriptural portion, and I was quoting Rashi and as many other commentators as I could recall, an angel took my soup plate. That is to say, Miriam—not her mother as would have been appropriate—came within touching distance of me under the pretext of taking my bowl.

Her proximity was almost too much to bear. Though I longed to look more closely at her face, I pretended to be listening to her father's interpretation, all the while enthralled by the ethereal touch of Miriam's breath on my cheek.

After we sang grace, I politely asked Reb Vidal's permission to take his daughter for a walk—accompanied, of course.

"Well,"—he smiled genially—"if my wife feels up to it. I think we could all do with a little sunshine."

I rejoiced at the opportunity to be alone with Miriam. For in fact alone we were. Reb Vidal and his wife walked deliberately slowly, so that gradually Miriam and I were nearly fifty feet in front of them.

Again I was nervous, not knowing how to start the conversation, though I knew exactly how I planned to end it.

I soon discovered that though she looked demure, Miriam was far from shy. In some ways her attitude reminded me of Deborah. She took the initiative.

"Tell me, Daniel," she said in the first words she was officially sanctioned to address to me, "what exactly do you do?"

"Well, a whole lot of things," I answered awkwardly. "But mostly I teach. You see there are a lot of Jews scattered in upper New England who needed organizing. It's very hard to preserve your religious identity when you're outnumbered by the trees."

"Are they Orthodox?" she inquired.

"No, not exactly," I said hesitantly, not intending to avoid her question yet not wanting to disparage my own congregation either. "Before people can study, they need the light to read by. I view my job as kindling their souls so they can pursue their religion to whatever extent they desire. Can you understand that?"

"Yes. It's a new idea, I guess," she answered. "You might say you're helping them to repent."

Desperate with love as I was, I couldn't let this veiled criticism pass.

"I'm sorry, Miriam. They're guilty of nothing but ignorance. And for that you don't have to repent. When I started six years ago, the only word all these people knew was 'Amen.' Now all of them have reached at least 'The Lord our God, the Lord is One.' Now don't you think that's marvelous?"

She thought for a moment, perhaps wondering what her teachers might say about my radical philosophy. She then braved an answer. "That sounds very idealistic, Danny. But is that what you want to devote your life to?"

A crucial question. One with a veritable minefield of dangers.

"To be honest with you, Miriam," I said and looked straight into her beautiful brown eyes, "because I always want to be honest with you—I'm not really sure. I mean my father obviously wanted me to succeed him. But I had so many doubts."

"You mean of living up to the responsibility?"

"Yes, Miriam, I was very frightened. What about you?" I asked her. "What are your ambitions?"

"I have no ambitions," she replied. "I only have dreams."

"Well then, what do you dream of?"

"Being a good wife—an *eshes chayil*—to a pious, learned man."

"And you've found no one 'pious' enough yet?" I asked with no small amount of trepidation.

"I suppose so," she said with what seemed a touch of embarrassment. "But then there was that dream I spoke of . . ."

"Yes?" I encouraged her to speak her heart.

She lowered her eyes. "I dared to think that I could find a scholar like my father. One who knew not only how to pray . . ." She hesitated, and then said as if about to voice a daring thought, "But one who knew how to laugh as well. Because there's so much joy in our religion."

I did an inward somersault. "Well, I think I know how to laugh," I said.

"I know," she answered with a tiny smile. "From the minute I saw you singing in the bookshop, I knew that the Father of the Universe had sent you there for a reason. You have such joy, Daniel. It shimmers all around you like candlelight."

She stopped herself, blushing. "But I'm talking too much."

"No, no," I pleaded. "Go on, say more. Say anything you like."

692

She smiled self-consciously and, her voice nearly in a whisper, answered, "The rest is not for me to say."

———

First I requested a private meeting with Reb Vidal and formally asked for his daughter's hand. I think he would have said yes, but he was so overcome with emotion he merely threw his arms around me. Even in the depths of my insecurity I took this to be a positive sign.

Then, after proudly announcing it to the rest of the family, he proposed we wait another hour to be absolutely certain the stars were shining in New York too, so he could call my uncle to discuss the wedding contract.

My fingers fairly shook as I dialed the number. The minute I heard our phone picked up, I shouted, "It's me, Danny. I've got wonderful news!"

I was shocked by the overwhelming silence at the other end. I lowered my voice and said, "Mama, is that you? Is anything wrong?"

All around me I could hear the Vidals murmur with anxiety.

"Oh," they heard me say with what was left of my voice. "I'll get on the first plane."

Totally in shock, I slowly put down the receiver and addressed my hosts. "I'm afraid this conversation will have to wait. Something terrible has happened."

"What is it, Danny?" Miriam asked anxiously.

"My Uncle Saul . . . ," I mumbled. "They've been trying to find me in New Hampshire . . . My Uncle Saul's been shot."

Shot. I could scarcely believe the words as I pronounced them. From what my mother had been able to convey, I gathered that Efraim Himmelfarb, one of the Elders, had been so incensed by my uncle's political declaration in *The New York Times*, that he'd gone berserk, bought a gun, and fired it at close range during Sabbath morning services.

"How is he?" Reb Vidal asked in a voice echoing my own shock.

"He was hit several times," I muttered. "One of the bullets lodged in his head. They're operating on him right now, but the chances of him surviving are . . ."

"Fifty-fifty?" he asked hopefully.

"No," I replied, feeling hot coals in my chest. "A million to one."

In my distracted state, I was unable to cope with the full enormity of it and found myself retreating into an absurd intellectuality, pondering how Himmelfarb could justify dishonoring the Sabbath by *carrying* anything.

I heard Reb Vidal's compassionate words. "Sit down, Danny. I'll call and see about the planes."

I sat there frozen, thinking of my beloved uncle, my wise, courageous uncle, when I saw Miriam's hand before my face, holding a glass of sparkling water.

"Here, Daniel," she said gently, "you need it."

Strange, isn't it? At that moment, I had all I could do to restrain myself from reaching for her hand—for what I really needed was to touch her.

Reb Vidal slowly reentered the room.

"I'm sorry, Daniel," he said softly. "There's no flight till seven in the morning."

"No!" I blurted out. "He'll be dead by then. I'll drive."

"No, Danny—I forbid you." His strong hands gripped me by the shoulders. "There are some catastrophes we can't help and some we can avoid. I won't allow you to drive in the state you're in."

I knew he was right, but I was so desperate that I had to act. I looked at him and he understood.

"Do you want to go to *shul* and pray?"

I nodded.

He addressed his wife and daughter. "We're going to *daven*. You don't have to wait up."

"We'll wait up, Papa, we will," Miriam insisted. She glanced at me with affection.

As we were putting on our coats Reb Vidal remarked, "Daniel, I think there are many others of us who would like to pray as well for the Silczer Rav. Would you mind if I call them?"

"No," I murmured. "No, go right ahead," thinking perhaps a crowd could somehow help absorb part of my pain.

We remained in that small synagogue, about two dozen of us, saying psalms for several hours. No one left. Once in a while a worshiper went for a glass of water but otherwise they prayed without pause as if the fate of the world was at stake. I was assaulted by grief and guilt.

On the day of Eli's *bar mitzvah* I had spoken words that shaped the fate of our entire community. I had convinced Saul privately not to build our dormitory in the occupied territories. But he had assumed public responsibility from that moment on. And so received the bullet that was meant for me.

As the others were chanting their prayers I went up to the Holy Ark and fell to my knees.

"O Lord, God of my fathers, I humble myself before you. Let Saul live. Do not let the righteous suffer. Let your wrath be visited on me. Please grant me this, and I will serve you in faithfulness the rest of my days. Amen."

We stayed till dawn and after morning prayers walked home slowly, physically and emotionally exhausted. The women, who had clearly kept vigil with us, were waiting with hot rolls and coffee. I was afraid to ask if there were any messages. But Mrs. Vidal took the initiative.

"Danny, your mother called . . ."

"Yes?" I was barely able to draw breath.

"Your uncle—" she stammered. "They operated. They got the bullet. He's . . . alive."

"What?" I gasped.

"The surgeon himself says it was a miracle."

I was too shocked to speak. I exchanged glances with Reb Vidal, whose tired eyes seemed to mist over as he murmured, "Sometimes—perhaps even when our faith is at its weakest—the Father of the Universe gives us a sign that he has heard our prayers."

He was right. It was a sign to me.

I could avoid my destiny no longer.

78

Daniel

Mine was not a simple ordination. My uncle saw to it that I was tested by no fewer than four renowned sages—*Gedolei Hatorah*—from different sects all over the city.

In retrospect, what was most curious about it all was that I didn't study for my examination. I didn't stay up memorizing likely passages or anything that could have strengthened my performance in this truly sacred questioning. I went through it like a sleepwalker. I was in double shock. Haunted by the specter of gunshots fired at a rabbi standing near an open Ark—by someone who supposedly was one of us. And counterbalancing this horror was the enormous love and joy that I had found in Miriam.

At last I was my father's son. Rav Daniel Luria—the Silzcer Rebbe.

———

Even though it was a Thursday and I arrived a full half hour early, the synagogue was packed. As I walked down the aisle wearing an old *tallit* which had belonged to my father, worshipers rose, bowed their heads, and shouted words of greeting— "*Yasher-koyakh!* " "More power to you!" "May you live to one hundred and twenty!"

I ascended the three steps, stood before the Holy Ark, and prayed.

May my prayer be acceptable to Thee
in the abundance of Thy lovingkindness.

I turned toward the congregation, placed both my hands on the sloping table, and looked out. Beneath me was a sea of worshipers in what looked like a thousand white prayer shawls. Uncle Saul was seated in a wheelchair in the first row, Eli at his side.

I glanced up to the ladies' gallery, where I could see the shining eyes of the three people I loved most on earth—my mother, my sister, and sitting between them, my beloved Miriam, who would be my wife in three more weeks.

For an instant I was silent. And then I pronounced the only prayer appropriate for such an occasion:

Blessed art Thou, O Lord Our God,
King of the Universe, who has kept me alive
and sustained me and brought me to this
wonderful moment.

As, unbidden, the congregation began to pray, I covered my face with my hands. And wept.

79

Timothy

O n New Year's Eve, after the other guests—
worker priests, students, and assorted
neighbors—had left, Hardt took Tim into his study,
poured each of them a large *ginjinha,* and said,
"Let's drink."

"To anything in particular?" Tim asked.

Hardt responded by opening his desk drawer and
pulling out a thick stack of paper. He looked at Tim
and beamed.

"It's finished. This is the book von Jakob wants
so badly to suppress. As a token of fraternity I offer
it to you."

"I don't understand."

"It's yours," the older man insisted. "You can
read it tonight and burn it in the morning. Or you
can burn it right now." He paused and then said,

"Or—you can help me publish it. Happy New Year, Dom Timóteo."

Tim stood motionless as his friend left the room. Then slowly, he sat down behind the desk and trained the feeble lamplight on the manuscript. Hardt's university secretary had obviously spent many hours typing it, binding it, and affixing the title cover: *The Crucifixion of Love.*

He did not need to peruse all its four hundred and eighteen pages to know what they contained. Hardt's theme was the impossibility and, as he saw it, the futility of priestly sexual abstinence.

What was potentially explosive was the multitude of data. Hardt had facts, case histories, names and testimonies of prelates everywhere throughout the Catholic world who were willing not only to be interviewed but also to permit their names to be used. These men continued to perform their sacerdotal functions, at the same time admitting to personal relationships crowned by physical love.

Tim knew the history of the Church was strewn with fallen priests, with popes who lodged their "nephews" in the Apostolic Palace, but he was nonetheless struck dumb by the reports from America.

Richard Sipe, a Baltimore psychotherapist who had been a Benedictine monk, estimated that half the fifty thousand Roman Catholic priests in the United States were breaking their vows of celibacy.

And yet for all this, Ernesto Hardt had not composed a document intended to destroy the Church. Rather, he sought to vest with dignity the lives of men who both served God and their own emotional needs.

At four-thirty A.M., Tim had finished the last page and realized that Hardt's argument for the legitimate fulfillment of human desire in men who serve God was no better embodied than in his Brazilian friend's own life.

During breakfast the next morning, his host seemed to be deliberately avoiding the subject of his book, talking almost exclusively to the children. Nonetheless, as Tim chatted with Isabella, it became clear that she, too, was anxious to know his reaction.

A little after eight she hurried Alberto and Anita out the door, and they, with typical childish reluctance, set off toward the school organized by one of Dom Ernesto's worker priests.

At last, Hardt grinned at Tim and asked mischievously, "Did you sleep well, my brother?"

Timothy took the initiative. "I think your book is dangerous, seditious—and very important. Von Jakob has every reason to fear its publication."

"Good," Hardt smiled. "Then I have done my job well."

"I'm still amazed at how you could marshal such information by yourself."

"Oh, Timóteo, my name may appear on the

cover, but I have literally hundreds of co-authors who have helped me gather information throughout the world. Only this week my office at the university received a hand-delivered report from Czechoslovakia." He went on to explain that because the Church there had had to operate clandestinely for so long, secretly ordaining priests and even bishops, there was now an entire underground clergy, many of whom were married.

"Do you think von Jakob knows?"

Hardt shrugged. "I'm sure the Holy Father does. This may surprise you, but because we are so short of priests in the Upper Amazon, the Pope has just granted a dispensation to allow two married men to be ordained and serve there."

Tim was astounded. "How can he do something that goes against all he believes in?"

"Because he is a realist," Hardt responded. "And his duty as Christ's Vicar is to keep the Church alive. In this regard he and I are of one mind."

"So tell me what in Heaven's name I'm doing here," Tim demanded.

"Did it ever occur to you that God had chosen you to proclaim the truth rather than suppress it? Tell me honestly what you believe now."

Tim answered slowly and deliberately. "Well, speaking as a realist," he said, emphasizing the word, "if a married priest can serve in the Amazon, then why not in the Vatican?"

Hardt smiled at Tim with affection. "Thank you, brother. But what will you tell them in Rome?"

At this point Archbishop Hogan turned the tables.

"I know what you'd like me to say, Ernesto. But let me tell you something. The truth, however admirable, isn't always the best means to a worthy end. Never mind what happens to me, let's say you publish—and they excommunicate you."

"I'm not afraid," said Hardt.

"I know that, brother. But I don't want the Church to lose you—"

"But what can you do about it? Rome doesn't seem to care."

"Why don't we try to change that? Why don't you help me build something?"

"For example?" Hardt demanded.

"A hospital, to begin with," Timothy replied. "The greatest joy in my life as a priest has been the baptisms I've performed here." He paused and then said softly, "And my greatest pain—the funerals. Give me the chance to raise money for a children's hospital."

Hardt answered dismissively, "Until the people run the Church, you won't see hospitals springing up in the jungle."

"If you'll just give me time to try, Ernesto, I'll not only help you publish your book in English, I'll even translate it myself. I know some very rich laymen who would be sympathetic to our cause."

Hardt hesitated for a split second, and then spoke

with quiet emotion, "You said *our* cause, Dom Timóteo. For that alone, I'm willing to hold off the publication."

"For how long?" Tim asked.

"As long as necessary," Hardt replied. "Or, until you give up trying to raise that money."

———

The night before Tim was to leave for Rome, he stood solemnly before the fire with Ernesto and Isabella, groping for words to express his feelings.

The Brazilian priest was holding a sheaf of papers under one arm.

Suddenly, he let it drop into the flames.

"What did you do, Ernesto?" Tim asked confusedly.

"Now you don't have to tell a lie to the Holy Father," Hardt replied. "You can say with all honesty that you've seen me burn every page of my book."

"But Ernesto, I just asked you to wait—not destroy it."

Hardt grinned. "Oh, I'm afraid you can't tell the Romans I've 'destroyed' it. Actually, it's one of my going-away presents to you."

He went to his desk and pulled out several small black plastic disks.

"It may surprise you, my brother, but even universities at the edge of the jungle have computers these days. Be sure to wrap these in foil before going on the plane."

"But why?" Tim stammered, "Why are you giving them to me?"

"A precaution," Hardt explained. "If something should happen to me—or our computer—I would always have the security of knowing our book is in friendly hands. *Adeus*, Tim—pray for me."

The two men embraced.

80

Timothy

A Vatican car met him at the airport. Timothy used its telephone to call Father Ascarelli.

"No, my son, how could you have awakened me when—since your capricious departure—I've been obliged to do my own work? I've even had to train my left hand—"

"What?" Tim interrupted.

"Nothing, nothing." Ascarelli brushed off the question. "Why don't you come around first thing in the morning?"

"Thank you, Father, but may I see you for a few minutes now?"

"Of course, my son. I'll boil the kettle and make us both some tea."

Minutes later, the long black limousine pulled up in front of the Governatorio, and Tim, tightly clutching his valise, leapt out.

He stood breathless outside Ascarelli's apartment and knocked softly. From within he heard the approach of shuffling feet. The door opened and there was his mentor, wearing the same old threadbare bathrobe.

"Benvenuto, figlio mio."

As they hugged, Tim realized Ascarelli was affectionately patting his back with his left hand only. The entire right side of his body was rigid.

"What's happened to you, Father?" Tim asked anxiously.

"Nothing, nothing. A little injury."

As they sat down the scribe nonchalantly recounted that a mild stroke had cost him the use of his right hand. Now, in the eightieth year of his life, he was obliged to learn how to do everything with his left.

The whistle of the kettle interrupted their dialogue. Tim persuaded his overeager host to sit quietly while he made the tea.

He carefully placed a cup where the old man could reach it and then sat opposite him.

"Don't worry," the old man reassured him. "I'll still be around when you get your cardinal's biretta."

"Would you believe that I don't care about those things?" Tim protested. "I never did and I certainly don't now."

"Well, like it or not, the whole Secretariat is

buzzing with your achievement. All the time you were in Brazil, Hardt didn't write a single heretical word. I'm sure von Jakob will reward you."

"Wrong, Father. He's written plenty, he just hasn't published it—yet."

Tim then told Ascarelli of his experiences with Hardt and the bargain they had struck.

"A children's hospital—that sounds wonderful. But where do you expect to find the millions of dollars you need to build this worthy project? The world is full of generous Catholics, but they're only human. They want their monuments where their friends can see them on their way to work."

"Let that be my problem, Father. Now may I ask you a favor? I have a copy of Hardt's book."

"You what?" the old man asked excitedly. "Quickly—let me see it."

Tim reached into his valise and pulled out a four-inch-square object wrapped in aluminum foil.

The old man eyed it suspiciously. "What's that? A sandwich?"

"I can only say it's food for thought," Tim replied, unwrapping the package and revealing six computer discs. "Remember my thesis topic?"

"Of course. 'The Obstacles to Priestly Matrimony.' Why?"

Tim answered quietly, "This book demolishes the obstacles."

———

"Are you sure?" Cardinal von Jakob asked with the closest to a smile that Tim had ever seen on the Prussian's face.

"Yes, Your Eminence. I saw him burn the book myself."

"*Deo gratias,*" the Cardinal responded. "You've done an excellent job."

But evidently not a complete job. For the prelate then asked, "Did you make a note of his contacts—the sources of his information?"

"With respect, Eminence," Tim replied, trying to suppress his disdain for the Grand Inquisitor, "I fulfilled my assignment to the letter. No one gave me a microfilm camera or asked me to play James Bond."

The German nodded. "Yes, quite. Still—it's a pity you missed the opportunity. But I promise you the pontiff will be pleased."

Timothy's immediate reward was a small but elegant cubicle among the offices at the Apostolic Palace.

After unpacking the last of his books, he made his first call as a special Papal Assistant.

Principessa Santiori was delighted to hear his voice and—as Tim had hoped—invited him to lunch the next day.

"Everyone is talking about you, *caro.* Plan to stay late so I can hear about everything."

Flushed with optimism, Tim strolled briskly to the Governatorio to fulfill his previous night's promise of taking Father Ascarelli for dinner at Da Marcello in Trastevere.

No one answered his first knock. Perhaps the scribe was asleep. Tim banged even louder. Down the hallway, a *portiere* who had been vacuuming the long carpet scampered to his side.

"I'm sorry, Your Grace. I'm afraid they took Father Ascarelli to Santa Croce earlier this afternoon."

Tim went pale. "How bad is it?"

"Your Grace," said the janitor, "he's eighty years old. How good could it be?"

He ran the dozen blocks to the hospital, causing at least one cleric he passed to remark, "Another crazy Irishman like Murphy. They must all run."

Within five minutes of his arrival, Tim established that, although the scribe had suffered another stroke, he was still very much alive. Moreover, if he returned that evening, after Professor Rivieri examined the patient, perhaps he might be allowed to visit.

Tim nodded mutely and went immediately to the hospital chapel to pray.

Later, he walked along the Tiber as darkness fell upon the city—and his heart. He tried to prepare himself for a kind of grief he had never known, the imminent loss of a beloved parent.

When he returned, Professor Rivieri was awaiting him.

"I'm afraid he's suffered severe damage. It's only a question of time. . . ."

With the doctor's permission, Tim sat at the bedside, making lighthearted conversation, now and then reciting some of the Latin poetry he knew his friend loved.

He tried to smile whenever the sick man would attempt a feeble groan to correct a misquotation, knowing that pedantry was probably the only joy that remained to the old scholar.

———

Tim would have canceled the next day's luncheon with the principessa, had not Ascarelli insisted he "give priority to starving children rather than a dying old man."

He walked mournfully toward the palazzo, oblivious to the beauty of the day and the frenzy of the motorists.

The principessa's pleasure in seeing Tim was dampened by the sad news he brought. She immediately instructed her private secretary to send flowers to the scribe's room.

Tim was nervous. His previous fund-raising had been limited to appeals to re-roof a parish church. He wondered if he could even pronounce the vast sum he needed and had done nothing but rehearse articulating the numbers all during his walk.

After lunch, as they drank coffee on the patio, Tim studied his patroness's face. She had been deeply moved by his tales of the wretched children of Brazil, and he was now more confident of being able to make his appeal.

"Principessa, the children need a hospital. In this day and age, they shouldn't be dying of dysentery and measles."

"I quite agree," she replied sympathetically. "How much would such a hospital cost?"

Timothy's heart beat faster.

He took a sip of mineral water, and tried to say as matter-of-factly as he could, "They would need something in the neighborhood of eight million dollars."

There was a silence. The principessa merely absorbed what he had told her. At last she answered with fervor.

"There is no question, Timoteo. You must have that money. And I will personally see that you get it."

He was on the verge of tears.

"God bless you, Cristina." He hesitated for a moment, wondering if he should rise and throw his arms around her.

But then she took the initiative.

"Listen to me, Timoteo, we'll form a committee. I'll get the finest families in Rome—and believe me I know them all, even the ones not connected with the Church. I'll have them over for an evening, and you can address them. By the next social season we should be able to launch this charity with a magnificent gala. I promise you, even His Holiness will attend."

She had demonstrated the supremely Roman art of saying yes, but meaning no.

"Cristina," he said, growing angry, "as we sit here sipping coffee and planning social events, little children are in agony, dying in their mothers' arms. Surely, if you gathered these friends of yours one evening and I spoke to them, if they're anything as sensitive, as compassionate, as you, they'll write checks—large checks."

The principessa looked baffled. Had Timothy misconstrued the sincerity of her feelings, the genuineness of her offer to help?

"My dear boy," she said, as if explaining something to a simple child. "One cannot be so—how can I say it?—brutal, in demanding contributions. No matter how noble the cause, if my friends were obliged to donate money to every charity in Rome, they would have nothing left to live on."

"Oh, I doubt that," Tim replied. He was painfully embarrassed, but he sensed he would never have this opportunity again, so he spoke his mind.

"Principessa, you yourself could write that check and barely feel it."

"Please, Your Grace," she answered coolly. "You are speaking out of turn."

Tim rose and began to pace back and forth, trying to control his emotions.

"Look," he began his peroration. "At heart I'm just a naive kid from Brooklyn. I know nothing of the world of money. But even if I weren't its titular archbishop, I would know that your church, Santa Maria delle Lacrime, sits in so valuable a spot that the Vatican would pay you enough for it to build five hospitals."

"Are you mad?" she replied. "Are you suggesting I sell a church that has been in the Santiori family for centuries just to build some clinic for unknown people in the jungle?"

Tim battled to restrain his anger. She's a woman. She's alone. She's old. Still, he could not stop his words.

"Your Highness, you've got paintings in your dining room that would honor museums in the great cities of the world. Every other day we read about paintings fetching millions of dollars at auction. You have *rooms* of Old Masters."

He was sweating and breathless, and stopped to regain his composure.

The principessa had not lost hers. She simply said, "I think Your Grace should go now."

"I'm sorry," he said quietly. "I was carried away. Really, I apologize. . . ."

She smiled. "My dear Timothy, I have never met a purer soul than yours. I do admire you and will always think only the kindest thoughts of you."

He had been dismissed.

———

In earlier times, if he had suffered such a humiliating experience, Tim would have run to his mentor for advice and consolation. Now with Ascarelli on his deathbed, no doubt expecting him to return in glory, he was almost ashamed to visit the hospital.

When the sky had grown even darker than his mood, he finally went back. Professor Rivieri was waiting, a look of grave concern on his face. Timothy feared the worst.

"Is he dead, *Professore*?"

The doctor shook his head. "He's developed some cardiac complications. I doubt he'll last the night."

"Would he be lucid enough to know me?" Tim asked with concern.

"Yes, Archbishop Hogan. You're probably the only person he recalls by name." He added gravely, "He's requested that you give him Extreme Unction."

Timothy nodded. "Will you ask the hospital chaplain to lend me his stole and the other—" His voice broke.

The doctor placed his hand on Tim's shoulder and said gently, "Your Grace, he's lived a long and happy life. I think I see in him a patient ready to embrace death."

Fifteen minutes later, Tim was at the old man's bedside. He was breathing with great difficulty and, faithful servant of the Church that he was, used all the energy he could muster to repeat the words Tim requested. Of course, Tim performed the rite in Latin.

Thereafter, Tim sat and watched Ascarelli lapse into a sleep that would surely be his last. Yet he vowed not to leave his bedside lest the Jesuit awake even for an instant and find no comforting presence nearby.

At a little after eleven, his fidelity was rewarded. The scribe half-opened his eyes and whispered, "Is it you, Timoteo?"

"It is, Father. Try not to tire yourself."

"Don't worry, *figlio,*" he said, stopping every few syllables for breath. "As the poet said, *'Nox est perpetua una dormienda'* —I'll have a long night to rest."

To convey that he was still alive intellectually, he made Tim describe his encounter with the principessa. No, Tim thought to himself, I shouldn't be telling him this bad news. And yet if he's lucid enough to remember where I was this afternoon, he'd probably still enjoy his favorite sport— exposing hypocrisy.

Tim spun out the tale, making himself seem like a buffoon, trying to emphasize the comical aspect of it all. But when the anecdote ended, he could think of no witticism to cloak his bitter disappointment.

The scribe looked at Tim and sighed philosophically, a wordless way of saying, What do you expect from that kind of hypocrite? He then changed the subject.

"You know, Timoteo, for a pedant like myself, even dying is an educational experience. All afternoon while you were gone I kept thinking of the lines Sophocles wrote when he, too, had one foot in the grave. Remember the *Coloneus*—the old king addressing his daughters?"

His sweating brow wrinkled even further as he struggled to summon the quotation from memory. " 'A single word compensates for all the hardships of life, and that is . . . *love.*' " He looked at his young protégé with half-open eyes. "Do you recall it—the Greek was—"

" *'To philein,*' " Tim responded. "The human tie."

"You never fail me," Ascarelli smiled weakly. "And *that* is what has given meaning to my life. It is easy for a churchman to love God. It is harder to love one's fellow man. But if that were not important, why would we be put on earth? I bless God for bringing me you, Timoteo. He gave me someone to share my love of Him."

Exhausted, the old man let his head drop back onto the pillow. He was silent for what seemed minutes as he fought to gather the strength to speak.

But all he could add was, *"Grazie, figlio mio. . . ."*

Ten minutes later, Professor Rivieri arrived, checked for vital signs with his stethoscope, and then filled out a death certificate for the papal scribe, Father Paolo Ascarelli, S.J.

Tim felt abandoned.

———

Tim found Monsignor Murphy waiting in the doctor's office, together with Guillermo Martínez, Father General of the Society of Jesus.

The papal secretary acknowledged Tim's presence with a nod, and said to Father Martínez, "His Holiness is deeply saddened by Father Ascarelli's death. He offers the vehicles for a funeral cortege to bring Father Paolo to the family plot in Piemonte."

"Monsignor Murphy," Tim politely interrupted. "Can you arrange a place for me?"

Before the papal secretary could react, Father Martínez replied, "Without question, Your Grace. Paolo loved you. He spoke of you often with admiration and affection."

His throat muscles tightening, Tim managed to reply, "The feeling was mutual."

Two days later, Timothy found himself with four Jesuit priests and Father Martínez riding in a papal limousine heading north through the rich farmlands of the Po Valley. They were mourners to be sure, but the long life and peaceful death of Father Ascarelli was more a cause for reminiscence than grief.

The Ascarelli family plot stood high on a hill, so high that the shores of Lake Garda could be seen far below.

There they were joined by a group of Ascarelli's nephews, nieces, and cousins, as well as some old acquaintances, one of whom made a point of introducing himself as *Dottore* Leone, the family attorney.

The service was brief, and according to the specific wishes of Father Ascarelli's will, there was no eulogy.

The relatives then invited the visiting priests from Rome to join them at the family home for *collazione*.

The cars moved at a leisurely pace down through the glorious landscape of the Piemonte wine country, past a long stone wall, through a large metal gate. They drove through almost a quarter of a mile of vineyards to the main house where two long tables had been laid with various local specialities.

As the scribe would have wanted it, the meal following his interment was marked by toasts and happy anecdotes, making his funeral an affectionate celebration of his life.

Toward midafternoon, Dottore Leone approached Tim and politely inquired if he and the Father General could join him for a private talk. They followed the lawyer into a high-ceilinged library, with an antique desk placed by the large window, which stretched from floor to ceiling.

"I hope you don't think it inappropriate, but since we are a long way from Rome, I thought it sensible to discuss Paolo's will with you—since he's named you both as executors."

The Jesuit nodded in accord, but Timothy, somewhat surprised, muttered, "Yes, of course, *Dottore.*"

They all sat, and Leone pulled an envelope from a briefcase he had left near the window.

"Actually, the instructions are quite straightforward. There is the small matter of a codicil, but I doubt if that would cause either of you any difficulty." Leone put on his reading glasses, perused the document, then slapped it down.

"Bah, the legalese of this testament is so ugly—and I have every right to say so since I wrote it myself. May I just summarize?"

Both churchmen nodded. The lawyer removed his spectacles and began.

"As Paolo was the only son, his father left the vineyards principally to him—with a token for his sisters, may they rest in peace. As a loyal Jesuit, Paolo wishes the Society of Jesus to assume complete ownership and use the profits to further their work—and here he was quite specific—in the Third World. He respectfully asks the Father General to seek the advice of Archbishop Hogan, who, at the time of signing this document, was working with the poor in Brazil."

Timothy and Father Martínez exchanged glances, a silent communion in which both men wordlessly expressed their willingness to work together to fulfill Ascarelli's wishes.

Timothy turned to the lawyer. "What else, *Dottore*?" he inquired.

"Why nothing, Your Grace. That's alpha and omega. Each year when the harvest is sold, you will have to meet and decide how Paolo's share is distributed. I am also an executor but I have no vote in this matter."

Father Martínez spoke first. "I hope there's a sum sufficient to establish an annual Latin prize in Paolo's honor at a seminary in the vicinity."

The attorney's eyes widened. "Perhaps I have understated the matter. Father Ascarelli lived only on his papal wages, and hence I have invested his share for more than thirty years. This alone could probably construct several large schools."

"As much as that?" the Jesuit leader said with amazement.

Leone smiled. "Oh, he left you two some real problems, I can tell you. I have no doubt you'll spend many months each year debating how to expend the annual endowment."

"And how much would that be?" asked Father Martínez, breathless.

"Well, the price of wine is rising every year," the attorney replied. "And the Barolo these vineyards produce is of the finest quality. Last year alone I put nearly three billion lire into the Trust."

Timothy, who had been unable to make any sound, now gasped. It was a staggering sum, nearly two million dollars. He suddenly found that only Latin could express his stupefaction. *"Deo gratias,"* he exclaimed.

"Ah no," the Father General corrected him good-humoredly. "*Ascarellio gratias!*" He turned to the lawyer and asked, "Do I recall you mentioning a codicil?"

"Yes," Leone answered. "The day before he died, Paolo called me to discuss Archbishop Hogan's desire to build a children's hospital in Brasília. He instructed me to urge you both to make this a priority and left a note to that effect, witnessed by two nurses. Of course, it was not notarized, but—"

The Father General raised his hand to stop the lawyer's oration.

"We need no legalism in this matter, *Avvocato*. Paolo's words had the only witness necessary."

Tim smiled and explained. "Father Martínez means Almighty God."

———

As the priests prepared for the long journey home, Timothy walked among the Ascarelli vineyards. He could now see that they stretched to the horizon. When he was too far from the others to be heard, he looked up at the crimson sky and called exultantly, "God bless you, Father Ascarelli. You've saved thousands of sick children." He added in a whisper, "And my soul as well."

By the time the convoy had returned to Rome, though emotionally and physically spent, Tim knew he would not be able to rest until he had prayed for his beloved mentor's soul.

At 11:30 P.M., St. Peter's Square was empty and dimly lit. Tim could hear the echoing of his feet on the cobblestones as he walked. When he reached the main entrance, he was surprised to find the huge bronze doors locked.

He chastised himself for not remembering that the great Basilica closed at sunset and would not open again until first light. As he slowly made his way down the Via della Conciliazione toward the river, he recalled the words of Christ in Matthew, chapter six. When you pray, do not be like those who pray in public so that they are noticed. Rather, pray privately—and He will answer.

And in the manner the Saviour preached, Tim whispered in his heart.

Our Father Who art in heaven, Hallowed be thy name. Thy kingdom come. Thy will be done, on earth as it is in heaven.

EPILOGUE

81

Timothy

The Auxiliary Bishop of Chicago was gazing out of his office window at the gray streets of his domain—the largest Catholic diocese in America. He was dictating to a young graduate of St. Mary's of the Lake, whose pencil raced to keep up with his torrent of words.

The phone rang and the younger priest answered.

"Oh," he remarked, suddenly awestruck, "Oh, my . . ."

"Who is it?" the bishop inquired.

"It's Rome, Your Excellency," the young man whispered breathlessly. "I can't believe I'm really talking to the Vatican—even though it's only an operator."

"Find out who's calling," George Cavanagh ordered, trying to act as if this were an everyday occurrence.

His secretary made the inquiry and then related, "It's someone called Timothy Hogan."

"My dear Jerzy," George said with mock indignation. "You're referring to a distinguished archbishop and papal nuncio." He took the phone. "*Salve,* Your Grace. To what do I owe the honor of this call?"

"Can you spare me five minutes?" Tim asked in a voice that seemed somewhat muffled to George, but whose tone he ascribed to a bad connection.

"For you, Timmo, I can even stretch it to six. What's on your mind?"

First, Tim reported Ascarelli's death.

"I'm really sorry," George said, "I know how much he meant to you."

"Thanks. George, I've got something momentous to discuss with you," Tim said somberly. "Are you alone?"

The Auxiliary Bishop of Chicago looked up at his secretary and said politely, "Will you excuse me, Jerzy? This is a very confidential matter."

The young man nodded and withdrew.

"Okay, Timmo. Unless my enemies are bugging this line, we're on our own."

"Oh," Tim responded. "Are you serious about having enemies?"

"Of course. I wouldn't be doing my job if I didn't. Now tell me how I can help you."

"I read somewhere that you're on the Advisory

Board of something called the Catholic Press of America. Am I right?"

"Yeah," George replied, "except it's the *New* Catholic Press of America. Don't tell me you've written a book?"

"Better than that," Tim retorted. "How would you like to publish the English translation of Ernesto Hardt's treatise in favor of married clergy?"

"Ernesto Hardt?" There was reverence in his voice. "How soon can I see the manuscript?"

"Well," Tim replied. "On the off chance that despite the trappings of power you had maintained your principles, I've already sent you some floppy disks by FedEx. They're in Portuguese, but I think I'll have the English translation finished within a month."

"I assume you want to remain anonymous, right, Timmo?"

"No, George. If you think my translation's good enough, you can print my name."

"Excuse me, brother, but in gratitude I oughta tell you that's not exactly a clever career move."

"That's all right," Tim replied. "I don't have a career."

"What?" George said with amazement.

"You'd better sit down. It's a long story."

George listened intently to the narrative of Tim's inner journey with Hardt as his guide. At the end he was deeply moved.

"To be honest, I don't know what to say. A part of me wanted to see you on St. Peter's throne. But another part of me thinks what you're doing is worthy of sainthood. Do you want me to help you find a teaching job in the States?"

"No, George. I think I'm taking a sabbatical from the Church."

"To do what?"

"I'm sorry, Your Excellency. The only clue I can give you is that my motivation is I John 4:8. Thanks for everything. God bless you."

As the line went dead, George Cavanagh quoted the gospel passage half-aloud: " 'He that loveth not, knoweth not God—For God is love.' "

He pondered for a moment and then thought to himself, I hope it's someone as pious and pretty as that girl I saw you with in Jerusalem.

82

Deborah

E li eyed the visitor to his *srif* with suspicion.
"Are you her son?" the stranger asked.

He was tall and tanned, his hair bleached white
from the sun. Yet he clearly did not belong here, for
he spoke hesitantly—in awkward American-
accented Hebrew.

"Would you prefer to speak English?" Eli inquired.

"Yes, thank you," said the man. "I'm a bit rusty
in the holy language. May I come in?"

Though a moody teenager, Eli was never impolite. Yet there was something about this visitor that
grated, something that annoyed him. He replied in a
surly tone to discourage the man.

"My mother isn't here. She doesn't get back
from teaching till after five."

"Oh, she teaches?" said the visitor.

"Why are you asking all these questions?" Eli challenged him.

"Because I'm an old friend," the American asserted. "And I've come a long way to see her."

"What do you call 'long'?" the boy demanded.

"Would Brazil impress you?" The man smiled.

"Are you kidding me?"

"No. Now if I said 'please' in Portuguese, would you let me come in? You're being pretty rude."

"Yes," Eli conceded, "I suppose you're right. I'm sorry. It's just . . . I wasn't expecting anyone. Would you like a coffee or a Coke?"

"Have you got anything stronger?"

"Well," the boy remarked sarcastically, "if you need something really strong, you can get a beer in the canteen."

"That's okay. I'll take the coffee if it isn't too much trouble."

Eli deliberately turned his back to start the electric kettle and to allow himself time to absorb the shock he had sustained. He hoped he had camouflaged it, but looking inward, he could not see the stranger eyeing *him* with wonder.

Nor could he imagine that the visitor was thinking, I know this boy. Not just because he has traces of Deborah's features—there's something more. I recognize his manner.

As Eli opened the cabinet and reached for the can of instant coffee, he glanced at the yellowed newspaper clipping that Deborah had hung inside the door. It was already as brittle as an autumn leaf.

He examined the photograph. It confirmed his suspicions. Then, still without turning, he asked, "Do you take sugar, Father?"

"One spoon, thank you. How did you know I was a priest? Is it that obvious, even in a sport shirt?"

Eli spun around.

"Oh, you don't look like a priest," he said, fixing the man with a level stare. "You look more like an archbishop to me."

"Really?" The visitor was taken aback, but resolved to engage this feisty youth at his own game. "Do you have many archbishops dropping by your kibbutz?"

"No," the boy answered. "You're actually the first. But it just so happens my father's in that business."

The stranger's expression froze. He was barely able to find words.

"You're not serious."

"Yes," Eli retorted acerbically. "It appears you weren't."

Now they stared at one another in silence, each seeing his own blue eyes in the face of the other.

"She never told me," Timothy murmured.

"Would it have mattered?"

"Yes." Tim's reply came from the very fiber of his being. "It would have mattered very much."

"Well, you're a little late, Reverend—you've even missed my *bar mitzvah*. But then of course you couldn't have been called to the Torah, anyway."

All right, Tim thought, recovering his self-possession now, I can give as good as I get.

"Listen, *boychik,* I can quote the Bible as well as you," he said.

"In Hebrew?"

"*And* Aramaic. And Syriac, if necessary. And while we're at it, when's the last time you studied the Dead Sea Scrolls?"

Eli was suddenly off balance.

There was a moment of mutual hesitation.

"Does my mother know you're coming?"

"No," Tim answered. "Until a few days ago I didn't know myself."

It was only when Tim said the words aloud that the full impact of their reality struck him. Seventy-two hours earlier he had stood at a crossroads in his life. He had served God with all his heart, and yet the hope of Heaven still could not fill the void. He knew he needed Deborah. He had always needed Deborah. But was it not presumptuous after all this time to assume that she would feel the same?

"How long are you staying?" the boy asked.

"That depends."

"On what?"

"On whether . . . your mother is . . . happy to see me."

"She won't be—if she has any sense. She deserves a real husband, not some kind of Christian astronaut who flies to earth every ten years or so."

"Fourteen," the older man corrected him, adding, "And you deserve a real father."

The boy shrugged. "I've done pretty well without one. What were you doing in Brazil, anyway?"

"That's certainly changing the subject," Tim remarked with amusement.

"Well what do you expect?" Eli said angrily, his voice breaking. "You waltz in here like the prophet Elijah and expect me to be happy to see you? Where the hell were you while I was growing up?"

He was nearly in tears.

Deeply moved, Tim wanted to embrace him.

"Please," he murmured, afraid to open his arms lest he crush this fragile being who was his own son. "Please don't cry."

"I'm not crying," Eli shouted. "Can't you see I'm pissed off? I'm mad as hell at you for walking out on my mother! You don't know what she's been through."

"And you?" Tim asked softly. "I can imagine you've been through a lot too."

"How?" Eli asked petulantly.

"Because I knew a young boy not unlike you who also had to grow up without a father—"

"Another one of yours?"

"No, I'm not interested in overpopulating the planet." He paused, then added urgently, "I never knew I had you. I swear I never knew—until I walked in here."

"You don't 'have' me. I'm not a package you can store and pick up when you want to. I'm a human being."

"What's your name, by the way?"

"Eli."

"As in Psalm Twenty-two, '*Eli, Eli lama azavtani*—' "

"Very clever, Archbishop. But if you've come to convert me, forget it."

"All I've come for is that cup of coffee."

Without a word, Eli turned, fetched the now-lukewarm mug, and brought it to his guest—who was staring at a photograph of Deborah holding a six-week-old baby. Eli was tempted to make a caustic remark, but something in the man's expression stopped him.

"How long till your mother gets home?" Tim asked, a slight tremor in his voice.

"I don't know," Eli responded. "Maybe half an hour. Were you planning to leave before that?"

"No—I was just wondering if you'd like to kick a football around."

"If you want," Eli said with an elaborate shrug. "There's always a game on the kibbutz field around now. In a half hour you can get your fair share of bruises."

"I think I can handle myself," Tim replied. "Where can I change?"

"In there," Eli pointed to the bedroom. "Do you need to borrow anything?"

"No, thanks." He suddenly smiled. "In fact I've got an outfit that'll knock your socks off."

"Don't tell me," the boy scoffed. "Your archbishop's suit?"

"Better than that. You'll see."

Moments later, Tim reemerged in the shiny blue uniform of the Brazilian soccer team. As the boy gasped, "Wow," the door opened.

"Eli," Deborah began. "What's going on? Whose car is that—?"

And then she saw him.

"My God."

They stared at each other. There were no words. Even after all this time, each knew exactly what the other was thinking.

"Deborah," he whispered at last. "You can't know how many times I've dreamed of this moment."

"Me too," she answered softly. "Only I didn't think it would be in this world." She turned to her son. "Have you met—"

"This is stupid," Eli cut her off, in a blustering attempt to disguise his feelings. "I'm going to get the hell out of here before things get too sentimental."

He raced out, trying to hold back his own tears.

———

They were alone. The two of them, after a million days and nights.

"Deborah, he's wonderful. You should be very proud."

"And you—?"

"Do I have the right? Love has to be earned. I haven't exactly been a frequent visitor."

"You never left my thoughts," she said, unafraid.

"Nor you mine," he confessed. "And I finally decided not to take the risk. . . ."

"What do you mean?"

"The leap of faith—the hope of being with you in the next life. I'd trade it all for being here right now." He hesitated, then asked, "Do you think we can start again?"

"No, my beloved." She smiled. "We'll just continue."

Acknowledgments

In the beginning there were words. Too many of them—and all in the wrong places. Linda Grey somehow found time while running a publishing house to put order into the chaos of my original manuscript. She is a brilliant and imaginative editor.

All roads may lead to Rome—and Jerusalem, for that matter. But they only bring you to the gates. I owe many debts to people who gave me access literally and spiritually to these great citadels of religion.

His Eminence Roger Cardinal Etchegaray, President of the Pontifical Council of Justice and Peace, welcomed a stranger to the Vatican, affording me a picture of life at the center of power I could not otherwise have obtained. His resourceful assistant, Sister Marjorie Keegan, provided informative documents while at the same time proving a surprising treasury of anecdotes about New York Jewish life.

Acknowledgments

Father Jacques Roubert, S.J., Regional Secretary in the Western European Assistancy of the General Curia, welcomed me to the world Jesuit headquarters at 5 Borgo Santo Spirito and gave me an understanding of the Society of Jesus that added a third dimension to everything I subsequently read.

I am grateful to Mishkenot Sha'ananim, a very special haven for those in the Arts, for allowing me to be their guest and absorb the unique atmosphere of Jerusalem.

Rabbi Hugo Gryn and his former associate, Rabbi Larry Tabick, read through the drafts to ferret out doctrinal lapses. I was reassured on certain points by Rabbi Doctor Louis Jacobs. Needless to say, any errors that remain are the result of my own stubbornness or carelessness.

Reverend Donald Doherty, M.M., of the Maryknoll Society and Reverend Michael Hilbert, S.J., of the Gregorian University provided helpful information regarding education for the priesthood.

The astonishing lapse from celibacy among the American Catholic clergy is documented by A. W. Richard Sipe in *A Secret World: Sexuality and the Search for Celibacy,* New York 1990.

I am also grateful to Reverend Edgar Wells, Rector of the Church of St. Mary the Virgin, New York City, and Miss Susan Rybarchyk for the Protestant viewpoint on certain issues; Ms. Irma Rabino and Rabbi Rhonda Nebel of the Jewish Theological Seminary (where I myself was briefly a student in the early 1950s); and Dr. Philip Miller and Ms. Sylvia Posner of Hebrew Union College.

Mr. Peter Govett and Mr. Howard Levine provided invaluable financial expertise. I am also indebted to Rita Antilety, Reverend Malcolm Foster, Don Galligan, Tonya Gomez, and Professor T. J. Luce.

I have had the privilege of talking to many truly remarkable individuals who confided their experiences to me, seminarians who understandably wish to remain anonymous and various members of the American Catholic Establishment, among them one whose pedigree includes the first American Catholic bishop as well as the first American-born saint, Mother Elizabeth Ann Seton.

Mr. and Mrs. Patrick Courtney—formerly Father Pat and Sister Margarita—shared with me their story of faith and love, which deserves a volume of its own.

———

It would be impossible to list a full bibliography of everything I consulted during the four years I spent writing this book. But I should signal my debt to the *Catholic Encyclopedia* and the *Encyclopaedia Judaica,* Penny Lernoux's *People of God, The Jesuits* by Malachi Martin, and Hayyim Schauss's *The Lifetime of a Jew.*

And, of course, the most important book of all, the Holy Bible.

E.S.   *Oxford, 1991*